DEATH IN HOLY ORDERS

WITHDRAWN

P. D. James was born in Oxford in 1920 and educated at Cambridge High School for Girls. From 1949 to 1968 she worked in the National Health Service and subsequently in the Home Office, first in the Police Department and later in the Criminal Policy Department. All that experience has been used in her novels. She is a Fellow of the Royal Society of Literature and of the Royal Society of Arts and has served as a governor of the BBC, a member of the Arts Council, where she was Chairman of the Library Advisory Panel, on the Board of the British Council, and as a magistrate in Middlesex and London. She is an Honorary Bencher of the Honourable Society of the Inner Temple. She has won awards for crime writing in Britain, America, Italy and Scandinavia, including the Mystery Writers of America Grandmaster Award and the National Arts Club Medal of Honor for Literature (US). She has received honorary degrees from seven British universities, was awarded an OBE in 1983, and was created a life peer in 1991. In 1997 she was elected President of the Society of Authors.

She lives in London and Oxford and has two daughters, five grandchildren and eight great-grandchildren.

P. D. JAMES

Death in Holy Orders

FABER & FABER

First published in 2001
by Faber & Faber Ltd
Bloomsbury House
74–77 Great Russell Street
London WC1B 3DA

Published by Penguin Books in association
with Faber and Faber in 2002
This Faber & Faber paperback edition first published in 2014

Pinted and bound by CPI Group (UK) Ltd, Croydon CR0 4YY

The right of P. D. James to be identified as author
of this work has been asserted in accordance with Section 77
of the Copyright, Designs and Patents Act 1988

A CIP record for this book
is available from the British Library

ISBN 978–0–571–30732–6

FSC
www.fsc.org
MIX
Paper from
responsible sources
FSC® C101712

2 4 6 8 10 9 7 5 3

For Rosemary Goad
For forty years editor and friend

Contents

Author's Note

In setting this story of murder and mystery in a Church of England theological college I would not wish to discourage candidates for the Anglican priesthood, nor to suggest for one moment that visitors to such a college in search of rest and spiritual renewal are in danger of finding a more permanent peace than they had in mind. It is the more important, therefore, to emphasize that St Anselm's is not based on any real theological college, past or present, and that its eccentric priests, its ordinands, staff and visitors are purely fictitious and exist only in the imagination of the writer and her readers.

I am grateful to a number of people who have kindly helped me by answering my questions; any errors, theological or otherwise, are my own. I am particularly grateful to the late Archbishop Lord Runcie, The Revd Dr Jeremy Sheehy, The Revd Dr Peter Groves, Dr Ann Priston OBE of The Forensic Science Service, and to my secretary, Mrs Joyce McLennan, whose help with this novel went far beyond her skill with a computer.

P. D. James

BOOK ONE

The Killing Sand

I

It was Father Martin's idea that I should write an account of how I found the body.

I asked, 'You mean, as if I were writing a letter, telling it to a friend?'

Father Martin said, 'Writing it down as if it were fiction, as if you were standing outside yourself, watching it happen, remembering what you did, what you felt, as if it were all happening to someone else.'

I knew what he meant, but I wasn't sure I knew where to begin. I said, 'Everything that happened, Father, or just that walk along the beach, uncovering Ronald's body?'

'Anything and everything you want to say. Write about the college and about your life here if you like. I think you might find it helpful.'

'Did you find it helpful, Father?'

I don't know why I spoke these words, they just came into my mind and I let them out. It was silly really, and in a way it was impertinent, but he didn't seem to mind.

After a pause he said, 'No, it didn't really help me, but then it was all a very long time ago. I think it might be different for you.'

I suppose he was thinking about the war and being taken prisoner by the Japanese, the awful events that happened in the camp. He never speaks about the war, but then why should he do so to me? But I don't think he speaks to anyone, not even to the other priests.

This conversation happened two days ago when we were walking together through the cloisters after Evensong. I don't go to Mass any more, not since Charlie died, but I do go to Evensong. It's a matter of courtesy really. It doesn't seem right working at the college, taking money from them, accepting all their kindness and never attending any of the services in the church. But perhaps I'm being too sensitive. Mr Gregory lives in one of the cottages, as I do, and teaches Greek part-time, but he never attends church except when there is music he wants to hear. No one ever presses me to attend, they never even asked why I stopped coming to Mass. But of course they noticed; they notice everything.

When I got back to my cottage I thought about what Father Martin had said and whether perhaps it might not be a good idea. I've never had any difficulty about writing. At school I was good at composition and Miss Allison, who taught us English, said she thought I might have the talent to be a writer. But I knew that she was wrong. I haven't any imagination, not the kind novelists need. I can't make things up. I can only write about what I see and do and know – and sometimes what I feel, which isn't as easy. Anyway I always wanted to be a nurse, even from childhood. I'm sixty-four and retired now, but I still keep my hand in here at St Anselm's. I'm partly the Matron, dealing with minor illnesses, and I also look after the linen. It's an easy job but I've got a weak heart and I'm lucky to be working. The college make it as easy as possible for me. They've even provided a lightweight trolley so that I'm not tempted to carry heavy bundles of linen. I ought to have said all this before. And I haven't even written down my name. It's Munroe, Margaret Munroe.

I think I know why Father Martin suggested it would be helpful if I began writing again. He knows that I used to write

4

a long letter to Charlie every week. I think he's the only person here except Ruby Pilbeam who does know that. Every week I'd sit down and remember what had happened since the last letter, the small unimportant things which wouldn't be unimportant to Charlie: the meals I ate, the jokes I heard, stories about the students, descriptions of the weather. You wouldn't think there would be much to tell in a quiet place like this on the edge of the cliffs, remote from anywhere, but it was surprising what I found to write to him. And I know Charlie loved the letters. 'Keep on writing, Mum,' he would say when he was home on leave. And I did.

After he was killed, the Army sent me back all his belongings and there was the bundle of letters among them. Not every one I'd written, he couldn't have kept them all, but he did keep some of the longest. I took them on to the headland and made a bonfire. It was a windy day, as it often is on the east coast, and the flames roared and spat and changed direction with the wind. The charred pieces of paper rose and whirled about my face like black moths and the smoke stung my nose. It was odd because it was only a little fire. But what I'm trying to say is that I know why Father Martin suggested I should write this account. He thought that writing something – anything – might help to bring me back to life. He's a good man, perhaps he's even a holy man, but there's so much he doesn't understand.

It seems strange to be writing this account without knowing who, if anyone, will ever see it. And I'm not sure whether I'm writing for myself or for some imaginary reader to whom everything about St Anselm's will be new and strange. So perhaps I ought to write something about the college, to set the scene, as it were. It was founded in 1861 by a pious lady called Miss Agnes Arbuthnot, who wanted to ensure that there would always be 'devout and learned young men ordained to the Catholic priesthood in the Church of England'. I've put in the inverted commas because those are her words. There's a booklet about her in the church and that's how I know. She gave the buildings, the land and nearly all her furniture, and enough money – so she thought – to keep the college going for ever. But there never is enough money and now St Anselm's has to be mainly financed by the Church. I know that Father Sebastian and Father Martin are afraid that the Church is planning to close it down. This fear is never openly discussed, and certainly not with the staff, though we all know. In a small and isolated community like St Anselm's news and gossip seem to be carried, unspoken, on the wind.

Apart from giving the house, Miss Arbuthnot built the north and south cloisters at the back to provide rooms for the students, and a set of guest-rooms linking the south cloister to the church. She also built four cottages for staff, arranged in a semicircle on the headland about a hundred yards from the college. She named them after the four evangelists. I am in St Matthew, the most southerly. Ruby Pilbeam, who is the cook-housekeeper, and her husband, the general handyman, are in St Mark. Mr Gregory is in St Luke, and in the northern cottage, St John, is Eric Surtees who helps Mr Pilbeam. Eric keeps pigs, but more as a hobby than to provide pork for the college. There are just the four of us with part-time cleaning women from Reydon and Lowestoft to help out, but there are never more than twenty ordinands and four resident priests and we manage. None of us would be easy to replace. This windswept desolate headland with no village, no pub, no shop, is too remote for most people. I like it here but even I can find it frightening and a little sinister. The sea is eating away the sandy cliffs year by year and sometimes I stand on the edge

6

looking out to sea and can imagine a great tidal wave rearing up, white and glistening, racing towards the shore to crash over the turrets and towers, the church and the cottages, and wash us all away. The old village of Ballard's Mere has been under the sea for centuries and sometimes on windy nights folks say it's possible to hear the faint ringing of church bells from the buried towers. And what the sea didn't take was destroyed in a great fire in 1695. Nothing of the old village now remains except the medieval church, which Miss Arbuthnot restored and made part of the college, and the two crumbling red brick pillars fronting the house, which are all that are left of the Elizabethan manor house that stood on the site.

I'd better try to explain something about Ronald Treeves, the boy who died. After all, his death is what this is supposed to be about. Before the inquest the police questioned me, asking how well I had known him. I suppose I knew him better than most of the staff here, but I didn't say much. There wasn't much I could tell. I didn't think it was my place to gossip about the students. I knew that he wasn't popular but I didn't tell them that. The trouble was that he didn't really fit in and I think he knew that he didn't. For one thing, his father was Sir Alred Treeves who runs an important armaments company and Ronald liked us to know that he was the son of a very rich man. The things he owned showed it too. He had a Porsche while the other students make do with cheaper cars – if they have a car at all. And he talked about his holidays in expensive and remote places that other students wouldn't be able to travel to, at least not in vacations.

All that might have gained him popularity in some colleges, but not here. Everyone is snobbish about something, don't let them tell you differently, but here it isn't about money. It isn't really about family either, although you'd do better as the son of a curate than you would as the son of a pop star. I suppose what they really care about is cleverness – cleverness and good looks and wit. They like people who can make them laugh. Ronald wasn't as clever as he thought he was and he never made anyone laugh. They thought he was dull, and of course when he realized that he became duller. I didn't say any of this to the police. What would have been the point? He was dead. Oh, and I think he was a bit of a snooper too, always wanting to know what was going on, asking questions. He didn't get much out of me. But some evenings he would turn up at the cottage and sit and talk while I knitted and listened. The students are discouraged from visiting the staff cottages except by invitation. Father Sebastian likes us to have our privacy. But I didn't mind him really. Looking back on it, I think he was lonely. Well, he wouldn't have bothered with me otherwise. And I remembered my Charlie. Charlie wasn't dull or unpopular or boring, but I like to think that, if he'd ever been lonely and wanted to sit quietly and talk, there would have been someone like me to give him a welcome.

When the police arrived they asked me why I had gone looking for him on the beach. But, of course, I hadn't. About twice a week I take a solitary walk after I've had lunch, and when I set out I didn't even realize that Ronald was missing. And I wouldn't have started looking on the beach. It's difficult to think what could happen to anyone on a deserted shore. It's safe enough if you don't clamber over the groynes or walk too close to the cliffs, and there are notices about the dangers of both. All the students are warned when they first arrive about the risk of swimming alone or walking too close to the unstable cliffs.

In Miss Arbuthnot's time it was possible to get down to the beach from the house, but the encroaching sea has changed all that. Now we have to walk about half a mile south of the college to the only place where the cliffs are low and firm enough to support some half-dozen rickety wooden steps with a handrail. Beyond this point is the darkness of Ballard's Mere, surrounded by trees and separated from the sea only by a narrow bank of shingle. Sometimes I walk as far as the mere and then turn back, but that day I went down the steps to the beach and started walking northward.

After a night of rain it was a fresh, lively day, the sky blue with scudding clouds, the tide running high. I rounded a slight promontory and saw the deserted beach stretching out before me with its narrow ridges of shingle and the dark lines of the old weed-encrusted groynes crumbling into the sea. And then, about thirty yards ahead, I saw what looked like a black bundle lying at the foot of the cliff. I hurried up to it and found a cassock, neatly folded, and beside it a brown cloak, also carefully folded. Within a few feet the cliff had slithered and tumbled and now lay in great clumps of compacted sand, tufts of grass and stones. I knew at once what must have happened. I think I gave a little cry, and then I began scraping away at the sand. I knew a body must be buried underneath it, but it wasn't possible to know where. I remember the gritty sand under my nails and how slow progress seemed, so that I began kicking the sand with my feet as if in anger, spraying it high so that it stung my face and got into my eyes. Then I noticed a sharp-edged spar of wood about thirty yards towards the sea. I fetched it and used it to start probing. After a few minutes it struck something soft and I knelt and began working again with my hands. Then I saw that what it had struck were two sand-encrusted buttocks, covered in fawn corduroy.

After that I couldn't go on. My heart was pounding and I had no more strength. I felt, obscurely, that I had humiliated whoever lay there, that there was something ridiculous and almost indecent about the two exposed mounds. I knew that he must be dead and that all my feverish haste hadn't really been important. I couldn't have saved him and now I couldn't bear to go on alone, uncovering him inch by inch, even if I'd had the strength. I had to get help, to break the news of what had happened. I think I knew even then whose body it was, but suddenly I remembered that all the ordinands' brown cloaks have name tabs. I turned back the collar of the cloak and read the name.

I remember stumbling down the beach on the firm edge of sand between the banks of pebbles and somehow dragging myself up the steps to the top of the cliff. I began running along the cliff road to the college. It was only a half-mile but the road seemed endless and the house seemed to recede with every painful step. My heart was beginning to pound and my legs felt as if the bones were dissolving. And then I heard a car. Looking back I saw it turning from the access road and coming towards me along the rough track bordering the cliff edge. I stood in the middle of the track and waved my arms and the car slowed. I saw that it was Mr Gregory.

I can't remember how I broke the news. I have a picture of myself standing there, caked in sand, hair blowing in the wind, gesticulating towards the sea. He didn't say anything, but silently opened the car door and I got in. I suppose it would have been sensible to drive on to the college but, instead, he turned the car and we got out at the steps to the beach. I've wondered since whether he didn't believe me and wanted to see for himself before calling for help. I can't remember the walk and the last clear picture is of us standing together by Ronald's body. Still without speaking Mr Gregory knelt in the sand and began digging with his hands. He was wearing leather gloves and that made it easier for him. We both worked in silence, feverishly shifting the sand, working up to the top of the body.

Above the corduroy trousers Ronald was wearing only a grey shirt. We uncovered the back of his head. It was like uncovering an animal, a dead dog or a cat. The deeper sand was still moist and his straw-coloured hair was matted with it. I tried to brush it away and it felt cold and gritty on my palms.

Mr Gregory said sharply, 'Don't touch him!', and I took my hand away quickly as if it had been burned. Then he said very quietly, 'We'd better leave him now, just as we found him. It's clear who it is.'

I knew that he was dead, but somehow I thought we ought to turn him over. I had some ridiculous idea that we could give him mouth-to-mouth breathing. I knew it wasn't rational, but I still felt we ought to do something. But Mr Gregory took off his left glove and put two fingers against Ronald's neck. Then he said, 'He's dead, but of course he's dead. There's nothing we can do for him.'

We were both silent for a moment, kneeling there on each side of him. We must have looked as if we were praying, and I would have said a prayer for him only I couldn't think of the right words. And then the sun came out and suddenly the scene looked as if it wasn't real, as if the two of us were being photographed in colour. Everything was bright and clear-edged. The grains of sand on Ronald's hair shone like pin-points of light.

Mr Gregory said, 'We must get some help, call the police. Do you mind waiting here with him? I won't be long. Or you can come with me if you prefer, but I think it would be better if one of us stayed.'

I said, 'You go. You'll be quicker in the car. I don't mind waiting.'

I watched him as he walked as briskly as the shingle allowed towards the mere, then round the promontory and out of sight. A minute later I heard the sound of the car as he drove towards the college. I half-slid down the sand a little way from the body and settled myself on the pebbles, wriggling to make myself more comfortable and digging in my heels. The pebbles beneath the surface were still damp from the night rain and the cold wetness seeped through the cotton of my slacks. I sat with my arms folded round my knees, looking out over the sea.

And sitting there I thought of Mike for the first time in years. He was killed when his motorcycle skidded off the A1 and into a tree. We had been home from our honeymoon for less than two weeks; we had known each other for less than a year. What I felt at his death was shock and disbelief, not grief. I thought at the time that it was grief but I know better now. I was in love with Mike but I didn't love him. That comes with living together and caring for each other and we never had the time. After he died I knew that I was Margaret Munroe, widow, but I felt that I was still Margaret Parker, spinster, aged twenty-one, a recently qualified nurse. When I discovered I was pregnant, that too seemed unreal. The baby, when he arrived, seemed nothing to do with Mike or our brief time together, and nothing to do with me. All that came later and perhaps it was the stronger because it came late. When Charlie died I mourned for both of them, but I still can't clearly recall Mike's face.

I was aware of Ronald's body behind me, but it was a comfort not to be sitting at his side. Some people taking watch beside the dead find their presence companionable, but I didn't feel that, not with Ronald. All I felt was a great sadness. It wasn't for that poor boy, it wasn't even for Charlie or Mike or for myself. It was a universal sadness which seemed to permeate everything round me, the fresh breeze against my cheek, the sky where there were a few massed clouds moving almost deliberately, it seemed, across the blue, and the sea itself. I found myself thinking of all the people who had lived and died on this coast, and of the bones lying a mile out under the waves in the great churchyards. Their lives must have mattered at the time to themselves and the people who cared about them, but now they were dead and it would have been just the same if they had never lived. In a hundred years no one will remember Charlie, Mike or me. All our lives are as insignificant as a single grain of sand. My mind felt emptied, even of sadness. Instead, gazing out to sea, accepting that in the end nothing really matters and that all we have is the present moment to endure or enjoy, I felt at peace.

I suppose I was sitting in a kind of trance because I didn't see or hear the three approaching figures until there was the loud crunch of shingle and they had almost reached me. Father Sebastian and Mr Gregory were trudging side by side. Father Sebastian had wrapped his black cloak tightly round him against the wind. Both their heads were bent and they walked purposefully as if they were marching. Father Martin was a little way behind, lurching as he struggled with difficulty over the shingle. I remember thinking that it was unkind of the other two not to wait for him.

I felt embarrassed to be discovered sitting. I got up, and Father Sebastian said, 'Are you all right, Margaret?'

I said, 'Yes Father', and then stood aside as the three of them walked up to the body.

Father Sebastian made the sign of the cross, then said, 'This is a disaster.'

Even at the time I thought it was a strange word to use and I knew that he wasn't just thinking at that moment of Ronald Treeves; he was thinking of the college.

He bent down and put his hand against the back of Ronald's neck and Mr Gregory said, quite sharply, 'He's dead of course. Better not disturb the body any further.'

Father Martin was standing a little apart. I saw his lips moving and I think he was praying.

Father Sebastian said, 'If you, Gregory, will go back to the college and watch for the police, Father Martin and I will stay here. Margaret had better go with you. This has been a shock for her. Take her to Mrs Pilbeam, if you will, and explain what's happened. Mrs Pilbeam will make her some hot tea and look after her. Neither of them are to say anything until I inform the college. If the police want to talk to Margaret they can do so later.'

It's funny, but I remember feeling a slight sense of resentment that he had spoken to Mr Gregory almost as if I wasn't there. And I didn't really want to be taken to Ruby Pilbeam's cottage. I like Ruby, who has always managed to be kind without being interfering, but all I wanted was to go home.

Father Sebastian came up and laid a hand on my shoulder. He said, 'You've been very brave, Margaret, thank you. Go with Mr Gregory now and I'll come to see you later. Father Martin and I will sit here with Ronald.'

It was the first time he had spoken the boy's name.

In the car Mr Gregory drove for a few minutes in silence, then said, 'That's a curious death. I wonder what the Coroner – or, come to that, the police – will make of it.'

I said, 'Surely it was an accident.'

'A curious accident, wouldn't you say?' I didn't reply, then he said, 'This isn't the first dead body you've seen, of course. You'll be accustomed to death.'

'I'm a nurse, Mr Gregory.'

I thought of the first body I'd seen all those years ago as an eighteen-year-old probationer, the first body I'd laid out. Nursing was different in those days. We used to lay out the dead ourselves and it was done with great reverence and in silence behind the screens. My first ward sister used to join us to say a prayer before we began. She told us that this was the last service we could render our patients. But I wasn't going to talk to Mr Gregory about that.

He said, 'Seeing a dead body, any body, is a comforting reassurance that we may live as men but we die as animals. Personally I find that a relief. I can't imagine any greater horror than eternal life.'

I still didn't reply. It's not that I dislike him: we hardly ever meet. Ruby Pilbeam cleans his cottage once a week and does his washing. It's a private arrangement they have. But he and I have never been on chatting terms and I wasn't in the mood to begin now.

The car turned westward between the twin towers and into the courtyard. Releasing his seatbelt and helping me with mine, he said, 'I'll walk with you to Mrs Pilbeam's. She may not be in. If not, you had better come to my cottage. What we both need is a drink.'

But she was in and I was glad of it after all. Mr Gregory reported the facts very briefly and said, 'Father Sebastian and Father Martin are with the body now and the police will arrive very soon. Please don't mention this to anyone else until Father Sebastian returns. He'll then speak to the whole college.'

After he had gone Ruby did indeed make tea, hot and strong

and very comforting. She fussed over me but I can't remember the words or the gestures. I didn't say much but she didn't expect me to. She treated me as if I were ill, settling me in one of the easy chairs before the fireplace, switching on two bars of the electric fire in case I felt cold with shock, and then drawing the curtains so that I could have what she described as 'a good long rest'.

I suppose it was about an hour before the police arrived, a youngish sergeant with a Welsh accent. He was kind and patient and I answered his questions quite calmly. There wasn't, after all, very much to tell. He asked me how well I'd known Ronald, the last time I'd seen him and whether he'd been depressed lately. I said I'd last seen him the previous evening walking towards Mr Gregory's cottage, I suppose for his Greek lesson. Term had only just started and that's all I had seen of him. I got the impression that the police sergeant – I think his name was Jones or Evans, a Welsh name anyway – was sorry he'd asked the question about Ronald being depressed. Anyway, he said that it all looked quite straightforward, asked Ruby the same questions and then left.

Father Sebastian broke the news of Ronald's death to the whole college when they assembled before five o'clock Evensong. Most of the ordinands had guessed by then that something tragic had happened; police cars and a mortuary van don't arrive in secret. I didn't go to the library so I never heard what Father Sebastian said. All I wanted by then was to be alone. But later in the evening the senior student, Raphael Arbuthnot, brought me a small pot of blue African violets with the sympathy of all the ordinands. One of them must have driven into Pakefield or Lowestoft to buy them. When he gave them to me, Raphael bent down and kissed my cheek. He said, 'I'm so sorry, Margaret.' It was the kind of thing people say at a *time like that, but it didn't sound commonplace. What it sounded like was an apology.*

It was two nights later that the nightmares began. I have never suffered from nightmares before, not even when I was a student nurse and first encountered death. The dreams are horrible, and now I sit in front of the television until late every evening, dreading the moment when tiredness drives me to bed. The dream is always the same. Ronald Treeves is standing beside the bed. He is naked and his body is plastered with damp sand. It is matted in his fair hair and over his face. Only the eyes are free of sand, and they gaze at me reproachfully as if asking why I didn't do more to save him. I know that there was nothing I could have done. I know that he was dead long before I came upon his body. But still he appears night after night, with that accusing reproachful gaze, the damp sand falling in clumps from his plain, rather pudgy face.

Perhaps now that I have written it down he will leave me in peace. I don't think I am a fanciful woman, but there is something strange about his death, something I ought to remember but which lies nagging at the back of my mind. Something tells me that Ronald Treeves's death wasn't an end but a beginning.

2

The call to Dalgliesh came at ten-forty a.m., just before he returned to his office after a meeting with the Community Relations Branch. It had gone on later than scheduled – such meetings invariably did – and there were only fifty minutes before he was due to join the Commissioner in the Home Secretary's office at the House of Commons. Time, he thought, for a coffee and to make a couple of outstanding telephone calls. But he had hardly reached his desk when his PA put her head round the office door.

'Mr Harkness would be grateful if you would see him before you leave. He's got Sir Alred Treeves with him.'

So now what? Sir Alred wanted something, of course; people who came to see senior officers of the Yard usually did. And what Sir Alred wanted he invariably got. You didn't run one of the most prosperous multinational corporations without knowing instinctively how to control the intricacies of power, in small matters as in large. Dalgliesh knew of his reputation; you could hardly live in the twenty-first century and be ignorant of it. A fair, even generous employer of successful staff, a liberal supporter of charities from his trust funds, a respected collector of twentieth-century European art; all of which could be translated by the prejudiced as a ruthless pruner of failures, a well-advertised supporter of fashionable causes and an investor with an eye for long-term capital gain. Even his reputation for rudeness was ambiguous. Since it was indiscriminate and the powerful suffered with the weak it had merely gained him an admirable reputation for honest egalitarianism.

Dalgliesh took the lift to the seventh floor with little expectation of pleasure but considerable curiosity. At least the meeting would be relatively short; he would have to leave by quarter-past to walk that convenient half-mile to the Home Office. When it came to priorities, the Home Secretary took precedence over even Sir Alred Treeves.

The Assistant Commissioner and Sir Alred were standing by Harkness's desk and both turned to face Dalgliesh as he entered. As often with people who feature prominently in the media, the first impression of Treeves was disconcerting. He was stockier and less ruggedly handsome than he appeared on television, the facial contour less defined. But the impression of latent power and a certain self-conscious enjoyment of it was even stronger. It was his foible to dress as a prosperous farmer: except on the most formal occasions he wore well-tailored tweeds. There was indeed something of the countryman about his person: the broad shoulders, the burnish on the cheeks and over the prominent nose, the unruly hair that no barber could entirely discipline. It was very dark, almost black, with a silver streak swept back from the middle of the forehead. In a man more concerned with his appearance, Dalgliesh could have suspected that it had been dyed.

As Dalgliesh entered, Treeves's glance under his bushy eyebrows was direct and frankly appraising.

Harkness said, 'I think you know each other.'

They shook hands. Sir Alred's hand was cold and strong but he withdrew it at once as if to emphasize that the gesture had been a formality. He said, 'We have met. A Home Office conference in the late eighties, wasn't it? On policy in the inner cities. I don't know why I got mixed up in it.'

'Your Corporation made a generous donation to one of the schemes organized under the inner cities initiatives. I think you wanted to satisfy yourself that it was likely to be usefully spent.'

'I dare say. Not much chance of that. Young people want well-paid jobs worth getting up in the morning for, not training for work that doesn't exist.'

Dalgliesh recalled the occasion. It had been the usual highly organized public relations exercise. Few of the senior officers or ministers present had expected much to come of it, and little had. Treeves, he remembered, had asked a number of pertinent questions, had expressed scepticism at the answers and had left before the Minister's summing up. Why exactly had he chosen to attend, chosen indeed to contribute? Perhaps that, too, had been a public relations exercise.

Harkness made a vague gesture towards the black swivel chairs ranged in front of the window and murmured something about coffee.

Treeves said, curtly, 'No thank you, I won't take coffee.' His tone implied that he had been offered an esoteric beverage inappropriate to ten forty-five in the morning.

They seated themselves with something of the portentous wariness of three Mafia bosses meeting to settle their several spheres of interest. Treeves looked at his watch. Specific time had no doubt been allowed for this encounter. He had come at his own convenience with no prior notice and no forewarning of what he had in mind. That, of course, had given him the advantage. He had arrived with every confidence that a senior officer would find time for him, and he had been right.

Now he said, 'My elder son, Ronald – he was adopted by the way – was killed ten days ago in a cliff fall in Suffolk. Sand fall would be a more accurate description; those cliffs south of Lowestoft have been eaten away by the sea since the seventeenth century. He was suffocated. Ronald was a student at St Anselm's Theological College at Ballard's Mere. It's a High Church establishment for the training of Anglican priests. Smells and bells.' He turned to Dalgliesh. 'You know about this sort of thing, don't you? Wasn't your father a parson?'

And how, Dalgliesh wondered, did Sir Alred know that? Probably at some time he'd been told it, half-recalled the fact and asked one of his minions to check before setting out for this meeting. He was a man who believed in having as much information as possible about the people with whom he was to deal. If it was to their discredit so much the better, but any personal detail that the other party didn't know he possessed was a satisfying and potentially useful accession of power.

Dalgliesh said, 'He was a Norfolk rector, yes.'

Harkness asked, 'Your son was training for the ministry?'

'I'm not aware that what he was being taught at St Anselm's would have qualified him for any other job.'

Dalgliesh said, 'There was a mention of the death in the broadsheets but I don't remember reading about the inquest.'

'You wouldn't. It was kept pretty quiet. Accidental death. It should have been an open verdict. If the Warden of the college and most of the staff hadn't been sitting there like a row of black-gowned vigilantes the Coroner would probably have found the courage to return a proper verdict.'

'You were there, Sir Alred?'

'No. I was represented but I was in China. There was a complicated contract to be negotiated in Beijing. I came back for the cremation. We brought the body back to London for that. They had some kind of memorial service – a requiem I think they called it – at St Anselm's, but neither my wife nor I attended. It's not a place where I ever felt at home. Immediately after the inquest I arranged for my chauffeur with another driver to collect Ronald's Porsche, and the college handed over his clothes, his wallet and his watch. Norris – he's my driver – brought back the parcel. There wasn't much. The students aren't encouraged to have more than the minimum of clothes, a suit, two pairs of jeans with the usual shirts and pullovers, shoes and that black cassock which the students are required to wear. He had some books, of course, but I told the college that they could have those for the library. It's odd how quickly you can tidy away a life. Then two days ago I received this.'

Unhurriedly he took out his wallet and unfolded a sheet of paper, then passed it to Dalgliesh. Dalgliesh glanced at it, and handed it to the Assistant Commissioner. Harkness read it aloud.

'"Why don't you ask some questions about your son's death? Nobody really believes it was an accident. Those priests will cover up anything to keep their good name.

There are a number of things going on in that college which ought to be brought into the light. Are you going to let them get away with it?"'

Treeves said, 'I regard that as coming close to an accusation of murder.'

Harkness handed the paper to Dalgliesh. He said, 'But without evidence, with no motive alleged and no suspect named, isn't it as likely to be the work of some prankster, perhaps someone who wants to make trouble for the college?'

Dalgliesh handed the paper back to Treeves, but it was waved away impatiently.

Treeves said, 'Obviously it's a possibility, among others. I imagine you won't rule that out. Personally I take a more serious view. Produced on a computer, of course, so no chance of that usual little "e" out of alignment which always crops up in crime fiction. You needn't trouble to test for fingerprints, I've had that done. Confidentially, of course. No result, but I didn't expect one. And the writer is educated, I'd say. He – or she – has got the punctuation right. In this under-educated age I'd suggest that means someone middle-aged rather than young.'

Dalgliesh said, 'And written in a way likely to spur you into action.'

'Why do you say that?'

'You're here, sir, aren't you?'

Harkness asked, 'You said that your son was adopted. What was his background?'

'He had none. His mother was fourteen when he was born, his father a year older. He was conceived against a concrete pillar in the Westway underpass. He was white, healthy and new-born – a desirable commodity in the adoption market. To put it bluntly, we were lucky to get him. Why the question?'

'You said that you were taking this as an accusation of murder. I was wondering who, if anyone, would benefit from his death.'

'Every death benefits someone. The only beneficiary here is my second son, Marcus, whose trust fund when he reaches thirty will now be augmented and his eventual inheritance greater than it might otherwise have been. As he was at school at the relevant time, we can exclude him.'

'Ronald hadn't written or spoken to you about being depressed or unhappy?'

'Not to me, but then I'm probably the last person he would have confided in. But I don't think we're understanding each other. I'm not here to be interrogated or to take part in your investigation. I've told you the little I know. Now I want you to take it over.'

Harkness glanced at Dalgliesh. He said, 'It's a matter, of course, for the Suffolk Police. They're an efficient force.'

'I've no doubt they are. Presumably they get inspected by Her Majesty's Inspector of Constabulary and certified as efficient. But they were part of the original inquiry. I want you to take it over. Specifically, I want Commander Dalgliesh to take it over.'

The Assistant Commissioner looked at Dalgliesh and seemed about to protest, then thought better of it.

Dalgliesh said, 'I'm due to take some leave next week and I plan to be in Suffolk for about a week. I know St Anselm's. I could have a word with the local police and with people at the college and see if there is a prima facie case for taking the matter further. But with the inquest verdict and your son's body cremated it's highly unlikely that anything new will come to light now.'

Harkness found his voice. 'It's unorthodox.'

Treeves got to his feet. 'It may be unorthodox, but it seems to me perfectly sensible. I want discretion, that's why I don't intend to go back to the local people. There was enough fuss in the local papers when the news of his death broke. I don't want headlines in the tabloids suggesting that there was something mysterious about the death.'

Harkness said, 'But you think there was?'

'Of course there was. Ronald's death was either an accident, suicide or murder. The first is improbable, the second inexplicable, which leaves the third. You'll get in touch with me, of course, when you have reached a conclusion.'

He was rising from his chair when Harkness asked, 'Were you happy, Sir Alred, about your son's choice of career?' He paused, then added, 'Job, vocation, whatever.'

Something in his tone, an uneasy compromise between tact and interrogation, made it apparent that he hadn't expected his question to be well-received, and it wasn't. Sir Alred's voice was quiet, but held an unmistakable warning. 'What precisely is that supposed to mean?'

Having started, Harkness had no intention of being intimidated. 'I was wondering whether your son had anything on his mind, a particular cause of worry.'

Sir Alred deliberately glanced at his wrist-watch. He

said, 'You're suggesting suicide. I thought I'd made my position clear. That's out. Out. Why the hell should he kill himself? He'd got what he wanted.'

Dalgliesh said quietly, 'But if it wasn't what you wanted?'

'Of course it wasn't what I wanted! A job with no future. The C of E will be defunct in twenty years if the present decline continues. Or it'll be an eccentric sect concerned with maintaining old superstitions and ancient churches – that is if the State hasn't taken them over as national monuments. People might want the illusion of spirituality. No doubt by and large they believe in God, and the thought that death might be extinction isn't agreeable. But they've stopped believing in heaven and they're not afraid of hell, and they won't start going to church. Ronald had education, intelligence, opportunities. He wasn't stupid. He could have made something of his life. He knew what I felt and the matter was closed between us. He certainly wasn't going to stick his head under a ton of sand to disoblige me.'

He got to his feet and nodded briefly to Harkness and Dalgliesh. The interview was over. Dalgliesh went down in the lift with him and then walked with him to where the chauffeur-driven Mercedes had glided to a stop. The timing, as he had expected, was perfect.

He had turned away when he was peremptorily called back.

Thrusting his head out of the window, Sir Alred said, 'It's occurred to you, I imagine, that Ronald could have been killed elsewhere and his body moved to the beach?'

'I think you can assume, Sir Alred, that it will have occurred to the Suffolk Police.'

'I'm not sure I share your confidence. It's a thought anyway. Worth bearing in mind.'

He made no move to order his chauffeur, sitting immobile and expressionless as a statue at the wheel, to drive off. Instead he said as if on impulse, 'Now here's a matter that intrigues me. It occurred to me in church actually. I show my face from time to time, the annual City service, you know. I thought that when I had a spare moment I'd follow it up. It's about the Creed.'

Dalgliesh was adept at concealing surprise. He asked gravely, 'Which one, Sir Alred?'

'Is there more than one?'

'Three actually.'

'Good God! Well, take any one. They're much the same, I suppose. How did they start? I mean, who wrote them?'

Dalgliesh, intrigued, was tempted to ask whether Sir Alred had discussed his question with his son, but prudence prevailed. He said, 'I think a theologian would be more useful to you than I am, Sir Alred.'

'You're a parson's son, aren't you? I thought you'd know. I haven't the time to go asking around.'

Dalgliesh's mind spun back to his father's study at the Norfolk rectory, to facts either learned or picked up from browsing in his father's library, to words he seldom spoke now but which seemed to have lodged in his mind since childhood. He said, 'The Nicene Creed was formulated by the Council of Nicaea in the fourth century.' The date inexplicably came to mind. 'I think it was 325. The Emperor Constantine called the Council to settle the belief of the Church and deal with the Arian Heresy.'

'Why doesn't the Church bring it up to date? We don't look to the fourth century for our understanding of medicine or science or the nature of the universe. I don't look to the fourth century when I run my companies. Why look to 325 for our understanding of God?'

Dalgliesh said, 'You'd prefer a Creed for the twenty-first century?' He was tempted to ask whether Sir Alred had it in mind to write one. Instead he said, 'I doubt whether any new council in a divided Christendom would arrive at a consensus. The Church no doubt takes the view that the bishops at Nicaea were divinely inspired.'

'It was a council of men, wasn't it? Powerful men. They brought to it their private agendas, their prejudices, their rivalries. Essentially it was about power, who gets it, who yields it. You've sat on enough committees, you know how they work. Ever known one that was divinely inspired?'

Dalgliesh said, 'Not Home Office working parties, admittedly.' He added, 'Are you thinking of writing to the Archbishop, or perhaps the Pope?'

Sir Alred gave him a sharp suspicious look but apparently decided that, if he were being teased, he would ignore or collude in it. He said, 'Too busy. Anyway it's a bit outside my province. Still, it's interesting. You'd think that it would have occurred to them. You'll let me know if anything turns up at St Anselm's. I'll be out of the country for the next ten days, but there's no hurry. If the boy was murdered I shall know what to do. If he killed himself, well that's his business, but I'd like to know that too.'

He nodded and abruptly withdrew his head. He said to the driver, 'All right, Norris, back to the office.'

The car glided away. Dalgliesh stared after it for a moment. With Alred what you saw was what you got. Hadn't that been an over-confident, even presumptuous assessment? The man was more complex than that, in his mixture of naivety and subtlety, of arrogance and that far-ranging curiosity which, alighting incongruously on a subject, invested it immediately with the dignity of his personal interest. But Dalgliesh was still puzzled. The verdict on Ronald Treeves, even if surprising, had at least been merciful. Was there some other more intriguing reason than parental concern for his insistence on a further inquiry?

He returned to the seventh floor. Harkness was staring out of the window. Without turning, he said, 'An extra-ordinary man. Had he anything else to say?'

'He'd like to rewrite the Nicene Creed.'

'The idea's absurd.'

'But probably less harmful to the human race than most of his other activities.'

'I meant this proposal to waste the time of a senior officer reopening the inquiry into his son's death. Still, he's not going to let it rest. Will you set it up with Suffolk or shall I?'

'Better keep it as low-key as possible. Peter Jackson transferred there last year as AC. I'll have a word with him. And I know something of St Anselm's. I stayed there as a boy for three summers. I don't suppose any of the same staff are there, but they'll probably see my arrival as more or less natural in the circumstances.'

'Do you think so? They may live remote from the

29

world but I doubt they'll be that naïve. A Commander of the Met taking an interest in the accidental death of a student? Well, we haven't much choice. Treeves isn't going to let this go and we can hardly send a couple of sergeants to start nosing about on someone else's patch. But if it is a suspicious death, Suffolk will have to take over whether Treeves likes it or not, and he can give over thinking that they can mount a murder investigation in secret. There's this to be said for murder, once it's out in the open we all stand on equal ground. That's one thing even Treeves can't manipulate to suit his convenience. It's odd, though, isn't it? I mean, it's odd his bothering, making a personal matter of it. If he wants to keep it out of the press, why resurrect it? And why take the letter seriously? He must get his share of letters from lunatics. You'd expect him to chuck this away with the rest of the rubbish.'

Dalgliesh was silent. Whatever the motive of the sender, the message hadn't struck him as the work of someone deranged. Harkness moved closer to the window and stood, shoulders hunched, peering out as if the familiar panorama of towers and spires had suddenly become interestingly strange to him.

Without turning, he said, 'He didn't show any pity for the boy, did he? And it can't have been easy for him – the kid, I mean. He gets adopted, presumably because Treeves and his wife thought they couldn't have children, and then she gets pregnant and a proper son arrives. The genuine article, your own flesh and blood, not a kid chosen for you by the Social Services department. And it isn't unusual. I know a case. The adopted child always feels that he's in the family under false pretences.'

The words had been spoken with barely controlled vehemence. There was a moment's silence, then Dalgliesh said, 'That may account for it, that or guilt. He couldn't love the boy when he was alive, can't even grieve for him now he's dead, but he can see that he gets justice.'

Harkness turned and said brusquely, 'What use is justice to the dead? Better to concentrate on justice for the living. But you're probably right. Anyway, do what you can. I'll put the Commissioner in the picture.'

He and Dalgliesh had been on Christian name terms for eight years, yet he spoke as if he were dismissing a sergeant.

3

The file for the meeting with the Home Secretary was ready on his desk, the annexes tabbed; his PA, as always, had been efficient. As he put the papers in his briefcase and went down in the lift Dalgliesh freed his mind from the preoccupations of the day and let it range free on the windswept coast of Ballard's Mere.

So he was going back at last. Why, he wondered, hadn't he returned before? His aunt had lived on the coast of East Anglia, at first in her cottage and then in the converted mill, and on his visits he could easily have made the journey to St Anselm's. Had it been an instinctive reluctance to court disappointment, the knowledge that one returns to a well-loved place always under judgement, burdened by the sad accretion of the years? And he would return as a stranger. Father Martin had been on the staff when he last visited but must have retired long ago; he would be eighty by now. He would bring to St Anselm's only unshared memories. And he would come uninvited and as a police officer to reopen, with little justification, a case that must have caused the staff at St Anselm's distress and embarrassment and which they had hoped to put behind them. But now he was returning, and he found that the prospect was suddenly pleasant.

He walked unheeding the undistinguished bureaucratic half-mile between Broadway and Parliament

Square, but his mind inhabited a quieter, less frenetic scene: the sandy friable cliffs spilling on to a beach pitted with rain, the oak groynes half demolished by centuries of tides but still withstanding the sea's onslaughts, the grit road which had once run a mile inland but was now perilously close to the cliff edge. And St Anselm's itself, the two crumbling Tudor towers flanking the front courtyard, the iron-bounded oak door and, to the rear of the great brick and stone Victorian mansion, the delicate cloisters enclosing the west court, the northerly one leading directly to the medieval church which serves the community as its chapel. He remembered that the students had worn cassocks when they were in college and brown worsted cloaks with hoods as a protection against the wind, never absent from that coast. He saw them, now surpliced for Evensong, filing into the church stalls, smelled the incense-scented air, saw the altar, with more candles than his Anglican father would have thought proper, and above the altar the framed painting by Rogier van der Weyden of the Holy Family. Would that still be there? And was that other possession, more secret, more mysterious and more jealously guarded, still hidden in the college, the Anselm papyrus?

He had spent only three summer holidays at the college. His father had exchanged ministries with a priest from a difficult inner city parish to give him at least a change of scene and tempo. Dalgliesh's parents had been unwilling to immure him in an industrial city for most of the summer holiday and he had been invited to stay on at the rectory with the newcomers. But the news that The Revd Cuthbert Simpson and his wife had four children under the age of eight, including seven-year-old twins, had turned him against the idea; even at fourteen he had longed for privacy during the long holiday. So he had agreed to accept an invitation from the Warden at St Anselm's while being uneasily aware that his mother thought he would have shown a more generous spirit by offering to stay and help with the twins.

The college had been half empty with only a few overseas students choosing to remain. They and the priests had taken trouble to make his stay happy, setting up a wicket on the stretch of specially mown grass behind the church and bowling to him indefatigably. He remembered that the food had been greatly superior to school meals and, indeed, to those at the Rectory, and he had liked his guest-room even though it gave no view of the sea. But he had most enjoyed the solitary walks, south towards the mere or north towards Lowestoft, the freedom to use the library, the prevailing but never oppressive silence, the assurance that he could take possession of every new day in unquestioned liberty.

And then, during his second visit and on the third of August, there had been Sadie.

Father Martin had said, 'Mrs Millson's granddaughter is coming to stay with her in her cottage. She's about your age I think, Adam. It might be company for you.' Mrs Millson had been the cook, even then in her sixties and certainly long since retired.

And Sadie had been company of a sort. She was a thin fifteen-year-old with fine corn-coloured hair which hung down each side of a narrow face, and small eyes of a remarkable grey flecked with green which on their first meeting stared at him with a resentful intensity. But she seemed happy enough to walk with him, seldom speaking, occasionally picking up a stone to hurl into the sea, or suddenly spurting ahead with fierce determination, then turning to wait for him, rather like a puppy chasing after a ball.

He remembered one day after a storm, when the sky had cleared but the wind was still high and great waves were crashing in with as much vehemence as they had during the dark hours of the night. They had sat side by side in the shelter of a groyne, passing a bottle of lemonade from mouth to mouth. He had written her a poem – more, he remembered, an exercise in trying to imitate Eliot (his most recent enthusiasm) than a tribute to genuine feeling. She had read it with furrowed brow, the small eyes almost invisible.

'You wrote this?'

'Yes. It's for you. A poem.'

'No it isn't. It doesn't rhyme. A boy in our class – Billy Price – writes poems. They always rhyme.'

He said indignantly, 'It's a different kind of poem.'

'No it isn't. If it's a poem the words at the end of the lines have to rhyme. Billy Price says so.'

Later he had come to believe that Billy Price had a point. He got up, tore the paper into small pieces and dropped them on the wet sand, watching and waiting for the next tumbling wave to suck them into oblivion. So much, he thought, for poetry's famed erotic power. But Sadie's female mind, in achieving its elemental ends, operated a less sophisticated, more atavistic ploy. She said, 'Bet you daren't dive off the end of that groyne.'

Billy Price, he thought, would no doubt have dared to dive off the end of the groyne in addition to writing verse which rhymed at the end of each line. Without speaking he got up and tore off his shirt. Wearing only his khaki shorts he balanced on the groyne, paused, walked over a slither of seaweed to the end and dived headlong into the turbulent sea. It was less deep than he thought and he felt the scrape of pebbles rasping his palms before he surfaced. Even in August the North Sea was cold, but the shock of the chill was only temporary. What followed was terrifying. It felt as if he were in the grasp of some uncontrollable force, as if strong hands were seizing him by the shoulders and forcing him backwards and under. Spluttering, he tried to strike out, but the shore was suddenly obliterated by a great wall of water. It crashed over him and he felt himself drawn back, then tossed upwards into daylight. He struck out towards the groyne, which seemed with every second to be receding.

He could see Sadie standing now on the edge, arms flailing, her hair streaming in the wind. She was shouting something but he could hear nothing but the drumming in his ears. He gathered his strength, waiting for the wave to advance, making progress, then desperately trying to hold on to it before the backward tug lost the few feet he had gained. He told himself not to panic, to husband strength, to try and catch each forward movement. And at last, foot by painful foot, he made it and, gasping, clutched the end of the groyne. It was minutes before he was able to move, but she reached down her hand and helped pull him up.

They sat side by side on a ridge of pebbles and, without speaking, she took off her dress and began rubbing his back. When he was dry, still without speaking, she handed him his shirt. He remembered now that the sight of her body, of the small pointed breasts and the pink and tender nipples, had aroused not desire, but an emotion that he now recognized as a mixture of affection and pity.

Then she said, 'Do you want to go to the mere? I know a secret place.'

The mere would still be there, a stretch of dark still water separated from the lively sea by a bank of shingle, its oily surface hinting at unfathomable depths. Except in the worst storms, the stagnant mere and salt sea never met across that shifting barrier. At the edge of the tide the trunks of black fossilized trees stood like totem poles to some long-dead civilization. The mere was a famous haunt of sea birds, and there were wooden hides concealed among the trees and bushes, but only the most enthusiastic bird-watcher ever penetrated to this dark and sinister stretch of water.

Sadie's secret place had been the wooden hulk of a wrecked ship half-embedded in the sand on the spit of land between the sea and the mere. There were still a few rotting steps down to the cabin and there they had spent the rest of the afternoon and all the days that followed. The only light had come from slits in the planking and they had laughed to see how their bodies were striped, tracing the moving lines with their fingers. He would read or write or sit back silently against the curved wall of the cabin while Sadie imposed on their small world her ordered if eccentric domesticity. The picnics provided by her grandmother were carefully laid out on flat stones, the food to be ceremoniously handed to him and eaten when she decreed. Jam jars filled with water from the mere held reeds and grasses and unidentified rubber-leaved plants from fissures in the cliff. Together they scoured the beach for stones with holes to add to the necklace that she had strung on cord along the cabin wall.

For years after that summer the smell of tar, of warm rotting oak combined with the tang of the sea had held for him an erotic charge. Where, he wondered, was Sadie now? Probably married with a brood of golden-haired children – if their fathers hadn't been drowned, electrocuted or otherwise disposed of in Sadie's preliminary process of selection. It was unlikely that any trace of the wreck would remain. After decades of pounding the sea must now have claimed its prey. And long before the final plank was tossed into the advancing tide, the string of the necklace would have frayed and, at last, finally broken, letting slip those carefully gathered stones to fall in a heap on the sand of the cabin floor.

4

It was Thursday, 12 October and Margaret Munroe was writing the final entry in the diary.

Looking back over this diary since I began writing it, most of it seems so dull that I wonder why I persevere. The entries following Ronald Treeves's death have been little more than descriptions of my daily routine interposed with descriptions of the weather. After the inquest and the Requiem Mass it sometimes seemed as if the tragedy had been formally tidied away and he had never been here. None of the students speak of him, at least not to me, and nor do the priests. His body was never returned to St Anselm's, even for the Requiem. Sir Alred wanted it to be cremated in London, so it was removed after the inquest by London undertakers. Father John packed up his clothes and Sir Alred sent two men in a car to collect the bundle and drive back Ronald's Porsche. The bad dreams have begun to fade and I no longer wake up sweating, imagining that sand-caked, blind-eyed horror groping towards me.

But Father Martin was right. It has helped me, writing down all the details, and I shall go on writing. I find I look forward to that moment at the end of the day when I have tidied away my supper things and can sit down at the table with this notebook. I haven't any other talent but I do enjoy using words, thinking about the past, trying to stand outside the things that have happened to me and make sense of them.

But today's entry won't be dull or routine. Yesterday was different. Something important did happen and I need to write it down to make the account complete. But I don't know whether it would be right even to form the words. It isn't my secret, after all, and although no one will ever read this account but me, I can't help feeling that there are things which it's unwise to put down on paper. When secrets are unspoken and unwritten they are lodged safely in the mind, but writing them down seems to let them loose and give them the power to spread like pollen on the air and enter into other minds. That sounds fanciful, but there must be some truth in it or why do I feel so strongly that I ought to stop writing now? But there's no sense in carrying on with the diary if I leave out the most important facts. And there isn't any real risk that these words will be read even if I place the book in an unlocked drawer. So few people come here and those that do wouldn't rummage among my things. But perhaps I ought to take more care over privacy. Tomorrow I'll give some thought to that, but now I shall write it down as completely as I dare.

The oddest thing is that I wouldn't have remembered any of it if Eric Surtees hadn't brought me a present of four of his home-grown leeks. He knows that I enjoy them for supper with a cheese sauce, and he often comes up with gifts of vegetables from the garden. I'm not the only one; he gives them to the other cottages as well as to the college. Before he arrived I had been rereading my account of the finding of Ronald's body, and as I unwrapped the leeks that scene on the shore was fresh in my mind. And

40

then things came together and I suddenly remembered. It all came back as clear as a photograph and I recalled every gesture, every word spoken, everything except the names – and I'm not sure I ever knew them. It was twelve years ago but it could have been yesterday.

I ate my supper and took the secret to bed with me. This morning I knew that I must tell the person most concerned. Once I'd done that I would keep silent. But first I must check that what I remembered was right, and I made the telephone call when I went into Lowestoft this afternoon to shop. And then, two hours ago, I told what I knew. It isn't really my business and now there's nothing else I need do. And, after all, it was easy and simple and nothing to worry about. I'm glad I spoke. It would have been uncomfortable to go on living here knowing what I know and yet not speaking of it, wondering all the time if I was doing right. Now I needn't worry. But it still seems so odd that things wouldn't have come together and I wouldn't have remembered if Eric hadn't brought me a present of those leeks.

This has been an exhausting day and I'm very tired, perhaps too tired to sleep. I think I'll watch the beginning of Newsnight, *and then to bed.*

She carried her notebook from the table and placed it in the drawer of the bureau. Then she changed her spectacles for the pair most comfortable for watching television, switched on the set and settled herself in the high winged armchair with the remote control resting on its arm. She was getting a little deaf. The noise swelled alarmingly before she adjusted the volume and the introductory music came to an end. She would probably fall asleep in the chair, but the effort of getting up and going to bed seemed beyond her.

She was almost dozing when she felt a draught of cooler air and was aware, more by instinct than by sound, that someone had come into the room. The latch of the door clicked down. Stretching her head round the side of the chair she saw who it was and said, 'Oh, it's you. I expect you were surprised to find my light still on. I was just thinking of going to bed.'

The figure came up behind the armchair and she bent her head upwards, looking up, waiting for a response. And then the hands came down, strong hands wearing yellow rubber gloves. They pressed against her mouth and closed her nose, forcing her head back against the chair.

She knew that this was death but she felt no fear, only an immense surprise and a tired acceptance. To struggle would have been useless, but she had no wish to struggle, only to go easily and quickly and without pain. Her last earthly sensation was the cold smoothness of the glove against her face and the smell of latex in her nostrils as her heart gave its last compulsive beat and was stilled.

5

On Tuesday, 17 October at five minutes to ten precisely, Father Martin made his way from the small turret room he occupied at the south of the house, down the twisting stairs and along the corridor to Father Sebastian's study. For the past fifteen years, Tuesday at ten a.m. had been set aside for the weekly meeting of all resident priests. Father Sebastian would make his report, problems and difficulties would be discussed, the details of next Sunday's Sung Eucharist and of other services in the week would be finalized, invitations to future preachers decided upon and any minor housekeeping matters disposed of.

Following the meeting, the senior student would be summoned for a private meeting with Father Sebastian. His job was to report any views, complaints or ideas that the small student body wished to communicate, and to receive any instructions and information the teaching staff wished him to pass on to his fellow ordinands, including details of the services for the following week. This was the extent of student participation. St Anselm's still adhered to an old-fashioned interpretation of *in statu pupillari*, and the demarcation between teachers and taught was both understood and observed. Despite this, the regime was surprisingly easygoing, particularly in regard to Saturday leave, provided students didn't depart until after five o'clock Evensong on Friday and were back in time for the ten o'clock Eucharist on Sunday.

Father Sebastian's office faced east over the porch and gave an uninterrupted view of the sea between the two Tudor towers. It was over-large for an office but, like Father Martin before him, he had refused to spoil its proportions by any partition. His part-time secretary, Miss Beatrice Ramsey, occupied the room next door. She worked there Wednesday to Friday only, achieving in those three days as much as most secretaries would achieve in five. She was a middle-aged woman of intimidating rectitude and piety, and Father Martin was always afraid that he might inadvertently let out a fart in her presence. She was totally devoted to Father Sebastian, but without any of the sentiment and embarrassing manifestations that a spinster's affection for a priest sometimes exhibits. Indeed, it seemed that her respect was for the office not the man and that she saw it as part of her duty to keep him up to the mark.

In addition to its size, Father Sebastian's office contained some of the most valuable objects bequeathed to the college by Miss Arbuthnot. Over the stone fireplace with the carved words which were at the core of St Anselm's theology, *credo ut intelligam*, hung a large Burne-Jones painting of crisp-haired young women of improbable beauty disporting themselves in an orchard. Earlier it had hung in the refectory but Father Sebastian, without explanation, had removed it to his office. Father Martin had tried to repress the suspicion that this had been less a sign of the Warden's affection for the painting or admiration for the artist than his desire that objects of particular value in the college should as far as possible grace his study and be under his eye.

This Tuesday it was to be a meeting of only three:

44

Father Sebastian, Father Martin and Father Peregrine Glover. Father John Betterton had an urgent dental appointment in Halesworth and had sent his apologies. Father Peregrine, the priest librarian, joined them within minutes. At forty-two he was the youngest of the priests in residence, but to Father Martin he often seemed the eldest. His chubby soft-skinned face was made more owl-like by large round horn-rimmed spectacles and his thick dark hair was cut in a fringe and only needed a tonsure to complete the resemblance to a medieval friar. This mildness of his face gave a false impression of his physical strength. Father Martin was always surprised when they stripped for swimming to see how firmly muscled was Father Peregrine's body. He himself swam now only on the hottest days, when he would splash apprehensively in the shallows on uncertain feet and watch in amazement as Father Peregrine, sleek as a dolphin, hurled his curved body into the surf. At the Tuesday meetings Father Peregrine spoke little and more usually to impart a fact than to express an opinion, but he was always listened to. Academically he was distinguished, having received a First in Natural Sciences at Cambridge before a second First in Theology and opting for the Anglican priesthood. At St Anselm's he taught Church History, sometimes with a disconcerting relevance to the development of scientific thought and discoveries. He valued his privacy and had a small room on the ground floor at the rear of the building next to the library which he resolutely refused to leave, perhaps because this hermitic and Spartan space reminded him of the monk's cell he secretly yearned to be occupying. It was next to the utility-room and his only concern was about the students' use of the noisy and somewhat antiquated washing machines after ten o'clock at night.

Father Martin placed three chairs in a partial ring before the window and they stood, bending their heads for the usual prayer which Father Sebastian spoke with no concession to the contemporary meaning of the first word.

'Prevent us, O Lord, in all our doings with thy most gracious favour, and further us with thy continual help; that in all our works, begun, continued, and ended in thee, we may glorify thy holy Name, and finally by thy mercy obtain everlasting life; through Jesus Christ our Lord, Amen.'

They composed themselves on the chairs, hands on their knees, and Father Sebastian began.

'The first thing I have to report today is somewhat disturbing. I have had a telephone call from New Scotland Yard. Apparently Sir Alred Treeves has expressed dissatisfaction with the verdict following the death of Ronald and has asked the Yard to investigate. A Commander Adam Dalgliesh will be arriving after lunch on Friday afternoon. Naturally I have undertaken to give him all the co-operation he requires.'

The news was received in silence. Father Martin felt a cold clutch at his stomach. Then he said, 'But the body has been cremated. There was an inquest and a verdict. Even if Sir Alred disagrees with it, I don't see what the police can discover now. And why Scotland Yard? Why a Commander? It seems a curious use of manpower.'

Father Sebastian gave his thin-lipped sardonic smile. 'I think we can take it that Sir Alred went to the top. Such men always do. And he would hardly ask the

Suffolk Police to reopen the case since they were the ones who made the preliminary investigation. As for the choice of Commander Dalgliesh, I understand that he was coming into the county anyway on a short holiday and that he knows St Anselm's. Scotland Yard is probably attempting to propitiate Sir Alred with the least inconvenience to us or trouble to themselves. The Commander mentioned you, Father Martin.'

Father Martin was torn between an unfocused apprehension and pleasure. He said, 'I was on the staff here when he stayed for three years during the summer holidays. His father was a Norfolk rector, I'm afraid I forget which parish. Adam was a delightful boy, intelligent and sensitive, I thought. Of course I don't know what he's like now. But I shall be glad to meet him again.'

Father Peregrine said, 'Delightful and sensitive boys have a habit of growing into insensitive and far from agreeable men. However, since we have no choice over his coming, I'm glad one of us can anticipate pleasure in the visit. I can't see what Sir Alred hopes to gain by this inquiry. If the Commander does reach the conclusion that there was a possibility of foul play, surely the local force will have to take over. Foul play is an odd expression. The word derives from Old English, but why the sporting metaphor? One would have expected foul act or foul deed.'

His fellow priests were too used to Father Peregrine's obsessive interest in semantics to think the suggestion worthy of comment. It was extraordinary, thought Father Martin, to hear those two words spoken aloud, words which, ever since the tragedy, no one at St Anselm's had allowed himself to say. Father Sebastian took them in his stride.

'The suggestion of foul play is, of course, ridiculous. If there had been any suggestion that the death was other than an accident, the evidence would have been brought out at the inquest.'

But there was, of course, a third possibility and it was one which was in all their minds. The verdict of accidental death had come as a relief to St Anselm's. Even so, this death had held the seeds of disaster for the college. It hadn't been the only death. Perhaps, thought Father Martin, that possible suicide had overshadowed Margaret Munroe's fatal heart attack. It had not been unexpected; Dr Metcalf had warned them that she might go at any time. And it had been a merciful death. She had been found by Ruby Pilbeam early the next morning, sitting peacefully in her chair. And now, only five days later, it was as if she had never been part of St Anselm's. Her sister, of whose existence they hadn't known until Father Martin went through Margaret's papers, had arranged the funeral, had come with a van for her furniture and belongings, and had cut the college out from the obsequies. Only Father Martin had understood how greatly Ronald's death had affected Margaret. Sometimes he thought that he was her only mourner.

Father Sebastian said, 'All the guest sets will be occupied this weekend. Apart from Commander Dalgliesh, Emma Lavenham will be arriving as arranged from Cambridge for her three days of lectures on the metaphysical poets. Then Inspector Roger Yarwood is coming from Lowestoft. He has been suffering from severe stress recently following the break-up of his marriage. He hopes to stay for a week. He has, of course, had nothing to do with the Ronald Treeves investigation. Clive Stannard is coming again for the weekend to continue his research into the domestic lives of the early Tractarians. As all the guest sets will be in use he had better go into Peter Buckhurst's room. Dr Metcalf wants Peter to remain in the sick-room for the present. He'll be warm and more comfortable there.'

Father Peregrine said, 'I'm sorry that Stannard is returning. I hoped I'd seen the last of him. He's an ungracious young man and his pretence of research is unconvincing. I sought his views on the effect of the Gorham case in modifying the Tractarian belief of J. B. Mozley and it was apparent he had no idea what I was talking about. I find his presence in the library disruptive – and so, I think, do the ordinands.'

Father Sebastian said, 'His grandfather was St Anselm's' lawyer and a benefactor of the college. I don't like to think that any member of the family is unwelcome. Still, that hardly entitles him to a free weekend whenever he fancies it. The work of the college must take precedence. If he applies again the matter will be tactfully dealt with.'

Father Martin said, 'And the fifth visitor?'

Father Sebastian's attempt to control his voice was not altogether successful. 'Archdeacon Crampton has telephoned to say that he will be arriving on Saturday and will stay until Sunday after breakfast.'

Father Martin cried, 'But he was here two weeks ago! Surely he's not proposing to become a regular visitor?'

'I fear he may. Ronald Treeves's death has reopened the whole question of the future of St Anselm's. As you know, my policy has been to avoid controversy, to continue our work quietly and to use what influence I have in Church circles to prevent closure.'

Father Martin said, 'There's no evidence to support closure except the policy of the Church to centralize all theological training in three centres. If this decision is rigidly enforced, then St Anselm's will close, but not because of the quality of our training or of the ordinands we produce.'

Father Sebastian ignored this restatement of the obvious. He said, 'There is, of course, another problem in regard to his visit. The last time the Archdeacon arrived Father John took a short holiday. I don't think he can do that again. But the presence of the Archdeacon is bound to be painful to him and, indeed, embarrassing for the rest of us if Father John is here.'

It would indeed, thought Father Martin. Father John Betterton had come to St Anselm's after some years in prison. He had been convicted of sexual offences against two boy servers in the church of which he was priest. To these charges he had pleaded guilty, but the offences had been more a question of inappropriate fondling and caresses than of serious sexual abuse, and a custodial sentence would have been highly unlikely had not Archdeacon Crampton busied himself in finding additional evidence. Previous choirboys, now young men, had been interviewed, additional evidence had been obtained and the police alerted. The whole incident had caused resentment and much unhappiness, and the prospect of having the Archdeacon and Father John under the same roof filled Father Martin with horror. He was torn with pity every time he saw Father John almost creeping about his duties, taking Communion but never celebrating, finding in St Anselm's a refuge rather than a job. The Archdeacon had obviously been doing what he saw as his duty, and perhaps it was unfair to assume that duty had not, in this case, been uncongenial. And yet to pursue a fellow-priest so remorselessly – and one for whom he held no personal antagonism, indeed had hardly ever met – seemed inexplicable.

Father Martin said, 'I wonder if Crampton was altogether – well – himself when he pursued Father John. There was something irrational about the whole business.'

Father Sebastian said sharply, 'In what way not altogether himself? He wasn't mentally ill, there's never been any suggestion surely . . . ?'

Father Martin said, 'It was shortly after his wife's suicide, a difficult time for him.'

'Bereavement is always a difficult time. I can't see how personal tragedy could have affected his judgement where the business of Father John was concerned. It was a difficult time for me after Veronica was killed.'

Father Martin had difficulty in repressing a slight smile. Lady Veronica Morell had been killed in a hunting fall on one of her regular returns to the family house she had never really left, and the sport that she had never been able, nor indeed intended, to give up. Father Martin suspected that, if Father Sebastian had to lose his wife, this was the way he would have preferred. 'My wife broke her neck out hunting' has a certain cachet lacking from 'my wife died of pneumonia'. Father Sebastian had shown no disposition to remarry. Perhaps being husband to the daughter of an earl, even one five years older than him and with more than a passing resemblance to the animals she adored, had rendered unattractive, even slightly demeaning, the prospect of allying himself to any less elevated woman. Father Martin, recognizing that his thoughts were ignoble, made a quick mental act of contrition.

But he had liked Lady Veronica. He recalled her rangy figure striding along the cloisters after the last service she had attended and braying to her husband, 'Your sermon was too long, Seb. Couldn't understand half of it and I'm sure the lads didn't.' Lady Veronica always referred to the students as lads. Father Martin sometimes imagined that she thought her husband was running a set of racing stables.

It was noticed that the Warden had always been at his most relaxed and cheerful when his wife was in college. Father Martin's imagination obdurately refused to encompass the idea of Father Sebastian and Lady Veronica in the matrimonial bed, but he had had no doubt, seeing them together, that they had liked each other very much indeed. It was, he thought, one more manifestation of the variety and peculiarities of the married state of which he, as a life-long bachelor, had never been more than a fascinated observer. Perhaps, he thought, a great liking was as important as love, and more durable.

Father Sebastian said, 'When Raphael arrives I shall, of course, speak to him about the Archdeacon's visit. He feels very strongly about Father John – indeed, he sometimes seems hardly rational on the subject. It isn't going to help things if he provokes an open quarrel. It could do nothing but harm to the college. He'll have to learn that the Archdeacon is both a trustee of the college and a guest and must be treated with the respect due to a priest.'

Father Peregrine said, 'Wasn't Inspector Yarwood the police officer in charge of the case when the Archdeacon's first wife committed suicide?'

His fellow priests looked at him in surprise. It was the kind of information Father Peregrine tended to acquire. It sometimes seemed that his subconscious was a repository of assorted facts and snippets of news which he could bring to mind at will.

Father Sebastian said, 'Are you sure? The Cramptons were living in North London at that time. He didn't move to Suffolk until after his wife's death. It would have been a matter for the Metropolitan Police.'

Father Peregrine said placidly, 'One reads these things. I remember the account of the inquest. I think you'll find that it was an officer called Roger Yarwood who gave evidence. He was a sergeant in the Metropolitan Police at the time.'

Father Sebastian creased his brow. 'This is awkward. I'm afraid that when they meet – as they inevitably will – it will bring back painful memories for the Archdeacon. But it can't be helped. Yarwood needs a period of rest and recuperation and the room has been promised. He was very useful to the college three years ago, before he was promoted, when he was on traffic duties and Father Peregrine backed into that stationary lorry. As you know, he's been coming to Sunday Mass fairly regularly and I think he finds it helpful. If his presence awakes distressing memories then the Archdeacon will have to cope with them as Father John copes with his. I shall arrange for

Emma to be in Ambrose immediately next to the church, Commander Dalgliesh in Jerome, then the Archdeacon in Augustine and Roger Yarwood in Gregory.'

They were in for an uncomfortable weekend, thought Father Martin. It would be deeply distressing for Father John to have to meet the Archdeacon, and Crampton himself was unlikely to welcome the encounter although it could hardly be unexpected; he must know that Father John was at St Anselm's. And if Father Peregrine were right – and he invariably was – a meeting between the Archdeacon and Inspector Yarwood was likely to embarrass them both. It would be difficult to control Raphael or to keep him apart from the Archdeacon; he was, after all, the senior ordinand. And then there was Stannard. Apart from any devious motives in coming to St Anselm's he was never an easy guest. Most problematic of all would be the presence of Adam Dalgliesh, an implacable reminder of unhappy events which they thought they had put behind them, viewing them with his experienced and sceptical eyes.

He was roused from his reverie by Father Sebastian's voice. 'And now I think we'll have our coffee.'

6

Raphael Arbuthnot came in and stood waiting with the graceful assurance that was typical of him. His black cassock with its row of covered buttons, unlike those of other ordinands, looked newly tailored, elegantly fitting; its dark austerity, contrasting with Raphael's pale face and shining hair, imposed a look which, paradoxically, was both hieratic and theatrical. Father Sebastian could never see him alone without a tinge of unease. He was himself a handsome man and had always valued – perhaps overvalued – handsomeness in other men and beauty in women. Only with his wife had it seemed unimportant. But he found beauty in a man disconcerting, even a little repellent. Young men, and particularly young English men, should not look like a slightly dissolute Greek god. It was not that there was anything androgynous about Raphael, but Father Sebastian was always aware that this was a beauty more likely to appeal to men rather than to women, even if it had no power to stir his own heart.

And there came again to mind the most insistent of the many worries which made it difficult to spend time with Raphael without a renewal of old misgivings. How valid really was his vocation? And should the college have agreed to take him on as an ordinand when he was already, as it were, part of the family? St Anselm's had been the only home he'd known since his mother, the last Arbuthnot, had dumped him on the college, a two-week-old baby, illegitimate and unwanted, twenty-five years ago. Wouldn't it have been wiser, perhaps indeed prudent, to have encouraged him to look elsewhere, to apply to Cuddesdon or St Stephen's House at Oxford? Raphael himself had insisted on training at St Anselm's. Hadn't there been the subtle threat that it was here or nowhere? Perhaps the college had been too accommodating in their anxiety not to lose to the Church the last of the Arbuthnots. Well, it was too late now and it was irritating how often these fruitless worries about Raphael would keep intruding on more immediate if mundane matters. Resolutely he put them aside and addressed himself to college concerns.

'A few minor details first, Raphael. Students who persist in parking in front of the college must do so more tidily. As you know, I prefer cars and motorcycles to be left outside the college buildings at the rear. If they have to be parked in the front courtyard, at least take some care. This is something which particularly irritates Father Peregrine. And will students please remember not to use the washing machines after Compline. Father Peregrine finds the noise distracting. And, now we are without Mrs Munroe, I have agreed that bed-linen for the present shall be changed fortnightly. The linen will be available in the linen-room and students should help themselves to what they require and change their own beds. We are advertising for a replacement but it may take some time.'

'Yes, Father. I'll mention these matters.'

'There are two more important items. This Friday we shall be having a visit from a Commander Dalgliesh of New Scotland Yard. Apparently Sir Alred Treeves is dissatisfied with the inquest verdict on Ronald and has asked the Yard to make enquiries. I don't know how long he will be with us, probably only for the weekend. Naturally we shall all co-operate with the Commander. That means answering his questions fully and honestly, not venturing opinions.'

'But Ronald's been cremated, Father. What can Commander Dalgliesh hope to prove now? Surely he can't overturn the findings of the inquest?'

'I imagine not. I think it's more a question of satisfying Sir Alred that there was a thorough investigation of his son's death.'

'But that's ridiculous, Father. The Suffolk Police were very thorough. What else can the Yard hope to discover now?'

'Very little, I imagine. Anyway, Commander Dalgliesh is coming and will occupy Jerome. There will be other visitors. Inspector Yarwood is arriving for a recuperative holiday. He needs rest and quiet and I imagine will take some of his meals in his room. Mr Stannard will be back continuing his research in the library. And Archdeacon Crampton is expected for a short visit. He will arrive on Saturday and plans to leave immediately after breakfast on Sunday. I have invited him to preach the homily at Compline on Saturday night. It will be a small congregation, but that can't be helped.'

Raphael said, 'If I'd known that, Father, I'd have taken good care not to be here.'

'I realize that. I expect you as senior student to be here at least until after Compline and to treat him with the courtesy that you should extend to a visitor, an older man and a priest.'

'I have no trouble with the first two, it's the third which sticks in my throat. How can he face us, face Father John, after what he's done?'

'I imagine, like the rest of us, he takes solace from the satisfaction of believing that at the time he did what he thought was right.'

Raphael's face flushed. He exclaimed, 'How can he think he was right – a priest hounding another priest into prison? It would be disgraceful if anyone did it. Coming from him it's abominable. And Father John – the gentlest, the kindest of men.'

'You forget, Raphael, that Father John pleaded guilty at his trial.'

'He pleaded guilty to misbehaviour with two young boys. He didn't rape them, he didn't seduce them, he didn't physically hurt them. All right, he pleaded guilty, but he wouldn't have been sent to prison if Crampton hadn't made it his business to start delving into the past, digging up those three youths, persuading them to come forward with evidence. What the hell business was it of his anyway?'

'He saw it as his business. We have to remember that Father John also pleaded guilty to those more serious charges.'

'Of course he did. He pleaded guilty because he felt guilty. He feels guilty at just being alive. But mainly it was to prevent those youths perjuring themselves in the witness-box. That's what he couldn't bear, the harm it would do them, the harm they'd do to themselves by lying in court. He wanted to spare them that, at the cost of going to prison.'

Father Sebastian said sharply, 'Did he tell you that? Have you actually discussed this with him?'

'Not really, not directly. But that's the truth of it, I know it is.'

Father Sebastian felt uncomfortable. That could well be. It was something he had thought out for himself. But this delicate psychological perception was appropriate to him as a priest; coming from a student he found it disconcerting. He said, 'You had no right, Raphael, to talk to Father John about this. He's served his sentence and he's come to live and work with us here. The past is behind him. It's unfortunate if he has to meet the Archdeacon but it won't be made easier for him or for anyone if you attempt to interfere. We all have our darkness within. Father John's is between him and God, or for him and his confessor. For you to intervene is spiritual arrogance.'

Raphael seemed hardly to have heard. He said, 'And we know why Crampton's coming, don't we? To nose about getting fresh evidence against the college. He wants to see us closed down. He made that obvious as soon as the Bishop appointed him as one of the trustees.'

'And if he's treated with discourtesy then he will be provided with the additional evidence he needs. I've kept St Anselm's open by such influence as I have and by carrying on quietly with my work, not by antagonizing powerful enemies. This is a difficult time for the college and Ronald Treeves's death didn't help.' He paused, then asked a question that until now he had left unspoken. He said, 'You must have discussed that death among yourselves. What view of it was taken by the ordinands?'

He saw that the question was unwelcome. There was a pause before Raphael replied. 'I think, Father, the general view was that Ronald killed himself.'

'But why? Did you have an opinion on that?'

The silence this time was longer. Then Raphael said, 'No, Father, I don't think we did.'

Father Sebastian went over to his desk and studied a sheet of paper. He said more briskly, 'I see the college will be fairly empty this weekend. Only four of you remaining. Remind me, will you, of why so many are on leave and so early in the term.'

'Three students have started parish training, Father. Rupert has been asked to preach at St Mark's and I think two students are going to hear him. Richard's mother has a fiftieth birthday coinciding with a twenty-fifth wedding anniversary and he has special leave for that. Then you remember that Toby Williams is being inducted to his first parish and quite a number of people will be supporting him. That leaves Henry, Stephen, Peter and myself. I was hoping I might have leave after Compline. I'll miss Toby's induction but I'd like to be present for his first parish Mass.'

Father Sebastian was still studying his paper. 'Yes, that seems to add up. You may leave after you've heard the Archdeacon preach. But aren't you down for a Greek lesson with Mr Gregory after Mass on Sunday? You'd better clear this with him.'

'I have, Father. He can fit me in on Monday.'

'Right, then I think that's all for this week, Raphael. You may as well take your essay. It's on the desk. Evelyn Waugh wrote in one of his travel books that he saw theology as the science of simplification whereby nebulous and elusive ideas are made intelligible and exact. Your essay is neither. And you misuse the word emulate. It is not synonymous with imitate.'

'Of course not. Sorry, Father. I can imitate you but I can't hope to emulate you.'

Father Sebastian turned away to hide a smile. He said, 'I would strongly advise you to attempt neither.'

As the door closed behind Raphael the smile lingered; and then the Warden remembered that he had extracted no promise of good behaviour. A promise, once given, would be kept, but there had been none. It was going to be a complicated weekend.

7

Dalgliesh left his flat overlooking the Thames at Queenshythe before first light. The building, now converted into modern offices for a financial corporation, had previously been a warehouse and the smell of spice, fugitive as memory, still lingered in the wide, sparsely furnished and wooden-clad rooms which he occupied on the top storey. When the building was sold for development he had resolutely resisted the prospective new owner's effort to buy out his long lease and at last, when Dalgliesh had rejected the final ridiculously high offer, the developers had conceded defeat and the top floor remained inviolate. Dalgliesh had now been provided, at the Company's expense, with his own unobtrusive door at the side of the building and a private and secure lift up to his flat at the cost of a higher rent but an extended lease. He suspected that the building had in the end been more than adequate for their needs and that the presence of a senior police officer on the top floor gave the nightwatchman a comforting if spurious sense of security. Dalgliesh retained what he valued: his privacy, emptiness beneath him at night and almost no noise during the daytime, and his wide view of the ever-changing life of the Thames borne beneath him on the tide.

He drove east through the City to the Whitechapel Road *en route* for the A12. Even as early as seven a.m.

the streets weren't empty of traffic and small groups of office workers were emerging from the Underground stations. London never entirely slept and he enjoyed this early-morning calm, the first stirrings of a life which within hours would become raucous, the comparative ease of driving along unencumbered streets. By the time he had reached the A12 and had thrown off the tentacles of Eastern Avenue, the first pink gash in the night sky had widened into a clear whiteness and the fields and hedges had lightened to a luminous grey in which trees and bushes, with the translucent delicacy of a Japanese water-colour, gradually gained definition and took on the first richness of autumn. It was, he thought, a good time of year to look at trees. Only in spring did they give greater delight. They were not yet denuded of leaves and the dark pattern of thrusting boughs and branches was becoming visible through a haze of fading green, yellow and red.

As he drove he thought about the purpose of this journey and analysed the reasons for his involvement – certainly unorthodox – in the death of an unknown young man, a death already investigated, defined by a coroner's inquest and as officially done with as the finality of the cremation which had reduced the body to ground bones. His offer to investigate hadn't been impulsive, little of his official life was so driven. And it hadn't altogether been a wish to get Sir Alred out of the office, although he was a man whose absence was usually preferable to his presence. He wondered again about the man's concern over the death of an adopted son for whom he had shown no signs of affection. But perhaps he, Dalgliesh, was being presumptuous. Sir Alred was, after all, a man who took care not to betray sentiment. It was possible that he felt far more for his son than he had cared to reveal. Or was it that he was obsessed with the need to know the truth, however inconvenient, however unpalatable, however difficult to ascertain? If so, that was a reason with which Dalgliesh could sympathize.

He made good time and in under three hours had reached Lowestoft. He hadn't driven through the town for years and on the previous visit had been struck by its depressing air of deterioration and poverty. The sea-front hotels, which in more prosperous times had catered for the summer holidays of the middle classes, now advertised bingo sessions. Many of the shops were boarded up and the people walked grey-faced with discouraged steps. But now there seemed to be something of a renaissance. Roofs had been replaced, houses were being repainted. He felt that he was entering a town which was looking with some confidence to its future. The bridge leading to the docks was familiar to him and he drove across it with a lifting of the heart. Along this road he had cycled in boyhood to buy the freshly-landed herrings on the quay. He could recall the smell of the glistening fish as they slid from the buckets into his rucksack, the heaviness of it bumping his shoulders as he cycled back to St Anselm's with his gift of supper or breakfast for the fathers. He smelled the familiar tang of water and tar, and gazed with remembered pleasure at the boats in the harbour, wondering whether it were still possible to buy fish on the quay. Even if it were, he would never again carry a gift back to St Anselm's with the same excitement and sense of achievement as in those boyhood days.

He had rather expected the police station to be similar to those remembered from childhood, a detached or terraced house adapted for police use, its metamorphosis marked by the blue lamp mounted outside. Instead he saw a low modern building, the façade broken by a line of dark windows, a radio mast rising with impressive authority from the roof, and the Union flag flying from a pole at the entrance.

He was expected. The young woman at the reception desk greeted him in her attractive Suffolk voice as if it only needed his arrival to complete her day.

'Sergeant Jones is expecting you, sir. I'll give him a ring and he'll be right down.'

Sergeant Irfon Jones was dark, lean-featured, his sallow skin, only lightly tanned by wind and sun, contrasting with hair that was almost black. His first words of greeting immediately established his nationality.

'Mr Dalgliesh is it? I'm expecting you, sir. Mr Williams thought we could use his office, if you'll come this way. He was sorry to miss you, and the chief is in London at an ACPO meeting, but you'll know that. If you'll just sign in, sir.'

Following him through the side door with its opaque glass panel and down a narrow corridor, Dalgliesh said, 'You're a long way from home, Sergeant.'

'I am that, Mr Dalgliesh. Four hundred miles to be exact. I married a Lowestoft girl, see, and she's an only child. Her mam's none too good so Jenny's best near home. When I got a chance I transferred from the Gower. It suits me well enough, as long as I'm by the sea.'

'A very different sea.'

'A very different coast, and both of them just as

dangerous. Not that we get many fatalities. The poor lad is the first for three and a half years. Well, there are signs up and people hereabouts know the cliffs are dangerous. They should do by now. And the coast's isolated enough. It's not as if you get families with children. In here, sir. Mr Williams has cleared his desk. Not that there's much in the way of vital evidence to look at, you might say. You'll have coffee? It's here, see. I'll just have to switch it on.'

There was a tray with two cups, their handles neatly aligned, a cafetière, a tin labelled 'coffee', a jug of milk and an electric kettle. Sergeant Jones was quickly competent if a little fussy over the procedure, and the coffee was excellent. They seated themselves in two low bureaucratic chairs placed before the window.

Dalgliesh said, 'You were called out to the beach, I believe. What exactly happened?'

'I wasn't the first on the scene. That was young Brian Miles. He's the local PC. Father Sebastian telephoned from the college and he got there as soon as he could. He didn't take long, not more than half an hour. When he arrived there were only two people by the body, Father Sebastian and Father Martin. The poor lad was dead all right, anyone could see that. But he's a good boy, is Brian, and he didn't like the look of it. I'm not saying he thought it was a suspicious death, but there's no denying it was an odd one. I'm his supervisory officer so he got on to me. I was here when the call came through just before three, and as Doc Mallinson – he's our police surgeon – happened to be in the station, we went to the scene together.'

Dalgliesh said, 'With the ambulance?'

'No, not at that time. I believe in London the Coroner has his own ambulance, but here we have to use the local service when we want to move a body. It was out on a call so it took maybe an hour and a half to get him moved. When we got him to the mortuary I had a word with the Coroner's officer and he thought the Coroner would almost certainly ask for forensics. He's a very careful gentleman is Mr Mellish. That's when it was decided to treat it as a suspicious death.'

'What exactly did you find at the scene?'

'Well, he was dead, Mr Dalgliesh. Doc Mallinson certified that at once. But it didn't need a doctor to tell you he was gone. Dead about five to six hours, Doc Mallinson thought. Of course, he was still pretty well buried when we got there. Mr Gregory and Mrs Munroe had uncovered most of the body and the top of his head, but his face and arms weren't visible. Father Sebastian and Father Martin stayed at the scene. There was nothing either of them could do but Father Sebastian insisted on staying until we'd uncovered the body. I think he was wanting to pray. So we dug the poor lad out, turned him over, got him on a stretcher and Doc Mallinson had a closer look at him. Not that there was anything really to see. He was caked with sand and he was dead. That was about it.'

'Were there any visible injuries?'

'Not that we could see, Mr Dalgliesh. Of course, when you are called to an accident like that you always wonder a bit, don't you? Stands to reason. But Doc Mallinson could find no signs of violence, no crack in the back of his head or anything like that. Of course, there was no knowing what Doc Scargill might find at the PM. He's our regional forensic pathologist. Doc Mallinson said he couldn't do any more except assess the time of death and we'd have to wait for the autopsy. Not that we thought there was anything suspicious about the death, mind you. Seemed plain enough at the time. He was burrowing about in the cliff too close to the overhanging ledge and it came down on him. That's what it looked like and that's what they found at the inquest.'

'So didn't anything strike you as strange or suspicious?'

'Well, strange more than suspicious. It was a funny position he was in – head down, like a rabbit or a dog burrowing into the cliff.'

'And nothing was found close to the body?'

'There were his clothes, his brown cloak and a long black garment with buttons – a cassock, isn't it? Very neat they were.'

'Nothing that could have been a weapon?'

'Well, only a spar of wood. We dug it out when we were uncovering him. It was lying pretty close to his right hand. I thought we'd better bring it back to the station with us in case it was important, but not much notice was taken. I've got it here, though, if you'd like to see it, sir. I can't think why it wasn't thrown away after the inquest. We got nothing from it, no prints, no blood.'

He went to a cupboard at the end of the room and drew out an object wrapped in plastic. It was a spar of pale wood about two and a half feet long. Examining it closer, Dalgliesh could see traces of what looked like blue paint.

Sergeant Jones said, 'It's not been in the water, sir, not to my eyes. He may have found it on the sand and picked it up, not meaning anything in particular. It's a kind of instinct, picking things up on the beach. Father Sebastian suggested that it came from an old bathing hut the college had demolished just above the steps to the beach. Apparently Father Sebastian thought the old blue and white one was a bit of an eyesore and something simple in plain wood would be better. So that's what they did. It's used as well to house the rigid inflatable they keep in case swimmers get into difficulties. The old hut was beginning to break up anyway. But not all of it had been taken away and there were still a few rotting planks piled there. They've all gone now, I dare say.'

'What about footprints?'

'Well, they're the first thing you look for. The boy's were covered by the fall of sand but we did find a single broken line further up the beach. They were his all right, we had his shoes, see. But he walked along the shingle most of the way and so could anyone have done. The sand was well scuffled at the scene. You'd expect that with Mrs Munroe and Mr Gregory and the two priestly gentlemen not worrying where they put their feet.'

'Were you yourself surprised at the verdict?'

'Well, I must say I was. An open verdict would have seemed more logical, like. Mr Mellish sat with the jury, he likes to do that if the case is a bit complicated or there's public interest, and the jury were unanimous, all eight of them. There's no denying that an open verdict is never satisfactory and St Anselm's is highly respected hereabouts. They're isolated, I don't deny it, but the young men preach at local churches and they do a bit of good in the community. Mind you, I'm not saying that the jury were wrong. Anyway, that's what they found.'

Dalgliesh said, 'Sir Alred can hardly complain about the thoroughness of the investigation. I don't see that you could have done more.'

'Nor do I, Mr Dalgliesh, and the Coroner said the same.'

There seemed nothing more to be learned and after thanking Sergeant Jones for his help and for the coffee, Dalgliesh left. The spar of wood with its trace of blue paint had been wrapped and labelled. Dalgliesh took it with him because it seemed expected of him, rather than because he thought it would be of use.

At the far end of the parking lot a man was loading cardboard boxes into the back seat of a Rover. Looking round, he saw Dalgliesh getting into the Jaguar, gazed fixedly at him for a moment and then, as if coming to a sudden resolution, walked over. Dalgliesh found himself gazing into a prematurely aged face which looked racked by lack of sleep or pain. It was a look which he had seen too often before not to recognize.

'You must be Commander Adam Dalgliesh. Ted Williams said you'd be looking in. I'm Inspector Roger Yarwood. I'm on sick-leave and here to collect some of my gear. I just want to say that you'll be seeing me at St Anselm's. The fathers take me in from time to time. It's cheaper than a hotel and the company's better than in the local loony-bin, which is the usual alternative. Oh, and the food's better.'

The words came out in a fluent stream as if rehearsed, and there was a look both challenging and shamed in the dark eyes. The news was unwelcome. Perhaps unreasonably, Dalgliesh had thought that he would be the only visitor.

70

As if sensing this reaction, Yarwood said, 'Don't worry, I shan't be joining you in your room after Compline for a jar. I want to get away from police gossip and I dare say you do too.'

Before Dalgliesh could do more than shake hands, Yarwood gave a quick nod, turned away and walked quickly back to his car.

8

Dalgliesh had said that he would arrive at the college after lunch. Before leaving Lowestoft he found a delicatessen and bought hot rolls, a pat of butter, some coarse-textured pâté and a half-bottle of wine. As always when driving in the country, he had come provided with a glass and with a thermos of coffee.

Leaving the town, he took side roads and then a rutted and overgrown lane just wide enough for the Jaguar. There was an open gate giving a wide view over the autumn fields and here he parked to eat his picnic. But first he turned off his mobile phone. Leaving the car, he leaned against the gatepost and shut his eyes to listen to the silence. These were the moments he craved in an over-busy life, the knowledge that no one in the world knew exactly where he was or could reach him. The small almost indistinguishable sounds of the countryside came to him on the sweet-smelling air, a distant unidentifiable bird-song, the susurration of the breeze in the tall grasses, the creaking of a branch over his head. After he had finished his lunch he walked vigorously down the lane for a half-mile, then returned to the car and made his way back to the A12 and towards Ballard's Mere.

And here, a little sooner than expected, was the turning; the same huge ash, but now ivy-covered and looking close to decay, and to his left the two trim cottages with their ordered front gardens. The narrow road, little more than a lane, was slightly sunken and the tangled winter hedge topping the bank obscured the view of the headland so that nothing could be seen of the distant St Anselm's except, when the hedges thinned, the occasional glimpse of tall brick chimneys and the southern dome. But as he reached the cliff edge and turned north on the gritty coastal track it came into distant view, a bizarre edifice of brick and layered stone looking as bright and unreal as a cardboard cut-out against the strengthening blue of the sky. It seemed to move towards him rather than he towards it, and it bore with it inexorably the images of adolescence and the half-remembered swinging moods of joy and pain, of uncertainty and shining hope. The house itself seemed unchanged. The twin stumps of crumbling Tudor brick with clumps of weed and grass lodged in the crevices still stood sentinel at the entrance to the front courtyard and, driving between them, he saw again the house in all its complicated authority.

In his boyhood it had been fashionable to despise Victorian architecture and he had viewed the house with a proper if half-guilty disdain. The architect, probably over-influenced by the original owner, had incorporated every fashionable feature: high chimneys, oriel windows, a central cupola, a southern tower, a castellated façade and an immense stone porch. But now it seemed to him that the result was less monstrously discordant than it had seemed to the eye of youth and that the architect had at least achieved a balance and a not unpleasing proportion in his dramatic mixture of medieval romanticism, of Gothic revival and pretentious Victorian domesticity.

He had been awaited, his arrival looked for. Even before he had closed the door of the car the front door opened and a frail limping figure in a black cassock came carefully down the three stone steps.

He recognized Father Martin Petrie instantly. The recognition came with a shock of surprise that the former Warden should still be in residence – he must be at least eighty. But here unmistakably was the man whom in boyhood he had revered and, yes, loved. Paradoxically the years fell away yet asserted their inexorable depredations. The bones of the face were more prominent above the lean and scrawny neck; the long swathe of hair crossing the brow, once a rich brown, was now silver-white and as fine as a baby's; the mobile mouth with its full lower lip was less firm. They clasped hands. For Dalgliesh it was like holding disjointed bones encased in a delicate suede glove. But Father Martin's grasp was still strong. The eyes, although shrunken, were the same luminous grey and the limp, a relic of his war service, was more pronounced, but he could still walk without a stick. And the face, always gentle, still held the unmistakable grace of spiritual authority. Looking into Father Martin's eyes, Dalgliesh realized that it wasn't only as an old friend that he was being welcomed; what he saw in Father Martin's gaze was a mixture of apprehension and relief. He marvelled again, and not without guilt, that he had stayed away for all these years. He had returned fortuitously, and almost on impulse; now he wondered for the first time what exactly was awaiting him at St Anselm's.

Leading him into the house, Father Martin said, 'I'm afraid I must ask you to move your car on to the grass behind the house. Father Peregrine dislikes seeing cars parked in the front courtyard. But there's no hurry. We've put you in your old set: Jerome.'

They entered the wide hall with its floor of chequered marble, its great oak staircase leading up to the galleried rooms above. Memory came flooding back with the smell of incense, furniture polish, old books and food. Except for the addition of a small room to the left of the entrance, nothing seemed to have altered. Its door stood open and Dalgliesh could glimpse an altar. Perhaps, he thought, the room was an oratory. The wooden statue of the Virgin with the Christ-child in her arms still stood at the bottom of the stairs, the red lamp still glowed beneath it, and there was still a single vase of flowers on the plinth at its foot. He paused to look at it and Father Martin waited patiently at his side. The carving was a copy, and a good one, of a Madonna and Child in the Victoria and Albert Museum, he couldn't remember by whom. It had none of the doleful piety common to such statues, no symbolic representation of the agonies to come. Both mother and child were laughing, the baby holding out his chubby arms, the Virgin, hardly more than a child, rejoicing in her son.

As they mounted the stairs, Father Martin said, 'You must be surprised to see me. Officially I have retired, of course, but the college has kept me on to help with the pastoral theology teaching. Father Sebastian Morell has been Warden here for the last fifteen years. I expect you'd like to revisit old haunts, but Father Sebastian will be expecting us. He'll have heard your car, he always does. The Warden's office is the same room as when you last visited.'

The man who stood up from his desk and came forward to greet them was very different from the gentle-faced Father Martin. He was over six feet tall and younger than Dalgliesh had expected. The light brown hair, only slightly tinged with grey, was brushed back from a fine high forehead. An uncompromising mouth, slightly hooked nose and long chin gave strength to a face which could have held a too-conventional if austere handsomeness. Most remarkable were the eyes; they were a clear dark blue, a colour which Dalgliesh found disconcertingly at odds with the keenness of the look which they fixed upon him. It was the face of a man of action, perhaps a soldier, rather than an academic. The well-tailored cassock of black gabardine seemed an incongruous garb for a man who exuded such latent power.

Even the furnishings of the room were discordant. The desk, holding a computer and printer, was aggressively modern, but on the wall above hung a carved wooden crucifix which could have been medieval. The opposite wall held a collection of *Vanity Fair* cartoons of Victorian prelates, the bewhiskered and shaven faces, lean, rubicund, etiolated or mildly pious, confident above the pectoral crosses and the lawn sleeves. On each side of the stone fireplace with its carved motto were framed prints of people and landscapes which presumably held a special place in the owner's memory. But above the fireplace was a very different picture. It was a Burne-Jones oil, a beautiful romantic dream exuding the artist's famed light which never was on land or sea. Four young women, garlanded and wearing long pink and brown dresses of flowered muslin, were grouped round an apple tree. One was sitting with a book open before her, a kitten cradled in her right arm; one had laid a lyre lightly aside and was gazing pensively into the distance; the two others were standing, one with a raised arm plucking a ripe apple, the other holding open her apron to receive the fruit with delicate long-fingered hands. Dalgliesh noticed against the right wall another Burne-Jones object: a two-drawer sideboard on high straight legs with castors, and two painted panels, one of a woman feeding birds, the other of a child with lambs. He had a memory both of the picture and the sideboard, but surely they had been in the refectory on his previous visits. Their shining romanticism seemed at odds with the clerical austerity of the rest of the room.

A welcoming smile transformed the Warden's face, but was so brief that it could have been no more than a spasm of the muscles.

'Adam Dalgliesh? You're very welcome. Father Martin tells me that it's been a long time since you were last here. We could wish your return was on a happier occasion.'

Dalgliesh said, 'I could wish it too, Father. I hope that I shan't have to inconvenience you for too long.'

Father Sebastian motioned to the armchairs one each side of the fireplace, and Father Martin drew up one of the chairs from the table for himself.

When they were seated, Father Sebastian said, 'I have to admit that I was surprised when your Assistant Commissioner rang. A Commander of the Metropolitan Police sent to report on the handling by a provincial force of a matter that, although tragic for all those intimately involved, is hardly a major incident and that has been the subject of an inquest and is now officially closed. Isn't that a little extravagant of manpower?' He paused, then added, 'Or irregular?'

'Not irregular, Father. Unconventional perhaps. But I was coming to Suffolk and it was thought it would save time and perhaps be more convenient for the college.'

'It has at least the advantage that it brings you back to us. We shall, of course, answer your questions. Sir Alred Treeves hasn't had the courtesy to approach us directly. He didn't attend the inquest – we understood he was abroad – but he did send a solicitor to hold a watching brief. As I remember, he expressed no dissatisfaction. We have had very few dealings with Sir Alred and haven't found him an easy man. He never made any bones about his dislike of his son's choice of profession – it would not, of course, be regarded by Sir Alred as a vocation. It's difficult to understand his motives in wanting to reopen the case. There are only three alternatives. Foul play is out of the question; Ronald had no enemies here and no one stood to gain by his death. Suicide? That is, of course, a distressing possibility, but there was no evidence either in his recent behaviour or in his conduct here to suggest that degree of unhappiness. There remains accidental death. I would have expected Sir Alred to accept the verdict with some relief.'

Dalgliesh said, 'There was the anonymous letter which I think the Assistant Commissioner spoke to you about. If Sir Alred hadn't received that I don't expect I should be here.'

Taking it out of his wallet he handed it over. Father Sebastian glanced at it briefly, then said, 'Obviously produced by a computer. We have computers here – one you see in my office.'

'You have no idea who could have sent it?'

Father Sebastian had hardly glanced at it before handing it back with a gesture of contemptuous dismissal. 'None. We have our enemies. Perhaps that's too strong a word; it would be more accurate to say we have people who would prefer this college not to exist. But their opposition to us is ideological, theological or financial, a question of Church resources. I can't believe that any would sink to this crude calumny. I'm surprised Sir Alred took it seriously. As a man of power he can't be unused to anonymous communications. We shall, of course, give you any help we can. No doubt you will want first to visit the place where Ronald died. Please forgive me if I leave Father Martin to accompany you. I have a visitor this afternoon and other rather urgent matters awaiting attention. Evensong is at five o'clock, if you wish to join us. Afterwards I have drinks here before dinner. We don't serve wine at meals on Fridays, as I expect you remember, but when we have guests it seems reasonable to offer them sherry before the meal. We have four other visitors this weekend. Archdeacon Crampton, a trustee of the college; Dr Emma Lavenham, who comes once a term from Cambridge to introduce the students to the literary heritage of Anglicanism; Dr Clive Stannard, who is using our library for research; and another police officer, Inspector Roger Yarwood of the local force who is at present on sick-leave. None of them was present at the time of Ronald's death. If you are interested in knowing who was in residence at the time, Father Martin will be able to supply a list. Are we to expect you for dinner?'

'Not tonight, Father, if you'll excuse me. I hope to be back for Compline.'

'Then I shall see you in church. I hope you will find your rooms comfortable.'

Father Sebastian got to his feet; obviously the interview was over.

9

Father Martin said, 'I expect you'd like to visit the church on the way to your rooms.'

It was obvious that he took Dalgliesh's agreement, even enthusiasm, for granted and indeed Dalgliesh wasn't unwilling. There were things in the little church that he had looked forward to seeing again.

He said, 'The van der Weyden Madonna is still above the altar?'

'Yes, indeed. That and the *Doom* are our two main attractions. But perhaps the word attractions isn't quite appropriate. I don't mean that we encourage visitors. We don't get many and they always come by appointment. We don't advertise our riches.'

'Is the van der Weyden insured, Father?'

'No, it never has been. We can't afford the premium and, as Father Sebastian has said, the picture is irreplaceable. Money doesn't buy another. But we do take care. Of course, being so isolated helps and we now have a modern alarm system operating. The panel is inside the door leading from the northern cloister to the sanctuary, and the alarm also covers the main south door. I think the system was installed well after your visit here. The Bishop insisted that we take advice on security if the painting is to remain in the church and, of course, he was right.'

Dalgliesh said, 'I seem to remember that the church was open all day when I was here as a boy.'

'Yes indeed, but that was before the experts decided that the painting was genuine. It distresses me that the church has to be kept locked, particularly in a theological college. That's why, when I was Warden, I installed the small oratory. I expect you saw it to the left of the door when you came in. The oratory itself can't be consecrated because it's part of another building, but the altar is and it does provide a place for the students to go for private prayer or for meditation when the church is locked after services.'

They passed through the cloakroom at the rear of the house, which gave access to the door to the north cloister. Here the room was bisected by a row of coat-hooks above a long bench, each hook with a receptacle underneath for outdoor shoes and boots. Most of the hooks were empty but about half a dozen held brown hooded cloaks. No doubt the cloaks, like the black cassocks the students wore indoors, had been prescribed by the formidable founder, Agnes Arbuthnot. If so, she had probably remembered the force and bitterness of the east winds on this unprotected coast. To the right of the cloakroom the half-open door to the utility-room gave sight of four large washing machines and a dryer.

Dalgliesh and Father Martin passed from the dimness of the house into the cloister and the faint but pervasive smell of High Anglican academe gave way to fresh air and the sunlit silent courtyard. Dalgliesh experienced, as he had as a boy, the sense of moving back in time. Here, red brick embellished Victoriana was replaced by stone simplicity. The cloisters with their narrow and slender pillars ran round the three sides of the cobbled courtyard. They were paved with York stone behind which a row of identical oak doors led to the two-storey student accommodation. The four apartments for visitors faced the west front of the main building and were separated from the church wall by a wrought-iron gate behind which could be glimpsed the empty acres of pale scrub-land and the richer green of the far fields of sugar beet. In the middle of the courtyard a mature horse-chestnut was already showing its autumnal decrepitude. From the foot of the gnarled trunk from which sections of bark were breaking away like scabs, small branches had sprouted, the young leaves as green and tender as the first shoots of spring. Above them the huge boughs were hung with yellow and brown and the dead leaves lay curled on the cobbles as dried and brittle as mummified fingers among the polished mahogany of the fallen chestnuts.

Some things, thought Dalgliesh, were new to him in this long-remembered scene, among them surely the rows of unadorned but elegantly shaped terracotta pots at the foot of the pillars. They must have made a brave show in summer but now the distorted stems of the geraniums were woody and the few remaining flowers only a puny reminder of past glories. And surely the fuchsia climbing so vigorously over the west-facing wall of the house had been planted since his time. It was still heavy with flowers but the leaves were already fading and the fallen petals lay in drifts like spilt blood.

Father Martin said, 'We'll go in through the sacristy door.'

He drew out a large key-ring from the pocket of his

cassock. 'I'm afraid it takes me a little time to find the right keys. I know I ought to know them by now, but there are so many of them, and I'm afraid I shall never get used to the security system. It's set to give us a whole minute before we have to punch in the four digits but the bleep is so low that now I can hardly hear it. Father Sebastian dislikes loud noise, particularly in the church. If the alarm is set off, it makes a terrifying jangle in the main building.'

'Shall I do it for you, Father?'

'Oh no thank you, Adam. No. I'll manage. I never have difficulty in remembering the number because it's the year Miss Arbuthnot founded the college, 1861.'

And that, thought Dalgliesh, was a number that might easily occur to the mind of a prospective intruder.

The sacristy was larger than Dalgliesh remembered and obviously served as vestry, cloakroom and office. To the left of the door leading into the church was a row of coat-hooks. Another wall was occupied with ceiling-high fitted cupboards for vestments. There were two upright wooden chairs and a small sink with a draining-board beside a cupboard whose Formica top held an electric kettle and a cafetière. Two large tins of white paint and a small one of black, with brushes in a jam jar at their side, were neatly stacked against the wall. To the left of the door and under one of the two windows was a large desk fitted with drawers and holding a silver cross. Above it was a wall-mounted safe. Seeing Dalgliesh's eyes on it, Father Martin said, 'Father Sebastian had the safe installed to hold our seventeenth-century silver chalices and paten. They were bequeathed to the college by Miss Arbuthnot and are very fine.

Previously, because of their value, they were kept in the bank but Father Sebastian felt that they should be used and I think he was right.'

Beside the desk was a row of framed sepia photographs, nearly all of them old, some obviously dating back to the early days of the college. Dalgliesh, interested in old photographs, moved over to look at them. One, he thought, must be of Miss Arbuthnot. She was flanked by two priests, each in cassock and biretta, both taller than herself. To Dalgliesh's fleeting but intense scrutiny there was no doubt which was the dominant personality. So far from seeming diminished by the black clerical austerity of her custodians, Miss Arbuthnot stood perfectly at ease, fingers loosely clasped over the folds of her skirt. Her clothes were simple but expensive; even in a photograph it was possible to see the sheen of the high-buttoned silk blouse with its leg-of-mutton sleeves and the richness of the skirt. She wore no jewellery except for a cameo brooch at her neck and a single pendant cross. Beneath the strong upward sweep of hair which looked very fair, the face was heart-shaped, the eyes with their steady gaze wide-spaced under straight and darker brows. Dalgliesh wondered what she would have looked like if ever this slightly intimidating seriousness had broken into laughter. It was, he thought, the photograph of a beautiful woman who took no joy in her beauty and who had looked elsewhere for the gratifications of power.

Memory of the church came back to him with the smell of incense and candle smoke. They moved down the northern aisle and Father Martin said, 'You'd like, of course, to see the *Doom* again.'

The *Doom* could be illumined by a light fixed to a nearby pillar. Father Martin lifted his arm and the tenebrous indecipherable scene sprang into life. They were facing a vivid depiction of the last judgement, painted on wood, the whole shaped in a half-moon with a diameter of about twelve feet. At the head was the seated figure of Christ in glory, holding out his wounded hands over the drama below. The central figure was obviously St Michael. He was holding a heavy sword in his right hand and, in his left, dangling scales in which he was weighing the souls of the righteous and the unrighteous. To his left, the Devil, with scaly tail and grinning lascivious jaws, the personification of horror, prepared to claim his prize. The virtuous lifted pale hands in prayer, the damned were a squirming mass of black pot-bellied, open-mouthed hermaphrodites. Beside them a group of lesser devils with pitchforks and chains were busily shoving their victims into the jaws of an immense fish with teeth like a row of swords. To the left Heaven was depicted as a castellated hotel with an angel as door-keeper welcoming in the naked souls. St Peter in cope and triple tiara was receiving the more important of the blessed. All were naked but still wearing the accoutrements of rank; a cardinal in his scarlet hat, a bishop in his mitre, a king and queen both crowned. There was, thought Dalgliesh, little democracy about this medieval vision of Heaven. All the blessed, to his eyes, wore expressions of pious boredom; the damned were considerably more lively, more defiant than regretful, as they were plunged feet first down the fish's throat. One, indeed, larger than the rest, was resisting his fate and making what looked like a finger to nose gesture of contempt towards the figure of St Michael. The *Doom*, originally more prominently displayed, was designed to terrify medieval congregations into virtue and social conformity literally through the fear of hell. Now it was viewed by interested academics or by modern visitors for whom the fear of hell no longer had power and who sought heaven in this world, not in the next.

As they stood regarding it together, Father Martin said, 'Of course it's a remarkable *Doom*, probably one of the best in the country, but I can't help wishing we could put it somewhere else. It probably dates from about 1480. I don't know whether you've seen the Wenhaston *Doom*. This is so like it that it must have been painted by the same monk from Blythburgh. While theirs was left outside for some years and has been restored, ours is far more in its original condition. We were lucky. It was discovered in the 1930s in a two-storeyed barn near Wisset where it was used to partition a room, so it's been in the dry probably since the 1800s.'

Father Martin switched off the light and prattled on happily. 'We had a very early circular tower standing by itself – you may know the one at Bramfield – but that has long since gone. This was a seven-sacrament font but as you can see, little of the carving remains. Legend has it that the font was dredged up from the sea in a great storm in the late 1700s. We don't know, of course, whether it was originally here or belongs to one of the drowned churches. Many centuries are represented here. As you see, we still have four seventeenth-century box pews.'

Despite their age, it was the Victorians who came to mind when Dalgliesh saw box pews. Here the squire and his family could sit in wood-enclosed privacy, unseen by the rest of the congregation and hardly viewed from the pulpit. He pictured them closeted together and wondered whether they took with them cushions and rugs or provided themselves with sandwiches, drinks and perhaps even a discreetly covered book to alleviate the hours of abstinence and the tedium of the sermon. As a boy his mind had been much exercised with wondering what the squire would do if he suffered from a weak bladder. How could he, or indeed the rest of the congregation, sit through the two services on Sacrament Sunday, through long sermons or when the Litany was said or sung? Was it perhaps usual to have a chamber-pot tucked away under the wooden seat?

And now they were walking up the aisle towards the altar. Father Martin moved to a pillar behind the pulpit and put up his hand to a switch. Immediately the gloom of the church seemed to deepen into a darkness as, with dramatic suddenness, the painting glowed into life and colour. The figures of the Virgin and St Joseph, fixed in their silent adoration for over five hundred years, seemed for a moment to float away from the wood on which they were painted to hang like a trembling vision on the still air. The Virgin had been painted against a background of intricate brocade in gold and brown which in its richness emphasized her simplicity and vulnerability. She was seated on a low stool with the naked Christ-child resting on a white cloth on her lap. Her face was a pale and perfect oval, the mouth tender under a narrow nose, the heavily-lidded eyes under thinly-arched brows fixed on the child with an expression of resigned wonder. From a high smooth forehead the strands of crimped auburn hair fell over her blue mantle to the delicate hands and fingers barely touching in prayer. The child gazed up at her with both arms raised as if foreshadowing the crucifixion. St Joseph, red-coated, was seated to the right of the painting, a prematurely aged, half-sleeping custodian, heavily leaning on a stick.

For a moment Dalgliesh and Father Martin stood in silence. Father Martin didn't speak until he had turned off the light. Dalgliesh wondered whether he had been inhibited from mundane conversation while the painting was working its magic.

Now he said, 'The experts seem to agree that it's a genuine Rogier van der Weyden, probably painted between 1440 and 1445. The other two panels probably showed saints with portraits of the donor and his family.'

Dalgliesh asked, 'What is its provenance?'

'Miss Arbuthnot gave it to the college the year after we were founded. She intended it as an altar-piece and we have never considered having it anywhere else. It was my predecessor, Father Nicholas Warburg, who called in the experts. He was very interested in paintings, particularly Netherlands Renaissance, and had a natural curiosity to know whether it was genuine. In the document which accompanied the gift, Miss Arbuthnot merely described it as part of an altar triptych showing St Mary and St Joseph, possibly attributable to Rogier van der Weyden. I can't help feeling that it would be better if we'd left it like that. We could just enjoy the painting without being obsessed with its safety.'

'How did Miss Arbuthnot acquire it?'

'Oh, by purchase. A landed family was disposing of some of its art treasures to help keep the estate going.

That kind of thing. I don't think Miss Arbuthnot paid very highly for it. There was the doubt about the attribution and, even if genuine, this particular painter wasn't as well known or as highly regarded in the 1860s as he is today. It's a responsibility, of course. I know that the Archdeacon feels very strongly that it ought to be moved.'

'Moved where?'

'To a cathedral, perhaps, where greater security would be possible. Perhaps even to a gallery or a museum. I believe he has even suggested to Father Sebastian that it should be sold.'

Dalgliesh said, 'And the money given to the poor?'

'Well, to the Church. His other argument is that more people should have a chance to enjoy it. Why should a small remote theological college add this to our other privileges?'

There was a note of bitterness in Father Martin's voice. Dalgliesh didn't speak and after a pause his companion, as if feeling that he may have gone too far, went on.

'These are valid arguments. Perhaps we ought to take account of them, but it's difficult to visualize the church without the altar-piece. It was given by Miss Arbuthnot to be placed above the altar in this church and I think we should strongly resist any suggestion that it should be moved. I could willingly part with the *Doom*, but not with this.'

But as they turned away Dalgliesh's mind was busy with more secular considerations. It hadn't taken Sir Alred's words about the vulnerability of the college to remind him how uncertain its future must be. What long-term future was there for the college, its ethos out of sympathy with the prevailing views of the Church, educating only twenty students, occupying this remote and inaccessible site? If its future was now in balance, the mysterious death of Ronald Treeves might be the one factor that tipped the scales. And if the college closed, what happened to the van der Weyden, to the other expensive objects bequeathed to it by Miss Arbuthnot, to the building itself? Remembering that photograph, it was difficult to believe that she hadn't, however reluctantly, envisaged this possibility and made provision for it. One returned, as always, to the central question: who benefits? He would like to have asked Father Martin, but decided it would be both tactless and, in this place, inappropriate. But the question would have to be asked.

The four sets of accommodation for guests had been named by Miss Arbuthnot after the four doctors of the Western Church: Gregory, Augustine, Jerome and Ambrose. After this theological conceit, and having decided that the four cottages for staff should be called Matthew, Mark, Luke and John, inspiration had apparently faltered and the sets for the students were less imaginatively but more conveniently identified by numbers in the north and south cloisters.

Father Martin said, 'You used to be in Jerome when you were here as a boy. Perhaps you remember. It's our one double now, so the bed should be comfortable. It's the second along from the church. I've no key for you, I'm afraid. We never have had keys to the guest-rooms. Everything is safe here. If you do have any papers you feel should be locked away, Miss Ramsey will look after them. She will be here at nine o'clock on Monday. I hope you'll be comfortable, Adam. As you see, the sets have been refurbished since your last visit.'

They had indeed. Where before the sitting-room had been a cosy, overcrowded repository for odd items of furniture which looked as if they were the rejects of the parish jumble sale, it was now as starkly functional as a student's study. Nothing here was superfluous; unfussy and conventional modernity had replaced individuality. There was a table with drawers, which could also serve as a desk, set before the window which gave a view westwards over the scrubland, two easy chairs, one each side of the gas fire, a low table and a bookcase. To the right of the fireplace was a cupboard with a Formica top holding a tray with an electric kettle, a teapot and two cups and saucers.

Father Martin said, 'There's a small refrigerator in that cupboard and Mrs Pilbeam will put in a pint of milk each day. As you will see when you go upstairs, we've installed a shower in what was part of the bedroom. You'll remember that when you were here last you had to walk along the cloisters and use one of the bathrooms in the main house.'

Dalgliesh did remember. It had been one of the pleasures of his stay to walk out in his dressing-gown into the morning air, a towel round his shoulders, either to the bathroom or to walk the half-mile to the bathing hut for a pre-breakfast swim. The small modern shower was a poor substitute.

Father Martin said, 'I'll wait for you here while you unpack if I may. There are two things I want to show you.'

The bedroom was as simply furnished as the room beneath. There was a double wooden bed with a bedside table and reading lamp, a fitted cupboard, another bookcase and an easy chair. Dalgliesh unzipped his travelling bag and hung up the one suit he had thought it necessary to bring. After a brief wash he rejoined Father Martin who was standing at the window looking out over the headland. As Dalgliesh entered he took a folded sheet of paper from the pocket of his cloak.

He said, 'I have something you left here when you

were fourteen. I didn't send it on because I wasn't sure whether you'd be happy to know that I'd seen it, but I've kept it and perhaps you'd now like it back. It's four lines of verse. I suppose you could call it a poem.'

And that, thought Dalgliesh, was an unlikely supposition. He suppressed a groan and took the paper held out to him. What youthful indiscretion, embarrassment or pretension was now to be resurrected from the past to his discomfort? The sight of the handwriting, familiar and yet strange and to his eyes, despite the careful calligraphy, a little tentative and unformed, jolted him back over the years more strongly than an old photograph because it was more personal. It was difficult to believe that the boyish hand which had moved over this quarter sheet of paper was the same as the hand that now held it.

He read the lines silently.

The Bereaved

'Another lovely day,' you said in passing,
Dull-voiced, and moved unseeing down the street.
You didn't say, 'Please wrap your jacket round me,
Outside the sun, inside the killing sleet.'

It brought back another memory, one which was common in his childhood: his father taking a burial service, the richness of the clods of earth heaped beside the bright green of artificial grass, a few wreaths, the wind billowing his father's surplice, the smell of flowers. Those lines, he remembered, had been written after the burial of an only child. He remembered, too, that he had worried over the adjective in its last line, thinking the two vowel sounds were too similar yet unable to find a suitable substitute.

Father Martin said, 'I thought they were remarkable lines for a fourteen-year-old. Unless you want them back I should like to keep them.'

Dalgliesh nodded and handed over the paper silently. Father Martin folded it back in his pocket with something of the satisfaction of a child.

Dalgliesh said, 'There was something else you wanted to show me.'

'Yes indeed. Perhaps we could sit down.'

Again Father Martin slipped a hand into his deep cloak pocket. He brought out what looked like a child's exercise book rolled up and bound with a rubber band. Smoothing it out on his lap and folding his hands over it as if he were protecting it, he said, 'Before we go to the beach I'd like you to read this. It's self-explanatory. The woman who wrote it died of a heart attack on the evening of the final entry. It may have no significance whatsoever for Ronald's death. I've shown it to Father Sebastian and that's his view. He thinks it can safely be ignored. It could mean nothing, but it worries me. I thought it would be a good idea to show it to you here where we have no chance of being interrupted. The two entries I'd like you to read are the first and the last.'

He handed over the book and sat in silence until Dalgliesh had read it. Dalgliesh asked, 'How did you come by it, Father?'

'I looked for it and found it. Margaret Munroe was found dead in her cottage by Mrs Pilbeam at six-fifteen on Friday 13 October. She was on her way to the college and was surprised to see a light on so early in St Matthew's

Cottage. After Dr Metcalf – he's the general practitioner who looks after us at St Anselm's – had seen the body and it had been removed, I thought about my suggestion that Margaret should write an account of finding Ronald and wondered whether in fact she had done so. I found this under her stack of writing paper in the drawer of a small wooden desk she had in her cottage. There had been no serious attempt to conceal it.'

'And as far as you can tell no one else knows of this diary's existence?'

'No one except Father Sebastian. I'm sure Margaret wouldn't have confided even in Mrs Pilbeam, who was the member of staff closest to her. And there was no sign that a search had been made of the cottage. The body looked perfectly peaceful when I was called. She was just sitting in her chair with her knitting in her lap.'

'And you have no idea what she's referring to?'

'None. It must have been something she saw or heard on the day of Ronald's death which sparked off memory, that and Eric Surtees's gift of leeks. He's a handyman here, helping Reg Pilbeam. But, of course, you know that from the diary. I can't think what it could have been.'

'Was her death unexpected?'

'Not really. She'd had a serious heart condition for some years. Dr Metcalf and the consultant she saw in Ipswich both discussed with her the possibility of a heart transplant, but she was adamant that she didn't want an operation of any kind. She said that scarce resources should be used on the young and on parents bringing up children. I don't think Margaret cared very much whether she lived or died after her son was killed. She wasn't morbid about it, it was just that she wasn't enough attached to life to fight for it.'

Dalgliesh said, 'I'd like to keep this diary, if I may. Father Sebastian may be right, it could be totally without significance, but it's an interesting document if one is considering the circumstances of Ronald Treeves's death.'

He put the exercise book away in his briefcase, shut it and set the combination lock. They sat for another half-minute in silence. It seemed to Dalgliesh that the air between them was heavy with unspoken fears, half-formed suspicions, a general sense of unease. Ronald Treeves had died mysteriously and a week later the woman who had found his body, and who had subsequently discovered a secret which she felt was important, was herself dead. It could be no more than a coincidence. There was so far no evidence of foul play, and he shared what he guessed was Father Martin's reluctance to hear those words spoken aloud.

Dalgliesh said, 'Did you find the verdict of the inquest surprising?'

'A little surprising. I would have expected an open verdict. But the thought that Ronald could have killed himself, and by an act so appalling, is one we here can hardly bear to let into our minds.'

'What sort of a boy was he? Was he happy here?'

'I'm not sure that he was, although I don't think any other theological college would have suited him better. He was intelligent and hard-working but singularly lacking in charm, poor boy. He was curiously judgemental for someone young. I would have said he combined a certain insecurity with considerable self-satisfaction. He had no particular friends – not that particular friendships are encouraged – and I think he may have been lonely. But there was nothing in his work or his life here to suggest despair or that he was tempted to the grievous sin of self-destruction. Of course, if he did kill himself, then we must be in some way to blame. We should have seen that he was suffering. But then, he gave no indication.'

'And you were happy about his vocation?'

Father Martin took his time before replying. 'Father Sebastian was, but I wonder whether he may not have been influenced by Ronald's academic record. He wasn't as clever as he thought he was, but he was clever. I had my doubts. It seemed to me that Ronald was desperate to impress his father. Obviously he couldn't measure up in his father's world, but he could choose a career which would offer no possible comparison. And with the priest-hood, particularly the Catholic priesthood, there's always the temptation of power. Once ordained, he would be able to pronounce absolution. That at least is something his father couldn't do. I have not said this to anyone else and I could be wrong. When his application was considered I felt I was in some difficulty. It is never easy for a Warden to have his predecessor still in college. This was a matter on which I didn't feel it right to oppose Father Sebastian.'

But it was with a sense of deepening if illogical unease that Dalgliesh heard Father Martin say, 'And now I expect you would like to see where he died.'

II

Eric Surtees left St John's Cottage by the back door and walked between his neat rows of autumn vegetables to commune with his pigs. Lily, Marigold, Daisy and Myrtle came galumphing across to him in a squealing mass and raised their pink snouts to sniff his coming. Whatever his mood, a visit to his self-built piggery and its railed enclosure could meet his need. But today, as he leant over and scratched Myrtle's back, nothing could lift the weight of anxiety that lay like a physical load on his shoulders.

His half-sister, Karen, was due to arrive in time for tea. Usually she drove from London every third weekend and, whatever the weather, those two days always remained sunlit in his memory and warmed and lightened the weeks between. In the last four years she had changed his life. He couldn't now imagine his life without her. Normally her coming this weekend would be a bonus; she had been with him only the Sunday before. But he knew that she was coming because she had something to ask of him, a request to make which he had refused the previous week and knew that he must somehow find the strength to refuse again.

Leaning over the fence of the pigsty he thought back over the last four years, about himself and Karen. The relationship hadn't at first been propitious. He had been twenty-six when they met; she was three years younger, and for the first ten years of her life her existence had been unknown to him and his mother. His father, a travelling representative for a large publishing conglomerate, had successfully run two establishments until, after ten years, the financial and physical strain and the complications of the balancing act had become too much for him and he had thrown in his lot with his mistress and departed. Neither Eric nor his mother had been particularly sorry to see him go; there was nothing she enjoyed more than a grievance and her husband had now handed her one which kept her in a state of happy indignation and fierce battling for the final ten years of her life. She fought, but unsuccessfully, to own the London house, insisted on having custody of the only child (there was no battle there), and conducted a long and acrimonious dispute about the allocation of income. Eric had never seen his father again.

The four-storey house was part of a Victorian terrace near the Oval underground station. After his mother's protracted death from Alzheimer's disease he stayed on alone, having been informed by his father's solicitor that he could continue to do so rent-free until his father died. Four years ago a massive heart attack killed him instantly while on the road, and Eric discovered that the house had been left jointly to him and his half-sister.

He had seen her for the first time at his father's funeral. The event – it could hardly be dignified by a more ceremonial name – had taken place at a North London crematorium without benefit of clergy, indeed without benefit of mourners except for himself and Karen and two representatives of the firm. The disposal had taken only minutes.

Coming out of the crematorium his half-sister had said without preamble, 'That's how Dad wanted it. He never went in for religion. He didn't want any flowers and he didn't want any mourners. We'll have to talk about the house, but not now. I have an urgent appointment at the office. It hasn't been easy to get off.'

She hadn't invited him to drive back with her and he went home alone to the empty house. But next day she had called. He vividly remembered opening the door. She was wearing, as she had at the funeral, tight black leather trousers, a baggy red sweater and high-heeled boots. Her hair looked spiky, as if it had been brilliantined, and there was a glittering stud in the left of her nose. Her appearance was conventionally *outré* but he found to his surprise that he rather liked the way she looked. They moved into the rarely used front room without speaking and she looked round with an appraising then dismissive glance at the leavings of his mother's life, the cumbersome furniture which he had never bothered to replace, the dusty curtains hung with the pattern towards the street, the mantelshelf crowded with gaudy ornaments brought back from his mother's holidays in Spain.

She said, 'We've got to make a decision about the house. We can sell now and each take half the profit, or we can let. Or, I suppose, we could spend a bit of capital on doing some adaptations and convert it into three studio flats. This won't be cheap, but Dad left an insurance policy and I don't mind spending it, as long as I get a higher proportion of the rents. What are you thinking of doing, by the way; I mean, did you expect to stay here?'

He said, 'I don't really want to stay in London. I was thinking, if we sell the house, I'd have enough money to buy a small cottage somewhere. I might try market gardening, something like that.'

'Then you'd be a fool. It'd need more capital than you're likely to get and there's no money in it anyway, not on the kind of scale you're thinking of. Still, if you want to get out, I suppose you're keen on selling.'

He thought: she knows what she wants to do and it will happen in the end, no matter what I say. But he didn't really greatly care. He followed her from room to room, in a kind of wonder.

He said, 'I don't mind keeping it on if that's what you want.'

'It's not what I want, it's what's the most sensible thing for us both. The housing market's good at present and likely to get better. Of course if we do convert, it will lessen its value as a family residence. On the other hand, it would bring us in a regular income.'

And that inevitably was what had happened. She had, he knew, begun by despising him, but as they worked together her attitude perceptibly changed. She was surprised and gratified to discover how good he was with his hands, how much money was saved because he could paint and paper walls, put up shelves, install cupboards. He had never bothered to improve the house which had been his home only in name. Now he discovered unexpected and satisfying skills. They employed a professional plumber, an electrician and a builder for the major work, but much of it was done by Eric. They became involuntary partners. On Saturdays they would shop for second-hand furniture, for bargains in bed-linen and cutlery, showing each other their trophies with the happy triumph of children. He showed her how to use a blow-torch safely, insisted on the proper preparation of the woodwork before painting despite her protests that it wasn't necessary, amazed her by the careful dedication with which he measured up and fitted the kitchen units. As they worked she gossiped about her own life, the freelance journalism in which she was beginning to make a name, her pleasure in achieving a by-line, the bitchiness and gossip and small scandals of the literary world on the fringe of which she worked. It was a world which he found terrifyingly alien. He was glad he was not required to enter it. He dreamed of a cottage, a kitchen garden and perhaps his secret passion of keeping pigs.

And he could remember – of course he could – the day when they became lovers. He had fixed slatted wooden blinds to one of the south-facing windows and they were emulsion-painting the walls together. She was a messy worker and half-way through announced that she was hot, sticky, splattered with paint and would take a shower. It would be a chance to test the efficiency of the newly installed bathroom. So he too had stopped painting and had sat cross-legged, resting against the one unpainted wall, watching the light slant in through the half-open blinds to lattice the paint-splattered floor and letting happy contentment bubble up like a spring.

And then she had come in. She had twisted a towel round her waist but was otherwise naked, and she was carrying a large bath-mat over her arm. Laying it down, she had squatted there and laughing at him, had held out her arms. In a kind of trance he had knelt in front of her and whispered, 'But we can't, we can't. We're brother and sister.'

'Only half-brother, half-sister. All to the good. Keep it in the family.'

He had muttered, 'The blind, it's too light.'

She had sprung up and pulled the blind shut. The room was almost dark. She came back to him and held his head against her breasts.

It had been for him the first time and it changed his life. He knew that she didn't love him and he didn't yet love her. During that and subsequent astonishing love-making he had shut his eyes and indulged all his private fantasies, romantic, tender, violent, shameful. The imaginings tumbled into his brain and were made flesh. And then one day for the first time, when they were making love more comfortably on the bed, he had opened his eyes and looked into hers and had known that this was love.

It was Karen who had found for him the job at St Anselm's. She had had an assignment in Ipswich and had picked up a copy of the *East Anglian Daily News*. Returning that night, she had come to the house in which he was now picnicking in the basement while the work continued, and had brought the paper with her.

'This might suit you. It's a handyman's job at a theological college just south of Lowestoft. That should be lonely enough for you. They're offering a cottage and apparently there's a garden, and I dare say you could persuade them to let you keep hens if you wanted.'

'I don't want hens, I'd rather have pigs.'

'Well pigs then, if they're not too smelly. They're not paying much, but you should get two hundred and fifty pounds a week from the rents here. You could probably save some of that. What do you think?'

He had thought it almost too good to be true.

She said, 'Of course they might want a married couple, but it doesn't say so. But we'd better get moving on it. I'll drive you down tomorrow morning if you like. Phone up now and ask for an appointment, they give a number.'

Next day she had driven him to Suffolk, leaving him at the gate of the college saying she would return and wait for him in an hour. He had been interviewed by Father Sebastian Morell and Father Martin Petrie. He had worried in case they had wanted a clerical reference or asked him if he were a regular churchgoer, but religion hadn't been mentioned.

Karen had said, 'You'll be able to get a reference from the Town Hall, of course, but you'd better prove that you're a good handyman. It's not an office drudge they're looking for. I've brought a camera along. I'll take photographs of those cupboards, shelves and fitments you've put up and you can show them the Polaroids. You've got to sell yourself, remember.'

But he didn't need to sell himself. He'd answered their questions simply and had taken out his Polaroids with a rather touching eagerness which had shown them how much he wanted the job. They had taken him to view the cottage. It was larger than he had expected or wanted, but it lay some eighty yards from the back of the college with an unobstructed view across the shrubland and with a small untended garden. He hadn't mentioned the pigs until he had worked there for over a month, but when he did no one had raised any objection. Father Martin had said a little nervously, 'They won't get out, will they, Eric?' as if he had been proposing to cage Alsatians.

'No, Father. I thought I could build a sty and enclosure for them. I'll show you the drawings, of course, before I buy the wood.'

'What about the smell?' Father Sebastian enquired. 'I'm told pigs don't smell, but I can usually smell them. Of course I may have a more sensitive nose than most people.'

'No, they won't smell, Father. Pigs are very clean creatures.'

So he had his cottage, his garden, his pigs, and once every three weeks he had Karen. He couldn't think of a life more satisfactory.

At St Anselm's he had found the peace that all his life he had been looking for. He couldn't understand why it was so necessary to him, this absence of noise, of controversy, of the pressures of discordant personalities. It wasn't as if his father had ever been violent towards him. For most of the time he hadn't even been present, and when he was present his parents' discordant marriage had been more a matter of grumbling and muttered grievances than of raised voices or open anger. What he saw as his timidity seemed to have been part of his personality since childhood. Even when working in the Town Hall – hardly the most provocative or exhilarating of jobs – he had held apart from the occasional spats of ill-feeling, the minor feuds which some workers seemed to find necessary, indeed to provoke. Until he knew and loved Karen no company in the world had seemed more desirable than his own.

And now, with this peace, this sanctuary, his garden

and his pigs, a job he enjoyed doing and was valued for, and Karen's regular visits, he had found a life that suited every corner of his mind and fibre of his being. But with the appointment of Archdeacon Crampton as a trustee everything changed. The fear of what Karen might demand of him was only an added worry to the overwhelming anxiety that had come with the arrival of the Archdeacon.

On the occasion of the Archdeacon's first visit, Father Sebastian had said to him, 'Archdeacon Crampton may call in to see you, Eric, sometime on Sunday or Monday. The Bishop has appointed him as a trustee and I expect there will be questions he will find it necessary to ask.'

There had been something in Father Sebastian's voice as he spoke the last words which had put Eric on guard.

He said, 'Questions about my job here, Father?'

'About the terms of your employment, about anything which enters his mind, I have no doubt. He may want to look round the cottage.'

He had wanted to look round the cottage. He had arrived shortly after nine o'clock on Monday morning. Karen, unusually, had stayed for Sunday night and had left in a hurry at half-past seven. She had had an appointment in London at ten o'clock and had already left it dangerously late; the Monday morning traffic on the A12 was bad, particularly as it approached London. In the rush – and Karen was always in a rush – she had forgotten that her bra and a pair of knickers were still hanging on the clothes-line at the side of the cottage. They were the first thing that the Archdeacon saw as he came down the path.

Without introducing himself, he said, 'I didn't realize you had a visitor.'

Eric snatched the offending articles from the line and stuffed them into his pocket, realizing even as he did so that the act, in its mixture of embarrassment and furtiveness, was a mistake.

He said, 'My sister has been here for the weekend, Father.'

'I'm not your father. I don't use that term. You can call me Archdeacon.'

'Yes, Archdeacon.'

He was very tall, certainly over six foot, square-faced with bright darting eyes under thick but well-shaped eyebrows, and a beard.

They walked down the path towards the pigsty in silence. At least, thought Eric, there was nothing he could complain about in the state of the garden.

The pigs greeted them with far louder squealing than was normal. The Archdeacon said, 'I hadn't realized you kept pigs. Do you provide pork for the college?'

'Sometimes, Archdeacon. But they don't eat much pork. Their meat comes from the butcher in Lowestoft. I just keep pigs. I asked Father Sebastian if I could and he gave permission.'

'How much of your time do they take up?'

'Not much, Fath . . . Not much, Archdeacon.'

'They seem extremely noisy, but at least they don't smell.'

There was no answer to that. The Archdeacon turned back to the house and Eric followed him. In the sitting-room he mutely offered one of the four upright rush-bottomed chairs round the square table. The Archdeacon seemed not to notice the invitation. He stood with his back to the fireplace and surveyed the room: the two armchairs – one a rocker, one a Windsor chair with a padded cushion in patchwork – the low bookcase along the whole of one wall, the posters which Karen had brought with her and fixed to the wall with Blu Tack.

The Archdeacon said, 'I suppose the stuff you've used to put up these posters doesn't damage the wall?'

'It shouldn't. It's specially made. It's like chewing gum.'

Then the Archdeacon pulled out one of the chairs sharply and sat down, motioning Eric to the other. The questions which followed were not aggressively put but Eric felt that he was a suspect under interrogation, accused of some as yet unnamed crime.

'How long have you worked here? Four years, isn't it?'

'Yes, Archdeacon.'

'And your duties are what, precisely?'

His duties had never been precise. Eric said, 'I'm a general handyman. I mend anything that gets broken if it isn't electrical, and I do the outside cleaning. That means I wash down the cloister floor, sweep up the courtyard, and clean the windows. Mr Pilbeam is responsible for the inside cleaning and there's a woman comes in from Reydon to help.'

'Hardly an onerous job. The garden looks well kept. You're fond of gardening?'

'Yes, very fond.'

'But it's hardly large enough to supply vegetables for the college.'

'Not all the vegetables, but I grow too much for my own use so I take the surplus up to the kitchen for Mrs Pilbeam and sometimes I give vegetables to people in the other cottages.'

'Do they pay for them?'

'Oh no, Archdeacon. Nobody pays.'

'And what do you get paid for these not very arduous duties?'

'I get the minimum wage based on five hours' work a day.'

He didn't say that neither he nor the college had worried too much about hours. Sometimes the work was done in less than five hours, sometimes it took longer.

'And in addition you get this cottage rent-free. You pay, no doubt, for your own heating, lighting and, of course, your own Council Tax.'

'I pay my Council Tax.'

'And what about Sundays?'

'Sunday is my day off.'

'I was thinking of church. You attend the church here?'

He did occasionally attend church, but only for Even-song when he would sit at the back and listen to the music and Father Sebastian's and Father Martin's measured voices, speaking words which were unfamiliar but beautiful to hear. But that couldn't be what the Arch-deacon meant.

He said, 'I don't usually go to church on Sunday.'

'But didn't Father Sebastian ask you about that when he appointed you?'

'No, Archdeacon. He asked me whether I could do the job.'

'He didn't ask you whether you were a Christian?'

And here at least he had an answer. He said, 'I am Christian, Archdeacon. I was christened when I was a baby. I've got a card somewhere.' He looked vaguely around as if the remembered card with its record of the christening, its sentimental picture of Christ blessing the little children might suddenly materialize.

There was a silence. He realized that the answer had been unsatisfactory. He wondered whether he ought to offer coffee, but surely nine-thirty was too early. The silence lengthened and then the Archdeacon got up.

He said, 'I see that you live very comfortably here and Father Sebastian seems pleased with you, but nothing lasts for ever, however comfortable. St Anselm's has existed for a hundred and forty years, but the Church – indeed the world – has changed a great deal in that time. I would suggest that if you do hear of another job that might suit you, you should seriously consider applying for it.'

Eric said, 'You mean that St Anselm's might close?'

He sensed that the Archdeacon had gone further than he had intended.

'I'm not saying that. These matters needn't concern you. I'm just suggesting for your own good that you shouldn't think that you have a job here for life, that's all.'

And then he left. Standing at the door Eric watched him striding across the headland towards the college. He was seized with an extraordinary emotion. His stomach churned and there was a taste bitter as bile in his mouth. In a life in which he had carefully avoided strong emotion he was feeling an overpowering physical response for the second time in his life. The first had been the realization of his love for Karen. But this was different. This was as powerful, but more disturbing. He knew that what he was feeling for the first time in his life was hatred for another human being.

12

Dalgliesh waited in the hall while Father Martin went to his room to collect his black cloak. When he reappeared, Dalgliesh said, 'Shall we take the car as far as we can?' He himself would have preferred to walk but he knew that, for his companion, the trudge along the beach would be tiring, and not only physically.

Father Martin accepted the suggestion with obvious relief. Neither of them spoke until they reached the point where the coastal track curved westward to join the Lowestoft road. Dalgliesh gently bumped his Jaguar on to the verge, then leaned over to help Father Martin with his seat belt. He opened the door for him and they set out for the beach.

Now that the track had ended, they were walking a narrow path of sand and well-trodden grass between the waist-high banks of bracken and a tangle of bushes. In places the bushes arched over the path and they walked in tunnelled dimness in which the surge of the sea had become no more than a distant rhythmic moan. Already the bracken was showing its first brittle gold and it seemed that every step they took on the spongy turf released the pungent nostalgic smells of autumn. They came out of the semi-darkness and saw the mere stretching before them, its dark sinister smoothness separated only by some fifty yards of shingle from the tumbling brightness of the sea. It seemed to Dalgliesh that there were fewer black tree stumps standing like prehistoric monuments guarding the mere. He looked for any trace of the wrecked ship but could see only a single black spar shaped like a shark's fin breaking the smooth stretch of the sand.

Here the access to the beach was so easy that the six wooden steps half-covered with sand and the single handrail were hardly necessary. At the top of the steps and built in a small hollow was an unpainted oak hut, rectangular and larger than an ordinary beach hut. Beside it was a heap of wood covered by a tarpaulin. Dalgliesh lifted an edge and saw a neatly-piled heap of planks and fractured timber, half painted blue.

Father Martin said, 'It's the remains of our old bathing hut. It was rather like the painted ones on Southwold beach but Father Sebastian thought it looked incongruous here on its own. It had become dilapidated and something of an eyesore so we took the opportunity to demolish it. Father Sebastian thought that a plain wooden shack, unpainted, would look better. This coast is so lonely that it's hardly needed when we come to bathe, but I suppose one should have somewhere to undress. We don't want to encourage our reputation for eccentricity. The hut also houses our small rescue boat. Swimming can be hazardous on this coast.'

Dalgliesh hadn't brought with him the spar of wood, nor had it been necessary. He had no doubt that it had come from the hut. Had Ronald Treeves picked it up casually as one sometimes did a spar of wood found on the beach with no particular purpose except perhaps to hurl it into the sea? Had he found it here or further along the shingle? Had he taken it with the intention of using it to prod down the overhanging ledge of sand over his head? Or had there been a second person carrying that spar of broken timber? But Ronald Treeves had been young and presumably fit and strong. How could he have been forced into that suffocating sand without some mark on his body?

The tide was retreating and they walked down to the strip of smooth damp sand at the edge of the curling waves, climbing over two groynes. They were obviously new and the ones he remembered from his boyhood visits lay between them, no more now than a few square-topped posts sunk deeply in the sand, linked with rotting planks.

Hitching up his cloak to climb over the green and slimy end of a groyne, Father Martin said, 'The European Community provided these new groynes. They're part of the defences against the sea. They've altered the appearance of the shore in some places. I expect there's more sand now than you remember.'

They had walked about two hundred yards when Father Martin said quietly, 'This is the place,' and began walking towards the cliff. Dalgliesh saw that there was a cross sticking into the sand made from two pieces of driftwood tightly bound.

Father Martin said, 'We placed the cross here the day after we found Ronald. So far it has stayed in place. Perhaps passers-by haven't liked to disturb it. I don't suppose it will last for long. Once we get the winter storms the sea will reach this far.'

Above the cross the sandy cliff was a rich terracotta and looked in places as it if had been sliced with a spade. At the cliff edge a fringe of grasses trembled in the gently moving air. To left and right there were several places where the cliff face had shifted, leaving deep cracks and crevices beneath overhanging ledges. It would, he thought, have been perfectly possible to lie with one's head under such a ledge and prod upwards with a stick, bringing down a half-ton of heavy sand. But it would take an extraordinary act of will or of desperation. He could think of few more dreadful ways to die. And if Ronald Treeves had wanted to kill himself, surely to swim out to sea until cold and exhaustion overcame him was a more merciful option? So far the word suicide had not been mentioned between him and Father Martin, but now he felt that it had to be said.

'This is a death, Father, which looks more like suicide than accident. But if Ronald Treeves wanted to kill himself, why not swim out to sea?'

'Ronald would never have done that. He was frightened of the sea. He couldn't even swim. He never bathed when the others came to swim and I don't think I have ever seen him walking on the beach. That's one of the reasons why I find it surprising that he chose to come to St Anselm's instead of applying to one of the other theological colleges.' He paused and said, 'I was afraid that you might think that suicide was more likely than accident. The possibility is deeply distressing to us all. If Ronald killed himself without us even knowing that he was so unhappy, then we failed him unforgivably. I can't really believe that he came here with the intention of committing what for him would have been a grave sin.'

Dalgliesh said, 'He took off his cloak and cassock and folded them neatly. Would he do that if he were just intending to scramble up the cliff?'

'He might do. It would be difficult to scramble up anywhere wearing either. There was something particularly poignant about those clothes. He had placed them so precisely, the sleeves folded inwards. It was as if he had packed them for a journey. But then, he was a careful boy.'

Dalgliesh thought, but why climb the cliff? If he was searching for something, what could it possibly be? These friable ever-changing banks of compacted sand with a thin stratum of pebbles and stones were hardly a reasonable hiding-place. There were, he knew, occasional interesting finds to be made, including pieces of amber or human bones washed up from graveyards now long under the sea. But if Treeves had glimpsed such an object, where was it now? Nothing of interest had been found by his body except that single spar of wood.

They walked back along the beach in silence, Dalgliesh accommodating his long stride to Father Martin's less certain steps. The elderly priest had bent his head to the wind and drawn his black cloak tightly around him. For Dalgliesh it was like walking with the personification of death.

When they were back in the car, Dalgliesh said, 'I'd like to have a word with the member of staff who found Mrs Munroe's body – a Mrs Pilbeam, wasn't it? And it would be helpful if I could speak to the doctor but it's difficult to think of the justification for that. I don't want to arouse suspicion where none exists. This death has been distressing enough without that.'

Father Martin said, 'Dr Metcalf is due to look in at the college this afternoon. One of the students, Peter Buckhurst, is recovering from glandular fever. It started at the end of last term. His parents are serving overseas so we kept him for the holidays to ensure that he got some care and nursing. When he calls, George Metcalf usually takes the opportunity to exercise his two dogs if he has half an hour or so to spare before his next appointment. We may catch him.'

They were fortunate. As they drove between the towers and into the courtyard, they saw a Range Rover parked at the front of the house. Dalgliesh and Father Martin got out of the car as Dr Metcalf came down the steps, carrying his case and turning to wave goodbye to someone unseen within the house. The doctor was revealed as a tall, weather-beaten man who must, thought Dalgliesh, be nearing retirement. He made his way to the Range Rover and opened the door to be greeted with loud barking; two Dalmatians sprang out and hurled themselves against him. Shouting imprecations, the doctor took out two large bowls and a plastic bottle which he unscrewed, pouring water into the bowls. There was an immediate sound of slurping and much wagging of strong white tails.

As Dalgliesh and Father Martin approached, he called out, 'Good afternoon, Father. Peter is recovering well, no need to worry. He ought to get out a bit more now. Less theology and more fresh air. I'll just take Ajax and Jasper as far as the mere. All well with you I hope?'

'Very well thank you, George. This is Adam Dalgliesh from London. He'll be with us for a day or two.'

The doctor turned to look at Dalgliesh and, while shaking hands, gave an approving nod as if physically he had passed muster.

Dalgliesh said, 'I'd been hoping to see Mrs Munroe

while I was here, but I'm too late. I'd no idea she was so ill, but I understand from Father Martin that the death wasn't unexpected.'

The doctor took off his jacket, dragged a voluminous sweater from the car and substituted walking boots for his shoes. He said, 'Death still has the power to surprise me. You think a patient won't last a week and they're sitting up and making a nuisance of themselves a year later. Then you expect they're good for at least another six months and arrive to find they've slipped away in the night. That's why I never give patients an estimate of how long they've got. But Mrs Munroe knew her heart was in a bad state – she was a nurse after all – and her death certainly didn't surprise me. She could have gone any time. We both knew that.'

Dalgliesh said, 'Which meant that the college was spared the distress of a second post-mortem so soon after the first.'

'Good Lord yes! None was necessary. I'd been seeing her regularly; indeed, I called in the day before she died. I'm sorry you missed her. Was she an old friend? Did she know you were coming to visit?'

'No,' said Dalgliesh, 'she didn't know.'

'A pity. If she'd had that to look forward to she might have hung on. You never know with heart patients. You never know with any patients, come to that.'

He gave a valedictory nod and strode off, the dogs leaping and trotting at his side.

Father Martin said, 'We could see if Mrs Pilbeam's in her cottage now, if you like. I'll just take you to the door and introduce you, and then leave you together.'

13

At St Mark's Cottage the door to the porch was wide open and light spilled across the red tiled floor and touched with brightness the leaves of the plants in terra-cotta pots which were ranged on low shelves on either side. Father Martin had hardly raised his hand to the knocker when the inner door opened and Mrs Pilbeam, smiling, stood aside to welcome them in. Father Martin made a brief introduction and left, after hesitating at the door as if uncertain whether he was expected to pronounce a benediction.

Dalgliesh entered the small over-furnished sitting-room with a reassuring and nostalgic sense of stepping back into childhood. In just such a room had he sat as a boy while his mother made her parish visits, sitting, legs dangling, at the table eating fruitcake or, at Christmas, mince pies, hearing his mother's low, rather hesitant voice. Everything about the room was familiar: the small iron fireplace with the decorated hood; the square central table covered with a red chenille cloth and with a large aspidistra in a green container at the centre; the two easy chairs, one a rocker, placed at each side of the fireplace; the ornaments on the mantelshelf, two Staffordshire dogs with pouting eyes, an over-decorated vase with the words 'Present from Southend' and an assortment of photographs in silver frames. The walls were hung with Victorian prints in their original walnut frames: *The*

Sailor's Return, *Grandpapa's Pet*, a group of unconvincingly clean children and parents processing to church across a meadow. The south window was wide open giving a view of the headland, and the narrow sill was covered with a variety of small containers holding cacti and African violets. The only discordant note was the large television set and video recorder dominant in the corner.

Mrs Pilbeam was a short, plumply compact woman with an open wind-tanned face under fair hair which had been carefully combed into waves. She had been wearing a flowered apron over her skirt but now took it off and hung it on a peg behind the door. She motioned Dalgliesh to the rocking chair and they sat facing each other, Dalgliesh resisting the temptation to lie back and set it comfortably rocking.

Watching him glancing at the pictures, she said, 'They were left to me by my gran. I grew up with those pictures. Reg thinks they're a bit sentimental but I like them. They don't paint like that nowadays.'

'No,' said Dalgliesh, 'they don't.'

The eyes looking into his were gentle but they were also intelligent. Sir Alred Treeves had been adamant that the investigation should be discreet but that didn't mean secrecy. Mrs Pilbeam was as entitled as Father Sebastian to the truth, or at least as much of it as was necessary.

He said, 'It's about the death of Ronald Treeves. His father, Sir Alred, couldn't be in England for the inquest and he has asked me to make some enquiries about what exactly happened so that he can be satisfied that the verdict was right.'

Mrs Pilbeam said, 'Father Sebastian told us you'd be

coming over asking questions. Bit of a funny idea of Sir Alred's, isn't it? You'd think he'd be happy to leave things be.'

Dalgliesh looked at her. 'Were you happy with the verdict, Mrs Pilbeam?'

'Well, I didn't find the body and I didn't go to the inquest. It wasn't really anything to do with me. But it seemed a bid odd. Everyone knows those cliffs are dangerous. Still, the poor lad's dead now. I don't see what good his dad hopes to do by raking it all up.'

Dalgliesh said, 'I can't, of course, speak to Mrs Munroe but I wondered whether she talked to you about finding the body. Father Martin says that you were friends.'

'Poor woman. Yes, I suppose we were friends, although Margaret was never one for calling in unexpectedly. Even when her Charlie was killed I never felt we were really close. He was a captain in the Army and she was so proud of him. She said that that was all he'd ever wanted to be, a soldier. He got captured by the IRA. I think he was doing something secret and they tortured him to find out what it was. When the news came I moved in with her just for a week. Father Sebastian asked me to, but I would have done it anyway. She didn't stop me. I don't think she noticed. But if I put food in front of her she took a mouthful or so. I was glad when she suddenly asked me to go. She said, "I'm sorry, Ruby, I've been such bad company. You've been very kind, but please go now." So I went.

'Watching her, all those months afterwards, it was like someone being tortured in Hell and not being able to make a sound. Her eyes got immense but the rest of her seemed to shrivel up. I thought she was, well, not getting over it – you don't, do you – not if it's your child? – but that she was beginning to take an interest in life again. I thought so, we all did. But then they let those murderers out of prison under the Good Friday agreement and she couldn't take that. And I think she was lonely. It was the boys that she loved – they were always boys to her – looking after them when they were sick. But I think they were a bit shy with her after Charlie died. The young don't like to watch unhappiness, and who can blame them?'

Dalgliesh said, 'They'll have to watch it and cope with it once they're priests.'

'Oh they'll learn, I dare say. They're good lads.'

Dalgliesh asked, 'Mrs Pilbeam, did you like Ronald Treeves?'

The woman waited before answering. 'It wasn't my place to think whether I liked him or not. Well, it wasn't anyone's place really. In a small community it doesn't do to have favourites. That's something Father Sebastian has always been against. But he wasn't a popular boy and I don't think he felt at home here. He was a bit too pleased with himself and too critical about other people. That usually comes from insecurity, doesn't it? And he never let us forget that his father was rich.'

'Was he particularly friendly with Mrs Munroe, do you know?'

'With Margaret? Well, I suppose you could say he was. He used to call there quite a bit, I do know that. The students are only supposed to go to the cottages by invitation, but I have a feeling he used to drop in on Margaret. Not that she ever complained. I can't think what they found to talk about. Maybe they both liked the company.'

'Did Mrs Munroe ever speak to you about finding the body?'

'Not much and I didn't like to ask. Of course it all came out at the inquest and I read about it in the papers, but I didn't go. Everyone else here was talking about it, though not when Father Sebastian was within earshot. He hates gossips. But I suppose I got all the details one way or another – not that there were many to get.'

'Did she tell you that she was writing an account of it?'

'No, she didn't, but I'm not surprised. She was a great one for writing, was Margaret. Before Charlie was killed she used to write to him every week. When I came in to see her she'd be sitting at the table writing away, page after page. But she never told me she was writing about young Ronald. Now why would she want to do that?'

'You found her body, didn't you, when she had her heart attack? What happened then, Mrs Pilbeam?'

'Well, I saw her light on when I went over to the college just after six. I hadn't seen her for a couple of days – not to talk to – and I had a bit of a conscience. I thought I'd been neglecting her and that she might like to come in and have a bite of supper with me and Reg, and maybe watch television together. So I went over to her cottage. And there she was, dead in her chair.'

'Was the door unlocked or had you a key?'

'Oh, it was unlocked. We hardly ever lock our doors here. I knocked and when she didn't answer I went in. We always did that. And that's when I found her. She was quite cold, sitting there in her chair, stiff as a board with her knitting in her lap. One of the needles was still in her right hand, pushed into the next stitch. Of course I called Father Sebastian and he rang Dr Metcalf. Dr

Metcalf had come to see her only the day before. She had a terribly bad heart so there wasn't any problem about the death certificate. It was a good way for her to go really. We should all be so lucky.'

'And you didn't find any paper, any letter?'

'Not where you'd see them, and of course I wouldn't go rummaging around. What would I be doing that for?'

'Of course you wouldn't, Mrs Pilbeam. I just wondered whether there was a manuscript, a letter or a document on the table.'

'No, nothing on the table. There was one odd thing though. She couldn't have been knitting, not really.'

'Why do you say that?'

'Well, she was knitting a winter pullover for Father Martin. He'd seen one in a shop in Ipswich and described it to her and she thought she'd knit it for Christmas. But it was a really complicated design, a kind of cable with a pattern in between, and she told me how difficult it was. She wouldn't be knitting it without the pattern open in front of her. I've seen her many a time and she always had to refer to the pattern. And she was wearing the wrong spectacles, the ones she puts on to watch television. She always wore the gold-rimmed ones for close work.'

'And the pattern wasn't there?'

'No, only the needles and the wool in her lap. And she was holding the needle in a funny way. She didn't knit like I do, she told me it was the continental way. Very odd it looked. She used to hold the left needle kind of rigid and worked the other one round it. I thought at the time it was funny, seeing the knitting in her lap when she couldn't have been knitting.'

'But you didn't speak to anyone about it?'

'What point would there be? It didn't matter. Just one of those odd things. I expect she was feeling ill and just reached for her needles and the knitting and sat down in her chair forgetting about the pattern. But I miss her. It's odd having the cottage still empty and it seemed as if she disappeared overnight. She never talked about any family, but it turned out she had a sister living in Surbiton. She arranged for the body to be taken to London for cremation and she and her husband came down to clear up the cottage. There's nothing like death for bringing the family on the scene. Margaret wouldn't have wanted a Requiem Mass, but Father Sebastian arranged a very nice service in the church. We all had a part to play. Father Sebastian thought I might like to read a passage from St Paul, but I said I'd rather just say a prayer instead. Somehow I can't take St Paul. Seems to me he was a bit of a troublemaker. There were those little groups of Christians all minding their own business and getting along all right, by and large. No one's perfect. And then St Paul arrives unexpectedly and starts bossing and criticizing. Or he'd send them one of his fierce letters. Not the kind of letter I'd care to receive, and so I told Father Sebastian.'

'What did he say?'

'That St Paul was one of the world's great religious geniuses and that we wouldn't be Christians now if it hadn't been for him. I said, "Well Father, we'd have to be something," and asked what he thought we'd be. But I don't think he knew. He said he'd think about it, but if he did he never told me. He said that I raised questions not covered by the syllabus of the Cambridge Faculty of Theology.'

And those, thought Dalgliesh after he had refused her offer of tea and cake and left, were not the only questions Mrs Pilbeam had raised.

14

Dr Emma Lavenham left her Cambridge college later than she had hoped. Giles had taken lunch in hall and, while she completed her packing, had talked about matters that he said needed to be settled before she left. She sensed that he had been glad to delay her. Giles had never liked her termly absences when she went to give three days of lectures at St Anselm's College. He had never openly objected, probably sensing that she would have seen this as an inexcusable interference in her private life, but he had more subtle ways of expressing his dislike of an activity in which he had no part and which took place in an institution for which, as a proclaimed atheist, he had little respect. But he could hardly complain that her work in Cambridge suffered.

The late start meant that she didn't escape the worst of the Friday night traffic, and the periodic hold-ups left her with a resentment against Giles for his delaying tactics and an irritation with herself for not resisting them more effectively. At the end of last term she had begun to realize that Giles was becoming both more proprietorial and more demanding of time and affection. Now, with the prospect of a Chair in a northern university, his mind was turning towards marriage, perhaps because he saw it as the likeliest way of ensuring that she went with him. He had, she knew, definite ideas of what for him constituted a suitable wife. Unfortunately it seemed that she filled them. She resolved for the next three days at least that she would put that and all the problems of her university life firmly out of mind.

The arrangements with the college had started three years ago. Father Sebastian, she realized, had recruited her in his customary fashion. Feelers had been put out among his Cambridge contacts. What the college required was an academic, preferably young, to give three seminars at the beginning of each term on 'The Poetic Inheritance of Anglicanism', someone with a reputation – or in the process of making it – who could relate to the young ordinands and who would fit in with the ethos of St Anselm's. What that ethos was, Father Sebastian hadn't thought it necessary to explain. The post, Father Sebastian had later told her, had arisen directly from the wishes of the founder of the college, Miss Arbuthnot. Strongly influenced in this, as in other matters, by her High Church friends in Oxford, she had believed it was important that the newly-ordained Anglican priests should know something of the literary inheritance which was theirs. Emma, aged twenty-eight and recently appointed a university lecturer, had been invited to what Father Sebastian had described as an informal discussion about the possibility of her joining the community for those nine days a year. The post had been offered and accepted with the only proviso on Emma's part that the poetry should not be limited to Church of England writers nor restricted in time. She had pointed out to Father Sebastian that she would wish to include the poems of Gerard Manley Hopkins and to extend the period covered to include modern poets such as T. S. Eliot. Father Sebastian, having obviously satisfied himself that she was the right person for the job, seemed content to leave the details to her. Apart from appearing at the third of her seminars where his silent presence had had a somewhat intimidating effect, he had taken no further interest in the course.

Those three days at St Anselm's, preceded by a weekend, had become important to her, eagerly looked forward to and never disappointing. Cambridge wasn't without its tensions and anxieties. She had gained her university lectureship early – perhaps, she thought, too early. There was the problem of reconciling the teaching which she loved with the need to produce research, the responsibilities of administration and the pastoral care of students who increasingly spoke first to her about their problems. Many were the first of their family to attend university. They came laden with expectations and anxieties. Some who had done well in A level found the reading lists dauntingly long, others suffered from a homesickness they were ashamed to admit and felt inadequately equipped to confront this intimidating new life.

None of these pressures was made easier by the demands of Giles and the complications of her own emotional life. It was a relief to be part of the beautifully ordered and isolated peace of St Anselm's, to be talking about the poetry she loved to intelligent young men who weren't faced with the weekly essay, the half-acknowledged wish to please her with acceptable opinions, and who were unshadowed by the prospect of Tripos. She liked them and, while generally discouraging the occasional romantic or amorous approach, knew that they liked her, were pleased to see a woman in college, looked forward to her coming and saw her as an ally. And it wasn't only the students who welcomed her. She was greeted always as a friend. Father Sebastian's calm, somewhat formal welcome couldn't conceal his satisfaction at having once again picked the right person. The other fathers showed their more demonstrative happiness at her return.

While her visits to St Anselm's were an anticipated pleasure, her regular and dutiful returns home to her father were never undertaken without a heaviness of spirit. Since relinquishing his Oxford post he had moved to a mansion flat near Marylebone station. The red brick walls reminded her of the colour of raw meat and the heavy furniture, the dark-papered walls and net-shrouded windows created a permanent atmosphere of internal gloom which her father appeared never to notice. Henry Lavenham had married late and had lost his wife to breast cancer soon after the birth of their second daughter. Emma had been only three at the time and it later seemed to her that her father had transferred to the new baby all the love he had felt for his wife, reinforced by pity for the helplessness of the motherless child. Emma had always known herself to be the less loved. She had felt no resentment or jealousy of her sibling but had compensated for the lack of love by work and success. Two words had reverberated from her adolescence: brilliant and beautiful. Both had imposed a burden, the first the expectation of success which had come to her too easily to deserve credit; the second a puzzle, sometimes almost a torment. She had grown into beauty only in adolescence and would gaze into the mirror trying to define and evaluate this extraordinarily overvalued possession, already half aware that, while good looks and prettiness were benisons, beauty was a dangerous and less amenable gift.

Until her sister Marianne was eleven the two girls had been looked after by a sister of her father's, a sensible, undemonstrative and conscientious woman who was totally devoid of maternal instinct but knew her duty when she saw it. She had provided a stabilizing, unsentimental care but had departed into her private world of dogs, bridge and foreign travel as soon as she thought Marianne had been old enough to leave. The girls had seen her go without regret.

And now Marianne was dead, killed by a drunken driver on her thirteenth birthday, and Emma and her father were alone. When she returned to see him he showed her a scrupulous, almost painful courtesy. She wondered whether their lack of communication and avoidance of any demonstrative affection – which she could hardly call estrangement since what had they been other than strangers? – was the result of his feeling that now, over seventy and bereaved, it would be demeaning and embarrassing to demand from her the love which he had never previously shown any sign of needing.

And now, at last, she was nearing the end of her journey. The narrow road to the sea was seldom used except on summer weekends and this evening she was the only traveller. The road stretched before her, pale, shadowed and a little sinister in the fading light. As always when she came to St Anselm's she had the sensation of moving towards a crumbling coast, untamed, mysterious and isolated in time as well as space.

As she turned north along the track leading to St Anselm's and the high chimneys and tower of the house loomed blackly menacing against the darkening sky, she saw a short figure trudging about fifty yards ahead and recognized Father John Betterton.

Drawing up beside him she let down the window and said, 'Can I give you a lift, Father?'

He blinked, as if for a moment not recognizing her. Then he gave the familiar sweet and childish smile. 'Emma. Thank you, thank you. A lift will be welcome. I walked further than I intended round the mere.'

He was wearing a heavy tweed coat and had his binoculars slung round his neck. He got in, bringing with him, impregnated in the tweed, the dank smell of brackish water.

'Any luck with the bird-watching, Father?'

'Just the usual winter residents.'

They sat in companionable silence. There had been a time when, briefly, Emma had found it difficult to be at ease with Father John. That had been on her first visit three years ago when Raphael had told her about the priest's imprisonment.

He had said, 'Someone is bound to tell you at Cambridge if not here, and I'd rather you heard it from me. Father John confessed to abusing some young boys in his choir. That's the word they used, but I doubt there was much real abuse. He was sent to prison for three years.'

Emma had said, 'I don't know much about the law, but the sentence seems harsh.'

'It wasn't just the two boys. Another priest from a neighbouring parish, Matthew Crampton, made it his business to rake up further evidence and produced three young men. They accused Father John of worse enormities. According to them it was his early abuse that made them unemployable, unhappy, delinquent and antisocial. They were lying but Father John still pleaded guilty. He had his reasons.'

Without necessarily sharing Raphael's belief in Father John's innocence, Emma felt a great pity for him. He seemed like a man who had partly withdrawn into a private world, precariously preserving the core of a vulnerable personality as if he were carrying within himself something fragile which even a sudden movement might shatter. He was unfailingly polite and gentle and she could only detect his private anguish on those few occasions when she looked into his eyes and had to turn hers away from the pain. Perhaps he was also carrying a burden of guilt. Part of her still wished that Raphael hadn't spoken. She couldn't imagine what his life in prison must have been. Would any man, she wondered, willingly bring that hell on himself? And his life at St Anselm's couldn't be easy. He occupied a private apartment on the third floor with his unmarried sister who could charitably be described as eccentric. Although it was obvious to Emma on the few occasions when she had seen them together that he was devoted to her, perhaps even love was an added burden rather than a comfort.

She wondered whether she ought to say a word to him now about the death of Ronald Treeves. She had read a brief account in the national papers and Raphael, who for some reason made it his business to keep her in touch with St Anselm's, had telephoned with the news. After some thought she had written a brief and carefully worded letter of condolence to Father Sebastian and had received an even briefer reply in his elegant handwriting. It would surely be natural to speak of Ronald now to Father John, but something held her back. She sensed that the subject would be unwelcome, even painful.

And now St Anselm's was clearly in sight, roofs, the tall chimney stacks, turrets, tower and cupola seeming visibly to darken with the dying of the light. In front the two ruined pillars of the long-demolished Elizabethan gatehouse gave out their silent ambiguous messages; crude phallic symbols, indomitable sentinels against the steadily-advancing enemy, obstinately enduring reminders of the house's inevitable end. Was it, she wondered, the presence beside her of Father John or the thought of Ronald Treeves choking his last breath under that weight of sand that caused this upsurge of sadness and vague apprehension? She had never come to St Anselm's before except with joy; now she approached it with something very close to fear.

As they drew up to the front door it opened and she saw Raphael outlined against the light from the hall. He had obviously been looking out for her. He stood there in his dark cassock, motionless as if carved in stone, looking down on them. She remembered her first sight of him; she had stared in momentary disbelief and then laughed aloud at her inability to conceal her surprise. Another student, Stephen Morby, had been with them and had laughed with her.

'Extraordinary, isn't he? We were in a pub in Reydon and a woman came up and said, "Where did you come from, Olympus?" I wanted to leap on the table, bare my chest and cry out, "Look at me! Look at me!" Some hope.'

He had spoken without a trace of envy. Perhaps he realized that beauty in a man wasn't the gift it seemed, and indeed for Emma it was impossible to look at Raphael without a superstitious reminder of the bad fairy at the christening. She was interested, too, that she could look at him with pleasure but without having the least sexual response. Perhaps he appealed more to men than to women. But if he had power over either sex he appeared unconscious of it. She knew from the easy confidence with which he held himself that he knew that he was beautiful and that his beauty made him different. He valued his exceptional looks and thought the better of himself for possessing them, but he seemed hardly to care about their effect on others.

Now his face broke into a smile and he came down the steps towards her holding out his hand. In her present mood of half-superstitious apprehension the gesture seemed less a welcome than a warning. Father John, with a nod and a final smile, pattered off.

Raphael took Emma's laptop and suitcase from her. He said, 'Welcome back. I can't promise you an agreeable weekend but it might be interesting. We've got two policemen in residence – one from New Scotland Yard, no less. Commander Dalgliesh is here to ask questions about Ronald Treeves's death. And there's someone else even less welcome as far as I'm concerned. I intend to keep out of his way and recommend you do the same. Archdeacon Matthew Crampton.'

15

There was one more visit to be made. Dalgliesh returned briefly to his room, then went through the iron doorway in the gate between Ambrose and the flint wall of the church, and made his way along the eighty yards of track which led to St John's Cottage. It was now late afternoon and the day was dying in a gaudy western sky streaked with pink. Beside the path a fringe of tall and delicate grasses shivered in the strengthening breeze, then flattened under the sweep of a sudden gust. Behind him, the west-facing façade of St Anselm's was patterned with light and the three inhabited cottages shone like the bright outposts of a beleaguered fortress, emphasizing the dark outline of the empty St Matthew's.

As the light faded the sound of the sea intensified, its soft rhythmic moaning rising to a muted roar. He recalled from his boyhood visits how the last evening light always brought with it this sense of the sea surging in power, as if night and darkness were its natural allies. He would sit at the window of Jerome, looking out over the darkening scrubland, picturing an imagined shore where the crumbling sand-castles would be finally demolished, the shouts and laughter of the children silenced, the deck chairs folded and carried away, and the sea would come into its own, rolling the bones of drowned mariners around the holds of long-wrecked ships.

The door of St John's Cottage stood open and light spilled over the path leading to the neat wicket gate. He could still see clearly the wooden walls of the piggery to the right, and hear the muffled snorting and scuffling. He could smell the animals but the smell was neither strong nor unpleasant. Beyond the piggery he could just glimpse the garden, neat rows of clumped unrecognizable vegetables, the higher canes supporting the last of a crop of runner beans and, at the end of the garden, the gleam of a small greenhouse.

At the sound of his footsteps the figure of Eric Surtees appeared in the doorway. He seemed to hesitate and then, without speaking, stood aside and made a stiff gesture inviting him in. Dalgliesh knew that Father Sebastian had told the staff of his impending visit although he was unsure how much explanation had been given. He had a sense that he was expected but not that he was welcomed.

He said, 'Mr Surtees? I'm Commander Dalgliesh of the Metropolitan Police. I think Father Sebastian explained that I'm here to ask some questions about the death of Ronald Treeves. His father wasn't in England at the time of the inquest and he naturally wants to know as much as possible about the circumstances of his son's death. I'd like to talk for a few minutes if it's convenient.'

Surtees nodded. 'That's OK. Do you mind coming in here?'

Dalgliesh followed him into the room to the right of the passage. The cottage could not have been more different from Mrs Pilbeam's comfortable domesticity. Although there was a centre table of plain wood with four upright chairs, the room had been furnished as a workplace. The wall opposite the door had been fitted with racks from which hung a row of immaculately clean garden implements, spades, forks, hoes, together with shears and saws, while a bank of wooden compartments underneath held boxes of tools and smaller implements. There was a workbench in front of the window with a fluorescent light above. The door to the kitchen was open and from it came a powerful and disagreeable smell. Surtees was boiling up pigswill for his small herd.

Now he pulled out a chair from the table. It rasped along the stone floor. He said, 'If you'll just wait here, I'll wash. I've been seeing to the pigs.'

Through the open door Dalgliesh could see him at the sink washing vigorously, splashing water over his head and face. He seemed like a man cleaning himself of more than superficial dirt. Then he came back with the towel still round his neck and sat opposite Dalgliesh, stiffly upright, and with the strained look of a prisoner steeling himself for interrogation. Suddenly he said in an over-loud voice, 'Would you like tea?'

Thinking that tea might help to put him at ease, Dalgliesh said, 'If it's not too much trouble.'

'No trouble. I use tea-bags. Milk and sugar?'

'Just milk.'

He came back within minutes and placed two heavy mugs on the table. The tea was strong and very hot. Neither of them began to drink. Dalgliesh had seldom interviewed anyone who gave so strong an impression of guilty knowledge. But knowledge of what? It was ridiculous to imagine this timid-looking boy – surely he was little more than a boy – killing any living creature.

Even his pigs would have their throats cut in the sanitized, strictly-regulated killing-ground of an authorized abattoir. It wasn't, Dalgliesh saw, that Surtees lacked strength for a physical encounter. Under the short sleeves of his checked shirt the muscles of his arms stood out like cords and his hands were rough, and so incongruous in size with the rest of his body that they looked as if they had been grafted on. The delicate face was tanned by sun and wind, and the open buttons of the rough cotton shirt showed a glimpse of skin as white and soft as a child's.

Lifting his mug, Dalgliesh said, 'Have you always kept pigs or only since you came to work here? That was four years ago, wasn't it?'

'Just since I came here. I've always liked pigs. When I got this job Father Sebastian said it would be all right to have about half a dozen if they weren't too noisy and didn't smell. They're very clean animals. People are quite wrong to think they smell.'

'Did you construct the piggery yourself? I'm surprised you used wood. I thought pigs could destroy almost anything.'

'Oh, they can. It's only wood on the outside. Father Sebastian insisted on that. He hates concrete. I lined it with breezeblocks.'

Surtees had waited until Dalgliesh began drinking before raising his own mug. Dalgliesh was surprised how much he relished the tea. He said, 'I know very little about pigs, but I'm told they're intelligent and companionable.'

Surtees visibly relaxed. 'Yes, they are. They're one of the most intelligent animals. I've always liked them.'

'Lucky for St Anselm's. It means they get bacon which doesn't smell of chemicals or exude that unappetizing, smelly liquid. And properly hung pork.'

'I don't really keep them for the college. I keep them – well, for companionship really. Of course, they have to go to be killed eventually and that's a problem now. There are so many EU regulations about abattoirs and always having a vet in attendance that people don't want to accept just a few animals. And then there's the problem of transport. But there's a farmer, Mr Harrison, just outside Blythburgh who helps with that. I send my pigs to the abattoir with his. And he always hangs some of the pork for his own use so I can supply the fathers with a decent joint occasionally. They don't eat much pork but they like to have the bacon. Father Sebastian insists on paying for it, but I think they should get it free.'

Dalgliesh wondered, as he had before, at the capacity of men to be genuinely fond of their animals, to have a lively regard for their welfare and minister to their needs with devotion, and at the same time be so easily reconciled to their slaughter. Now he got down to the business of his visit.

He said, 'Did you know Ronald Treeves, know him personally, that is?'

'Not really. I knew he was one of the ordinands and I saw him about the place, but we didn't really talk. I think he was a bit of a loner. I mean, when I did see him about the place he was usually on his own.'

'What happened on the day he died? Were you here?'

'Yes, I was here with my sister. It was the weekend and she was visiting. We didn't see Ronald that Saturday and the first we knew he was missing was when Mr Pilbeam came round and asked if he'd been here. We said he hadn't. We didn't hear anything else until I went out at about five o'clock to sweep up some fallen leaves from the cloisters and the courtyard and to wash down the stones. It had been raining the day before and the cloisters were a bit muddy. I usually go up to sweep and hose the cloisters after the services, but Father Sebastian had asked me after Mass to hose them down before Evensong. I was doing that when Mr Pilbeam told me that they'd found Ronald Treeves's body. Later on, before Evensong, Father Sebastian got us all together in the library and told us what had happened.'

'It must have been a very great shock for you all.'

Surtees was looking down at his hands, still clasped and resting on the table. Suddenly he jerked them both out of sight like a guilty child and hunched forward. He said in a low voice, 'Yes. A shock. Well it was, wasn't it?'

'You seem to be the only gardener at St Anselm's. Do you grow for yourself or for the college?'

'Mostly vegetables for myself and for anyone who needs them, really. I don't grow enough for the college, not when all the ordinands are in residence. I suppose I could extend the garden but it would take too much time. The soil's quite good considering it's close to the sea. My sister usually takes vegetables back to London when she comes, and Miss Betterton likes to have them. She cooks for herself and Father John. Mrs Pilbeam too, for herself and Mr Pilbeam.'

Dalgliesh said, 'Mrs Munroe left a diary. She mentioned that you'd been kind enough to bring her some leeks on October 11th, the day before she died. Do you remember doing that?'

There was a pause, then Surtees said, 'Yes, I think so. Perhaps I did. I can't remember.'

Dalgliesh said gently, 'It wasn't so long ago, was it? Just over a week. Are you sure you can't remember?'

'I do remember now. I took the leeks up in the evening. Mrs Munroe used to say she liked leeks with cheese sauce for supper, so I took some to St Matthew's Cottage.'

'And what happened?'

He looked up, genuinely puzzled. 'Nothing. Nothing happened. I mean, she just said thank you and took them in.'

'You didn't go into the cottage?'

'No. She didn't ask me and I wouldn't have wanted to. I mean, Karen was here and I wanted to get back. She stayed on that week until Thursday morning. I went up on chance really. I thought Mrs Munroe might have been with Mrs Pilbeam. If she hadn't been at home I'd have left the leeks at the door.'

'But she was at home. Are you sure that nothing was said, that nothing happened? You just handed her the leeks?'

He nodded. 'I just handed them to her and left.'

It was then that Dalgliesh heard the sound of an approaching car. Surtees's ears must have caught it simultaneously. He pushed back his chair with obvious relief and said, 'That'll be Karen. She's my sister. She's coming for the weekend.'

And now the car had stopped. Surtees hurried out. Dalgliesh, sensing his anxiety to speak to his sister alone, perhaps to warn her of his presence, followed him quietly and stood in the open doorway.

A woman had got out of the car, and now she and her brother stood close together regarding Dalgliesh. Without speaking, she turned and began lugging a large rucksack and an assortment of plastic bags out of the car, then slammed the door. Lumbered with the assorted packages they came down the path.

Surtees said, 'Karen, this is Commander Dalgliesh from New Scotland Yard. He's asking questions about Ronald.'

She was hatless, her dark hair cropped into short spikes. A heavy gold loop in each ear emphasized the paleness of the delicately-boned face. Her eyes were narrow under thin arched brows, the irises dark and glitteringly bright. With a pursed mouth heavily outlined in gleaming red lipstick, her face was a carefully designed pattern in black, white and red. The glance she gave Dalgliesh was initially hostile, a reaction to an unexpected and unwanted visitor. As their eyes held, it became appraising and then wary.

They moved together into the workroom. Karen Surtees dumped her rucksack on the table. Nodding to Dalgliesh, she said to her brother, 'Better get these ready-prepared meals from M & S into the freezer straight away. There's a case of wine in the car.'

Surtees looked from one to the other, then went out. Without speaking the girl began dragging an assortment of clothes and tins from the rucksack.

Dalgliesh said, 'You're obviously not wanting visitors at present but, as I'm here, it will save time if you can answer a few questions.'

'Ask away. I'm Karen Surtees, by the way. Eric's

half-sister. You're a bit late on the job, aren't you? Not much point now asking questions about Ronald Treeves. There's been an inquest. Accidental death. And there isn't even a body to exhume. His dad had him cremated in London. Didn't they bother to tell you that? Anyway, I don't see what it's got to do with the Met. I mean, isn't it for the Suffolk Police?'

'Essentially yes, but Sir Alred has a natural curiosity about his son's death. I was coming into the county so he asked me to find out what I could.'

'If he really wanted to know how his son died he'd have gone to the inquest. I suppose he's got a guilty conscience and wants to show that he's a concerned dad. What's he worried about anyway? He's not saying that Ronald was murdered?'

It was odd to hear that doom-laden word spoken so easily. 'No, I don't think he's saying that.'

'Well, I can't help him. I only met his son once or twice when he was out walking and we'd say "good morning" or "nice day", the usual meaningless platitudes.'

'You weren't friends?'

'I'm not friends with any of the students. And if by friends you mean what I think you mean, I come down here to get a change from London and to see my brother, not to fuck the ordinands! Not that it would do them much harm, to look at them.'

'You were here the weekend Ronald Treeves died?'

'That's right. I arrived Friday night, much the same time as today.'

'Did you see him that weekend?'

'No, neither of us did. The first we knew he was missing was when Pilbeam came down to ask if he had been here. We said he hadn't. End of story. Look, if there's anything else you want to know, can it wait till tomorrow? I'd like to settle in, get unpacked, have some tea, know what I mean? Getting out of London was hell. So if it's all right by you, I'll leave it for now, not that there's anything else to say. As far as I was concerned he was just one of the students.'

'But you must have formed an opinion about the death, both of you. You must have talked about it.'

Surtees had finished stowing away the food and now came in from the kitchen. Karen looked at him. She said, 'Of course we talked about it, the whole bloody college must have talked about it. If you want to know, I thought he'd probably killed himself. I don't know why and it's none of my business. As I said, I hardly knew him but it seemed a very odd accident. He must have known that the cliffs are dangerous. Well, we all know, there are enough warning notices. What was he doing on the beach anyway?'

'That,' said Dalgliesh, 'is one of the questions.'

He had thanked them and was turning to go when a thought struck him. He said to Surtees, 'The leeks you took to Mrs Munroe, how were they wrapped? Can you remember? Were they in a bag or did you carry them unwrapped?'

Surtees looked puzzled. 'I can't remember. I think I wrapped them in newspaper. That's what I usually do with the vegetables, the large ones anyway.'

'Can you remember what newspaper you used? I know it isn't easy.' Then, as Surtees didn't reply, he added, 'Was it a broadsheet or a tabloid? Which newspaper do you take?'

It was Karen who finally answered. 'It was a copy of the *Sole Bay Weekly Gazette*. I'm a journalist. I tend to notice newspapers.'

'You were here in the kitchen?'

'I must have been, mustn't I? Anyway, I saw Eric wrapping the leeks. He said he was taking them up to Mrs Munroe.'

'You don't happen to remember the date of the paper?'

'No, I don't. I remember the paper because, like I said, I tend to look at newspapers. Eric opened it at the middle page and there was a picture of a local farmer's funeral. He wanted his favourite heifer to attend so they led the beast to the grave with black ribbons tied to its horns and round its neck. I don't think they'd have actually let it into the church. Just the kind of shot picture editors love.'

Dalgliesh turned to Surtees: 'When does the *Sole Bay Gazette* come out?'

'Every Thursday. I don't usually read it until the weekend.'

'So the paper you used was probably the one from the previous week.' He turned to Karen and said, 'Thank you, you've been very helpful,' and saw again in her eyes that swift appraising glance.

They followed him to the door. As he turned at the gate he saw them standing close together watching, as it seemed, until they could be sure he had actually left. Then simultaneously they turned and the door closed behind them.

16

After his solitary dinner at the Crown in Southwold, Dalgliesh had planned to return to St Anselm's in time to attend Compline. But the meal, which was too excellent to be hurried, took longer than expected and by the time he had got back and parked the Jaguar, the service had started. He waited in his rooms until a beam of light fell over the courtyard and he saw that the south door of the church had been opened and the small congregation was coming out. He made his way to the sacristy door where Father Sebastian finally emerged and turned to lock up behind him.

Dalgliesh said, 'May we speak, Father? Or would you prefer it to wait until tomorrow?'

He knew that it was the practice at St Anselm's for the college to keep silence after Compline, but the Warden replied, 'Will it take long, Commander?'

'I hope not, Father.'

'Then now, if you wish. Shall we go to my study?'

Once there the Warden took his seat behind the desk and motioned Dalgliesh to a chair before him. This was to be no comfortable chat in the low chairs before the fire. The Warden had no intention of beginning the conversation or of asking Dalgliesh what conclusions, if any, he had reached about Ronald Treeves's death. Instead he waited in a silence which, although not unfriendly, gave the impression that he was exercising patience.

Dalgliesh said, 'Father Martin has shown me Mrs Munroe's diary. Ronald Treeves seems to have spent more time with her than one might expect and it was, of course, she who found the body. That makes any reference to him in her diary important. I am thinking particularly of the last entry, the one she wrote on the day she died. You didn't take it seriously, the evidence that she had discovered a secret and was worried by it?'

Father Sebastian said, 'Evidence? What a forensic word, Commander. I did take it seriously because it was obviously serious for her. I had misgivings about our reading a private diary, but as Father Martin had encouraged her to keep it, he was interested to see what she had written. Perhaps it was a natural curiosity, although I can't help feeling that the diary should have been destroyed unread. The facts, however, seem to be plain. Margaret Munroe was an intelligent, sensible woman. She discovered something which worried her, confided in the person concerned and was satisfied. Whatever the explanation she was given, it put her mind at rest. Nothing would have been gained and much harm done if I had started probing. You're not suggesting that I should have called the college together and asked whether any of them had a secret which they had shared with Mrs Munroe? I preferred to take her written word that the explanation she was given had made no further action necessary.'

Dalgliesh said, 'Ronald Treeves seems to have been something of a loner, Father. Did you like him?'

It was a dangerously provocative question, but Father Sebastian took it unflinchingly. Watching him, Dalgliesh thought that he detected a slight hardening of the handsome face, but he couldn't be certain.

The Warden's answer, when it came, might have held an implied rebuke but his voice betrayed no resentment. 'In my relations with the ordinands I don't concern myself with questions of liking or disliking, nor would it be proper to do so. Favouritism, or perceived favouritism, is particularly dangerous in a small community. Ronald was a singularly charmless young man, but since when has charm been a Christian virtue?'

'But you did concern yourself with the question of whether he was happy here?'

'It is not the business of St Anselm's to promote private happiness. I would have concerned myself had I thought that he was unhappy. We take our pastoral responsibility for students very seriously. Ronald neither sought help nor gave any indication that he was in need of it. That doesn't exclude my own culpability. Ronald's religion was important to him and he was deeply committed to his vocation. He would have had no doubt that suicide is a grave sin. The act could not have been impulsive; there was that half-mile walk to the mere, the trudge along the shore. If he killed himself it could only have been because he was in despair. I should have known this about any student and I didn't.'

Dalgliesh said, 'The suicide of the young and healthy is always mysterious. They die and no one knows why. Perhaps even they wouldn't have been able to explain.'

The Warden said, 'I was not asking for your absolution, Commander. I was merely setting out the facts.'

There was a silence. Dalgliesh's next question was equally stark but it had to be asked. He wondered whether he was being too direct, even tactless, in his questioning but he judged that Father Sebastian would welcome directness and despise tact. More was understood between them than was being spoken.

He said, 'I was wondering who would benefit if the college were closed.'

'I would, among others. But I think that any questions of that kind could more properly be answered by our lawyers. Stannard, Fox and Perronet have served the college since its inception and Paul Perronet is at present a trustee. Their office is in Norwich. He could tell you something of our history, if you're interested. I know that he does work occasionally on Saturday mornings. Would you like me to make an appointment? I'll see if I can get him at home.'

'That would be helpful, Father.'

The Warden stretched out his hand to the telephone on his desk. He had no need to check the number. After he had pressed down the digits there was a short pause, then he said, 'Paul? It's Sebastian Morell. I'm ringing from my office. I have with me Commander Dalgliesh. You remember we spoke on Thursday night about his visit? He has a number of questions about the college that I would be glad if you would answer ... Yes, anything he asks. There's nothing you need withhold ... That's good of you, Paul. I'll hand you over.'

Without speaking, he passed the receiver to Dalgliesh. A deep voice said, 'Paul Perronet here. I shall be in my office tomorrow morning. I have an appointment at ten, but if you can come early, say nine o'clock, that should give us time enough. I'll be here from eight-thirty. Father Sebastian will give you the address. We're very close to the cathedral. I'll see you at nine o'clock then. Just so.'

When Dalgliesh had regained his seat, the Warden said, 'Is there anything else tonight?'

'It would be helpful, Father, if I could have a sight of Margaret Munroe's staff record, if you still have it.'

'It would of course have been confidential were she still with us. As she is dead, I can see no objection. Miss Ramsey keeps it in a locked cabinet next door. I'll fetch it for you.'

He went out, and Dalgliesh could hear the rasp of the steel cabinet drawer. Within seconds the Warden was back and handed over a stiff manila folder. He didn't enquire what possible relevance Mrs Munroe's file could have to the tragedy of Ronald Treeves's death and Dalgliesh thought he knew why. He recognized in Father Sebastian an experienced tactician who wouldn't ask a question if he judged the reply would be either unforthcoming or unwelcome. He had promised co-operation and would give it, but he would store up each of Dalgliesh's intrusive and unwelcome requests until the opportune moment came to point out how much had been demanded, how small the justification and how ineffective the result. No one would be more adept at luring his adversaries on to ground they could not legitimately defend.

Now he said, 'Do you wish to take the file away, Commander?'

'For the night, Father. I'll return it tomorrow.'

'Then if there is nothing else for the present, I'll say good-night.'

He rose and opened the door for Dalgliesh. It could have been a gesture of politeness. To Dalgliesh it smacked more of a headmaster ensuring that a recalcitrant parent was finally taking himself off.

The door to the south cloister was open. Pilbeam had not yet locked up for the night. The courtyard, lit only by the dim wall lights along the cloisters, was very dark and only two of the students' rooms, both in the south cloister, showed even a chink of light. As he turned towards Jerome, he saw that two figures were standing together outside the door of Ambrose. One he had been introduced to at tea and the pale head shining under the wall light was unmistakable. The other was a woman. Hearing his footsteps she turned towards him and as he reached his door their eyes met and for a second held as if in mutual amazement. The light fell on a face of grave and astounding beauty, and he experienced an emotion that now came rarely, a physical jolt of astonishment and affirmation.

Raphael said, 'I don't think you've met. Emma, this is Commander Dalgliesh who has come all the way from Scotland Yard to tell us how Ronald died. Commander, meet Dr Emma Lavenham who arrives from Cambridge three times a year to civilize us. After virtuously attending Compline we decided, quite separately, to walk out and look at the stars. We met at the edge of the cliff. Now, like a good host, I'm seeing her back to her rooms. Good-night, Emma.'

His voice and stance were proprietorial and Dalgliesh sensed her slight withdrawal. She said, 'I was perfectly capable of finding my own way back. But thank you, Raphael.'

It looked for a moment as if he were about to take her hand, but she said a firm 'Good-night', which seemed to embrace them both, and went quickly into her sitting-room.

Raphael said, 'The stars were disappointing. Good-night, Commander. I hope you have everything you need.' He turned and strode briskly across the cobbles of the courtyard to his room in the north cloister.

For some reason which he found difficult to explain, Dalgliesh felt irritated. Raphael Arbuthnot was a facetious young man who was undoubtedly too handsome for his own good. Presumably he was a descendant of the Arbuthnot who had founded St Anselm's. If so, how much was he likely to inherit if the college were forced to close?

Resolutely he settled at the desk and opened Mrs Munroe's file, sifting through each of the papers. She had come to St Anselm's on 1 May 1994 from Ashcombe House, a hospice outside Norwich. St Anselm's had advertised both in the *Church Times* and in a local paper for a resident woman to be in charge of the linen and to help generally with the housekeeping. Mrs Munroe's heart condition had recently been diagnosed and her letter of application stated that nursing had become too heavy for her and that she was looking for a residential post with lighter duties. Her references from the matron of the hospice had been good, though not over-enthusiastic. Mrs Munroe, who had taken up her post on 1 June 1988, had been a conscientious and dedicated nurse, but was perhaps a little too reserved in her relationships with others. Nursing the dying had become both physically and mentally too exhausting for her, but the hospice thought she would be able to undertake some light nursing responsibilities at a college of healthy young men and would be happy to do so in addition to being in charge of the linen. Once arrived, it seemed that she was seldom absent. There were very few applications to Father Sebastian for leave and it seemed that she preferred to spend holidays in her cottage where she was joined by her only child, an army officer. The general impression gained from the file was of a conscientious, hard-working, essentially private woman with few interests outside her son. There was a note on the file that he had been killed eighteen months after her arrival at St Anselm's.

He put the file in the desk drawer, showered and went to bed. Clicking off the light he tried to compose himself for sleep, but the preoccupations of the day refused to be banished. He was standing again on the beach with Father Martin. He saw in imagination that brown cloak and cassock as precisely folded as if the boy had been packing for a journey, and perhaps that is how he had seen it. Had he really taken them off to clamber up a few yards of unstable sand layered with stones and precariously held together with clumps of grassy earth? And why make the attempt? What if anything did he hope to reach, to discover? This was a stretch of coast where from time to time parts of long-buried skeletons would appear under the sand or in the cliff face, washed up generations ago from the drowned graveyards now lying a mile away under the sea. But nothing had been apparent to any of those at the scene. Even if Treeves had glimpsed the smooth curve of a skull or the end of a long bone jutting from the sand, why would he have found it necessary to take off his cassock and cloak before attempting to reach it? To Dalgliesh's mind there had been something more significant in that neatly-folded pile of clothes. Hadn't it been a deliberate, almost ceremonial, laying aside of a life, of a vocation, perhaps even of a faith?

From thoughts of that dreadful death his mind, torn between pity, curiosity and conjecture, turned to Margaret Munroe's diary. He had read the paragraphs of the final entry so often that he could have recited them by heart. She had discovered a secret so important that she couldn't bring herself to record it except obliquely. She had spoken to the person most concerned, and within hours of that disclosure she was dead. Given the state of her heart, that death could have happened at any time. Perhaps it had been hastened by anxiety, the need to confront the implications of her discovery. But it could have been a convenient death for someone. And how easy such a murder would be. An elderly woman with a weak heart alone in her cottage, a local doctor who had seen her regularly and would have no difficulty in giving a death certificate. And why, if she was wearing the spectacles she used for watching television, had her knitting been in her lap? And if she had been watching a programme when she died, who had turned off the set? All these oddities could, of course, be explained. It was the end of the day and she was tired. Even if more evidence came to light – and what evidence could there be? – there was little hope of solving the mystery now. Like Ronald Treeves she had been cremated. It struck him that St Anselm's was oddly prompt in disposing of its dead, but that was unfair. Both Sir Alred and Mrs Munroe's sister had cut the college out of the obsequies.

He wished he had actually seen Treeves's body. It was always unsatisfactory to have evidence at second hand and no photographs had been taken of the scene. But the accounts had been clear enough, and what they pointed to was suicide. But why? Treeves would have seen the act as a sin, a mortal sin. What could have been strong enough to drive him to such a horrific end?

17

Any visitor to an historic county town or city quickly becomes aware in his or her peregrinations that the most attractive houses in the centre are invariably the offices of lawyers. Messrs Stannard, Fox & Perronet were no exception. The firm was housed within walking distance of the cathedral in an elegant Georgian house separated from the pavement by a narrow band of cobbles. The gleaming front door with its lion's-head knocker, the glistening paintwork, the windows unsmudged by city grime reflected the frail morning sunlight, and the immaculate net curtains all proclaimed the respectability, prosperity and exclusiveness of the firm. In the reception office, which had obviously once been part of a larger, finely-proportioned front room, a fresh-faced girl looked up from her magazine and greeted Dalgliesh in a pleasant Norfolk accent.

'Commander Dalgliesh, isn't it? Mr Perronet is expecting you. He said to ask you to go straight up. It's the first floor at the front. His PA doesn't come in on Saturdays, there's only the two of us, but I could easily make you coffee if you'd like it.'

Smiling, Dalgliesh thanked her, declined the offer and made his way up the stairs between framed photographs of previous members of the firm.

The man who was waiting for him at the door of his office and moved forward was older than his voice on the telephone had suggested, certainly in his late fifties. He was over six feet tall, bony, with a long jaw, mild grey eyes behind horn-rimmed spectacles, and straw-coloured hair which lay in lank strands across a high forehead. It was the face of a comedian rather than of a lawyer. He was formally dressed in a dark pin-stripe suit, obviously old but extremely well cut, its orthodoxy belied by a shirt with a broad blue stripe and a pink bow-tie with blue spots. It was as if he were aware of some discordance of personality or an eccentricity which he was at pains to cultivate.

The room into which Dalgliesh was led was much as he had expected. The desk was Georgian and clear of paper or filing trays. There was an oil painting, no doubt of one of the founding fathers, above the elegant marble fireplace, and the water-colour landscapes, carefully aligned, were good enough to be by Cotman, and probably were.

'You won't take coffee? Very wise. Too early. I go out for mine at about eleven. A stroll up to St Mary Mancroft. Gives me a chance to get out of the office. I hope this chair isn't too low. No? Take the other if you prefer. Father Sebastian has asked me to answer any questions you care to ask about St Anselm's. Just so. Of course, if this were an official police inquiry I should have a duty as well as a wish to co-operate.'

The mildness of his grey eyes was deceptive. They could be searching. Dalgliesh said, 'Hardly an official inquiry. My position is ambiguous. I expect Father Sebastian has told you that Sir Alred Treeves is unhappy about the verdict at the inquest on his son. He's asked the Met to make a preliminary investigation to see if there's a case for taking the matter further. I was due to be in the county and I know something of St Anselm's, so it seemed expedient and economical for me to make this visit. Of course, if there is any suggestion of a criminal case the matter will become official and pass into the hands of the Suffolk Constabulary.'

Paul Perronet said, 'Dissatisfied with the verdict, is he? I should have thought it would have come as something of a relief.'

'He thought the evidence for accidental death was inconclusive.'

'So it may have been, but there was no evidence of anything else. An open verdict might have been more appropriate.'

Dalgliesh said, 'Coming at a difficult time for the college, the publicity must have been unwelcome.'

'Just so, but the tragedy was handled with great discretion. Father Sebastian is skilled in these matters. And St Anselm's certainly has had worse publicity. There was the homosexual scandal in 1923 when the priest lecturer in church history – one Father Cuthbert – fell passionately in love with one of the ordinands and they were discovered by the Warden *in flagrante delicto*. They cycled off together on Father Cuthbert's tandem bicycle to Felixstowe docks and freedom, having, I presume, changed from their cassocks into Victorian knickerbockers. An engaging picture, I always think. And then there was a more serious scandal in 1932 when the then Warden converted to Rome and took half the teaching staff and a third of the ordinands with him. That must have sent Agnes Arbuthnot reeling in her grave! But it's true that this latest publicity comes at an unfortunate time. Just so.'

'Were you at the inquest yourself?'

'Yes I attended, representing the college. This firm has represented St Anselm's since its foundation. Miss Arbuthnot – indeed the Arbuthnot family generally – had a dislike of London, and when her father later moved into Suffolk and built the house in 1842 he asked us to take over his legal affairs. We were out of the county, of course, but I think he wanted an East Anglian firm rather than one necessarily in Suffolk. Miss Arbuthnot carried on the association after her father's death. One of the senior partners here has always been a trustee of the college. Miss Arbuthnot provided for this in her will and stated that he should be a communicant member of the Church of England. I'm the present trustee. I don't know what we'll do in the future if all the partners here are Roman Catholics, Nonconformists or plain unbelievers. I suppose we'll have to persuade someone to convert. Up to now, though, there has always been a suitably qualified partner.'

Dalgliesh said, 'It's an old firm, isn't it?'

'Founded in 1792. No Stannards in the firm now. The last one is an academic, one of the new universities, I believe. But we have a young Fox coming on – young vixen rather. Priscilla Fox, qualified only last year and very promising. I like to see continuity.'

Dalgliesh said, 'I understand from Father Martin that the death of young Treeves may hasten the closure of St Anselm's. As a trustee, is that your view?'

'I'm afraid so. Hasten, mind you, not cause. The Church, as I expect you know, has a policy of centralizing its theological teaching in fewer centres, but St Anselm's has always been something of an anomaly. It may close more quickly now, but closure, alas, is inevitable. Not just a question of church policy and resources. The ethos is out of date. St Anselm's has always had its critics – "élitist", "snobbish", "too isolated", even "the students too well fed". The wine is certainly remarkably fine. I take care not to make my quarterly visits in Lent or on a Friday. But most of it is bequeathed. Doesn't cost the college a penny. Old Canon Cosgrove left them his cellar five years ago. The old man had a fine palate. Should keep them going till they close.'

Dalgliesh said, 'And if and when they do, what happens to the buildings, the contents?'

'Didn't Father Sebastian tell you?'

'He told me that he would be among the beneficiaries, but referred me to you for the details.'

'Just so. Just so.'

Mr Perronet got up from the desk and opened a cupboard to the left of the fireplace. He brought out with some effort a large box labelled ARBUTHNOT in white paint.

He said, 'If you're interested in the history of the college, and I take it you are, perhaps we should begin at the beginning. It's all here. Yes indeed, you can read the story of a family in one large black tin box. I'll begin with Agnes Arbuthnot's father, Claude Arbuthnot, who died in 1859. He manufactured buttons and buckles – buttons for those high boots the ladies used to wear, ceremonial buttons and buckles, that kind of thing – at a factory outside Ipswich. Did extremely well and made himself a very rich man. Agnes, born in 1820, was the eldest child. After her was Edwin, born in 1823, and Clara, born two years later. We needn't trouble ourselves with

Clara. Never married and died of TB in 1849 in Italy. Buried in Rome in the Protestant cemetery – in very good company, of course. Poor Keats! Well, that's what they did in those days, travelled to the sun in the hope of a cure. The voyage was enough to kill them. Pity she didn't go to Torquay and rest up there. Anyway, exit Clara.

'It was the old man Claude, of course, who built the house. He'd made his pile and he wanted something to show for it. Just so. He left the house to Agnes. The money was divided between her and the son, Edwin, and I gather there was some dissension over the bestowal of the property. But Agnes cared for the house and lived in it and Edwin didn't, so she got it. Of course, if her father, a rigid Protestant, had known what she was going to do with it, things might have been different. Still, you can't follow your property beyond the grave. He bequeathed it to her and that was that. It was the year after his death that she went to stay with a school friend in Oxford, came under the influence of the Oxford Movement and decided to found St Anselm's. The house was there, of course, but she built on the two cloisters, restored and incorporated the church and built the four cottages for staff.'

Dalgliesh said, 'What happened to Edwin?'

'He was an explorer. Except for Claude the males in the family seem all to have had an itch for travel. Actually, he was part of some notable digs in the Middle East. He rarely came back to England and died in Cairo in 1890.'

Dalgliesh said, 'Was he the one who gave the St Anselm papyrus to the college?'

And now the eyes behind the horn-rimmed spectacles grew wary. There was a silence before Perronet spoke. 'So you know about that. Father Sebastian didn't say.'

'I know very little. My father was in on the secret and, although he was always discreet, I picked up hints when he and I were at St Anselm's. A fourteen-year-old boy has sharper ears and a more inquisitive mind than adults sometimes realize. My father told me a little and made me promise to keep it secret. I don't think I was much interested in doing anything else.'

Perronet said, 'Well, Father Sebastian said to answer all your questions but there's not much I can tell you about the papyrus. You probably know as much as I. It was certainly given to Miss Arbuthnot in 1887 by her brother and he was certainly capable of forging it or having it forged. He was a man fond of practical jokes and this would have appealed to him. He was a fervent atheist. Can an atheist be fervent? Anyway, he was anti-religion.'

'What is the papyrus exactly?'

'It purports to be a communication from Pontius Pilate to an officer of the guard regarding the removal of a certain body. Miss Arbuthnot took the view that it was a forgery and most wardens who have seen the letter since have agreed. I haven't myself been shown it but my father was and so, I believe, was old Stannard. My father had no doubt that it wasn't genuine, but he said that, assuming it to have been forged, it had been done with considerable cleverness.'

Dalgliesh said, 'It's strange that Agnes Arbuthnot didn't have it destroyed.'

'Oh, not strange I think. No, I wouldn't call it strange.

There's a note about it here among the papers. I'll just give you the gist if you don't mind. She took the view that, if it were destroyed, her brother would make the matter public and the fact of its destruction would serve to prove its authenticity. Once destroyed no one could prove that it wasn't a fake. She left careful instructions that it was to be preserved in the possession of each successive Warden, to be passed over to his successor only at his death.'

Dalgliesh said, 'Which means that Father Martin has it at present.'

'That's right. Father Martin will have it somewhere in his possession. I doubt if even Father Sebastian knows where. If you require any further information about the letter you should speak to him. I can't see how it's relevant to the death of young Treeves.'

Dalgliesh said, 'Nor can I at present. What happened to the family after Edwin Arbuthnot's death?'

'He had a son, Hugh, born in 1880, killed in action on the Somme in 1916. My grandfather died in that action. The dead of that war still march through all our dreams don't they? He left two sons, the elder Edwin, born in 1903, never married, and died in Alexandria in 1979. Then there was Claude, born in 1905. He was the grandfather of Raphael Arbuthnot who is a student at the college at the present. But that, of course, you know. Raphael Arbuthnot is the last of the family.'

Dalgliesh said, 'But he doesn't inherit?'

'No. Unfortunately he's not legitimate. Miss Arbuthnot's will was detailed and specific. I don't think the dear lady ever really envisaged that the college would be closed, but my predecessor here who was dealing with the family's affairs at the time pointed out that this eventuality should be provided for. Just so. The will states that the property and all objects in the college and the church that were the gift of Miss Arbuthnot and are present at the time of closure should be divided in equal shares between any direct descendants of her father, provided such descendants were legitimate in English law and communicant members of the Church of England.'

Dalgliesh said, 'An unusual wording, surely, "legitimate in English law".'

'Not really. Miss Arbuthnot was typical of her class and age. Where property was concerned the Victorians were always alive to the possibility of a foreign claimant of doubtful legitimacy born of an irregularly contracted foreign marriage. There are some notorious cases. Failing a legitimate heir, the property and the contents are to be divided, again in equal shares, between the priests resident in the college at the time of its closure.'

Dalgliesh said, 'Which means that the beneficiaries are Father Sebastian Morell, Father Martin Petrie, Father Peregrine Glover and Father John Betterton. That's a little hard on Raphael, isn't it? I suppose there's no doubt about the legitimacy?'

'On the first point I would have to agree. The unfairness has not, of course, escaped Father Sebastian. The question of closing the college first arose seriously two years ago and he spoke to me then. He somewhat naturally is unhappy about the terms of the will and suggested that, in the event of closure, some arrangement should be arrived at between the beneficiaries to ensure that Raphael benefits. Normally, of course, bequests can be varied by agreement of the beneficiaries, but the matter here is complicated. I told him that I couldn't give quick or easy answers to any questions relating to the disposal of the property. There is, for example, the extremely valuable painting in the church. Miss Arbuthnot gave it to the church particularly to be used above the altar. If the church is to remain consecrated, should it be moved or should some arrangement be made whereby whoever is responsible for the church can acquire it? The recently appointed trustee, Archdeacon Crampton, has been agitating to have it removed now, either to a place of greater safety or to be sold for the benefit of the diocese generally. He would like to have all the valuable items removed. I have told him that I would regret any such premature action, but he may well get his way. He has considerable influence, and such action would, of course, ensure that the Church rather than individuals will benefit when the college closes.

'Then there is the problem of the buildings. I confess I can't see an obvious use for them and they may well not be standing in twenty years' time. The sea is advancing rapidly along that coast. The erosion, of course, considerably affects their value. The contents, even without the picture, are likely to be more valuable, the silver, the books and the furnishings particularly so.'

Dalgliesh said, 'And then there's the St Anselm papyrus.'

Again he thought the reference was unwelcome.

Perronet said, 'Presumably that too will pass to the beneficiaries. That could create a particular difficulty. But if the college closes and there is subsequently no Warden, then the papyrus will form part of the estate.'

'But it is, presumably, a valuable object, authentic or otherwise.'

Paul Perronet said, 'It would have considerable value to anyone interested either in money or in power.'

Like Sir Alred Treeves, thought Dalgliesh. But it was difficult to imagine Sir Alred deliberately introducing his adopted son into the college with the purpose of getting hold of the St Anselm papyrus, even if he had evidence of its existence.

He said, 'There's no doubt, I suppose, of Raphael's illegitimacy?'

'Oh indeed no, Commander, indeed no. His mother when pregnant made no secret of the fact that she was neither married nor had any wish to be. She never revealed the name of the father, although she did express her contempt and hatred for him. After the child was born she literally dumped him at the college in a basket with a note which said, "You are supposed to go in for Christian charity so practise it on this bastard. If you want money, ask my father". The note is here among the Arbuthnot papers. It was an extraordinary thing for a mother to do.'

It was indeed, thought Dalgliesh. Women did abandon their children, sometimes they even murdered them. But there had been a calculated brutality about this rejection and by a woman surely not without money and friends.

'She went abroad immediately and I believe travelled extensively in the Far East and India for the next ten years or so. I believe that for most of the time she was in the company of a friend, a woman doctor, who committed suicide just before Clara Arbuthnot returned to England. Clara died of cancer in Ashcombe House, a hospice outside Norwich, on 30 April 1988.'

'Without ever seeing the child?'

'She neither saw nor took any interest in him. Of course, she died tragically young. Things might have changed. Her father, who was over fifty when he married, was an old man by the time his grandson was born, couldn't have coped and didn't want to. But he did set up a small trust fund. The Warden here at the time was made legal guardian after the grandfather's death. Effectively the college has been Raphael's home. The fathers have, on the whole, done extremely well by the boy. They thought it right he should go away to prep school and have the company of other boys and I think this was wise. Then, of course, there was public school. The trust fund just ran to the fees. But he's been at the college for most of the holidays.'

The telephone on the desk rang. Paul Perronet said, 'Sally tells me my next caller has arrived. Is there anything else you need to know, Commander?'

'Nothing, thank you. I'm not sure how relevant any of this will prove, but I'm glad to be put in the picture. Thank you for taking so much time over the matter.'

Perronet said, 'We seem to have travelled very far from that poor boy's death. You will, of course, let me know the result of your enquiries. As a trustee I have an interest. Just so.'

Dalgliesh promised that he would. He made his way up the sunlit street towards the soaring splendour of St Mary Mancroft. This, after all, was supposed to be a holiday. He was entitled to spend at least an hour on his own pleasures.

He pondered what he had learned. It was an odd coincidence that Clara Arbuthnot had died in the same hospice where Margaret Munroe had been a nurse. But perhaps not so very odd. Miss Arbuthnot might well have wanted to die in the county of her birth, the job at St Anselm's would have been advertised locally and Mrs Munroe had been looking for a post. But the two women could not have met. He would have to check the dates, but it was clear in his own mind. Miss Arbuthnot had died a month before Margaret Munroe had taken up her post at the hospice.

But the other fact he had learned was an uncomfortable complication. Whatever the truth about Ronald Treeves's death, it had brought nearer the closure of St Anselm's College. And when that closure took place, four members of the staff would become very rich men.

He had decided that St Anselm's would welcome his absence for most of the day, but had told Father Martin that he would be in for dinner. After two hours' satisfying exploration of the city, he found a restaurant where neither food nor décor were pretentious and ate a simple lunch. There was something else he needed to do before returning to the college. Consulting the telephone directory at the restaurant, he discovered the address of the publishers of the *Sole Bay Weekly Gazette*. Their office, from which they published a number of local papers and magazines, was a low brick building rather like a garage close to one of the road junctions outside the city. There was no problem in obtaining back copies of the paper. Karen Surtees's memory had not been at fault, the issue for the week before Mrs Munroe's death did indeed carry a picture of the ribbon-bedecked heifer at her owner's graveside.

Dalgliesh had parked in the forecourt in front of the building and now returned to the car and studied the newspaper. It was a typical provincial weekly, its preoccupation with local life and rural and small-town interests a refreshing relief from the predictable concerns of the national broadsheets. Here were reports from the villages of whist drives, sales of work, darts competitions, funerals and meetings of local groups and associations. There was a page of photographs of brides and grooms, heads together, smiling into the camera, and several pages of advertisements for houses, cottages and bungalows with pictures of the properties. Four pages were devoted to personal notices and other advertisements. Only two items hinted at the less innocent concerns of the wider world. Seven illegal immigrants had been discovered in a barn and it was suspected that they had been brought in on a local boat. The police had made two arrests in connection with the finding of cocaine, raising suspicion that there could be a local dealer.

Folding the paper, Dalgliesh reflected that his hunch had come to nothing. If anything in the *Gazette* had sparked off Margaret Munroe's memory, the secret had died with her.

18

The Revd Matthew Crampton, Archdeacon of Reydon, drove to St Anselm's by the shortest route from his vicarage at Cressingfield just south of Ipswich. He drove towards the A12 with the comfortable assurance that he had left the parish, his wife and his study in good order. Even in youth he had never left home without the assumption, never voiced aloud, that he might not return. It was never a serious worry but the thought was always there, like other unacknowledged fears which curled like a sleeping snake in the pit of his mind. It sometimes occurred to him that he lived his whole life in the daily expectation of its ending. The small diurnal rituals which this involved had nothing to do with a morbid preoccupation with mortality, nor with his faith, but were more, he acknowledged, a legacy of his mother's insistence every morning on clean under-clothes, since this might be the day on which he would be run over and exposed to the gaze of nurses, doctors and the undertaker as a pitiable victim of maternal unconcern. As a boy he had sometimes pictured the final scene: himself stretched out on a mortuary slab and his mother comforted and gratified by the thought that he had at least died with his pants clean.

He had tidied away his first marriage as methodically as he tidied his desk. That silent visitation at the corner of the stair or glimpsed through his study window, the sudden shock of hearing a half-remembered laugh, were mercifully supine, overlaid by parish duties, the weekly routine, his second marriage. He had consigned his first marriage to a dark oubliette of his mind and shot the bolt, but not before he had almost formally passed sentence on it. He had heard one of his parishioners, the mother of a child who was dyslexic and slightly deaf, describing how her daughter had been 'statemented' by the local authority and had understood that this meant that the child's needs had been assessed and appropriate measures agreed on. So, in a very different context but with equal authority, he had statemented his marriage. The words, unspoken, had never been consigned to paper, but mentally he could recite them as if he were speaking of a casual acquaintance, and always of himself in the third person. That brief and final disposal of a marriage was written on his mind, pictured always in italics.

Archdeacon Crampton married his first wife soon after he became vicar of his inner-city parish. Barbara Hampton was nearly twenty years younger, beautiful, wilful and disturbed – a fact which her family had never disclosed. The marriage had at first been happy. He knew himself to be the fortunate husband of a woman he had done little to deserve. Her sentimentality was taken for kindness; her easy familiarity with strangers, her beauty and her generosity made her very popular in the parish. For months the problems were either unacknowledged or not spoken of. And then the church wardens and parishioners would call at the vicarage when she was away and tell their embarrassed stories. The outbursts of violent temper, the screaming, the insults, incidents which he had thought happened only to and with him, had spread into the parish. She refused treatment, arguing that it was he who was sick. She began to drink more steadily and more heavily.

One afternoon four years after the wedding he was due to go out to visit sick parishioners and, knowing that she had gone to bed that afternoon pleading tiredness, had gone to see how she was. Opening the door he thought that she was sleeping peacefully and left, not wishing to disturb her. On his return that evening he found that she was dead. She had taken an overdose of aspirin. The inquest returned a verdict of suicide. He blamed himself for having married a woman too young for him, and unsuitable to be a vicar's wife. He found happiness in a second and more appropriate marriage but he never ceased to mourn his first wife.

That was the story as mentally he recited it, but now he returned to it far less often. He had married again within eighteen months. An unmarried vicar, particularly one who has been tragically widowed, is inevitably regarded as the lawful target of the parish matchmakers. It seemed to him that his second wife had been chosen for him, an arrangement in which he had happily acquiesced.

Today he had a job to do, and it was one he relished while convincing himself that it was a duty: to persuade Sebastian Morell that St Anselm's had to be closed and to find any additional evidence that would help to make that closure as speedy as it was inevitable. He told himself, and believed, that St Anselm's – expensive to maintain, remote, with only twenty carefully-selected students, over-privileged and élitist – was an example of everything that was wrong with the Church of England. He admitted, and mentally congratulated himself on his honesty, that his dislike of the institution extended to its Principal – why on earth should the man be called Warden? – and that dislike was strongly personal, going well beyond any difference in churchmanship or theology. Partly, he admitted, it was class resentment. He thought of himself as having fought his way to ordination and preferment. In fact little struggle had been necessary; in his university days his path had been smoothed by not ungenerous grants and his mother had always indulged her only child. But Morell was the son and the grandson of bishops and an eighteenth-century forebear had been one of the great Prince Bishops of the Church. The Morells had always been at home in palaces and the Archdeacon knew that his adversary would put out his tentacles of family and personal influence to reach the sources of power in Whitehall, the universities and the Church, and wouldn't yield an inch of ground in the fight to keep his fiefdom.

And there had been that dreadful horse-faced wife of his, God only knew why he had married her. Lady Veronica had been in residence at the college on the Archdeacon's first visit, long before he was appointed as a trustee, and had sat on his left at dinner. The occasion had not been a happy one for either of them. Well, she was dead now. At least he would be spared that braying, offensively upper-class voice which it took centuries of arrogance and insensitivity to develop. What had she or her husband ever known of poverty and its humiliating deprivations, when had they ever had to live with the violence and the intractable problems of a decayed inner-city parish? Morell had never even served as a parish priest except for two years in a fashionable provincial town. And why a man of his intellectual ability and reputation should be content to be principal of a small isolated theological college was something of a mystery to the Archdeacon and, he suspected, not only to him.

But there could, of course, be an explanation and it lay in the terms of Miss Arbuthnot's deplorable will. How on earth had her legal advisers allowed her to make it? Of course, she couldn't have known that the pictures and the silver she had given to St Anselm's would so appreciate in value over nearly a century and a half. In recent years St Anselm's had been supported by the Church. It was morally just that when the college became redundant, the assets should go to the Church or to Church charities. It was inconceivable that Miss Arbuthnot had intended to make multimillionaires of the four priests fortuitously in residence at the time of the closure, one of them aged eighty and another a convicted child abuser. He would make it his business to ensure that all valuables were removed from the college before it was formally closed. Sebastian Morell could hardly oppose the move without laying himself open to the accusation of selfishness and greed. His devious campaign to keep St Anselm's open was probably a ruse to conceal his interest in the spoils.

The battle lines had been formally drawn and he was on his confident way to what he expected would be a decisive skirmish.

19

Father Sebastian knew that he would have to have a confrontation with the Archdeacon before the weekend was over, but he didn't intend it to take place in the church. He was prepared, even eager, to stand his ground, but not before the altar. But when the Archdeacon said that he would like now to see the Rogier van der Weyden, Father Sebastian, having no excuse for not accompanying him, and feeling that merely to hand over the keys would be uncivil, consoled himself with the thought that the visit would probably be short. What, after all, could the Archdeacon object to in the church except perhaps the lingering smell of incense? He made a resolution to keep an even temper and if possible to restrict the conversation to superficialities. Surely in church two priests could talk to each other without acrimony.

They made their way down the north cloister to the sacristy door without speaking. Nothing was said until Father Sebastian had switched on the light illuminating the picture, and they stood side by side regarding it in silence.

Father Sebastian had never found words adequate to describe the effect on him of this sudden revelation of the image and he didn't attempt to find them now. It was a full half-minute before the Archdeacon spoke. His voice boomed unnaturally loud in the silent air.

'It shouldn't be here, of course. Haven't you ever given serious thought to having it moved?'

'Moved where, Archdeacon? It was given to the college by Miss Arbuthnot precisely to be placed in the church and over the altar.'

'Hardly a safe place for something so valuable. What's it worth, do you think? Five million? Eight million? Ten million?'

'I've no idea. As far as safety is concerned the altar-piece has been in place for over a hundred years. To where exactly do you propose it should be removed?'

'To somewhere safer, somewhere where other people can enjoy it. The most sensible course – and I've discussed this with the Bishop – would be to sell it to a museum where it would be on public view. The Church, or indeed any worthwhile charity, could find a good use for the money. The same applies to the two most valuable of your chalices. It is inappropriate that objects of such value should be kept for the private satisfaction of twenty ordinands.'

Father Sebastian was tempted to quote a verse of scripture – 'For this ointment might have been sold for much, and given to the poor' – but prudently forbore. But he couldn't keep the note of outrage from his voice.

'The altar-piece is the property of this college. It will certainly not be sold while I am Warden, nor will it be removed. The silver will be kept in the sanctuary safe and used for the purpose for which it was made.'

'Even though its presence means that the church has to be kept locked and is unavailable to the ordinands?'

'It isn't unavailable. They have only to ask for the keys.'

'The need to pray is sometimes more spontaneous than remembering to ask for a key.'

'That's why we have the oratory.'

The Archdeacon turned away and Father Sebastian walked over to switch off the light. His companion said, 'In any case, when the college is closed the picture will have to be removed. I don't know what the diocese has in mind for this place – I mean the church itself. It's too remote to serve again as a parish church even as part of a team ministry. Where would you get a congregation? It's unlikely that whoever buys the house will want a private chapel, but you never know. It's difficult to see who would be interested in buying. Remote, inconvenient to run, difficult to reach and with no direct access to the beach. It would hardly be suitable for a hotel or convalescent home. And with the coast erosion there's no certainty it will be here in twenty years' time.'

Father Sebastian waited until he could be sure of speaking calmly. 'You talk, Archdeacon, as if the decision to close St Anselm's has already been taken. I assumed that, as Warden, I would be consulted. No one yet has spoken or written to me.'

'Naturally you will be consulted. All the necessary tedious processes will be followed. But the end is inevitable, you know that perfectly well. The Church of England is centralizing and rationalizing its theological training. Reform is long overdue. St Anselm's is too small, too remote, too expensive and too élitist.'

'Elitist, Archdeacon?'

'I use the word deliberately. When did you last accept an ordinand from the state educational system?'

'Stephen Morby came through the state system. He's probably our most intelligent ordinand.'

'The first, I suspect. And, no doubt, by way of Oxford and with the required First. And when will you accept a woman as ordinand? Or a woman priest on the staff for that matter?'

'No woman has ever applied.'

'Precisely. Because women know when they're not wanted.'

'I think that recent history would disprove that, Archdeacon. We have no prejudices. The Church, or rather Synod, has made its decision. But this place is too small to cope with women ordinands. Even the larger theological colleges are finding it difficult. It's the ordinands who suffer. I will not preside over a Christian institution in which some members refuse to take the sacrament at the hands of others.'

'And élitism isn't your only problem. Unless the Church adapts itself to meet the needs of the twenty-first century, it will die. The life your young men live here is ridiculously privileged, totally remote from the lives of the men and women they will be expected to serve. The study of Greek and Hebrew have their place, I'm not denying that, but we need also to look at what the newer disciplines can offer. What training do they receive in sociology, in race relations, in inter-faith co-operation?'

Father Sebastian managed to keep his voice steady. He said, 'The training provided here is among the best in the country. Our inspection reports make that plain. And it's ludicrous to claim that anyone here is out of touch with the real world or isn't being trained to minister to that world. Priests have gone out from St Anselm's to serve in the most deprived and difficult areas here and overseas. What about Father Donovan who died of typhoid in the East End because he wouldn't leave his flock, or Father Bruce martyred in Africa? And there are others. St Anselm's has educated two of the century's most distinguished bishops.'

'They were bishops for their age, not ours. You're talking about the past. I'm concerned with the needs of the present, particularly of the young. We won't bring people to the faith with outworn conventions, an archaic liturgy, and a Church that is seen as pretentious, boring, middle-class – racist even. St Anselm's has become irrelevant to the new age.'

Father Sebastian said, 'What is it that you want? A Church without mystery, stripped of that learning, tolerance and dignity that were the virtues of Anglicanism? A Church without humility in the face of the ineffable mystery and love of Almighty God? Services with banal hymns, a debased liturgy and the Eucharist conducted as if it were a parish bean-feast? A Church for Cool Britannia? That is not how I conduct services at St Anselm's. I'm sorry, I recognize that there are legitimate differences in how we view the priesthood. I wasn't being personal.'

The Archdeacon said, 'Oh, but I think you were. Let me be frank, Morell.'

'You have been frank. And is this the place for it?'

'St Anselm's will be closed. It has served the past well, no doubt, but it is irrelevant to the present. Its teaching is good, but is it any better than was that of Chichester, Salisbury, Lincoln? They had to accept closure.'

'It will not be closed. It will not be closed in my lifetime. I'm not without influence.'

'Oh we know that. That's exactly what I'm complaining about – the power of influence, knowing the right people, moving in the right circles, a word in the right ear. That view of England is as out of date as the college. Lady Veronica's world is dead.'

But now Father Sebastian's barely controlled anger found trembling release. He could hardly speak but the words, distorted with hatred, came out at last in a voice he hardly recognized as his own. 'How dare you! How dare you even mention my wife's name!'

They glared at each other like pugilists. It was the Archdeacon who found voice. 'I'm sorry, I've been intemperate and uncharitable. The wrong words in the wrong place. Shall we go?'

He made as if to hold out his hand and then decided against it. They walked in silence along the north wall to the door of the sacristy. Father Sebastian suddenly halted. He said, 'There's someone here with us. We're not alone.'

They stood for a few seconds and listened. The Archdeacon said, 'I can hear nothing. The church is obviously empty except for us. The door was locked and the alarm set when we arrived. There's no one here.'

'Of course not. How could there be? It was just a feeling I had.'

Father Sebastian set the alarm, locked the outside door to the sacristy behind them, and they passed together into the north cloister. The apology had been uttered but words had been spoken by both which Father Sebastian knew could never be forgotten. He was filled with self-disgust at his loss of control. Both he and the Archdeacon had been at fault, but he was the host and he was the more responsible. And the Archdeacon had only articulated what others thought, others were saying. He felt the descent of a profound depression and with it came a less familiar emotion and one more acute than apprehension. It was fear.

20

Afternoon tea on Saturdays at St Anselm's was an informal affair, laid out in the students' sitting-room at the back of the house for those who had indicated that they would be in. The number was usually small, particularly if there was a football match worth attending within reasonable distance.

The time was three o'clock and Emma, Raphael Arbuthnot, Henry Bloxham and Stephen Morby were lazing in Mrs Pilbeam's sitting-room which lay between the main kitchen and the passage leading into the south cloister. It was from this same passage that a flight of steep stairs led down to the cellar. The kitchen with its four-oven Aga, its shining steel working surfaces and modern equipment, was out of bounds to the students. It was here in her small sitting-room next door with its single gas stove and square wooden table that Mrs Pilbeam often chose to cook scones and cake and prepare tea. The room was cosily domestic, even a little shabby in contrast to the surgical cleanliness of the uncluttered kitchen. The original fireplace with its decorated iron hood was still in place and, although the glowing nuggets were now synthetic and the fuel was gas, it gave a comforting focus to the room.

The sitting-room was very much Mrs Pilbeam's domain. The mantelshelf held some of her personal treasures, most of them brought back from holidays by former students: a decorated teapot, an assortment of mugs and jugs, the china dogs she liked, and even a small gaudily-dressed doll whose thin legs dangled over the edge of the mantelshelf.

Mrs Pilbeam had three sons, now widely scattered, and Emma guessed that she enjoyed those weekly sessions with the young as much as the ordinands welcomed the relief from the masculine austerity of their daily routine. Like them, Emma took comfort from Mrs Pilbeam's maternal but unsentimental affection. She wondered whether Father Sebastian altogether approved of her joining in these informal get-togethers. She had no doubt that he knew; little that went on in college escaped Father Sebastian's notice.

This afternoon there were only the three students present. Peter Buckhurst, still convalescent from glandular fever, was resting in his room.

Emma was curled among the cushions of a wicker chair to the right of the fireplace, with Raphael's long legs stretched out from the opposite chair. Henry had spread a section of the Saturday edition of *The Times* over one end of the table while at the other Stephen was being given a cookery lesson by Mrs Pilbeam. His north-country mother, in the immaculate terraced house in which he had been brought up, believed that sons should not be expected to help with the housework; so had her own mother believed and her mother before her. But Stephen, while at Oxford, had become engaged to a brilliant young geneticist with more egalitarian, less accommodating views. This afternoon, with the encouragement of Mrs Pilbeam and the occasional criticisms of his fellow ordinands, he was tackling pastry-making and was now rubbing a mixture of lard and butter into the flour.

Mrs Pilbeam remonstrated, 'Not like that, Mr Stephen. Use your fingers gently, lift up your hands, and let the mixture trickle down into the bowl. That way it collects plenty of air.'

'But I feel a right Charlie.'

Henry said, 'You look a right Charlie! If your Alison could see you now she'd have grave doubts about your ability to father the two brilliant children you're no doubt planning for.'

'No, she wouldn't,' said Stephen, and gave a happy reminiscent smile.

'That still looks a funny colour. Why don't you go to the supermarket? They sell perfectly good pastry from the freezer.'

'There's nothing like home-made pastry, Mr Henry. Don't discourage him. Now that looks about right. Start adding the cold water. No, don't reach for the jug. It has to go in a spoonful at a time.'

Stephen said, 'I had quite a good recipe for chicken casserole when I had digs at Oxford. You just buy pieces of chicken from the supermarket, then add a tin of mushroom soup. Or you can have tomato, any soup really. It always comes out all right. Is this done, Mrs P?'

Mrs Pilbeam peered into the bowl where the dough had finally been formed into a glistening lump. 'We'll be doing casseroles next week. Looks quite good. Now we'll wrap it in cling film and put it in the fridge to rest.'

'Why does it want to rest? I'm the one who's exhausted! Does it always go that colour? It looks kind of dingy.'

Raphael roused himself and said, 'Where's the sleuth?'

It was Henry who answered, eyes still on his paper. 'Not in until dinner apparently. I saw him driving off immediately after breakfast. I must say I saw him go with some relief. He isn't exactly a comfortable presence about the place.'

Stephen asked, 'What can he possibly hope to discover? He can't reopen the inquest. Or can he? Can you have a second inquest on a cremated body?'

Henry looked up, said 'I imagine not without difficulty. Ask Dalgliesh, he's the expert,' and returned to *The Times*.

Stephen went to the sink to wash the flour from his hands. He said, 'I've a bit of a conscience about Ronald. We didn't take much trouble over him, did we?'

'Trouble? Were we expected to take trouble? St Anselm's isn't a prep school.' Raphael's voice assumed a high pedantic half-whine. '"This is young Treeves, Arbuthnot, he'll be in your dormitory. Keep an eye on him, will you. Show him the ropes." Perhaps Ronald thought he was back at school, that awful habit he had of labelling everything. Name tabs on all his clothes, sticky labels on everything else. What did he think we were going to do, steal from him?'

Henry said, 'Every sudden death produces predictable emotions: shock, grief, anger, guilt. We've got over the shock, we didn't feel much grief and we've no reason to feel angry. That leaves guilt. There's going to be a boring uniformity about our next confessions. Father Beeding will get tired of hearing the name Ronald Treeves.'

Intrigued, Emma asked, 'Don't the priests at St Anselm's hear your confessions?'

Henry laughed. 'Good Lord, no. We may be incestuous

but we're not as incestuous as that. A priest comes twice a term from Framlingham.' He had finished with his paper and now folded it carefully.

'Talking of Ronald, did I tell you that I saw him on the Friday evening before he died?'

Raphael said, 'No, you didn't. Saw him where?'

'Leaving the piggery.'

'What was he doing there?'

'How do I know? Scratching the pigs' backs, I suppose. Actually, I thought he was distressed, for a moment even crying. I don't think he saw me. He blundered past me on to the headland.'

'Did you say anything about this to the police?'

'No, I didn't say anything to anyone. All the police asked me – with, I thought, a crashing lack of tact – was whether I thought Ronald had any reason to kill himself. Leaving the piggery the night before, even in a state of distress, would hardly warrant sticking your head under a ton of sand. And I couldn't be certain what I'd seen. He almost brushed against me but it was dark. I could have imagined it. Eric said nothing presumably, or it would've been brought out at the inquest. Anyway Ronald was seen later that evening by Mr Gregory who said that he was all right during his Greek lesson.'

Stephen said, 'It was odd though, wasn't it?'

'Odder in retrospect than it seemed at the time. I can't get it out of my mind. And Ronald does rather hang about the place, doesn't he? Sometimes he seems more physically present, more real, than he was when he was alive.'

There was a silence. Emma hadn't spoken. She looked across at Henry and wished, as she often did, that she had some clue to his character. She remembered a conversation with Raphael soon after Henry had joined the college.

'Henry puzzles me, doesn't he you?'

She had said, 'You all puzzle me.'

'That's good. We don't want to be transparent. Besides, you puzzle us. But Henry – what's he doing here?'

'Much the same as you, I imagine.'

'If I earned half a million clear each year with the prospect of another million bonus for good behaviour every Christmas, I doubt I'd want to give it up for seventeen thousand a year if you're lucky, and not even a decent vicarage any longer. They've been sold off to yuppie families with a taste for Victorian architecture. All we'll get is some ghastly semi with parking space for the second-hand Fiesta. Remember that uncomfortable passage in St Luke, the rich young man turning away sorrowful because he had great possessions? I can see myself in him all right. Luckily I'm poor and a bastard. Do you think God has arranged that we're never faced with temptations that He knows perfectly well He hasn't given us the strength to resist?'

Emma had said, 'The history of the twentieth century hardly supports that thesis.'

'Perhaps I'll put the idea to Father Sebastian, suggest I might work it up into a sermon. On second thoughts, perhaps not.'

Raphael's voice recalled her to the present. He said, 'Ronald was a bit of a drag on your course, wasn't he? The careful preparation so that he could think of intelligent questions to ask, all that assiduous scribbling.

He was probably taking down useful passages for future sermons. There's nothing like an infusion of verse to raise the mediocre to the memorable, especially if the congregation doesn't realize that you're quoting.'

Emma said, 'I did sometimes wonder why he came. The seminars are voluntary, aren't they?'

Raphael gave a hoarse, half ironic, half mirthful laugh; it jarred on Emma. 'Yes, my dear, absolutely. It's just that in this place voluntary doesn't quite mean the same as it does elsewhere. Let's say some behaviour is more acceptable than others.'

'Oh dear. And I thought you all came because you enjoy the poetry.'

Stephen said, 'We do enjoy the poetry. The trouble is that there are only twenty of us. That means that we're always under scrutiny. The priests can't help it, it's a question of numbers. That's why the Church thinks that sixty is about the right size for a theological college – and the Church is right. The Archdeacon has a point when he says we're too small.'

Raphael said crossly, 'Oh the Archdeacon. Do we have to talk about him?'

'All right, we won't. He's an odd mixture though, isn't he? Admittedly the Church of England is four different churches, not one, but where exactly does he fit in? He's not a clap-happy. He's a Bible evangelical, yet he accepts women priests. He's always saying that we must change to serve the new century, but he's hardly representative of liberal theology, and he's uncompromising on divorce and abortion.'

Henry said, 'He's a Victorian throw-back. When he's here I feel I'm in a Trollope novel, except that the roles have got reversed. Father Sebastian ought to be Archdeacon Grantly with Crampton playing Slope.'

Stephen said, 'No, not Slope. Slope was a hypocrite. The Archdeacon is at least sincere.'

Raphael said, 'Oh he's sincere all right. Hitler was sincere. Genghis Khan was sincere. Every tyrant's sincere.'

Stephen said mildly, 'He's not a tyrant in his parish. Actually, I think he's a good parish priest. Don't forget I spent a week's secondment there last Easter. They like him. They even like his sermons. As one of the church-wardens said, "He knows what he believes and he gives it to us straight. And there's not a person in this parish in grief or need who hasn't been grateful to him." We see him at his worst; he's a different man when he's here.'

Raphael said, 'He pursued a fellow-priest and got him jailed. Is that Christian charity? He hates Father Sebastian; so much for brotherly love. And he hates this place and all it stands for. He's trying to get St Anselm's closed.'

Henry said, 'And Father Sebastian is working to keep it open. I know where my money is.'

'I'm not so sure. Ronald's death didn't help.'

'The Church can't close down a theological college because one of the students gets himself killed. Anyway, he's due to go after breakfast on Sunday. Apparently he's needed back in the parish. Only two more meals to get through. You'd better behave yourself, Raphael.'

'I've had a finger-wagging from Father Sebastian. I shall attempt to exercise impressive control.'

'And if you fail, you'll apologize to the Archdeacon before he leaves in the morning?'

'Oh no,' said Raphael. 'I've a feeling no one will be apologizing to the Archdeacon in the morning.'

Ten minutes later, the ordinands had left for tea in the students' sitting-room. Mrs Pilbeam said, 'You look tired, Miss. Stay and have a bite of tea with me if you like. Now that you are cosy it would be more peaceful.'

'I'd like that, Mrs P, thank you.'

Mrs Pilbeam drew up a low table beside her and placed on it a large cup of tea and a buttered scone with jam. How good it was, thought Emma, to be sitting in peace and with another woman, hearing the creak of the wicker chair as Mrs Pilbeam settled herself, smelling the warm buttery scones and watching the blue flames of the fire.

She wished that they hadn't spoken about Ronald Treeves. She didn't realize how much that still-mysterious death could overshadow the college. And not only that death. Mrs Munroe had died naturally, peacefully, had perhaps been glad to go, but it was an added weight of loss in a small community where death's depredations would never go unnoticed. And Henry was right; one always felt guilt. She wished she had taken more trouble with Ronald, had been kinder and more patient. The mental picture of him half-stumbling from Surtees's cottage was a bur in the mind not easily to be shaken off.

And now there was the Archdeacon. Raphael's dislike of him was becoming obsessive. And it was more than dislike. There had been hatred in his voice; it wasn't an emotion she had expected to find at St Anselm's. She realized how much she had come to rely on these visits to the college. Familiar words from the Prayer Book floated into her mind. That peace which the world cannot give. But the peace had been broken in that image of a boy gasping open mouthed for air and finding only the killing sand. And St Anselm's was part of the world. The students might be ordinands and their teachers priests, but they were still men. The college might stand in defiant symbolic isolation between the sea and the acres of unpopulated headland, but the life within its walls was intense, tightly controlled, claustrophobic. What emotions might not flourish in that hothouse atmosphere?

And what of Raphael, brought up motherless in this seclusive world, escaping only to the equally masculine and controlled life of prep and public school? Did he really have a vocation or was he paying back an old debt in the only way he knew how? She found herself for the first time mentally criticizing the priests. Surely it should have occurred to them that Raphael should be trained at some other college. She had thought of Father Sebastian and Father Martin as possessing wisdom and goodness hardly comprehensible to those, like herself, who found in organized religion a structure for moral striving rather than the final repository of revealed truth. But she returned always to the same uncomfortable thought: the priests were still only men.

A wind was rising. She could hear it now as a soft irregular boom hardly distinguishable from the louder boom of the sea.

Mrs Pilbeam said, 'We're due for a high wind but I doubt we'll get the worst of it before morning. Still, the night will be rough enough, I reckon.'

They drank their tea in silence, then Mrs Pilbeam said, 'They're good lads, you know, all of them.'

'Yes,' said Emma, 'I know they are.' And it seemed to her that it was she who was doing the comforting.

21

Father Sebastian didn't enjoy afternoon tea. He never ate cake and took the view that scones and sandwiches only spoiled his dinner. He thought it right to put in an appearance at four o'clock when there were guests but usually only stayed long enough to drink his two cups of Earl Grey with lemon and welcome any new arrivals. This Saturday he had left the greetings to Father Martin, but at ten minutes past four thought it would be courteous to put in an appearance. But he was only half-way down the stairs when he was met by the Archdeacon rushing up towards him.

'Morell, I need to speak to you. In your office, please.'

And now what? thought Father Sebastian wearily as he mounted the stairs behind the Archdeacon. Crampton took the stairs two at a time and, once outside the office, seemed about to crash unceremoniously through the door. Father Sebastian, entering more quietly, invited him to take one of the chairs in front of the fire but was ignored, and the two men stood facing each other so closely that Father Sebastian could smell the taint of sourness on the other's breath. He found himself forced to meet the glare of two blazing eyes and was instantly and uncomfortably aware of every detail of Crampton's face: the two black hairs in the left nostril, the angry patches of red high on each cheekbone, and a crumb of what looked like buttered scone adhering to the edge of the mouth. He stood and watched while the Archdeacon took control of himself.

When Crampton spoke he was calmer, but the menace in his voice was unmistakable. 'What is that police officer doing here? Who invited him?'

'Commander Dalgliesh? I thought I explained . . .'

'Not Dalgliesh. Yarwood. Roger Yarwood.'

Father Sebastian said calmly, 'Like yourself, Mr Yarwood is a guest. He is a detective inspector of the Suffolk Constabulary and is taking a week's leave.'

'Was that your idea, to have him here?'

'He's an occasional visitor, and a welcome one. At present he's on sick-leave. He wrote to ask if he could stay for a week. We like him and are glad to have him.'

'Yarwood was the police officer who investigated my wife's death. Are you seriously telling me that you didn't know?'

'How could I know, Archdeacon? How could any of us know? It wasn't something he would speak about. He comes here to get away from his work. I can see that it's distressing for you to find him here and I am sorry it should have happened. Obviously his presence brings back very unhappy memories. But it's an extraordinary coincidence, no more. They happen every day. Inspector Yarwood transferred to Suffolk from the Metropolitan Police five years ago, I believe. It must have been shortly after your wife's death.'

Father Sebastian avoided using the word *suicide*, but he knew that it hung unspoken between them. The tragedy of the Archdeacon's first wife was well-known in clerical circles, as inevitably it would be.

The Archdeacon said, 'He must leave, of course. I'm not prepared to sit at dinner with him.'

Father Sebastian was torn between a sympathy that was genuine even if not strong enough to discomfort him, and a more personal emotion. He said, 'I'm not prepared to tell him to go. As I have said, he's a guest here. Whatever memories he brings to mind for you, surely it's possible for two adult men to sit at the same dinner-table without provoking outrage.'

'Outrage?'

'I find the word appropriate. Why should you be so angry, Archdeacon? Yarwood was doing his job. It wasn't personal between you.'

'He made it personal from the first moment he appeared in the vicarage. That man more or less accused me of murder. He came day after day, even when I was at my most grieving and vulnerable, pestering me with questions, querying every little detail of my marriage, personal matters that were nothing to do with him, nothing! After the inquest and the verdict I complained to the Met. I would have gone to the Police Complaints Authority but I hardly expected them to take it seriously and by then I was trying to put it behind me. But the Met did set up an inquiry and admitted that Yarwood had perhaps been over-zealous.'

'Over-zealous?' Father Sebastian fell back on a familiar bromide. 'I suppose he thought he was doing his duty.'

'Duty? It was nothing to do with duty! He thought he could make a case and a reputation. It would have been quite a coup for him, wouldn't it? Local vicar accused of murdering his wife. Do you know what harm that kind of allegation could do, in the diocese, in the parish? He tortured me and he enjoyed torturing me.'

Father Sebastian found it difficult to reconcile this accusation with the Yarwood he knew. He was aware of conflicting emotions; sympathy for the Archdeacon, indecision whether or not to speak to Yarwood, concern not to worry unnecessarily a man he suspected was still fragile both physically and mentally, and the need to get through the weekend without antagonizing Crampton further. All these worries came incongruously and ludicrously together in the overriding question of the placement at dinner. He couldn't seat the two police officers together; they would want to avoid any obligation to engage in professional chat and he certainly didn't want it at his dinner-table. (Father Sebastian never thought of the refectory at St Anselm's in terms other than 'his' dining-hall, 'his' dinner-table.) It was obvious that neither Raphael nor Father John could appropriately be seated either next to the Archdeacon or facing him. Clive Stannard was a dull guest at the best of times; he could hardly inflict him on Crampton or Dalgliesh. He wished that his wife were alive and in residence. None of this would be happening if Veronica were alive. He felt a prick of resentment that she had so inconveniently left him.

It was then that there was a knock on the door. Glad of any interruption, he called, 'Come', and Raphael entered. The Archdeacon took one look at him and said to Father Sebastian, 'You'll see to it then will you, Morell?' and went out.

Father Sebastian, although glad of the interruption,

was not in the mood to be welcoming and his 'What is it, Raphael?' was curt.

'It's about Inspector Yarwood, Father. He'd prefer not to have dinner with the rest of us. He wonders if it's possible for him to have something in his room.'

'Is he ill?'

'I don't think he's particularly well, but he didn't say anything about feeling ill. He saw the Archdeacon at tea and I gather he doesn't want to encounter him again if possible. He didn't stop to eat so I followed him back to his room to see if he was all right.'

'And did he tell you why he was upset?'

'Yes Father, he did.'

'He had no right to confide in you or anyone else here. It was unprofessional and unwise, and you should have stopped him.'

'He didn't say very much, Father, but what he did say was interesting.'

'Whatever he said should have remained unspoken. You'd better see Mrs Pilbeam and ask her to provide some dinner for him. Soup and a salad, something like that.'

'I think that's all he wants, Father. He said he'd like to be left alone.'

Father Sebastian wondered if he should speak to Yarwood, but decided against it. Perhaps what the man wanted, to be left alone, was the best course. The Archdeacon was due to leave next morning after an early breakfast as he wanted to be back in his parish to preach at the ten-thirty Sunday Parish Communion. He had hinted that someone of importance was to be in the congregation. With any luck the two men need not see each other again.

Wearily the Warden made his way down the stairs to the students' sitting-room and his two cups of Earl Grey tea.

22

The refectory faced south and was almost a replica in size and style of the library with the same barrelled roof and an equal number of high narrow windows, although these were devoid of figurative coloured glass and held instead panes of delicate pale green with a design of grapes and vine leaves. The walls between them were brightened by three large pre-Raphaelite paintings, all the gift of the founder. One, by Dante Gabriel Rossetti, showed a girl with flaming red hair seated at a window and reading a book which with imagination could be construed as devotional. The second, by Edward Burne-Jones, of three dark-haired girls dancing in a swirl of golden brown silk under an orange tree, was frankly secular, and the third and largest, by William Holman Hunt, showed a priest outside a wattle chapel baptizing a group of ancient Britons. They were not pictures which Emma coveted, but she had no doubt they were a valuable part of St Anselm's heritage. The room itself had obviously been designed as a family dining-room but one, she thought, intended for ostentation rather than practicality or intimacy. Even the traditionally large Victorian family would surely feel isolated and discomforted by this monument to paternal grandeur. St Anselm's had obviously made few changes in adapting the dining-room for institutional use. The oval carved oak table still held place in the centre of the room, but had been lengthened in the middle by six feet of plain wood. The chairs, including the ornate armed carver, were obviously original and, in place of the customary hatch into the kitchen, the food was served from a long sideboard covered with a white cloth.

Mrs Pilbeam waited at table with the help of two ordinands, the students taking this duty in turn. The Pilbeams ate the same meal, but at the table in Mrs Pilbeam's sitting-room. Emma, on her first visit, had been intrigued how well this eccentric arrangement worked. Mrs Pilbeam seemed to know by instinct the exact moment when each course in the dining-room was finished and made her appearance on time. No bells were rung and the first and main courses were eaten in silence while one of the ordinands read from a high desk to the left of the door. This duty, too, was taken in turn.

The choice of subject was left to the ordinand and the readings were not necessarily expected to be either from the Bible or from religious texts. During her visits Emma had heard Henry Bloxham read from *The Waste Land*, Stephen Morby give a lively reading of a P. G. Wodehouse *Mulliner* short story, while Peter Buckhurst had chosen *The Diary of a Nobody*. The advantage of the system for Emma, apart from the interest of the readings and the revelation of personal choice, was that she could enjoy Mrs Pilbeam's excellent cooking without the need to make small talk, the ritual turn to one side and the other.

With Father Sebastian presiding, dinner at St Anselm's had something of the formality of a private house. But when the reading and the two first courses were over, the previous silence seemed to facilitate conversation, which normally carried on happily while the reader caught up by taking his meal from the hotplate and the company finally moved for coffee into the students' sitting-room, or through the south door into the court-yard. Often the talk carried on until it was time for Compline. After Compline it was customary for ordinands to go to their own rooms and keep a silence.

Although by tradition each student took the next vacant chair, Father Sebastian himself arranged the seating of the guests and staff. He had placed Archdeacon Crampton on his left, Emma beside him, with Father Martin on her other side. On his right was Commander Dalgliesh, next to him Father Peregrine and then Clive Stannard. George Gregory dined only occasionally in college, but tonight he was present, seated between Stannard and Stephen Morby; Emma had expected to see Inspector Yarwood but he didn't arrive and no one commented on his absence. Three of the four students in residence took their seats and, like the rest of the company, stood behind their chairs ready for grace. It was only then that Raphael entered, buttoning up his cassock. He muttered an apology and, opening the book he was carrying, took his place at the reading desk. Father Sebastian spoke a Latin grace and there was a shuffling of chairs as they settled down to the first course.

Taking her seat next to the Archdeacon, Emma was aware of his physical nearness as she guessed he was of hers. She knew instinctively that he was a man who responded to women with a strong if suppressed sexuality. He was as tall as Father Sebastian but more sturdily built, broad-shouldered, bull-necked, and with strong handsome features. His hair was almost black, the beard just beginning to fleck with grey, his eyes deep-set under brows so well shaped that they could have been plucked. They gave a discordant hint of femininity to his dark, unsmiling masculinity. Father Sebastian had introduced him to Emma when they arrived in the dining-room and he had grasped her hand with a strength which conveyed no warmth and had met her gaze with a look of puzzled surprise, as if she were an enigma which it behoved him to solve before the dinner was over.

The first course had already been set out, baked aubergines and peppers in olive oil. There was a subdued clatter of forks as they began to eat and, as if he were waiting for this signal, Raphael started to read. He said, as if announcing a lesson in church, 'This is the first chapter of Anthony Trollope's *Barchester Towers*.'

It was a work with which Emma, who liked Victorian novels, was familiar, but she wondered why Raphael had chosen it. Ordinands did occasionally read from a novel, but it was more usual to choose a passage complete in itself. Raphael read well, and Emma found herself eating with almost over-fastidious slowness as her mind occupied itself with the setting and the story. St Anselm's was an appropriate house in which to read Trollope. Under its cavernous arched roof she could picture the Bishop's bedroom in the Palace at Barchester and Archdeacon Grantly watching at his father's deathbed, knowing that if the old man lived until the Government fell – as was hourly expected – he would have no hope of succeeding his father as Bishop. It was a powerful passage, that proud ambitious son sinking to his knees and praying that he might be forgiven the sin of wishing his father would die.

The wind had been rising steadily since early evening.

Now it was battering the house in great gusts like bursts of gunfire. During the worst of each onslaught Raphael would pause in his reading like a lecturer waiting for quietness from an unruly class. In the lulls his voice sounded unnaturally clear and portentous.

Emma became aware that all movement had ceased from the dark figure beside her. She glanced at the Archdeacon's hands and saw that they were clenched round his knife and fork. Peter Buckhurst was silently circulating with the wine, but the Archdeacon clamped his hand over his glass, white-knuckled, so that Emma half-expected it to smash under his palm. Watching the hand, it seemed to loom and become almost monstrous in imagination, the black hairs erect along the ridge of the fingers. She was aware, too, that Commander Dalgliesh, sitting opposite, had momentarily raised his eyes to the Archdeacon in a speculative glance. Emma couldn't believe that the tension, so strongly communicating itself to her from her companion, couldn't be felt by the whole table, but only Commander Dalgliesh seemed aware of it. Gregory was eating in silence but with evident satisfaction. He seldom looked up until Raphael began reading. Then he occasionally glanced at him with slightly quizzical amusement.

Raphael's voice continued as Mrs Pilbeam and Peter Buckhurst silently cleared the plates, and she brought in the main course: cassoulet with boiled potatoes, carrots and beans. The Archdeacon then made some attempt at recovery, but he ate almost nothing. At the end of the first two courses, which were to be followed by fruit and cheese and biscuits, Raphael closed the novel, went to the hotplate to collect his plate, and took his seat at the end of the table. It was then that Emma looked at Father Sebastian. His face was rigid and he was staring down the table at Raphael who, it seemed to Emma, was resolutely refusing to meet his eyes.

No one seemed anxious to break the silence until the Archdeacon, making an effort, turned to Emma and began a rather stilted conversation about her relationship with the college. When was she appointed? What was it that she taught? Did she find the students on the whole receptive? How did she personally think the teaching of English and religious verse related to the theological syllabus? She knew that he was trying to put her at ease, or at least making an attempt at conversation, but it sounded like an interrogation and she was uncomfortably aware that in the silence his questions and her answers sounded unnaturally loud. Her eyes kept straying to Adam Dalgliesh, on the Warden's right, to the dark head bent towards the fairer. They seemed to have plenty to talk about. Surely they wouldn't be discussing Ronald's death, not here at dinner. From time to time she sensed Dalgliesh's gaze fixed on her. Their eyes briefly met and she turned quickly away, then was angry with herself for the moment's embarrassed gaucherie and turned resolutely to endure the Archdeacon's curiosity.

Finally they moved into the sitting-room for coffee, but the change of venue did nothing to revive the conversation. It became a desultory exchange of platitudes and, long before it was time to get ready for Compline, the company broke up. Emma was one of the first to leave. Despite the storm she felt the need for fresh air and exercise before bed. Tonight she would give Compline a miss. It was the first time in all her visits that she had felt so strongly the need to get free of the house. But when she left by the door leading to the south cloister, the force of the wind struck her like a physical blow. Soon it would be difficult to stand upright. This was not a night for a solitary walk on a headland that had suddenly become unfriendly. She wondered what Adam Dalgliesh was doing. Probably he would feel it courteous to attend Compline. For her it would be work – there was always work – and an early bed. She walked along the dimly-lit southern cloister to Ambrose and solitude.

23

It was nine twenty-nine and Raphael, entering the sacristy last, found only Father Sebastian taking off his cloak before robing for the service. Raphael had his hand on the door leading into the church when Father Sebastian said, 'Did you choose that chapter of Trollope deliberately to upset the Archdeacon?'

'It's a chapter I'm fond of, Father. That proud ambitious man actually kneeling by his father's bedside, facing his secret hope that the Bishop will die in time. It's one of the most impressive chapters Trollope ever wrote. I thought we might all appreciate it.'

'I'm not asking for a literary appreciation of Trollope. You haven't answered my question. Did you choose it to discomfort the Archdeacon?'

Raphael said quietly, 'Yes, Father, I did.'

'Presumably because of what you learned from Inspector Yarwood before dinner.'

'He was distressed. The Archdeacon had more or less forced himself into Roger's room and confronted him. Roger blurted something out and told me afterwards that it was in confidence and that I must try to forget it.'

'And your method of forgetting was deliberately to select a chapter of prose that would not only be deeply upsetting to a guest in this house, but that would betray the fact that Inspector Yarwood had confided in you.'

'The passage, Father, wouldn't have been offensive to the Archdeacon unless what Roger told me was true.'

'I see. You were applying *Hamlet*. You created mischief and you disobeyed my instructions about how you should behave to the Archdeacon while he was our guest. We have some thinking to do, you and I. I must consider whether I can in conscience recommend you for ordination. You must consider whether you are really suited to being a priest.'

It was the first time Father Sebastian put into words the doubt which he had hardly dared acknowledge, even in thought. He made himself look into Raphael's eyes while he waited for a response.

Raphael said quietly, 'But have we really any choice, Father, either of us?'

What surprised Father Sebastian was not the reply, but the tone in which it was spoken. He heard in Raphael's voice what he saw also in his eyes, not defiance, not a challenge to his authority, not even the usual note of ironic detachment, but something more disturbing and painful; a trace of sad resignation which was, at the same time, a cry for help. Without speaking Father Sebastian finished robing, then waited for Raphael to open the sacristy door for him and followed him into the candle-lit gloom of the church.

24

Dalgliesh was the only member of the congregation at Compline. He seated himself half-way down the right aisle and watched as Henry Bloxham, wearing a white surplice, lit two candles on the altar and the row of candles in their glass shades along the choir stalls. Henry had shot back the bolts of the great south door before Dalgliesh's arrival, and Dalgliesh sat quietly, expecting to hear at his back the grinding creak of its opening. But neither Emma nor any of the staff or visitors arrived. The church was dimly lit and he sat alone in a concentrated calm in which the tumult of the storm seemed so distant that it was part of another reality. Finally Henry switched on the light over the altar and the van der Weyden stained the still air with light. Henry genuflected before the altar and returned to the sacristy. Two minutes later the four resident priests entered, followed by the ordinands and the Archdeacon. The white-surpliced figures, moving almost silently, took their places with an unhurried dignity and Father Sebastian's voice broke the silence with the first prayer.

'The Lord Almighty grant us a quiet night and a perfect end. Amen.'

The service was sung in plainsong and with a perfection born of practice and familiarity. Dalgliesh stood or knelt as appropriate and joined in the responses; he had no wish to play the part of a voyeur. He put all thoughts of Ronald Treeves and of death out of his mind. He was not here as a police officer; he was required to bring nothing with him but the acquiescence of the heart.

After the final Collect but before the blessing the Archdeacon moved from his stall to deliver the homily. He chose to stand in front of the altar-rail rather than to move down to the pulpit or reading desk. Dalgliesh reflected that it was just as well, since otherwise he would be preaching to a congregation of one, and almost certainly to the person he was least concerned to address. The homily was short, less than six minutes, but it was powerful and quietly delivered, as if the Archdeacon were aware that unwelcome words gained in intensity if softly spoken. He stood there, dark and bearded, like an Old Testament prophet while his surpliced audience sat, their eyes not turning to him, as still as if they were images in stone.

The theme of the homily was Christian discipleship in the modern world and it was an attack on nearly everything for which St Anselm's had stood for over a hundred years, and on everything Father Sebastian valued. The message was unambiguous. The Church could not survive to serve the needs of a violent, troubled and increasingly unbelieving century unless it returned to the fundamentals of the faith. Modern discipleship was not a matter of indulgence in archaic if beautiful language, in which words more often obscured than affirmed the reality of faith. There was a temptation to overvalue intelligence and intellectual achievement so that theology became a philosophical exercise in justifying scepticism. Equally seductive was an overemphasis on ceremony, vestments and disputed points of procedure, an obsession with competitive musical excellence which too often transformed a church service into a public performance. The Church was not a social organization within which the comfortable middle class could satisfy its craving for beauty, order, nostalgia and the illusion of spirituality. Only by a return to the truth of the gospel could the Church hope to meet the needs of the modern world.

At the end of the homily the Archdeacon returned to his stall and the ordinands and priests knelt while Father Sebastian spoke the final blessing. After the small procession had left the church, Henry returned to extinguish the candles and switch off the altar light. Then he came down to the south door to say a courteous good-night to Dalgliesh and to lock the door behind him. Except for those two words, neither spoke.

As he heard the rasp of the iron, Dalgliesh felt that he was being permanently shut out from something which he had never fully understood or accepted and which was now being finally bolted against him. Sheltered by the cloister from the full force of the gale, he made his way along the few yards from the church door to Jerome and bed.

BOOK TWO

Death of an Archdeacon

I

The Archdeacon didn't loiter after Compline. He and Father Sebastian disrobed in silence in the sacristy and he said a curt good-night before stepping out into the windswept cloister.

The courtyard was a vortex of sound and fury. An early rain had ceased but the strong southeaster, rising in strength, gusted and whirled about the horse-chestnut, set a hissing among the high leaves and bent the great boughs so that they rose and fell with the majestic slowness of a funeral dance. Frailer branches and twigs snapped off and fell like the sticks of spent fireworks on the cobbles. The south cloister was still clear but the fallen leaves, rolling and twisting across the courtyard, were already piling in a damp mush against the sacristy door and the wall of the north cloister.

At the entrance to the college, the Archdeacon scraped free the few leafy skeletons plastered against the sole and the toe of his black shoes and moved through the cloakroom into the hall. Despite the violence of the storm, the house was strangely silent. He wondered whether the four priests were still in the church or sacristy, perhaps holding an indignant meeting about his homily. The ordinands, he assumed, had gone to their rooms. There was something unusual, almost ominous, in the calm and faintly pungent air.

It wasn't yet ten-thirty. He felt restless and disinclined

for so early a night, but the outside exercise he had suddenly craved seemed impracticable and even dangerous in the darkness and the force of the wind. It was, he knew, customary at St Anselm's to keep silent after Compline and, although he had little sympathy with the convention, he wasn't anxious to be seen flouting it. There was, he knew, a television set in the ordinands' sitting-room, but the Saturday programmes were never much good and he was reluctant to disturb the calm. But he could probably find a book there, and there could be no objection to his watching the late ITV news.

But when he opened the door he saw that the room was occupied. The youngish man, who had been introduced to him at lunch as Clive Stannard, was watching a film and, turning at his entrance, seemed to resent the intrusion. The Archdeacon hovered for a moment, then said a brief good-night, let himself out through the door beside the cellar steps and battled his way across the courtyard to Augustine.

By ten-forty he was in his pyjamas and dressing-gown and ready for bed. He had read a chapter of St Mark's Gospel and said his usual prayers, but tonight both had been no more than a routine exercise in conventional piety. He knew the words of scripture by heart and had silently mouthed them, as if by slowness and careful attention to each word he could extract from them some meaning previously withheld. Taking off his dressing-gown he made sure that the window was secure against the storm and climbed into bed.

Memory is best held at bay by action. Now, lying rigidly between taut sheets, hearing the howling of the wind, he knew that sleep wouldn't come easily. The crowded and traumatic day had left his mind over-stimulated. Perhaps he should have battled against the wind and taken his walk. He thought about the homily, but with satisfaction rather than regret. He had prepared it with care and delivered it quietly but with passion and authority. These things had to be said and he had said them, and if the homily had further antagonized Sebastian Morell, if distress and dislike had hardened into enmity, well that couldn't be helped. It wasn't, he told himself, that he courted unpopularity; it was important to him to stand well with people he respected. He was ambitious and he knew that a bishop's mitre wasn't won by antagonizing a significant section of the Church, even if its influence was less powerful than once it had seemed. But Sebastian Morell was no longer as influential as he imagined. In this battle he could be sure that he was on the winning side. But there were, he reminded himself, battles of principles which had to be fought if the Church of England was to survive to serve the new millennium. Closing St Anselm's might be only a minor skirmish in that war, but it was one which would give him satisfaction to win.

So what was it then that he found so unsettling about St Anselm's? Why should he feel that here on this windswept desolate coast the spiritual life had to be lived at a greater intensity than elsewhere, that he and his whole past were under judgement? It wasn't as if St Anselm's had a long history of devotion and worship. Certainly the church was medieval; one could, he supposed, hear in that silent air the echo of centuries of plainsong, although it had never been apparent to him. For him a church was functional, a building for worship, not a place of worship. St Anselm's was only the creation of a Victorian spinster with too much money, too little sense and a taste for lace-trimmed albs, birettas and bachelor priests. Probably the woman had been half-mad. It was ridiculous that her pernicious influence should still govern a twenty-first-century college.

He shifted his legs vigorously in an attempt to loosen the constricting sheet. He wished suddenly that Muriel were with him, that he could turn to her stolid comfortable body and accepting arms for the temporary oblivion of sex. But even as in thought he reached for her, there came between them, as so often in the marital bed, the memory of that other body, arms delicate as a child's, the pointed breasts, the open exploring mouth moving over his body. 'You like this? And this? And this?'

Their love had been a mistake from the beginning, ill-advised and so predictably disastrous that he wondered now how he had been so self-deceived. The affair had been the stuff of cheap romantic fiction. It had even begun in the setting of much cheap romantic fiction, a cruise-ship in the Mediterranean. A clerical acquaintance, who was booked as a guest lecturer on a voyage to archaeological and historical sites in Italy and Asia, had fallen ill at the last minute and had suggested him as a substitute. He suspected that the organizers wouldn't have taken him if a better-qualified candidate had been available, but he had been surprisingly successful. Luckily on his cruise there had been no knowledgeable academics among the passengers. By conscientious preliminary preparation and by taking with him the best-written guides he had managed to keep ahead of the other passengers.

Barbara had been on board taking an educational

cruise with her mother and stepfather. She was the youngest passenger and he wasn't the only male to be enchanted with her. To him she had looked more like a child than a nineteen-year-old, and a child born out of her own time. The coal-black hair cut in a bob with a low fringe over immense blue eyes, the heart-shaped face and small full lips, the boyish figure emphasized by the very short cotton shifts she chose to wear, gave her a look of the 1920s. The older passengers, who had lived through the 30s and had a folk memory of that earlier frenetic decade, sighed nostalgically and murmured that she reminded them of the young Claudette Colbert. For him the image was false. She had no film-star sophistication, only a childish innocence and gaiety and a vulnerability that enabled him to interpret sexual desire as the need to cherish and protect. He couldn't believe his luck when she singled him out for the distinction of her favour and thereafter attached herself to him with proprietorial dedication. Within three months they were married. He was thirty-nine, she was just twenty.

Educated at a succession of schools dedicated to the religion of multiculturalism and liberal orthodoxy, she knew nothing about the Church but was avid for information and instruction. Only later did he realize that the relationship between teacher and taught was for her deeply erotic. She liked to be mastered, and not only physically. But none of her enthusiasms lasted, including her enthusiasm for marriage. The church where he was then vicar had sold off the large Victorian vicarage and built in its grounds a modern two-storey house of no architectural merit, but economical to run. It was not the house she had expected.

Extravagant, wilful, capricious, he early realized she was the antithesis of a suitable wife for an ambitious Church of England clergyman. Even the sex became overlaid with anxiety. She was at her most demanding when he was overtired or on the rare occasions when they had overnight visitors and he would become uncomfortably aware of the thinness of the bedroom walls as she murmured endearments which could so easily rise to shouted taunts and demands. At breakfast the next morning she would appear in her dressing-gown, openly flirtatious, lifting her arms so that the thin silk fell away, sleepy-eyed and triumphant.

Why had she married him? For security? To get away from the mother and stepfather she hated? To be cosseted, cared for, indulged? To feel safe? To be loved? He grew to dread her unpredictable moods, her outbreaks of screaming fury. He tried to shield them from the knowledge of the parish but soon the whispers came back to him. He remembered with burning embarrassment and resentment the visit of one of his church-wardens who happened to be a doctor. 'Your wife isn't my patient, of course, vicar, and I don't want to interfere, but she isn't well. I think you should try to get professional help.' But when he suggested that she might see a psychiatrist or even a general practitioner, he was greeted with sobbing accusations that he was trying to get rid of her, to have her put away.

Outside the wind, which for a few minutes had dropped in intensity, rose again to a howling crescendo. Usually he enjoyed listening to its fury from the safety of his bed; now this small and functional room seemed less a sanctuary than a prison. Since Barbara's death he had prayed for forgiveness for marrying her, for failing her in love and understanding; he had never asked for forgiveness for wishing her dead. Now, lying in this narrow bed, he began painfully to confront the past. It was not an act of will that drew back the bolts of that dark dungeon to which he had consigned his marriage. The visions that rose to pass through his mind were not of his choosing. Something – that traumatic encounter with Yarwood, this place, St Anselm's – worked together to ensure that he had no alternative.

Caught between a dream and a nightmare, he imagined himself in an interrogation room, modern, functional, characterless. And then he realized that it was the living-room of his old vicarage. He was seated on the sofa between Dalgliesh and Yarwood. They hadn't handcuffed him, not yet, but he knew that he had already been judged and found guilty, that they had all the evidence they needed. It rolled before his eyes in a grainy, secretly-filmed indictment. From time to time Dalgliesh would say 'stop there', and Yarwood would put out a hand. The image would be fixed while they viewed it in an accusing silence. All the petty transgressions and unkindnesses, as well as the major failure in love, passed before his eyes. And now at last they were viewing the final reel, the heart of darkness.

He was no longer squashed down on the sofa imprisoned between his two accusers. He had moved into the frame to re-enact every movement, every word, to experience every emotion as if for the first time. It had been the late afternoon of a sunless day in mid-October, a thin rain, fine as a mist, had been falling continuously for the last two days from a gunmetal sky. He had returned from two hours of visiting long-term sick and housebound parishioners. As always he had tried conscientiously to meet their individual and predictable needs; blind Mrs Oliver who liked him to read a passage of scripture and pray with her; old Sam Possinger who on every visit re-fought the Battle of Alamein; Mrs Poley, caged in her zimmer-frame, avid for the latest parish gossip; Carl Lomas, who had never set foot in St Botolph's but liked discussing theology and the defects of the Church of England. Mrs Poley, with his help, had edged her way painfully into the kitchen and made tea, taking from the tin the gingerbread cake she had baked for him. He had unwisely praised it four years ago on his first visit and was now condemned to eat it weekly, finding it impossible to admit that he disliked gingerbread. But the tea, hot and strong, had been welcome and would save him the trouble of making it at home.

He parked his Vauxhall Cavalier in the road and walked to his front door down the concrete path which dissected the spongy saturated lawn on which decaying rose petals were dissolving into the unmown grass. The house was totally silent and he entered, as always, with apprehension. Barbara had been sullen and fidgety at breakfast, and the restlessness and the fact that she hadn't bothered to dress were always a bad sign. At their lunch of soup from a carton followed by a salad, still in her dressing-gown, she had pushed her plate away saying that she was too tired to eat; she would go to bed for the afternoon and try to sleep.

She had said petulantly, 'You'd better go to your boring old parishioners. They're all you care about anyway. Don't disturb me when you get back. I don't want to hear about them. I don't want to hear about anything.'

He had not replied, but had watched with a surge of anger and helplessness as slowly she mounted the stairs, the silk belt of her dressing-gown trailing, her head drooping as if in an agony of despair.

Now, returning home and burdened with apprehension, he closed the front door behind him. Was she still in bed or had she waited for him to leave, then dressed and gone out on one of her destructive and humiliating insurgencies into the parish? He had to know. He mounted the stairs quietly; if she were asleep he had no wish to wake her.

The door to the bedroom was shut and he turned the doorknob gently. The room was in semi-darkness, the curtains partly-drawn across the one long window which gave a view of the rectangle of grass, rough as a field, the triangular beds which were the garden, and beyond to the rows of neat identical houses. He moved towards the bed and, as his eyes adjusted to the half-light, saw her clearly. She was lying on her right side, her hand curled against her cheek. The left arm was flung out over the bedclothes. Bending down he could hear her breathing, low and laboured, could smell the wine on her breath and a stronger, sweet, disagreeable stink which he identified as vomit. On the bedside table was a bottle of Cabernet Sauvignon. Beside it, lying on its side and with the screw-cap rolled a little apart, was a large empty bottle which he recognized. It had contained tablets of soluble aspirin.

He told himself that she was asleep, that she was drunk, that she needed to be left undisturbed. Almost instinctively he picked up the wine bottle and was about to judge how much she had drunk when something as strong as a warning voice made him put it down again. He saw that there was a handkerchief protruding from beneath the pillow. Taking it he wiped the bottle clean, then dropped the handkerchief on the bed. It seemed to him that his actions were as without volition as they were without sense. Then he left her, closing the door behind him, and went downstairs. He told himself again: she's asleep, she's drunk, she won't want to be disturbed. After half an hour he went to his study, calmly got the papers together for the six o'clock meeting of the Parochial Church Council and left the house.

He had no mental picture, no memory of the PCC meeting, but he could remember driving home with Melvyn Hopkins, one of the churchwardens. He had promised Melvyn to let him have a sight of the latest report of the Church's committee on social responsibility and had suggested that Melvyn accompany him to the Vicarage. And now the sequence of images was clear again. Himself apologizing for the fact that Barbara wasn't there and telling Melvyn that she had been unwell, going up again to the bedroom and again gently opening the door, seeing in the half-light the still figure, the wine bottle, the bottle of pills on its side. He went over to the bed. This time there was no low raucous breathing. Putting out his hand to her cheek he found that it was cold and knew that what he was touching was death. And then there came a memory, words heard or read from some forgotten source, but now terrifying in their implication. It was always wise to have someone with you when you found the body.

He couldn't relive the events of the church funeral

service or the cremation; he had no memory of either. In their place was a jumble of faces – sympathetic, concerned, frankly anxious – zooming at him out of darkness, distorted and grotesque. And now there was that one dreaded face. He was sitting on the sofa again, but this time with Sergeant Yarwood and a young uniformed boy who looked no older than one of his boy choristers and who sat silent throughout the interrogation.

'And when you returned to the house, from visiting your parishioners, shortly after five, you say, what exactly did you do, sir?'

'I've told you, sergeant. I went up to the bedroom to see if my wife was still sleeping.'

'When you opened the door, was the bedside lamp on?'

'No, it wasn't. The curtains were almost completely drawn and the room was in semi-darkness.'

'Did you go up to the body?'

'I've told you, sergeant. I just looked in, saw that my wife was still in bed and assumed that she was asleep.'

'And she went to bed – when was that?'

'At lunch-time. I suppose about half-past twelve. She said she wasn't hungry, that she was going to have a sleep.'

'Didn't you think it strange that she should still be sleeping after five hours?'

'No, I didn't. She said that she was tired. My wife often did sleep in the afternoons.'

'Didn't it occur to you that she might be ill? Didn't it occur to you to go up to the bed and make sure she was all right? Didn't you realize that she might urgently need a doctor?'

'I've told you – I'm tired of telling you – I thought she was asleep.'

'Did you see the two bottles on the bedside table, the wine and the soluble aspirin?'

'I saw the wine bottle. I guessed my wife had been drinking.'

'Did she take the bottle of wine up to bed with her?'

'No, she didn't. She must have come down for it after I left the house.'

'And carried it up to bed with her?'

'I suppose so. There was no one else in the house. Of course she took it up to bed with her. How else could it have got on the bedside table?'

'Well, that's the question, isn't it sir? You see, there were no fingerprints on the wine bottle. Can you explain how that could be?'

'Of course I can't. I assume she wiped them off. There was a handkerchief half-under the pillow.'

'Which you were able to see although you couldn't see the upturned bottle?'

'Not at the time. I saw it later when I found her body.'

And so the questions went on. Yarwood returned time and time again, sometimes with the young uniformed constable, but sometimes on his own. Crampton came to dread every ring at the door and could hardly bear to look out of the windows in case he saw that grey-coated figure moving resolutely up the path. The questions were always the same and his answers became unconvincing even to his own ears. Even after the inquest and the expected verdict of suicide the persecution continued. Barbara had been cremated weeks before. There was nothing left of her but a few handfuls of ground bones buried in a corner of the churchyard, and still Yarwood continued his inquiries.

Never had nemesis arrived in a less personable form. Yarwood looked like a doorstep salesman, doggedly persistent, inured to rejection, carrying with him like halitosis the taint of failure. He was slightly-built, surely only just tall enough to qualify for the police, sallow-skinned and with a high bony forehead and dark secretive eyes. He seldom looked directly at Crampton during the questioning but focused on the middle distance as if communing with an internal controller. His voice never varied from a monotone and the silence between the questions was pregnant with a menace which seemed to embrace more than his victim. He seldom gave notice of his coming but seemed to know when Crampton was at home and would wait with apparently docile patience at the front door until silently ushered in. There were never any preliminaries, only the insistent questions.

'Would you say it was a happy marriage, sir?'

The impertinence of it shocked Crampton into silence, then he found himself replying in a voice of such harshness that he could hardly recognize it: 'I suppose that for the police every relationship, even the most sacred, can be classified. You should hand out a marriage questionnaire, it would save everyone time. Tick the appropriate box: Very happy. Happy. Reasonably happy. A little unhappy. Unhappy. Very unhappy. Murderous.'

There was a silence, then Yarwood said, 'And which box would you tick, sir?'

In the end Crampton made a formal complaint to the Chief Constable and the visits ceased. He was told that after the inquiry it was accepted that Sergeant Yarwood had exceeded his authority, particularly in arriving alone and pursuing an investigation which had not been authorized. He remained in Crampton's memory as a dark accusing figure. Time, the new parish, his appointment to Archdeacon, his second marriage – nothing could assuage the burning anger which consumed him whenever he thought of Yarwood.

And now today the man had appeared again. He couldn't remember what exactly they had said to each other. He only knew that his own resentment and bitterness had been poured out in a torrent of angry vituperation.

He had prayed, at first regularly and then intermittently, since Barbara's death, asking forgiveness for his sins against her; impatience, intolerance, lack of love, failure to understand or to forgive. But the sin of wishing her dead had never been allowed to take root in his mind. And he had received his absolution to the lesser sin of neglect. It had come in the words of Barbara's general practitioner when they had met just before the inquest.

'One thing has been on my mind. If I'd realized when I came home that Barbara wasn't asleep – that she was in a coma – and had called for an ambulance, would it have made any difference?'

He had received the absolving reply: 'With the quantity she had taken and drunk, none at all.'

What was there about this place that forced him to confront the greater as well as the lesser lies? He had known she was in danger of death. He had hoped that she would die. He was in the eyes of his God, surely, as guilty of murder as if he had dissolved those tablets and forced them down her throat, as if he had held the glass of wine to her lips. How could he continue to minister to others, to preach the forgiveness of sins, when his own great sin was unacknowledged? How could he have stood up before that congregation tonight with this darkness in his soul?

He put out his hand and switched on the bedside lamp. It flooded the room with light, surely brighter than when, by that gentle glow, he had read his evening passage of scripture. He got out of bed and knelt, burying his head in his hands. It wasn't necessary to search for the words; they came to him naturally, and with them came the promise of forgiveness and peace. 'Lord be merciful to me, a sinner.'

It was while he was kneeling there that his mobile telephone on the bedside table broke the silence with its cheerfully incongruous tune. The sound was so unexpected, so discordant, that for five seconds he didn't recognize it. Then he got stiffly to his feet and put out his hand to answer the call.

2

Shortly before five-thirty Father Martin woke himself with a shriek of terror. He jerked up in bed and sat, rigid as a doll, staring wild-eyed into the darkness. Beads of sweat ran down his forehead and stung his eyes. Brushing them away he felt his skin taut and ice cold, as if already in the rigor of death. Gradually, as the horror of the nightmare ended, the room took shape around him. Grey forms, more imagined than seen, revealed themselves out of darkness and became comfortingly familiar; a chair, the chest of drawers, the footboard of his bed, the outline of a picture-frame. The curtains over the four circular windows were drawn but from the east he could see a thin sliver of the faint light which even on the darkest night hovered above the sea. He was aware of the storm. The wind had been rising all evening and by the time he had composed himself for sleep it was howling round the tower like a banshee. But now there was a lull more ominous than welcome and, sitting up rigidly, he listened to the silence. He heard no footfall on the stairs, no calling voice.

When the nightmares began two years earlier, he had asked to be given this small circular room in the southern tower, explaining that he liked the wide view of the sea and coast and was attracted by the silence and solitude. The stairs were becoming a tedious climb but at least he could hope that his waking screams would be unheard.

But somehow Father Sebastian had guessed the truth, or part of it. Father Martin remembered their brief conversation one Sunday after Mass.

Father Sebastian had said, 'Are you sleeping well, Father?'

'Reasonably so, thank you.'

'If you are disturbed by bad dreams I understand there is help available. I'm not thinking of counselling, not in the ordinary sense, but sometimes talking about the past with others who have suffered the same experience is said to be helpful.'

The conversation had surprised Father Martin. Father Sebastian had made no secret of his distrust of psychiatrists, saying that he would be more inclined to respect them if they could explain the medical or philosophical basis of their discipline, or could define for him the difference between the mind and the brain. But it had always surprised him how much Father Sebastian knew about what was going on under the roof of St Anselm's. The conversation had been unwelcome to Father Martin, the matter not pursued. He knew that he was not the only survivor of a Japanese prison camp who was being tormented in old age by horrors which a younger brain had been able to suppress. He had no wish to sit in a circle discussing his experiences with fellow-sufferers, although he had read that some found it helpful. This was something he had to deal with himself.

And now the wind was rising, a rhythmic moaning that rose to a howling and then screeching intensity, more a malignant manifestation than a force of nature. He urged his legs out of bed, pushed his feet into his bedroom slippers and pottered stiffly over to open the east-facing window. The cold blast was like a healing draught, cleaning his mouth and nostrils of the foetid stench of the jungle, drowning the all-too-human moans and screams with its wild cacophony, cleansing his mind of the worst of the images.

The nightmare was always the same. Rupert had been dragged back to the camp the night before and now the prisoners were lined up to watch his beheading. After what had been done to him the boy could hardly walk to the appointed place and sank to his knees as if with relief. But he made a last effort and managed to raise his head before the blade swung down. For two seconds the head remained in place, then slowly it toppled and the great red fountain spurted out like a last celebration of life. This was the image which night after night Father Martin endured.

On waking he was tortured always by the same questions. Why had Rupert tried to escape when he must have known it was suicide? Why hadn't he confided his purpose? Worst of all, why hadn't he himself stepped forward in protest before the blade fell, tried with his frail strength to seize it from the guard, and died with his friend? The love he had felt for Rupert, requited but unconsummated, had been the only love of his life. All else had been the exercise of a general benevolence or the practice of loving kindness. Despite the moments of joy, some even of a rare spiritual happiness, he carried always the darkness of that betrayal. He had no right to be alive. But there was one place where he could always find peace and he sought it now.

He took his bunch of keys from the bedside table,

shuffled over to the hook on the door and took down his old cardigan with the patches of leather on the elbows which he wore in winter under his cloak. He put the cloak over it, quietly opened the door and made his way down the stairs.

He needed no torch; a low light from a single bulb burned on each landing and the spiral staircase to the floor below, always a hazard, was kept well lit by the use of wall-mounted lights. There was a lull in the storm. The silence of the house was absolute, the muted moaning of the wind emphasizing an internal calm more portentous than the mere absence of human sounds. It was difficult to believe that there were sleepers behind the closed doors, that this silent air had ever echoed to the sound of hurrying feet and strong male voices, or that the heavy oak front door had not been closed and bolted for generations.

In the hall a single red light at the foot of the Virgin and Child cast a glow over the smiling face of the mother and touched with pink the chubby outstretched arms of the Christ-child. Wood was quickened into living flesh. He passed on his silent slippered feet across the hall and into the cloakroom. The row of brown cloaks was the first evidence of the house's occupation; they seemed to hang like forlorn relics of a long-dead generation. He could hear the wind very clearly now, and as he unlocked the door into the north cloister it rose suddenly into renewed fury.

To his surprise the light over the back door was off, as was the row of low-powered lights along the cloister. But when he stretched out his hand and pressed down the switch they came on and he could see that the stone floor was thick with leaves. Even as he closed the door behind him another gust shook the great tree and sent the drift of leaves around its trunk bowling and scurrying about his feet. They swirled about him like a flock of brown birds, pecked gently against his cheek and lay weightless as feathers on the shoulders of his cloak.

He scrunched his way to the door of the sacristy. It took a little time under the final light to identify the two keys and let himself in. He switched on the light beside the door, then punched out the code to silence the low insistent ringing of the alarm system, and went through into the body of the church. The switch for the two rows of ceiling lights over the nave was to his right and he put out his hand to press it down, then saw with a small shock of surprise but no anxiety that the spotlight which illuminated the *Doom* was on so that the west end of the church was bathed in its reflected glow. Without switching on the nave lights he moved along the north wall, his shadow moving with him on the stone.

Then he reached the *Doom* and stood transfixed at the horror that lay sprawled at his feet. The blood hadn't gone away. It was here in the very place in which he was seeking sanctuary, as red as in his nightmare, not rising like a strong feathered fountain but spread in blotches and rivulets over the stone floor. The stream was no longer moving but seemed to quiver and become viscous as he gazed. The nightmare hadn't ended. He was still trapped in a place of horror, but one which he couldn't now escape by waking. That or he was mad. He shut his eyes and prayed, 'Dear God, help me.' Then his conscious mind took hold and he opened his eyes and willed himself to look again.

His senses, unable to apprehend the whole scene in the enormity of its horror, were registering it by slow degrees, detail by detail. The smashed skull; the Archdeacon's spectacles lying a little apart but unbroken; the two brass candlesticks placed one on each side of the body as if in an act of sacrilegious contempt; the Archdeacon's hands stretched out, seeming to clutch at the stones but looking whiter, more delicate, than his hands had looked in life; the purple padded dressing-gown stiffening with his blood. Finally Father Martin raised his eyes to the *Doom*. The dancing devil in the front of the picture now wore spectacles, a moustache and a short beard, and his right arm had been elongated in a gesture of vulgar defiance. At the foot of the *Doom* was a small tin of black paint with a brush lying neatly over the lid.

Father Martin staggered forward and dropped to his knees beside the Archdeacon's head. He tried to pray but the words wouldn't come. Suddenly he needed to see other human beings, to hear human feet and human noises, to know the comfort of human companionship. Without thinking clearly he staggered to the west of the church and gave one vigorous tug on the bell pull. The bell sang out as sweetly as ever, but seeming to his ears clamorous in its dread.

Then he went to the south door and, with trembling hands, managed at last to draw back the heavy iron bolts. The wind rushed in, bringing with it a few torn leaves. He left it ajar and walked, more strongly and firmly now, back to the body. There were words he had to say and now he found the strength to say them.

He was still on his knees, the edge of his cloak trailing in the blood, when he heard footsteps and then a woman's voice. Emma knelt beside him and put her arms round his shoulders. He felt the soft brush of her hair against his cheek and could smell her sweet delicately-scented skin driving from his mind the metallic smell of the blood. He could feel her tremble but her voice was calm. She said, 'Come away, Father, come away now. It's all right.'

But it wasn't all right. It was never going to be all right again.

He tried to look up at her but couldn't raise his head; only his lips could move. He whispered, 'Oh God, what have we done, what have we done?' And then he felt her arms tighten in terror. Behind them the great south door was creaking wider open.

3

Dalgliesh usually had little difficulty in getting to sleep, even in an unfamiliar bed. Years of working as a detective had inured his body to the discomforts of a variety of couches and, provided he had a bedside light or a torch for the brief period of reading which was necessary for him before sleep came, his mind could usually let go of the day as easily as did his tired limbs. Tonight was different. His room was propitious for sleep; the bed was comfortable without being soft, the bedside lamp was at the right height for reading, the bedclothes were adequate. But he took up his copy of Seamus Heaney's translation of *Beowulf* and read the first five pages with a dogged persistence, as if this were a prescribed nightly ritual instead of a long-awaited pleasure. But soon the poetry took hold and he read steadily until eleven o'clock, then switched off the lamp and composed himself for sleep.

But tonight it didn't come. That welcome moment eluded him when the mind slips free of the burden of consciousness and sinks unafraid into its little diurnal death. Perhaps it was the fury of the wind keeping him awake. Normally he liked to lie in bed and fall asleep to the sound of a storm, but this storm was different. There would be a lull in the wind, a brief period of total anticipatory peace followed by a low moaning, rising into a howling like a chorus of demented demons. In these crescendos he could hear the great horse-chestnut groaning and had a sudden vision of snapping boughs, of the scarred trunk toppling, first as if reluctant and then in a terrifying plunge to thrust its upper branches through the bedroom window. And – always a vibrant accompaniment to the tumult of the wind – he could hear the pounding of the sea. It seemed impossible that anything living could stand up to this assault of wind and water.

In a period of calm he switched on the bedside light and looked at his watch. He was surprised to see that it was five thirty-five. So he must have slept – or at least dozed – for over six hours. He was beginning to wonder whether the storm had really spent its force when the moaning began again, and rose to another howling crescendo. In the lull that followed his ears caught a different sound, and one so familiar from childhood that he recognized it instantly: the peal of a church bell. It was a single peal, clear and sweet. For a second only he wondered if the sound was the remnant of some half-forgotten dream. Then reality took hold. He had been fully awake. He knew what he had heard. He listened intently but there was no further peal.

He acted swiftly. By long habit he never went to bed without carefully placing to hand the items he might need in an emergency. He pulled on his dressing-gown, rejected slippers in favour of shoes, and took a torch, heavy as a weapon, from his bedside table.

Leaving the apartment in darkness and guided only by the torch, he closed the front door quietly behind him, and stepped into a sudden gusting wind and a flurry of leaves which whirled round his head like a flock of frantic birds. The row of low-powered wall lights along both the north and south cloisters was sufficient only to outline the slender pillars and cast an eerie glow over the paving stones. The great house was in darkness and he saw no lights from any window except in Ambrose next door where he knew Emma was sleeping. Running past without pausing to call out to her, he felt a clutch of fear. A faint slit of light showed that the great south door of the church was ajar. The oak groaned on its hinges as he pushed it open then closed it behind him.

For a few seconds, no more, he stood transfixed by the tableau before him. There was no obstacle between him and the *Doom* and he saw it framed by two stone pillars, so brightly lit that the faded colours seemed to glow with an unimagined newly-painted richness. The shock of its black defacement paled before the greater enormity at his feet. The sprawled figure of the Archdeacon lay prone before it as if in an extremity of worship. Two heavy brass candlesticks stood ceremoniously one each side of his head. The pool of blood was surely more lusciously red than any human blood. Even the two human figures looked unreal; the white-haired priest in his spreading black cloak, kneeling and almost embracing the body, and the girl crouched beside him with an arm round his shoulder. For a moment, disorientated, he could almost imagine that the black devils had sprung from the *Doom* and were dancing round her head.

At the sound of the door she turned her head, then was instantly upright and ran towards him.

'Thank God you've come.'

She clutched at him and he knew, as he put his arms round her and felt the trembling of her body, that the gesture was an instinctive impulse of relief.

She broke free at once and said, 'It's Father Martin. I can't make him move.'

Father Martin's left arm, stretched over Crampton's body, had its palm planted in the pool of blood. Putting down his torch, Dalgliesh placed his hand on the priest's shoulder and said gently, 'It's Adam, Father. Come away now. I'm here. It's all right.'

But of course it wasn't all right. Even as he spoke the anodyne words, their falsity jarred.

Father Martin didn't move and the shoulder under Dalgliesh's touch was stiff as if locked in rigor mortis. Dalgliesh said again, more strongly: 'Let go, Father. You must come away now. There's nothing you can do here.'

And this time, as if the words had at last reached him, Father Martin allowed himself to be helped to his feet. He looked at his bloodied hand with a kind of childish wonder, then wiped it down the side of his cloak. And that, thought Dalgliesh, will complicate the examination for blood. Compassion for his companions was overlaid with more urgent preoccupations; the imperative to preserve the scene from contamination as far as possible, and the need to ensure that the method of murder was kept secret. If the south door had as usual been bolted, the killer must have come in from the sacristy and through the north cloister. Gently, and with Emma supporting the priest on his right side, he led Father Martin towards the row of chairs nearest the door.

He settled them both down and said to Emma, 'Wait here for a few minutes. I won't be long. I'll bolt the south door and go out through the sacristy. I'll lock it after me. Don't let anyone in.'

He turned to Father Martin: 'Can you hear me, Father?'

Father Martin looked up for the first time and their eyes met. The pain and horror were almost more than Dalgliesh could bear to meet.

'Yes, yes. I'm all right. I'm so sorry, Adam. I've behaved badly. I'm all right now.'

He was very far from all right, but at least he seemed able to take in what was being said.

Dalgliesh said, 'There's one thing I have to say now. I'm sorry if it sounds insensitive, the wrong time to ask, but it is important. Don't tell anyone what you have seen this morning. No one. Do you both understand that?'

They murmured a low assent, then Father Martin said more clearly, 'We understand.'

Dalgliesh was turning to go when Emma said, 'He isn't still here, is he? He isn't hiding somewhere in the church?'

'He won't be here, but I'm going to look now.'

He was unwilling to put on any more lights. Apparently only he and Emma had been woken by the church bell. The last thing he wanted was other people crowding the scene. He returned to the south door and shot its great iron bolt. Torch in hand, he made a swift but methodical examination of the church, as much for her satisfaction as his. Long experience had shown him almost immediately that this was no very recent death. He opened the gates to the two box pews and swept the torch over the seats, then knelt and looked beneath them. And here was a find. Someone had occupied the second pew. A portion of the seat was free of dust and when he knelt and shone the torch in the deep recess beneath it, it was apparent that someone had crouched there.

He ended his quick but thorough search and went back to the two seated figures. He said, 'It's all right, there's no one here but us. Is the sacristy door locked, Father?'

'Yes. Yes it is. I locked it after me.'

'Will you give me the keys, please.'

Father Martin fumbled in the pocket of his cloak and handed over a bunch. It took a little time for his shaking fingers to find the right keys.

Dalgliesh said again, 'I won't be long. I'll lock the door behind me. Will you be all right until I come back?'

Emma said, 'I don't think Father Martin ought to stay here long.'

'He won't have to.'

It should, thought Dalgliesh, take only a matter of minutes to fetch Roger Yarwood. Whichever force took on this investigation, he needed help now. There was, too, a question of protocol. Yarwood was an officer of the Suffolk Police. Until the Chief Constable decided which of his officers should take over, Yarwood would be temporarily in charge. He was relieved to find a handkerchief in his dressing-gown pocket and used this to ensure that he made no print on the sacristy door. Resetting the alarm and locking the door behind him, he plunged through a mush of fallen leaves, now inches deep in the north cloister, and hurried back to the guest apartments. Roger Yarwood, he remembered, was in Gregory.

The set was in darkness and he passed by the light of

the torch through the sitting-room and called up the stairs. There was no reply. He went up to the bedroom and found that the door was open. Yarwood had gone to bed, but now the bedclothes had been thrown back. Dalgliesh opened the door to the shower and found it was empty. He switched on the light and quickly checked the wardrobe. There was no overcoat and he could see no shoes other than Yarwood's slippers by the bed. Yarwood must at some time have walked out into the storm.

It would be pointless for him to start searching alone. Yarwood could be anywhere on the headland. Instead he went back at once to the church. Emma and Father Martin were sitting just as he had left them.

He said gently: 'Father, why don't you and Dr Lavenham go to her sitting-room. She can make some tea for you both. I expect Father Sebastian will want to speak to the whole College, but you could wait there quietly and rest for the time being.'

Father Martin looked up. His eyes held something of the piteous puzzlement of a child. He said, 'But Father Sebastian will want me.'

It was Emma who replied. 'Of course he will, but hadn't we better wait until Commander Dalgliesh has spoken to him? The best plan is to go to my sitting-room. There's everything there for making tea. I know I should like it.'

Father Martin nodded and got up. Dalgliesh said, 'Before you leave, Father, we must check whether the safe has been tampered with.'

They went into the sacristy and Dalgliesh asked for the combination. Then, with his handkerchief covering his fingers to preserve any prints which might be on the knob of the combination lock, he turned it carefully and opened the door. Inside, on top of a number of documents, was a large drawstring bag in soft leather. He took it to the desk and opened it to reveal, wrapped in white silk, two magnificent pre-Reformation jewelled chalices and a paten, a gift from the founder to St Anselm's.

Father Martin said quietly, 'Nothing is missing', and Dalgliesh returned the bag to the safe and turned the combination lock. So the motive wasn't robbery; but he hadn't for a moment supposed that it was.

He waited until Emma and Father Martin had left by the south door, then bolted it behind them and went out through the sacristy into the leaf-covered north cloister. The storm was beginning to spend its force and, although its devastation lay about him in snapped boughs and fallen leaves, the wind was abating now to little more than strong gusts. He let himself in through the north cloister door and made his way up two flights of stairs to the Warden's flat.

Father Sebastian came quickly to his knock. He was wearing a wool plaid dressing-gown but his tousled hair made him look curiously young. The two men gazed at each other. Even before he spoke Dalgliesh felt that the Warden knew the words he had come to speak. They were stark, but there was no easy or gentle way of giving this news.

He said, 'Archdeacon Crampton has been murdered. Father Martin found his body in the church immediately after half-past five this morning.'

The Warden put his hand in his pocket and drew out his wrist-watch. He said, 'And it's now just after six. Why wasn't I told earlier?'

'Father Martin rang the church bell to raise the alarm and I heard it. So did Dr Lavenham who was first on the scene. There were things I had to do. And now I must phone the Suffolk Police.'

'But isn't this a matter initially for Inspector Yarwood?'

'It would be. Yarwood is missing. May I use your office, Father?'

'Of course. I'll put on some clothes and join you. Does anyone else know of this?'

'Not yet, Father.'

'Then I must be the one to tell them.'

He closed the door and Dalgliesh made his way to the office on the floor below.

4

The Suffolk number he needed was in the wallet in his room, but after a couple of seconds' thought, he was able to recall it. Once his identity was established he was given the Chief Constable's number. After that it was quick and simple. He was dealing with men not unused to being woken with the need for decision and action. He reported fully but briefly; nothing needed to be said twice.

There was a silence of some five seconds before the Chief Constable spoke: 'Yarwood disappearing is a major complication. Alred Treeves is another, but less important. Still, I don't see how we can take this on. We can't waste time. The first three days are always the most vital. I'll speak to the Commissioner. But you'll want a search party?'

'Not yet. Yarwood may just have wandered off. He may even have returned by now. If not I'll get some of the students here to search at first light. I'll report when there's any news. If he's not found you'd better take over.'

'Right. Your own people will confirm, but I think you'd better assume that the case is yours. I'll discuss details with the Met but I imagine you'll want your own team.'

'That would be simpler.'

It was only then that, pausing again, the Chief

Constable said, 'I know something of St Anselm's. They're good people. Will you give Father Sebastian my sympathy. This is going to hurt them in more ways than one.'

In another five minutes the Yard had rung with the details which had been agreed. Dalgliesh would take the case. Detective Inspectors Kate Miskin and Piers Tarrant with Sergeant Robbins were on their way by car and the supporting team, a photographer and three scene-of-crime officers, would follow. Since Dalgliesh was already there, it wasn't considered necessary to incur the expense of a helicopter. The team would arrive by train at Ipswich and the Suffolk Police would arrange transport to the college. Dr Kynaston, the forensic pathologist with whom Dalgliesh usually worked, was already at a crime scene and likely to be tied up for the rest of the day. The local Home Office pathologist was on leave in New York but his substitute, Dr Mark Ayling, was on call and available. It would seem sensible to use him. Any urgent material for forensic examination could go either to the Huntingdon or to the Lambeth lab, depending on their workloads.

Father Sebastian had tactfully waited in the outer office while Dalgliesh was telephoning. Hearing that the conversation seemed finally to have ended, he came in and said, 'I should like now to go to the church. You have your responsibilities, Commander, but I have mine.'

Dalgliesh said, 'It's urgent first to get a search started for Roger Yarwood. Who is your most sensible ordinand for this kind of job?'

'Stephen Morby. I suggest he and Pilbeam take the Land Rover.'

He went to the telephone on his desk. It was quickly answered.

'Good morning, Pilbeam. Are you dressed? Good. Would you please wake Mr Morby and both of you come to my office immediately.'

The wait was not long before Dalgliesh heard footsteps hurrying up the stairs. A pause at the door and the two men came in.

He hadn't before seen Pilbeam. The man was tall, certainly over six foot, strongly built and thick-necked with a tanned and rugged country face under thinning straw-coloured hair. Dalgliesh thought that there was something familiar about him, then realized that he was remarkably like an actor whose name he couldn't recall but who frequently appeared in war films in the supporting role of inarticulate but dependable NCO who invariably died uncomplainingly in the last reel to the greater glory of the hero.

He stood waiting, totally at ease. Beside him Stephen Morby – no weakling – looked a boy. It was to Pilbeam that Father Sebastian spoke.

'Mr Yarwood is missing. I'm afraid he may have gone wandering again.'

'It was a bad night for wandering, Father.'

'Exactly. He may return any minute but I don't think we should wait. I want you and Mr Morby to take the Land Rover and look for him. Your mobile phone is working?'

'It is, Father.'

'Ring at once if there's any news. If he's not on the headland or near the mere don't waste time going further. It may then be a matter for the police. And Pilbeam . . .'

'Yes, Father.'

'When you and Mr Morby return, whether or not with Mr Yarwood, report at once to me without speaking to anyone else. That goes for you too, Stephen. Do you understand?'

'Yes, Father.'

Stephen Morby said, 'Something's happened, hasn't it? Something more than Mr Yarwood wandering off.'

'I shall explain when you return. You may not be able to do much until full light but I want you to get started. Take torches, blankets and hot coffee. And Pilbeam, I shall be speaking to the whole community at seven-thirty in the library. Will you ask your wife to be good enough to join us.'

'Yes, Father.'

They went out. Father Sebastian said, 'They're both sensible. If Yarwood is on the headland they'll find him. I thought it right to delay explanation until they return.'

'I think that was wise.'

It was becoming apparent that Father Sebastian's natural authoritarianism was quickly adjusting to unfamiliar circumstances. Dalgliesh reflected that to have a suspect taking an active part in the investigation was a novelty he could well dispense with. The situation would need careful handling.

The Warden said, 'You were right, of course. Finding Yarwood has priority. But now, perhaps, I may go where I should be, at the Archdeacon's side.'

'Some questions first, Father. How many keys to the church and who holds them?'

'Is this really necessary now?'

'Yes, Father. As you said, you have your responsibilities and I have mine.'

'And yours must take precedence?'

'For the present, yes.'

Father Sebastian was careful to keep his impatience out of his voice. He said, 'There are seven sets comprising the two keys to the sacristy door, one a security Chubb and one a Yale. The south door has bolts only. Each of the four resident priests holds a set, the other three are in the key cupboard next door in Miss Ramsey's office. It is necessary to keep the church locked because of the value of the altar-piece and silver but all ordinands may sign for the keys if they need to go to the church. The students, not the domestic staff, are responsible for the cleaning.'

'And the staff and visitors?'

'They only have access to the church when accompanied by a key-holder except during the times of the services. As we have four services a day, Morning Prayer, the Eucharist, Evening Prayer and Compline, they are hardly deprived. I dislike the restriction, but it is the price we pay for keeping the van der Weyden over the altar. The problem is that the young are not always conscientious about resetting the alarm. All the staff and the visitors have keys to the iron gate leading from the west court out to the headland.'

'And who in college will know the code for the alarm system?'

'I imagine everyone. We are guarding our treasures against intruders, not against each other.'

'What keys do the ordinands have?'

'They each have two keys, one to the iron gate which

is their usual mode of entrance, and one to the door either in the north or south cloister depending on the situation of their rooms. None of them has keys to the church.'

'And Ronald Treeves's keys were returned here after his death?'

'Yes. They're in a drawer in Miss Ramsey's office, but he didn't of course have keys to the church. And now I wish to go to the Archdeacon.'

'Of course. On the way, Father, we can check if the three spare sets of keys to the church are in the key cupboard.'

Father Sebastian didn't reply. As they passed through the outer office he went over to a narrow cupboard to the left of the fireplace. It was not locked. Inside were two rows of hooks holding named keys. There were three hooks on the first row labelled CHURCH. One was empty.

Dalgliesh said, 'Can you remember when you last saw the church keys, Father?'

Father Sebastian thought for a moment and said, 'I think it was yesterday morning before lunch. Some paint was delivered for Surtees to paint the sacristy. Pilbeam came in to collect a set of keys and I was here in the office when he signed for them, and still here when he returned them less than five minutes later.'

He went to the right drawer in Miss Ramsey's desk and drew out a book. 'I think you'll find here that this was the last entry for the keys. As you see, he held them for no more than five minutes. But the last person to see them would have been Henry Bloxham. He was responsible for making the church ready for Compline last night. I was here when he collected a set of keys and in my office next door when he returned them. If there had been a set missing he would have said so.'

'Did you actually see him return the keys, Father?'

'No. I was in my office but the door between the rooms was open and he called good-night. There will be no entry in the key book. Ordinands who collect the keys before a service are not required to sign it. And now, Commander, I must insist that we go to the church.'

The house was still in silence. They passed without speaking over the tessellated floor of the hall. Father Sebastian was moving towards the door through the cloakroom, but Dalgliesh said, 'We'll avoid the north cloister as far as possible.'

Nothing more was said until they reached the sacristy door. Father Sebastian fumbled for his keys, but Dalgliesh said, 'I'll do this, Father.'

He unlocked the door, locked it after them, and they passed into the church. He had left on the light over the *Doom* and the horror at its foot was clearly visible. Father Sebastian's steps didn't falter as he moved towards it. He didn't speak, but looked first at the desecration of the painting and then down at his dead adversary. Then he made the sign of the cross and knelt in silent prayer. Watching him, Dalgliesh wondered what words Father Sebastian was finding to communicate with his God. He could hardly be praying for the Archdeacon's soul; that would have been anathema to Crampton's uncompromising Protestantism.

He wondered, too, what words he would find appropriate if he were praying at this moment. 'Help me to solve this case with the least pain to the innocent, and protect my team.' The last time he remembered having prayed with passion and with the belief that his prayer was valid had been when his wife was dying, and it had not been heard – or, if heard, had not been answered. He thought about death, its finality, its inevitability. Was part of the attraction of his job the illusion it gave that death was a mystery that could be solved, and with the solution all the unruly passions of life, all doubts and all fears could be folded away like a garment.

And then he heard Father Sebastian speaking as if he had become aware of Dalgliesh's silent presence and needed to involve him, even if only as a listener in his secret ministry of expiation. The familiar words spoken in his beautiful voice were an affirmation not a prayer and they so uncannily echoed Dalgliesh's thoughts that he heard them as if for the first time, and with a *frisson* of awe.

'And thou, Lord, in the beginning has laid the foundation of the earth; and the heavens are the works of thine hands: they shall perish, but thou remainest; and they all shall wax old as doth a garment; and as a vesture shalt thou fold them up, and they shall be changed; but thou art the same, and thy years shall not fail.'

5

Dalgliesh shaved, showered and dressed with practised speed, and by twenty-five minutes past seven had again joined the Warden in his office. Father Sebastian looked at his wrist-watch. 'It's time to go to the library. I'll say a few words first and then you can take over. Is that acceptable?'

'Perfectly.'

It was the first time on this visit that Dalgliesh had been in the library. Father Sebastian switched on a series of lights which curved down over the shelves and immediately memory came rushing back of long summer evenings reading here under the sightless eyes of the busts ranged along the top of the shelves, of the western sun burnishing the leather spines and throwing gules of coloured light over polished wood, of long evenings when the boom of the sea seemed to strengthen with the dying light. But now the high barrelled ceiling was in gloom and the stained glass in the pointed windows was a black void patterned with lead.

Along the northern wall a row of bookshelves jutting at right angles between the windows formed cubicles, each with a double reading desk and chair. Father Sebastian went to the nearest cubicle, swung up two chairs and placed them together in the middle of the room. He said, 'We'll need four chairs, three for the women and one for Peter Buckhurst. He's not yet strong enough to stand for long – not that this will take long, I imagine. There's no point in putting out a chair for Father John's sister. She's elderly and hardly ever shows herself outside their flat.'

Without replying, Dalgliesh helped to carry the last two chairs and Father Sebastian arranged them in line, then stood back as if assessing the accuracy of their placement.

There was the sound of soft footfalls across the hall and the three ordinands, all wearing their black cassocks, came in together as if by prior arrangement and took their stand behind the chairs. They stood upright and very still, their faces set and pale, their eyes fixed on Father Sebastian. The tension they brought into the room was palpable.

They were followed in less than a minute by Mrs Pilbeam and Emma. Father Sebastian indicated the chairs with a gesture and without speaking the two women sat down, leaning a little towards each other as if there could be comfort even in the slight touch of a shoulder. Mrs Pilbeam, in recognition of the importance of the occasion, had taken off her white working overall and looked incongruously festive in a green woollen skirt and pale blue blouse adorned with a large brooch at the neck. Emma was very pale but had taken care in dressing, as if attempting to impose order and normality on the disruption of murder. Her brown low-heeled shoes were highly polished and she wore fawn corduroy trousers, a cream blouse which looked freshly ironed, and a leather jerkin.

Father Sebastian said to Buckhurst, 'Won't you sit, Peter?'

'I'd rather stand, Father.'

'I'd prefer you to sit.'

Without further demur Peter Buckhurst took the seat beside Emma.

Next came the three priests. Father John and Father Peregrine stood one at each end of the ordinands. Father Martin, as if recognizing an unspoken invitation, came and stood beside Father Sebastian.

Father John said, 'I'm afraid my sister is still asleep and I didn't like to wake her. If she's needed, perhaps she could be seen later?'

Dalgliesh murmured, 'Of course.' He saw Emma look at Father Martin with loving concern and half rise in her chair. He thought, she's kind as well as clever and beautiful. His heart lurched, a sensation as unfamiliar as it was unwelcome. He thought, Oh God, not that complication. Not now. Not ever.

And still they waited. Seconds lengthened into minutes before they again heard footsteps. The door opened and George Gregory entered, closely followed by Clive Stannard. Stannard had either overslept or had seen no reason to inconvenience himself. He had put on his trousers and a tweed jacket over his pyjamas and the striped cotton showed plainly at his neck and was ruched over his shoes. Gregory, in contrast, had dressed with care, his shirt and tie immaculate.

Gregory said, 'I'm sorry if I've kept you waiting. I dislike putting on my clothes before I've showered.'

He took his stand behind Emma and rested his hand on the back of her chair, then quietly slid it away, apparently feeling the gesture had been inappropriate. His eyes, fixed on Father Sebastian, were wary but

Dalgliesh thought he detected a hint of amused curiosity. Stannard was, he thought, frankly frightened and attempting to conceal it by a nonchalance which was as contrived as it was embarrassing.

He said, 'Isn't it a bit early for drama? I take it that something's happened. Hadn't we better know?'

No one replied. The door opened again and the last arrivals came in. Eric Surtees was in his working clothes. He hesitated at the door and cast a look of puzzled inquiry at Dalgliesh as if surprised to find him present. Karen Surtees, bright as a parrot in a long red sweater over green trousers, had taken time only to apply a coat of bright red lipstick. Her eyes, denuded of make-up, looked drained and full of sleep. After a moment's hesitation she took the vacant chair and her brother moved behind her. All those summoned were now present. Dalgliesh thought that they looked like an ill-assorted wedding group, reluctantly posing for an over-enthusiastic photographer.

Father Sebastian said, 'Let us pray.'

The exhortation was unexpected. Only the priests and the ordinands responded instinctively by bowing their heads and clasping their hands. The women seemed uncertain what was expected of them but, after a glance at Father Martin, stood up. Emma and Mrs Pilbeam bowed their heads and Karen Surtees stared at Dalgliesh with belligerent disbelief as if holding him personally responsible for the embarrassing débâcle. Gregory, smiling, stared straight ahead and Stannard frowned and shifted his feet. Father Sebastian spoke the words of the Morning Collect. He paused and then said the prayer which he had spoken at Compline some ten hours earlier.

'Visit, we beseech thee, O Lord, this place, and drive from it all the snares of the enemy; let thy holy angels dwell herein to preserve us in peace; and may thy blessing be upon us evermore; through Jesus Christ our Lord. Amen.'

There was a chorus of 'Amen', subdued from the women, more confident from the ordinands, and the group stirred. It was less a movement than a release of breath. Dalgliesh thought: They know now, of course they know. But one of them has known from the beginning. The women again sat down. Dalgliesh felt the intensity of the gaze fixed on the Warden. When he began speaking, his voice was calm and almost expressionless.

'Last night a great evil came into our community. Archdeacon Crampton has been brutally murdered in the church. His body was discovered by Father Martin at five-thirty this morning. Commander Dalgliesh, who was here as our guest on another matter, is still our guest but is now among us as a police officer investigating a murder. It will be our duty as well as our wish to give him every possible assistance by answering his questions fully and honestly and by doing nothing either by word or action to hinder the police or to make them feel that their presence here is unwelcome. I have telephoned those ordinands who are away this weekend and deferred for a week those due to return this morning. Those of us now here must try to continue the life and work of the college while co-operating fully with the police. I have put St Matthew's Cottage at Mr Dalgliesh's disposal and the police will be working from there. At Mr Dalgliesh's request the church and the access to the north cloister are both closed, as is the cloister itself.

Mass will be said in the oratory at the usual time and all services will be held there until the church has been reopened and made ready for divine service. The Archdeacon's death is now a matter for the police. Don't speculate, don't gossip among yourselves. Murder, of course, cannot be kept hidden. Inevitably this news will break, in the Church and in the wider world. I would ask you not to telephone or communicate the news in any way outside these walls. We can hope for at least one day of peace. If there are any matters worrying you, Father Martin and I are here.' He paused and then added, 'As always. And now I will ask Mr Dalgliesh to take over.'

His audience had listened in almost total silence. Only at the sonorous word *murdered* did Dalgliesh hear a quick intake of breath and a frail cry quickly suppressed which he thought came from Mrs Pilbeam. Raphael, white-faced, was so rigid that Dalgliesh feared he was about to keel over. Eric Surtees shot a terrified glance at his sister then looked quickly away and fixed his eyes on Father Sebastian. Gregory was frowning in intense concentration. The still cold air was charged with fear. Apart from Surtees's glance at his sister, none of them met each other's eyes. Perhaps, thought Dalgliesh, they were afraid of what they might see.

Dalgliesh was interested that Father Sebastian had made no mention of the absence of Yarwood, Pilbeam and Stephen Morby, and was grateful for his discretion. He decided to be brief. It wasn't his habit when investigating murder to apologize for the inconvenience caused; inconvenience to those involved was the least of murder's contaminating evils.

He said, 'It has been agreed that the Metropolitan Police shall take over this case. A small team of police officers and support services will be arriving this morning. As Father Sebastian has said, the church is closed, as is the north cloister and the door leading from the house to that cloister. I myself or one of my officers will be speaking to you all some time today. However, it would save time if we could establish one fact at once. Did anyone here leave his or her room last night after Compline? Did anyone go near or into the church? Did any of you see or hear anything last night that could have had a bearing on this crime?'

There was silence, then Henry said, 'I went out just after ten-thirty for some air and exercise. I walked briskly about five times round the cloisters and then went back to my room. I'm Number Two on the south cloister. I saw and heard nothing unusual. The wind was getting up strongly by then and blowing showers of leaves into the north cloister. That's chiefly what I remember.'

Dalgliesh said, 'You were the ordinand who lit the candles in church before Compline and opened the south door. Did you fetch the church key from the outer office?'

'Yes. I fetched it just before the service and returned it afterwards. There were three keys when I collected it, and three after I had taken it back.'

Dalgliesh said, 'I'll ask again. Did any of you leave your room after Compline?'

He waited for a moment but there was no response. He went on, 'I shall want to see the shoes and clothes that you were wearing yesterday evening and it will later be necessary to take the fingerprints of everyone in

St Anselm's for the purposes of elimination. I think that's all for the present.'

Again there was a silence, then Gregory spoke. 'A question for Mr Dalgliesh. Three people seem to be missing, among them an officer of the Suffolk Police. Is there any significance in that fact, I mean for the thrust of the investigation?'

Dalgliesh said, 'At present, none.'

This breaking of the silence provoked Stannard into querulous speech. He said, 'Can I ask why the Commander is assuming that this must be what I think the police describe as an inside job? While we are having clothes examined and fingerprints taken, the person responsible is probably miles away. After all, this place is hardly secure. I for one don't intend to sleep here tonight without a lock on my door.'

Father Sebastian said, 'Your concern is natural. I'm arranging for locks to be fitted to your room and to the four guest sets and keys to be provided.'

'And what about my question? Why the assumption that it must have been one of us?'

It was the first time that this possibility had been spoken aloud and it seemed to Dalgliesh that everyone present was determined to stare ahead as if any glance might convey an accusation. He said, 'No assumptions are being made.'

Father Sebastian said, 'The closing of the north cloister will mean that ordinands with rooms there will have temporarily to vacate them. With so many students absent, that applies at present only to you, Raphael. If you will hand over your keys, a key to room 3 in the south cloister and to the south corridor door will be given in exchange.'

'What about my things, Father, books and clothes? Can't I fetch them?'

'You must manage without them for the present. Your fellow students will be able to lend you what you need. I can't emphasize too strongly the importance of keeping away from any area which the police have put out of bounds.'

Without another word Raphael took a bunch of keys from his pocket, detached two and, stepping forward, handed them to Father Sebastian.

Dalgliesh said, 'I understand that all the resident priests have keys to the church. Could you please check now that they are in your possession?'

Father Betterton spoke for the first time. 'I'm afraid I haven't my keys with me. I always leave them on a chair by my bed.'

Dalgliesh still had Father Martin's bunch of keys which he had taken in the church, and now he moved to the other two priests, checking that the church keys were still on their rings.

He turned to Father Sebastian, who said, 'I think that's all that needs to be said at present. The timetable set up for today will be kept as far as possible. There will be no Morning Prayer but I propose to say Mass in the oratory at midday. Thank you.'

He turned and walked steadily out of the room. There was a shuffling of feet. The little company looked at each other and then, one by one, made for the door.

Dalgliesh had switched off his mobile telephone during the meeting, but now it rang. It was Stephen Morby.

'Commander Dalgliesh? We've found Inspector Yarwood. He'd fallen into a ditch about half-way down the approach road. I tried to ring earlier but couldn't get through. He's been partly lying in water and he's unconscious. We think he's broken a leg. We didn't like to move him because of making the injury worse, but we felt we couldn't leave him where he was. We got him out as carefully as we could and rang for an ambulance. He's being loaded into it now. They're taking him to Ipswich Hospital.'

Dalgliesh said, 'You did the right thing. How bad is he?'

'The paramedics think he should be all right but he hasn't regained consciousness. I'm going with him in the ambulance. I'll be able to tell you more when I get back. Mr Pilbeam is driving behind us so I'll come back with him.'

Dalgliesh said, 'Right. Be as quick as you can. You're both needed here.'

He gave the news to Father Sebastian. The Warden said, 'It's what I feared had happened. This has been the pattern of his illness. I understand it's a kind of claustrophobia and when it comes on him he has to get into the open air and walk. After his wife left him, taking the children, he used to disappear for days. Sometimes he walked until he collapsed and the police found him and brought him back. Thank God he's been found and, it seems, in time. And now perhaps, if you'll come to the study, we can discuss what you and your colleagues will need in St Matthew's Cottage.'

'Later, Father. I need first to see the Bettertons.'

'I think Father John went back to their flat. It's on the third floor on the north side. No doubt he'll be looking out for you.'

Father Sebastian had been too shrewd to speculate aloud about Yarwood's possible implication in the murder. But surely Christian charity only extended so far. With part of his mind he must have hoped that here was the best possible outcome: a killing by a man temporarily not responsible for his actions. And if Yarwood didn't survive, he would always remain a suspect. His death could be very convenient for someone.

Before making his way to the Bettertons' flat, Dalgliesh went back to his own apartment and rang the Chief Constable.

6

There was a bell beside the narrow oak door to the Bettertons' flat but Dalgliesh had barely pressed it before Father John appeared and ushered him in.

He said, 'If you wouldn't mind just waiting a moment, I'll fetch my sister. I think she's in the kitchen. We have a very small kitchen here in the flat and she prefers to eat separately rather than join the community for meals. I won't be a moment.'

The room in which Dalgliesh found himself was low-ceilinged but large with four ogee-shaped windows facing the sea. The room was over-furnished with what looked like the relics of earlier homes; low padded chairs with button backs, a sofa with a sagging seat facing the fireplace, its back covered with a throw in Indian cotton; a round central table in solid mahogany with six chairs discordant in age and style; a pedestal desk set between two of the windows; an assortment of small tables each laden with the miscellany of two long lives – photographs in silver frames, some porcelain figures, boxes in wood and silver and a bowl of pot-pourri whose stale and dusty perfume had long since spent itself on the stuffy air.

The wall to the left of the door was completely covered with a bookcase. Here was the library of Father John's youth, student days and priesthood, but there was also a row of black-covered volumes labelled *Plays of the Year*, dating back from the 30s and 40s. Beside them was a row of paperback detective stories. Dalgliesh saw that Father John was addicted to the women writers of the Golden Age: Dorothy L. Sayers, Margery Allingham and Ngaio Marsh. To the right of the door was propped a golf bag holding some half-dozen clubs. It was an incongruous object to find in a room which bore no other evidence of interest in sport.

The pictures were as varied as the other artefacts: Victorian oils, highly sentimental in subject but competent in execution, floral prints, a couple of samplers and water-colours which were probably the work of Victorian forebears – they looked too good to be the work of amateurs but not good enough for professionals. But despite the gloom the room was too obviously lived in, too idiosyncratic and too comfortable to be depressing. The two high-backed armchairs each side of the fire had beside them a table with an anglepoise lamp. Here brother and sister, facing each other, could sit and read in comfort.

As soon as Miss Betterton entered, Dalgliesh was struck by the odd disparity produced by the eccentric patterning of family genes. At first sight it was difficult to believe that the two Bettertons were closely related. Father John was short with a compact body and a gentle face which wore an air of perpetual anxious puzzlement. His sister was at least six inches taller with an angular body and sharp suspicious eyes. Only the similarity of the long-lobed ears, the droop of the eyelids and the small pursed mouths proclaimed any family likeness. She looked considerably older than her brother. Her steel-grey hair was pulled back into a pleat anchored to the top of her head by a comb from which the ends of her dry hair stuck out like an ornamental frieze. She was wearing a skirt in thin tweed almost to the floor, a striped shirt which looked as if it were one of her brother's, and a long fawn cardigan in which the moth-holes in the sleeves were clearly visible.

Father John said, 'Agatha, this is Commander Dalgliesh from New Scotland Yard.'

'A policeman?'

Dalgliesh put out his hand. He said, 'Yes, Miss Betterton, I'm a policeman.'

The hand which, after a second's delay, was pressed into his hand was cool and so thin that he could feel every bone.

She said, in that fluting upper-class voice which those who don't possess it find difficult to believe can ever be natural, 'I'm afraid you've come to the wrong place, my man. We haven't any dogs here.'

'Mr Dalgliesh doesn't have anything to do with dogs, Agatha.'

'I thought you said he was a dog handler.'

'No, I said Commander not dog handler.'

'Well we haven't any ships either.' She turned to Dalgliesh. 'Cousin Raymond was a Commander in the last war. The Royal Navy Volunteer Reserve, not the proper Navy. The Wavy Navy I believe they called them because of the wavy gold stripes on their sleeves. He got killed anyway so it made no difference. You may have noticed his golf clubs beside the door. One cannot imbue a niblick with much sentiment but one is reluctant to part with the clubs. Why aren't you in uniform, Mr Dalgliesh? I like to see a man in uniform. A cassock is not the same.'

'I'm a police commander, Miss Betterton. It's a rank peculiar to the Metropolitan Police, nothing to do with the Navy.'

Father John, obviously feeling that the dialogue had gone on long enough, interposed. His voice was kind but firm. 'Agatha dear, something very terrible has happened. I want you to listen carefully and stay very calm. Archdeacon Crampton has been found murdered. That's why Commander Dalgliesh needs to talk to you, to all of us. We must help him in any way we can to find out who was responsible for this terrible act.'

His exhortation to stay calm was unnecessary. Miss Betterton received the news without a flicker either of surprise or distress.

She turned to Dalgliesh. 'So you did need a sniffer dog after all. A pity you didn't think to bring one. Where was he murdered? I speak of the Archdeacon.'

'In the church, Miss Betterton.'

'Father Sebastian won't like that. Hadn't you better tell him?'

Her brother said, 'He has been told, Agatha. Everyone has.'

'Well he won't be missed, not in this house. He was an extremely unpleasant man, Commander. I refer to the Archdeacon, of course. I could explain to you why I take this view, but these are confidential family matters. You will understand, I'm sure. You look an intelligent and discreet officer. I expect that comes with being ex-Navy. Some people are better dead. I won't explain why the Archdeacon is among them but you can be assured that the world will be a more agreeable place without him. But you will have to do something about the body. It can't stay in the church. Father Sebastian wouldn't like that at all. What about the services? Won't it be in the way? I shan't attend, of course, I'm not a religious woman, but my brother does and I don't think he would like to walk over the Archdeacon's body. Whatever our private opinions of the man, that would not be agreeable.'

Dalgliesh said, 'The body will be moved, Miss Betterton, but the church will have to remain closed at least for a few days. I have some questions I need to ask you. Did either you or your brother leave your apartment here at any time after Compline yesterday?'

'And why should we wish to do that, Commander?'

'That's what I'm asking you, Miss Betterton. Did either of you leave the apartment after ten last night?'

He looked from one to the other. Father John said, 'Eleven o'clock is our bedtime. I didn't leave the flat after Compline or later and I'm sure Agatha didn't. Why should she?'

'Would either of you have heard if the other had left?'

It was Miss Betterton who replied, 'Of course not. We don't lie awake wondering what the other is doing. My brother is perfectly at liberty to wander about the house at night if he wishes, but I can't see why he should. I expect you're wondering, Commander, whether either of us killed the Archdeacon. I'm not a fool. I know where all this is leading. Well I didn't, and I don't suppose my brother did. He is not a man of action.'

Father John, visibly distressed, was vehement. 'Of course I didn't, Agatha. How can you think that.'

'I wasn't thinking it. The Commander was.' She

turned to Dalgliesh. 'The Archdeacon was going to turn us out. He told me. Out of this flat.'

Father John said, 'He couldn't do that, Agatha. You must have misunderstood him.'

Dalgliesh asked, 'When did this happen, Miss Betterton?'

'The last time the Archdeacon was here. It was a Monday morning. I went to the piggery to see if Surtees had any vegetables he could let me have. He's really very helpful when one runs out. I was just walking away when I met the Archdeacon. I expect he was coming to get some free vegetables too, or perhaps he wanted to see the pigs. I recognized him at once. Of course I didn't expect to see him and I may have been a little sharp in my greeting. I'm not a hypocrite, I don't believe in pretending to like people. As I'm not religious, I don't have to exercise Christian charity. And no one told me he was visiting the college. Why can't I be told these things? I wouldn't have known he was here now if Raphael Arbuthnot hadn't told me.'

She turned to Dalgliesh. 'I expect you've met Raphael Arbuthnot. He's a delightful boy and very clever. He has supper with us occasionally and we read a play together. He could have been an actor if the priests hadn't got hold of him. He can take any part and mimic every voice. It's a remarkable skill.'

Father John said, 'My sister is fond of the theatre. She and Raphael go up to London once a term for a morning's shopping, lunch and a matinée.'

Miss Betterton said, 'I think it means a lot to him, getting out of this place. But I'm afraid I don't hear as well as I used to. Actors today aren't trained to project their voices. Mumble, mumble, mumble. Do you think they have classes in mumbling at drama school and sit in a circle mumbling at each other? Even if we sit in the front of the stalls it's sometimes quite difficult. Of course I don't complain to Raphael. I wouldn't wish to hurt his feelings.'

Dalgliesh said gently, 'But what exactly did the Archdeacon say to you when you thought he was threatening to have you evicted from your apartment?'

'It was something about people being too ready to live off church funds and give little or nothing in return.'

Father John broke in. 'He wouldn't have said that, Agatha. Are you sure you're remembering correctly?'

'He may not have used those precise words, John, but that's what he meant. And then he said that I shouldn't take it for granted that I could stay here for the rest of my life. I understood him perfectly well. He was threatening to get us out.'

Father John, distressed, said, 'But he couldn't, Agatha. He hadn't the power.'

'That's what Raphael said when I told him about it. We were talking about it the last time he was here for supper. I said to Raphael, if he could get my brother put in prison, he can do anything. Raphael said, "Oh no he can't. I'll stop him."'

Father John, in despair at the way the interview was going, had moved over to the window. He said, 'There's a motorcycle coming along the coast road. How very odd. I don't think we're expecting anyone this morning. Perhaps it's a visitor for you, Commander.'

Dalgliesh moved beside him. He said, 'I shall have to leave you now, Miss Betterton. Thank you for your co-operation. I may have some other questions, and if so I will ask what time would be convenient for you to see me. And now, Father, could I please see your bunch of keys?'

Father John disappeared and returned almost immediately holding his key ring. Dalgliesh compared the two church keys with the ones on Father Martin's ring. He said, 'Where did you leave these keys last night, Father?'

'In the usual place, on my bedside table. I always leave the keys there at night.'

As he left, leaving Father John with his sister, he glanced at the golf clubs. The heads were uncovered, the metal of the irons shone clean. The mental picture was uncomfortably clear and convincing. It would need someone with a good eye, and there would be the difficulty of concealing the club until the moment had come to strike, the moment when the Archdeacon's attention was fixed on the vandalized *Doom*. But was that a problem? It could have been propped against the rear of a pillar. And with a weapon of that length there would be much less risk of bloodstains. He had a sudden and vivid picture of a fair-haired young man waiting motionless in the shadows, club in hand. The Archdeacon would not have left his bed and gone to the church if summoned by Raphael, but here was a young man who, on Miss Betterton's evidence, could mimic anyone's voice.

7

Dr Mark Ayling's arrival was as surprising as it was unexpectedly early. Dalgliesh was moving down the stairs from the Bettertons' flat when he heard the motor-cycle roaring into the courtyard. Pilbeam had unlocked the great door as he did each morning, and Dalgliesh stepped out into the half-light of a fresh-smelling day which, after the tumult of the night, held an exhausted calm. Even the thud of the sea was muted. The powerful machine circled the courtyard then came to a stop immediately in front of the main entrance. The rider removed his helmet, unstrapped a case from the pannier and, carrying his helmet under his left arm, came bound-ing up the steps with the insouciance of a motorbike courier delivering a routine package.

He said, 'Mark Ayling. Body in the church, is it?'

'Adam Dalgliesh. Yes, it's this way. We'll go through the house and out by the south door. I've secured the door from the house into the north cloister.'

The hall was empty and it seemed to Dalgliesh that Dr Ayling's feet rang unnaturally heavily on the tessellated floor. The pathologist could not be expected to sneak in but this was hardly a tactful arrival. He wondered whether he ought to have found Father Sebastian and effected an introduction, but decided against it. This wasn't, after all, a social call and the least delay the better. But he had no doubt that the pathologist's arrival had been noticed, and as they paced down the passage-way past the cellar steps to the south cloister door he had an uncomfortable if irrational feeling that he was guilty of a breach of good manners. To carry out a murder investigation in an atmosphere of barely suppressed non-co-operation and antagonism was, he reflected, less complicated than coping with the social and theological nuances of this present scene of crime.

They crossed the courtyard beneath the half-denuded boughs of the great horse-chestnut and came to the sacristy door without speaking.

As Dalgliesh unlocked it, Ayling asked, 'Where can I change my gear?'

'In here. It's part-vestry, part-office.'

Changing 'gear' apparently meant divesting himself of his leathers, putting on a brown three-quarter-length overall and exchanging his boots for soft slippers over which he drew white cotton socks.

As he locked the sacristy door behind them, Dalgliesh said, 'It's likely that the murderer came in by this door. I'm securing the church until the SOCOs arrive from London.'

Ayling disposed of his leathers tidily on the swivel chair in front of the desk and placed his boots neatly side by side. He asked, 'Why the Met? It's a Suffolk case.'

'There's a Suffolk DI staying in college at present. It makes a complication. I was here on another matter so it seemed sensible for me to take over for the present.'

The explanation appeared to satisfy Ayling.

They passed into the body of the church. The nave lights were dim, but sufficient, presumably, for a congregation who knew the liturgy by heart. They moved down to the *Doom*. Dalgliesh put up his hand to the spotlight. In the surrounding incense-laden gloom, which seemed in imagination to stretch beyond the church walls into an infinity of blackness, the beam blazed down with a shocking brilliance, brighter even than Dalgliesh remembered. Perhaps, he thought, it was the presence of another person that transformed the scene into an act of Grand Guignol; the actor's carefully arranged body lying still with practised art, the inspired touch of the two candlesticks placed at its head, himself a silent watcher in the shadow of the pillar, waiting for his cue.

Ayling, frozen momentarily into stillness by the unexpected glare, could have been assessing the effectiveness of the theatrical tableau. When he began his soft-footed prowl around the body he looked like a director assessing the camera angles, satisfying himself that the death pose was both realistic and artistically pleasing. Dalgliesh noticed details with greater clarity: the scuffed toe of the black leather slipper which had fallen from Crampton's right foot, how large and peculiar the naked foot now seemed, how ugly and elongated the big toe. With the face partly invisible, that single foot, now forever stilled, assumed a potency greater than if the body had been naked, provoking an upsurge of both pity and outrage.

Dalgliesh had met Crampton only briefly and had felt in his presence no more than a mild resentment at an unexpected and not particularly congenial guest. But now he felt as strong an anger as he had ever experienced at a murder scene. He found himself echoing words which were familiar although their precise source eluded him: 'Who hath done this thing?' He would discover the answer, and when he did, this time he would also find the proof, this time he would not close the file knowing the identity of the culprit, the motive and the means, but powerless to make an arrest. The burden of that past failure was still heavy upon him but with this case it would at last be lifted.

Ayling was still prowling cautiously round the body, never lifting his eyes from it, as if he had encountered some interesting but unusual phenomenon and was uncertain how it might react to scrutiny. Then he squatted by the head, sniffed delicately at the wound, and said, 'Who is he?'

'I'm sorry. I hadn't realized that you hadn't been told. Archdeacon Crampton. He's a recently-appointed trustee of this college and arrived Saturday morning.'

'Someone didn't like him, unless he surprised an intruder and this wasn't personal. Is there anything worth stealing?'

'The altar-piece is valuable but would be difficult to remove. There's no evidence that anyone has tried. There's valuable silver in the sacristy safe. The safe hasn't been tampered with.'

Ayling said, 'And the candlesticks are still here. Brass though – hardly worth stealing. Not much doubt about the weapon or the cause of death. A blow to the right of the cranium above the ear made by a heavy implement with a sharp edge. I don't know whether the first blow killed him, but it would certainly have felled him. Then the assailant struck again. Something like frenzy in the attack, I'd say.'

He straightened up, then lifted the unbloodied candle-stick with his gloved hand. 'Heavy. It'd take some strength. A woman could do it or an older man if they used both hands. Needed a bit of an eye though and he's not going to stand there with his back obligingly turned to a stranger – or to anyone he didn't trust come to that. How did he get in, Crampton I mean?'

Dalgliesh realized that here he had a pathologist not over concerned about the precise extent of his responsibilities.

'As far as I know he hadn't a key. He was either let in by someone already here or he found the door open. The *Doom* has been vandalized. He could have been enticed in.'

'That looks like an inside job. Cuts down on the number of your suspects very conveniently. When was he found?'

'At five-thirty. I was here about four minutes later. Judging by the appearance of the blood and the beginning of rigor in the side of the face I guessed that he had been dead about five hours.'

'I'll take his temperature but I doubt I can be more accurate. He died about midnight, give or take an hour.'

Dalgliesh asked, 'What about the blood? Would there have been much spurting?'

'Not with the first blow. You know how it is with head wounds on this site. You get bleeding into the cranial cavity. But he didn't stick at one blow, did he? For the second and subsequent strikes you'd get spurting. Could be more of a spatter than a strong stream. Depends how close he was to the victim when he struck the subsequent blows. If the assailant were right-handed I'd expect the right arm to be bloodied, perhaps even the chest.' He added, 'He'd expect that, of course. Could have come in his shirt and rolled up his sleeves. Could have worn a T-shirt, better still been naked. It's been known.'

Dalgliesh had heard nothing he hadn't thought out for himself. He said, 'Wouldn't the victim have found that a little surprising?'

Ayling ignored the interruption. 'He'd have to be quick though. He couldn't rely on the victim turning away from him for more than a second or two. Not much time to roll up a sleeve, get hold of a candlestick from where he'd placed it ready.'

'Where do you suppose that was?'

'Inside the box pew? A bit too far, perhaps. Why not just stand it up behind the pillar. He'd only need to hide one stick, of course. He could fetch the other from the altar afterwards to set up his little tableau. I wonder why he bothered to do that. Somehow I can't see it as an act of reverence.'

Finding Dalgliesh unresponsive, he said, 'I'll take his temperature and see if that helps to fix the time of death but I doubt whether I can put it closer than your original estimate. I'll be able to tell you more when I've had him on the table.'

Dalgliesh didn't wait to watch this first violation of the body's privacy, but walked slowly up and down the central aisle until, looking back, he saw that Ayling had finished and had got to his feet.

Together they returned to the sacristy. As the pathologist took off his working gown and zipped himself into his leathers, Dalgliesh said, 'Would you care for some coffee? I dare say it could be arranged.'

'No thanks. Pressure of time and they won't want to

see me. I should be able to do the PM tomorrow morning and I'll ring you, although I'm not expecting any surprises. The coroner will want the forensics done. He's careful like that. So will you, of course. I suppose I could use the Met lab if Huntingdon is busy. You won't want him moved until the photographer and SOCOs have finished but give me a ring when you're ready. I expect the people here will be glad to see the last of him.'

When Mark Ayling was ready to go, Dalgliesh locked the sacristy door and reset the alarm. For some reason he found difficult to define he was reluctant to take his companion through the house again.

He said, 'We can leave by the gate on to the headland. It'll save you being waylaid.'

They skirted the courtyard on the path of trodden grass. Across the scrubland Dalgliesh could see lights in the three occupied cottages. They looked like the lonely outposts of some beleaguered garrison. There was a light, too, in St Matthew's Cottage and he guessed that Mrs Pilbeam, probably with duster and vacuum cleaner, was making sure that it was clean and ready for occupation by the police. He thought again of Margaret Munroe and of that lonely dying which could have been so opportune, and there came to him a conviction that was as powerful as it was apparently irrational: that the three deaths were connected. The apparent suicide, the certified natural death, the brutal murder – there was a cord which connected them. Its strength might be tenuous and its path convoluted, but when he had traced it, it would lead him to the heart of the mystery.

In the front courtyard he waited until Ayling had mounted and roared away. He was turning to go back inside the house when he caught sight of the sidelights of a car. It had just turned from the approach road and was coming fast along the path. Within seconds he had identified Piers Tarrant's Alfa Romeo. The first two members of his team had arrived.

8

The call came through to Detective Inspector Piers Tarrant at six-fifteen. Within ten minutes he was ready to leave. He had been instructed to call for Kate Miskin on the way and reflected that this was unlikely to cause delay; Kate's flat on the Thames just beyond Wapping was on the route out of London he proposed to take. Detective Sergeant Robbins lived on the Essex border and would drive his own car to the scene. With luck, Piers hoped to overtake him. He let himself out of his flat and into the early Sunday morning quiet of the deserted streets. He collected his Alfa Romeo from the garage space which was his by courtesy of the City of London Police, slung his murder bag in the back, and set off eastward on the same route along which Dalgliesh had travelled two days before.

Kate was waiting for him at the entrance to the block where she had a flat overlooking the river. He had never been invited inside and nor had she ever seen the interior of his flat in the City. The river with its ever-changing light and shade, its dark surging tides and busy commercial life was her passion as the City was his. His flat comprised only three rooms above a delicatessen in a back street near St Paul's Cathedral. The camaraderie of the Met and his sexual life had no part in this private world. Nothing in the flat was superfluous and everything was carefully chosen and as expensive as he could afford. The City, its churches and alleys, its cobbled passages and seldom-visited courts, was both a hobby and a relief from his professional world. Like Kate, he was fascinated by the river, but as part of the City's life and history. He cycled each day to work and used his car only when he left London but, when he drove, it had to be a car he was happy to own.

Kate buckled herself into the seat beside him after a brief greeting and for the first few miles didn't speak, but he could sense her excitement as he knew she sensed his. He liked her and he respected her, but their professional relationship wasn't without its occasional small jags of resentment, irritation or competition. But this was something they shared, this surge of adrenalin at the beginning of a murder inquiry. He had sometimes wondered whether this almost visceral thrill wasn't uncomfortably close to blood-lust; certainly it held something of a blood sport.

After they had left Docklands behind them, Kate said, 'All right, put me in the picture. You read theology at Oxford. You must know something about this place.'

The fact that he had once read theology at Oxford was one of the few things about him she did know, and it had never ceased to intrigue her. Sometimes he could imagine that she believed he had gained some special insight or esoteric knowledge which gave him an advantage when it came to the consideration of motive and the infinite vicissitudes of the human heart. She would occasionally say, 'What use is theology? Tell me that. You chose to spend three years on it. I mean, you must have felt you would gain something from it, something useful or important.' He doubted whether she had

believed him when he had said that choosing theology
had given him a better chance of a place at Oxford than
opting for the history which he would have preferred.
He didn't tell her, either, what it was he had chiefly
gained: a fascination with the complexity of the intellectual bastions which men could construct to withstand
the tides of disbelief. His own disbelief had remained
unshaken but he had never regretted those three years.

Now he said, 'I know something about St Anselm's,
but not a lot. I had a friend who went on there after his
degree, but we lost touch. I've seen photographs of the
place. It's an immense Victorian mansion on one of the
bleakest parts of the East Coast. There are a number of
myths which have grown up around it. Like most myths
they're probably partly true. It's High Church – Prayer
Book Catholic maybe – I'm not really sure – with some
fancy Roman additions – strong on theology, opposed
to practically everything that's happened in Anglicanism
in the last fifty years, and you haven't a chance of getting
in without a first-class degree. But I'm told the food is
very good.'

Kate said, 'I doubt we'll get the chance to eat it. So
it's élitist, the college?'

'You could say that, but then so is Manchester United.'

'Did you think of going there?'

'No, because I didn't read theology with a view to
going into the Church. Anyway, they wouldn't have had
me. I didn't get a good enough degree. The Warden
tends to be particular. He's an authority on Richard
Hooker. All right, don't ask, he was a sixteenth-century
divine. You can take it from me that anyone who has
written the definitive work on Hooker is no intellectual

slouch. We could have trouble with The Revd Dr Sebastian Morell.'

'And the victim? Did AD say anything about him?'

'Only that he's an Archdeacon Crampton and was found dead in the church.'

'And what's an archdeacon?'

'A kind of Rottweiler of the Church. He – or it can be a she – looks after Church property, inducts parish priests. Archdeacons have charge of a number of parishes and visit them once a year. The spiritual equivalent of HM Inspector of Constabulary.'

Kate said, 'So it's going to be one of those self-contained cases with all the suspects under one roof and us having to pussyfoot around to avoid private calls to the Commissioner or complaints from the Archbishop of Canterbury. Why us anyway?'

'AD didn't talk for long. You know how he is. Anyway, he wanted us to get on the road. Apparently a DI from Suffolk was a visitor in the college last night. The Chief Constable apparently agrees that it would be inadvisable for them to take the case.'

Kate didn't question further, but Piers had the strong impression that she resented that he had taken the first call. She was, in fact, senior to him in terms of service although she had never made an issue of it. He wondered whether he should point out that AD had saved time by ringing him first since he had the faster car and would be driving, but decided against it.

As he expected, they overtook Robbins on the Colchester bypass. Piers knew that, had Kate been driving, they would have slackened speed to enable the team to arrive together. His response was to wave at Robbins and press down his foot on the accelerator.

Kate had put her head back and appeared to be dozing. Glancing at the strong good-looking face, he thought about their relationship. It had changed in the last two years since the publication of the Macpherson Report. Although he knew little about her life, he did know that she was illegitimate and had been brought up by a grandmother in the bleakest of inner-city areas and at the top of a high-rise building. Blacks had been her neighbours and her friends at school. To be told that she was a member of a Force where racism was institutionalized had filled her with a passionate resentment which he now realized had changed her whole attitude to her job. Politically far more sophisticated than she, and more cynical, he had tried to inject some calm into their heated discussions.

She had demanded, 'Given this report, would you join the Met if you were black?'

'No, but nor would I if I were white. But I have joined and I don't see why Macpherson should drive me out of my job.'

He knew where he wanted that job to take him, to a senior post in the anti-terrorist branch. That was where the opportunities now lay. In the meantime he was happy where he was, in a prestigious squad with a demanding boss he respected and enough excitement and variety to keep boredom at bay.

Kate said, 'Is that what they wanted then? To discourage blacks from joining and drive out decent non-racist officers?'

'For God's sake, Kate, let it rest. You're getting to be a bore.'

'The report says that an act is racist if the victim perceives it as such. I perceive this report as racist – racist against me as a white officer. So where do I go to complain?'

'You could try the race relations people, but I doubt you'll get any joy. Speak to AD about it.'

He didn't know whether she had, but at least she was still in the job. But he knew that he worked now with a different Kate. She was still conscientious, still hard-working, still dedicated to the task in hand. She would never let the team down. But something had gone; the belief that policing was a personal vocation as well as a public service and that you owed it more than hard work and dedication. He used to find this personal commitment in her over-romantic and naïve; now he realized how much he missed it. At least, he told himself, the Macpherson Report had destroyed for ever her over-deferential respect for the Bench.

By eight-thirty they were passing through the village of Wrentham, still wrapped in an early morning calm which seemed the more peaceful because hedges and trees showed the dilapidations of a night's storm which had hardly touched London. Kate quickened into aware-ness to consult her map and watch for the Ballard's Mere turning. Piers slackened speed.

He said, 'AD said it would be easy to miss. Look out for a large decaying ash on the right and a couple of flint cottages opposite.'

The ash, with its heavy cladding of ivy was unmissable, but as they turned into the road which was little more than a lane, one glance showed clearly what had happened. A large bough of the tree had been torn from the trunk and now lay along the grass verge looking in the growing light as bleached and smooth as a bone. From it sprouted dead branches like gnarled fingers. The main trunk showed the great wound where the branch had been torn away and the road, now passable, was still strewn with the debris of the fall: curls of ivy, twigs and a scatter of green and yellow leaves.

There were lights in the windows of both cottages. Piers drew to the side and hooted. Within seconds the figure of a stout middle-aged woman came down the garden path. She had a pleasant wind-tanned face under an unruly bush of hair and wore a brightly-flowered overall over what looked like layers of wool. Kate opened the window.

Piers leaned across and said, 'Good morning. You've had a spot of trouble here.'

'Come down she did at ten o'clock, right on the hour. It were the storm, you see. A real blow we had last night. Lucky we heard the fall – not that you could miss it for the noise she made. My husband was afraid there'd be an accident so he put out red warning lights both sides. Then, come morning, my Brian and Mr Daniels from next door got the tractor and pulled her off the road. Not that many folk come this way except to visit the fathers and the students at the college. Still, we thought better not wait for the council to move it.'

Kate asked, 'When did you clear the road, Mrs . . . ?'

'Finch. Mrs Finch. At half-past six. It were still dark, but Brian wanted to get it done before they was off to work.'

Kate said, 'Lucky for us. It was very kind of you, thank you. So no one could have got past by car in either direction between ten o'clock last night and half-past six this morning?'

'That's right, miss. There's only been a gentleman on a motorcycle – going to the college, no doubt. There's nowhere else to go on this road. He's not back yet.'

'And no one else has driven past?'

'Not that I saw, and I usually do see, the kitchen being at the front.'

They thanked her again, said their goodbyes, and moved off. Glancing back, Kate could see Mrs Finch watching them for a few seconds before re-latching the gate and waddling off up the garden path.

Piers said, 'One motorcycle and he hasn't returned. Could've been the pathologist, although you'd expect him to come by car. Well, we've got some news for AD. If this road is the only access . . .'

Kate had her eyes on the map. 'Which it is, for vehicles anyway. Then any murderer from outside the college must have arrived before ten p.m. and can't yet have left, not by road anyway. An inside job?'

Piers said, 'That's the impression I got from AD.'

The question of access to the headland was so important that Kate was about to say that it was surprising AD hadn't already sent someone to question Mrs Finch. But then she remembered. Until she and Piers arrived, who at St Anselm's could he have sent?

The narrow road was deserted. It was lower than the surrounding fields and edged with bushes so that it was with a shock of surprise and pleasure that Kate saw suddenly the great crinkled greyness of the North Sea.

To the north a Victorian mansion bulked large against the sky.

As they approached, Kate said, 'Good Lord, what a monstrosity! Who would have thought of building a house like that literally within yards of the sea?'

'No one. When it was built it wouldn't have been within yards of the sea.'

She said, 'You can't possibly admire it.'

'Oh I don't know. It has a certain confidence.'

A motorcyclist was approaching and roared past. Kate said, 'Presumably that was the forensic pathologist.'

Piers slowed down as they drove between two ruined pillars of red brick to where Dalgliesh was waiting.

9

St Matthew's Cottage would hardly have provided sufficient or suitable accommodation for a wide-spreading investigation, but Dalgliesh judged that it was adequate for the task in hand. There was no suitable police accommodation within miles and the bringing of caravans on to the headland would have been an illogical and expensive expedient. But being in college had its problems, including where they were to eat; in any human emergency or distress, from murder to bereavement, people still had to be fed and found beds. He recollected how, after his father's death, his mother's concern about how the Norfolk rectory could accommodate all the overnight guests expected, their foibles about what they could or could not eat, and what food should be provided for the whole of the parish had blunted at least temporarily the edge of grief. Sergeant Robbins was already coping with present problems, telephoning a list of hotels suggested by Father Sebastian to book accommodation for himself, Kate and Piers and the three Scene of Crime Officers. Dalgliesh would remain in his guest set.

The cottage was the most unusual incident room of his career. Mrs Munroe's sister, in removing every physical trace of occupation, had left the cottage so denuded of character that the very air was tasteless. The two small ground-floor rooms were furnished with obvious rejects from the guest sets, conventionally placed but producing only an atmosphere of dreary expedience. In the sitting-room to the left of the door a bentwood armchair with a faded patchwork cushion and a low slatted chair with a foot-rest had been placed on each side of the small Victorian grate. In the centre of the room was a square oak table with four chairs; two others were set against the wall. A small bookcase to the left of the fireplace held only a leather-covered Bible and a copy of *Through the Looking Glass*. The right-hand room looked slightly more inviting with a smaller table set against the wall, two mahogany chairs with bulbous legs, a shabby sofa and a matching armchair. The two upstairs rooms were empty. Dalgliesh judged that the sitting-room could best serve as an office and for interviews with the opposite room as a waiting-room, while one of the bedrooms, fitted with a telephone socket and an adequate number of electric points, could house the computer which the Suffolk Police had already provided.

The question of food had been settled. Dalgliesh baulked at the thought of joining the community for dinner. His presence would, he thought, inhibit even Father Sebastian's conversational powers. The Warden had extended an invitation, but had hardly expected it to be accepted. Dalgliesh would take his evening meal elsewhere. But it had been agreed that the college would provide soup and sandwiches or a ploughman's lunch at one o'clock for all the team. The question of payment had been tactfully ignored for the present by both parties but the situation was not without a touch of the bizarre. Dalgliesh wondered whether this might prove to be the first murder case in which the killer had provided accommodation and free food for the investigating officer.

They were anxious to get down to work, but first they must view the body. Dalgliesh with Kate, Piers and Robbins went over to the church, put on overshoes and made their way along the north wall to the *Doom*. He could be sure that none of his officers would attempt to anaesthetize horror by facetiousness or crude graveyard humour; any who did so wouldn't serve under him for long. He switched on the spotlight and they stood for a moment contemplating the body in silence. The quarry wasn't yet even a blurred figure on the horizon and his spoor had not been detected, but this was his work in all its crude enormity and it was right that they should see it.

Only Kate spoke. She asked, 'The candlesticks, sir, where would they normally be?'

'On the altar.'

'And when was the *Doom* last seen unvandalized?'

'At the nine-thirty service of Compline yesterday evening.'

They locked the church behind them, set the alarm, and returned to the incident room. And now they settled down for the preliminary discussion and briefing before they got to work. Dalgliesh knew that it couldn't be rushed. Information not given by him now, or imperfectly understood, could result in later delays, misunderstandings or mistakes. He embarked on a detailed but concise account of everything he had seen or done since his arrival at St Anselm's, including his investigation of Ronald Treeves's death and the contents of Margaret Munroe's diary. They sat together at the table, mostly in silence, making occasional notes.

Kate sat upright, her eyes fixed on her notebook except when, with disconcerting intensity, she raised them to Dalgliesh's face. She was dressed as she always was when on a case: in comfortable walking shoes, narrowly-cut trousers and a well-tailored jacket. Beneath it in winter, as now, she wore a cashmere roll-neck jumper, in summer a silk shirt. Her light brown hair was drawn back and worn in a short thick plait. She wore no discernible make-up, and her face, good looking rather than handsome, expressed what essentially she was: honest, reliable, conscientious but perhaps not wholly at peace with herself.

Piers, restless as always, could not sit still for long. After several apparent attempts at comfort he now sat with his legs wound round those of the chair and his arm flung round the back. But his mobile, slightly podgy face was alight with interest and the sleepy chocolate-brown eyes under the heavy lids held their usual look of quizzical amusement. Less obviously attentive than Kate, he still missed nothing. He was informally dressed in a green linen shirt with fawn linen trousers, an expensively creased informality which was as carefully considered as Kate's more conventional look.

Robbins, as neat and formal as a chauffeur, sat perfectly at ease at the end of a table and got up from time to time to brew more coffee and refill their mugs.

When Dalgliesh had finished his account, Kate said, 'What are we going to call this murderer, sir?'

Rejecting the usual soubriquets, the squad invariably chose a name at the beginning of the investigation.

Piers said, 'Cain would be appropriately biblical and short, if hardly original.'

Dalgliesh said, 'Cain it is. Now we get down to work. I want prints from everyone who was in college last night, including visitors and the staff in the cottages. The Archdeacon's prints can await the arrival of the SOCOs. You'd better make the others a priority before we make a start on the interviews. Then examine the clothes all the residents were wearing yesterday, and that includes the priests. I've checked the ordinands' brown cloaks. The right number are in place and look clean, but take another look.'

Piers said, 'He'd hardly have worn either a cloak or a cassock surely, why should he? If Crampton was enticed into the church he'd expect to find the caller waiting for him in his nightclothes – pyjamas or a dressing-gown. Then the blow must have been struck very quickly, seizing the moment when Crampton turned towards the *Doom*. Time maybe to roll up a pyjama sleeve. He'd hardly encumber himself with a heavy serge cloak. Of course he could have been naked, or partly naked, under a dressing-gown, and slipped it off. Even so, he'd have to be damned quick.'

Dalgliesh said, 'The pathologist made the not particularly original suggestion that he was naked.'

Piers went on, 'It's not all that fanciful, sir. After all, why show himself at all to Crampton? All he needs to do is to unbolt the south door and leave it ajar. Then he puts on the light to illuminate the *Doom* and hides behind a pillar. Crampton might be surprised to find no one waiting for him, but he'd go over to the *Doom* anyway, drawn to it by the light and because the caller had told him that it had been vandalized and exactly how.'

Kate said, 'Wouldn't he ring Father Sebastian before he went to the church?'

'Not till he'd seen for himself. He wouldn't want to make a fool of himself by raising the alarm unnecessarily. But I wonder what excuse the caller gave him to explain being in the church at that hour. A chink of light, perhaps? He was woken by the wind, looked out, saw a figure and got suspicious? But the question probably wasn't even raised. Crampton's first thought would have been to go to the church.'

Kate said, 'And if Cain had worn a cloak, why return it to the house and still retain the keys? The missing keys are the vital piece of evidence. The murderer couldn't risk having them in his possession. They would be easy enough to dispose of – chuck them anywhere on the headland – but why not return them? If he'd had the guts to sneak in and take them you'd think he'd have the guts to go back and return them.'

Piers said, 'Not if he was bloodstained, either his hands or his clothes.'

'But why should he be? We've gone over all that. And there's no hurry, he would have time to go back to his room and wash. He wouldn't expect the body to be discovered until the church was opened for morning prayer at seven-fifteen. There's one thing though.'

'Yes?' asked Dalgliesh.

'Doesn't the fact that the keys weren't returned point to the murderer being someone who lives outside the house? Any of the fathers had a legitimate reason for being there at any hour of the day or night. There would be no risk to them in returning the keys.'

Dalgliesh said, 'You're forgetting, Kate; they wouldn't need to take them. The four priests already have keys and I've checked. They're still on their key-rings.'

Piers said, 'But one of them might take a set precisely in order to throw suspicion on one of the staff, ordinands or guests.'

Dalgliesh said, 'It's a possibility, just as it's a possibility that the defacing of the *Doom* had nothing to do with the murder. There's a childish malice about it which doesn't tie up with the brutality of the killing. But the most extraordinary thing about this murder is why it was done in this way. If someone wanted Crampton dead, he could have been killed without any need to entice him into the church. None of the guest sets has a lock or key to the door. Anyone in college could have walked in to Crampton's room and killed him in his bed. Even an outsider wouldn't have had much difficulty provided he knew the layout of the college. An ornamental iron gate is one of the easiest to climb over.'

Kate said, 'But we know it can't have been an outsider apart from the missing keys. No car could have got past that fallen branch after ten o'clock. I suppose Cain could have come on foot, climbed over the tree or maybe walked along the beach. It wouldn't have been easy in last night's wind.'

Dalgliesh said, 'The murderer knew where to find the keys and the code for the alarm. It looks like an inside job but we keep an open mind. I'm just pointing out that if the murder had been committed in a less spectacular and bizarre way it would have been difficult to bring it home to anyone at St Anselm's. The possibility would always have remained that someone did get in, perhaps a casual thief who got to know that doors were unlocked and killed Crampton in a panic because he woke at the wrong moment. It isn't likely, but it couldn't have been discounted. This murderer not only wanted Crampton dead, he wanted the crime fixed firmly in St Anselm's. Once we've discovered why we'll be on the way to solving it.'

Sergeant Robbins had been sitting quietly a little apart, making notes. Two of his many accomplishments were the ability to work unobtrusively and to write shorthand, but his memory was so reliable and precise that the notes were hardly necessary. Although the most junior, he was a member of the team and Kate found herself waiting for Dalgliesh to bring him in. Now he said, 'Any theory, Sergeant?'

'Not really, sir. It's almost certainly an inside job and whoever did it is perfectly happy for us to know that. But I'm wondering whether the altar candlestick could be part of that. Can we be certain it was the weapon? OK, it's bloody, but it could have been taken from the altar and used after Crampton was dead. The PM wouldn't be able to show – not conclusively anyway – whether the first blow was struck with the candlestick, only whether there are traces on it of Crampton's blood and brain.'

Piers said, 'What's your thinking? Isn't the central puzzle the difference between an obviously premeditated murder and the frenzy of the attack?'

'Let's suppose it wasn't premeditated. We're fairly sure that Crampton must have been lured there, presumably to be shown the desecration of the *Doom*. Someone is waiting for him. And then there's an angry exchange. Cain loses control and strikes out. Crampton falls. Then Cain, standing over a dead man, sees a way of pinning it on the college. He takes the two candlesticks, uses one to strike Crampton again, and sets both of them up at his head.'

Kate said, 'It's possible, but that would mean that Cain had something ready to hand, something heavy enough to crack a skull.'

Robbins went on, 'It could be a hammer, any sort of heavy tool, a garden implement. Suppose he saw the gleam of a light in the church last night and went to investigate, arming himself with anything he had handy. Then he finds Crampton there, they have a violent quarrel and he strikes out.'

Kate objected. 'But why would anyone go into the church at night alone armed with any kind of a weapon? Why not ring someone in the house?'

'He might prefer to investigate, and perhaps he didn't go alone. Perhaps he had someone with him.'

A sister maybe, thought Kate. It was an interesting theory.

Dalgliesh was for a moment silent, then he said, 'We've a lot to do between the four of us. I suggest we get started.'

He paused, wondering whether to speak what was in his mind. They had one murder clear before them; he didn't want to complicate the investigation with matters which might not be relevant. On the other hand it was important that his suspicions should be kept in mind.

He said, 'I think we have to see this murder in the context of two previous deaths, Treeves and Mrs Munroe. I have a hunch – no more at this stage – that they're connected. The link may be fragile but I think it's there.'

The suggestion was greeted by a few seconds of

silence. He felt their surprise. Then Piers said, 'I thought you were more or less satisfied, sir, that Treeves killed himself. If Treeves was murdered, it would be too much of a coincidence to have two killers in St Anselm's. But surely Treeves's death was either suicide or an accident? Look at the facts as you've set them out. The body was found two hundred yards from the only access to the beach. Difficult to carry him over that shore and he'd hardly walk willingly with his killer. He was strong and healthy. You couldn't bring down half a ton of sand on his head unless you had first drugged him, made him drunk or knocked him out. None of these things happened. You said the PM was thorough.'

Kate spoke directly to Piers. 'OK, let's accept it was suicide. But suicide has to have a reason. What drove him to it? Or who? There could be a motive there.'

'But not for Crampton's murder, surely. He wasn't even at St Anselm's at the time. We have no reason to suppose he ever met Treeves.'

Kate went doggedly on. 'Mrs Munroe remembered something from her past which worried her. She speaks to the person concerned and shortly afterwards she's dead. It strikes me that her death is suspiciously convenient.'

'For whom, for God's sake? She had a bad heart. She could have died any time.'

Kate reiterated, 'She wrote that diary entry. There was something she remembered, something she knew. And she would have been the easiest person of all to kill, an elderly woman with a weak heart, particularly if she had no reason to fear her killer.'

Piers protested. 'OK, she knew something. That

doesn't mean it was important. It could have been some minor peccadillo, something Father Sebastian and those priests wouldn't approve of but which no one else would take seriously. And now she's cremated, this cottage cleared and the evidence, if any, gone for good. Whatever she remembered, it happened twelve years ago anyway. Who's going to do murder for that?'

Kate said, 'She found Treeves's body, remember.'

'What's that to do with it? The diary note is explicit. She didn't remember that incident from her past when she saw the body, she remembered when Surtees brought her some leeks from his garden. It was then that things came together, the present and the past.'

Kate said, 'Leeks – a leak. Could it be a play on the word?'

'For God's sake, Kate, that's pure Agatha Christie!' Piers turned to Dalgliesh. 'Are you saying, sir, that we are now investigating two murders, Crampton's and Mrs Munroe's?'

'No. I'm not proposing to jeopardize a murder inquiry for the sake of a hunch. What I am saying is that there could be a connection and that we should keep it in mind. There's a lot to do so we'd better get on with it. The priority is the fingerprinting and questioning the priests and ordinands. That's for you, Kate, with Piers. They've seen enough of me. So has Surtees, so you'd better see him and his sister. There's an advantage in facing them with someone new. We're not going to get far until Inspector Yarwood is well enough to be questioned. According to the hospital that should be by Tuesday if we're lucky.'

Piers said, 'If there's a chance he might have a vital

298

clue, or if he's a suspect, shouldn't he be kept unobtrusively under guard?'

Dalgliesh said, 'He is being kept unobtrusively under guard. Suffolk are helping there. He was out of his room that night. He could even have seen the murderer. That's why I'm not leaving him without protection.'

There was the sound of a car bumping across the headland. Sergeant Robbins went to the window. 'Mr Clark and the SOCOs have arrived, sir.'

Piers looked at his watch. 'Not bad, but they'd have been better driving the whole way. It's getting out of Ipswich that takes the time. Lucky the train didn't foul up.'

Dalgliesh said to Robbins, 'Ask them to bring their gear in here. They can use the second bedroom. And they'll probably want coffee before they start.'

'Yes sir.'

Dalgliesh decided that the Scene of Crime Officers could change into their search clothes in the church, but well away from the actual scene. Brian Clark, the head of the team and inevitably called Nobby, hadn't worked with Dalgliesh before. Calm, unemotional and humourless, he was not the most inspiring of colleagues, but he came with a reputation for thoroughness and reliability and, when he did condescend to communicate, spoke sense. If there were anything to find, he would find it. He was a man who distrusted enthusiasm and even the most potentially valuable clue was apt to be greeted with, 'All right, lads, keep calm. It's only a palm print, it's not the Holy Grail.' He also believed in the separation of functions. His job was to discover, collect and preserve the evidence, not to usurp the job of the detective. For Dalgliesh, who encouraged teamwork and was receptive to ideas, this reserve amounting to taciturnity was a disadvantage.

Now, and not for the first time, he missed Charlie Ferris, the SOCO who had been on the job when he had investigated the Berowne/Harry Mack murders. They too had taken place in a church. He could clearly recall Ferris – small, sandy-haired, sharp-featured and lithe as a greyhound – prancing gently like an eager runner awaiting the starting pistol, recall too the extraordinary working garb which the Ferret had devised for the job: the diminutive white shorts and short-sleeved sweat-shirt, the tight-fitting plastic cap which made him look like a swimmer who had forgotten to take off his underclothes. But the Ferret had retired to run a pub in Somerset where his orotund bass, so incongruous in his slight frame, was adding power to the village church choir.

A different pathologist, a different team of SOCOs, soon to have their name changed again. He supposed that he was lucky still to have Kate Miskin. But now was not the time to concern himself with Kate's morale, or with her possible future. Perhaps, he thought, it was increasing age which made him less tolerant of change.

But at least the photographer was familiar. Barney Parker was past retirement age and now worked on a part-time basis. He was a voluble, wiry, eager-eyed, jaunty little man who had looked exactly the same for all the years Dalgliesh had known him. His other part-time job was taking wedding photographs and perhaps this soft-focus beautifying of brides provided a relief from the uncompromising starkness of his police work. He had, indeed, something of the irritating importunity of a wedding photographer, looking round at the scene as if to ensure that there were no other bodies anxious for his attention. Dalgliesh almost expected him to chivvy them all for the family line-up. But he was an excellent photographer whose work couldn't be faulted.

Dalgliesh walked over to the church with them, passing through the sacristy and skirting the murder scene. They changed in a pew near the south door in a silence which Dalgliesh judged had nothing to do with the sacredness of the scene, and stood like a little group of spacemen in their white cotton oversuits and hoods, watching Nobby Clark follow Dalgliesh back towards the sacristy. With the hood of his suit puckered round his face and his slightly protruding upper teeth, Dalgliesh thought that Clark needed only a pair of ears to make him look like a large disgruntled rabbit.

Dalgliesh said, 'The murderer almost certainly came in through the sacristy door from the north cloister. That means the cloister floor will need examining for prints although I doubt you'll get anything useful under this weight of leaves. No knob on the door, but the prints of almost everyone here could validly be on any part of the door.'

Moving into the church, he said, 'There's a possibility of prints on the *Doom* and on the wall beside it, although he would've been crazy not to wear gloves. This candlestick on the right has traces of blood and hair, but again we'll be lucky to get prints. What is interesting is here.' He led the way up the central aisle to the second box pew. 'Someone has hidden himself under the seat. There's a considerable amount of dust which has been disturbed.

I don't know whether you'll get prints on the wood, but it's a possibility.'

Clark said, 'Right sir. What about the team's lunch? There doesn't seem to be a pub near and I don't want to break off. I'd like as much natural light as possible.'

'The college is providing sandwiches. Robbins will be fixing beds for the night. We can look at progress tomorrow.'

'I think I'll need more than two days, sir. It's those leaves in the north cloister. They'll all need shifting and examining.'

Dalgliesh doubted whether any joy would result from this tedious exercise, but had no wish to discourage Clark's obvious attention to detail. He said a last word to the other two members of the team and left them to it.

IO

Before the individual interviews began, the finger-printing of everyone at St Anselm's had priority. The task fell to Piers and Kate. Both knew that Dalgliesh preferred all women to be fingerprinted by a member of their own sex. Before they began, Piers said, 'It's a long time since I've done this. You'd better see to the women as usual. Seems an unnecessary refinement to me. Anyone would think it was a form of rape.'

Kate was making the preparations. She said, 'You could see it as a form of rape. Innocent or not innocent, I'd hate to have some police officer grabbing hold of my fingers.'

'It's hardly a grab. Looks as if we've got a full waiting-room except for the priests. Who do we start with?'

'Better make it Arbuthnot.'

Kate was interested in the different reactions of the suspects who presented themselves during the next hour with varying degrees of meekness. Father Sebastian, arriving with his fellow-priests, was grimly co-operative, but could not resist a moue of distaste when Piers took his fingers to cleanse them in soap and water, then firmly rolled them on the inkpad. He said, 'Surely I can do it for myself.'

Piers was unconcerned. 'I'm sorry, sir. It's a question of making sure we get a good print at the edges. A matter of experience really.'

Father John didn't speak from start to finish but his face was deathly white and Kate saw that he was shaking. Throughout the brief procedure he kept his eyes closed. Father Martin was frankly interested, and gazed with almost childish wonder at the complicated pattern of whorls and loops which proclaimed his unique identity. Father Peregrine, his eyes straining towards the college to which he was impatient to return, seemed hardly aware of what was happening. Only when he caught sight of his ink-smeared fingers was he provoked to grumble that he hoped the stain would be easily washed off and that ordinands should ensure that their fingers were thoroughly clean before coming to the library. He would put up a note on the board.

None of the ordinands or staff made any difficulty, but Stannard came prepared to see the procedure as a gross infringement of civil liberty. He said, 'I suppose you have authority for doing this?'

Piers said calmly, 'Yes sir, with your consent, under the provisions of the Police and Criminal Evidence Act. I think you know the legislation.'

'And if I didn't consent I've no doubt you could get some kind of court order. After you've made an arrest – if you ever get that far – and I'm proved innocent, I take it my prints will be destroyed. How can I be sure they will?'

'You have the right to witness the destruction if you make an application.'

'And I will,' he said as his fingers were placed on the inkpad. 'You can be bloody sure I will.'

Now they had finished and the last to be fingerprinted,

Emma Lavenham, had left. Kate said, with such careful casualness that even she found her tone unnatural, 'What do you suppose AD thinks about her?'

'He's a heterosexual male and a poet. He thinks what any heterosexual male and a poet thinks when he meets a beautiful woman. What I think, come to that. He'd like to take her to the nearest bed.'

'Oh come on, d'you have to be that crude? Can't any of you think of a woman except in terms of bed?'

'What a puritan you are, Kate. You asked me what he'd think, not what he'd do. He has all his instincts under control, that's his trouble. She's an anomaly here, isn't she? Why do you think Father Sebastian imported her? To provide a temporary exercise in resisting temptation? You'd think a pretty boy would be a better bet. The four we've met so far, though, seem a depressingly hetero bunch to me.'

'And you'd know, of course.'

'So would you. Talking of beauty, what do you think of the Adonis Raphael?'

'The name's too appropriate, isn't it? I wonder if he'd look the same if he'd been christened Albert. Too good looking, and he knows it.'

'Turn you on?'

'No, and nor do you. Time to make some visits. Who shall we start with? Father Sebastian?'

'At the top?'

'Why not? And after that AD wants me with him when he interviews Arbuthnot.'

'Who'll take the lead with the Warden?'

'Me. To begin with anyway.'

'You think he'll open up more to a woman? You may be right, but I shouldn't bank on it. These priests are used to the confessional. That makes them good at keeping secrets, including their own.'

II

Father Sebastian had said, 'You will, of course, wish to see Mrs Crampton before she leaves. I'll send you a message when she's ready. If she should want to visit the church I assume that would be permissible.'

Dalgliesh replied briefly that it would. He wondered whether Father Sebastian had taken it for granted that if Mrs Crampton wished to see where her husband had died, he would be the one to escort her. Dalgliesh had other ideas but judged that now was not the time to argue the point; Mrs Crampton might not wish to visit the church. Whether she did or not, it was important that they met.

The message that she was ready to see him was brought to the incident room by Stephen Morby, who was now being used by Father Sebastian as a general messenger. Dalgliesh had noticed how much Morell disliked the telephone.

When he entered the Warden's office Mrs Crampton got up from her chair and came towards him, holding out her hand and regarding him steadily. She was younger than Dalgliesh had expected, heavily-breasted above a neat waist and with a pleasant open and unadorned face. She was hatless and her short mid-brown hair, brushed to shininess, looked expensively cut; he could almost believe she had come straight from the hairdresser if the idea were not preposterous. She was wearing a tweed suit in blue and fawn with a large cameo brooch in the lapel. It was obviously modern and looked incongruous against the country tweed. Dalgliesh wondered whether it had been a gift from her husband and she had fastened it in her jacket as a badge of allegiance or defiance. A short travelling coat lay across the back of a chair. She was perfectly calm and the hand which clasped Dalgliesh's was cold but firm.

Father Sebastian's introduction was brief and formal. Dalgliesh said the customary words of sympathy and regret. He had spoken them to the family of a murder victim more times than he could remember: to him they always sounded insincere.

Father Sebastian said, 'Mrs Crampton would like to visit the church and has asked that you go with her. If I'm needed you'll find me here.'

They walked together through the south cloister and across the cobbles of the courtyard to the church. The Archdeacon's body had been removed but SOCOs were still busy in the building and one of them was now clearing the leaves from the north cloister, carefully examining each one. There was already a clear path to the sacristy door.

The church struck cold and Dalgliesh was aware that his companion shivered. He asked, 'Would you like me to fetch your coat?'

'No thank you, Commander. I shall be all right.'

He led the way to the *Doom*. It was not necessary to tell her that this was the place; the stones were still stained with her husband's blood. Unselfconsciously and a little stiffly she knelt. Dalgliesh moved away and walked up the central aisle.

Within a few minutes she had joined him. She said, 'Shall we sit down for a little while? I expect you have some questions you want to ask.'

'I could ask them in Father Sebastian's office or in the incident room in St Matthew's Cottage if that would be more comfortable for you.'

'I shall be more comfortable here.'

The two SOCOs had moved tactfully into the sacristy. They sat for a brief moment in silence, then she said, 'How did my husband die, Commander? Father Sebastian seemed reluctant to say.'

'Father Sebastian hasn't been told, Mrs Crampton.'

Which didn't, of course, mean he didn't know. Dalgliesh wondered whether this possibility had occurred to her. He said, 'It's important for the success of the investigation that the details are kept secret for the present.'

'I understand that. I shall say nothing.'

Dalgliesh said gently, 'The Archdeacon was killed by a blow to the head. It would have been very sudden. I don't think he suffered. He may not even have had time to feel shock or fear.'

'Thank you, Commander.'

Again there was a silence. It was curiously companionable and he was in no hurry to break it. Even in her grief, which she was bearing with stoicism, she was restful to be with. Was it this quality, he wondered, which had drawn the Archdeacon to her? The silence lengthened. Glancing at her face he saw the glister of a tear on her cheek. She put up a hand to brush it away but when she spoke her voice was steady.

'My husband was not welcome in this place, Commander, but I know that no one at St Anselm's could possibly have killed him. I refuse to believe that a member of a Christian community could be capable of such evil.'

Dalgliesh said, 'This is a question I have to ask. Had your husband any enemies, anyone who might wish him harm?'

'No. He was much respected in the parish. One might say that he was loved, although it wasn't a word he would have used. He was a good, compassionate and conscientious parish priest and he never spared himself. I don't know whether anyone has told you that he was a widower when we married. His first wife committed suicide. She was a very beautiful but disturbed woman and he was greatly in love with her. The tragedy affected him deeply, but he had come through it. He was learning how to be happy. We were happy together. It's cruel that all his hopes should come to this.'

Dalgliesh said, 'You said that he wasn't welcome at St Anselm's. Was this because of theological differences or were there other reasons? Did he discuss his visit here with you?'

'He discussed everything with me, Commander, everything that hadn't been told him in confidence as a clergyman. He felt that St Anselm's had outgrown its usefulness. He wasn't the only one who felt that. I think even Father Sebastian realizes that the college is an anomaly and will have to close. There were differences of churchmanship, of course, which didn't make things any easier. And then I expect you know about the problem of Father John Betterton.'

Dalgliesh said carefully, 'I gained the impression that there was a problem but I don't know the details.'

'It's an old and rather tragic story. Some years ago Father Betterton was found guilty of sexual offences against some of his choirboys and was sentenced to prison. My husband uncovered part of the evidence and was a witness at the trial. We weren't married at the time – it was shortly after his first wife's death – but I know it caused him much distress. He did what he saw as his duty and it caused him a great deal of pain.'

Dalgliesh privately thought that the greater pain had been suffered by Father John.

He said, 'Did your husband say anything to you before coming on this visit, anything to suggest that he might have arranged to meet someone here or that he had reason to suppose that this visit would be particularly difficult?'

'No, nothing. I'm sure no meeting was arranged other than with the people here. He wasn't looking forward to the weekend but he wasn't dreading it either.'

'And had he been in touch with you since he arrived yesterday?'

'No, he hadn't telephoned and I wouldn't have expected him to. The only call I had apart from parish business was from the diocesan office. Apparently they'd lost my husband's mobile phone number and wanted it for the records.'

'What time was this call?'

'Quite late. I was surprised because it must have been after the office was closed. It was just before half-past nine on Saturday.'

'Did you speak to the person who rang? Was it a man or a woman?'

'It sounded like a man. I thought at the time that it

was a man, although I couldn't swear to it. No, I didn't really speak except to give the number. He just said thank you and rang off at once.'

Of course he did, thought Dalgliesh. He wouldn't want to speak an unnecessary word. All he wanted was the number he could get in no other way, the number he would ring that night from the church to summon the Archdeacon to his death. Wasn't this the answer to one of the problems at the heart of the case? If Crampton had been lured to the church by a call on his mobile, how had the caller discovered the number? It wouldn't be difficult to trace that nine-thirty call and the result could be damning for someone at St Anselm's. But there still remained a mystery. The murderer – better still think of him as Cain – wasn't unintelligent. This crime had been carefully planned. Wouldn't Cain have expected Dalgliesh to speak to Mrs Crampton? Wasn't it possible – no, more than possible – that the telephone call would come to light? Another possibility occurred to Dalgliesh. Could this have been precisely what Cain had intended?

12

After the fingerprinting, Emma collected some papers she needed from her guest set and was setting off for the library when she heard quick footsteps in the south cloister and Raphael caught up with her.

He said, 'There's something I want to ask you. Is this a good time?'

Emma was about to say, 'If it isn't going to take too long', but after a glance at his face, stopped herself. She didn't know whether he was seeking comfort but he certainly looked in need of it. She said instead, 'It's a good time. But haven't you a tutorial with Father Peregrine?'

'That's postponed. I've been sent for by the police. I'm on my way now to be grilled. That's why I needed to see you. I suppose you wouldn't be willing to tell Dalgliesh that we were together last night? After eleven o'clock's the crucial time. I've got an alibi of sorts until then.'

'Together where?'

'In your set or mine. I suppose I'm asking if you'd say that we slept together last night.'

Emma stopped walking and turned to face him. She said, 'No I wouldn't! Raphael, what an extraordinary thing to ask. You're not usually so crass.'

'But not an extraordinary thing to do – or is it?'

She began striding quickly ahead but he kept pace

with her. She said, 'Look, I don't love you and I'm not in love with you.'

He broke in, 'That's a nice distinction. But you might just think it possible. The idea might not utterly repel you.'

Emma turned to face him. 'Raphael, if I had slept with you last night I wouldn't be ashamed to admit it. But I didn't, I wouldn't and I shan't lie. Apart from the morality of lying, it would be stupid and dangerous. Do you think it would deceive Adam Dalgliesh for a moment? Even if I were a good liar – and I'm not – he'd know. It's his business to know. D'you want him to think you killed the Archdeacon?'

'He probably thinks it already. The alibi I've got isn't worth much. I went to keep Peter company to help him through the storm, but he was asleep before midnight and I could easily have crept out. I expect that's what Dalgliesh will believe I did do.'

Emma said, 'Assuming he does suspect you – which I doubt – he'll certainly do so more strongly if you start fabricating an alibi. It's so unlike you, Raphael. It's stupid, pathetic and insulting to both of us. Why?'

'Perhaps I wanted to find out what you thought of the idea in principle.'

She said, 'You don't sleep with a man in principle, you sleep with him in the flesh.'

'And, of course, Father Sebastian wouldn't like it.'

He had spoken with casual irony, but Emma didn't miss the note of bitterness in his voice.

She said, 'Of course he wouldn't. You're one of his ordinands and I'm a guest here. Even if I wanted to sleep with you – which I don't – it would be a breach of good manners.'

That made him laugh, but the sound was harsh. He said, 'Good manners! Yes, I suppose that's a consideration. It's the first time I've been turned down with that excuse. The etiquette of sexual morality. Perhaps we should introduce a seminar into the ethics syllabus.'

She asked again, 'But why, Raphael? You must have known what answer you'd get.'

'It's just that I thought that if I could make you like me – or perhaps even love me a little – I wouldn't be in such a muddle. Everything would be all right.'

She said more kindly, 'But it wouldn't. If life is a muddle we can't look for love to make it all come right.'

'But people do.'

They were standing together in silence outside the south door. Emma turned to go in. Suddenly Raphael stopped and took her hand and, bending, kissed her on the cheek. He said, 'I'm sorry, Emma. I knew it was no good really. I just had a dream. Please forgive me.'

He turned, and she watched him striding back through the cloister and waited until he had passed through the iron gate. She let herself into the college, confused and unhappy. Could she have been more sympathetic, more understanding? Did he want to confide and should she have encouraged him? But if things were going wrong for him – and she thought they were – what use was it looking to someone else to put them right? But in one sense hadn't she done just that herself with Giles? Tired of the importunities, the demands for love, the jealousies and rivalries, hadn't she decided that Giles, with his status, his strength, his intelligence, could provide her with at least a semblance of commitment so that she could be left alone to get on with that part of her life which she valued most, her work? She knew now that it had been a mistake. It had been worse than a mistake, it had been wrong. After she returned to Cambridge she would be honest with him. It wasn't going to be an agreeable parting – Giles wasn't used to rejection – but she wouldn't think further about it now. That future trauma was nothing compared to the tragedy at St Anselm's of which inescapably she was a part.

13

Just before twelve o'clock Father Sebastian rang Father Martin, who was sitting in the library marking essays, and asked if he might have a word. This was his usual practice, to telephone personally. From the first days of his taking over as Warden he had been careful never to summon his predecessor through an ordinand or a member of staff; the new and very different reign would not be marked by a tactless exercise of authority. For most men the prospect of a previous Warden staying on in residence and in a part-time teaching post would have been to invite disaster. It had always been considered seemly for the outgoing Warden not only to depart in well-organized dignity, but to take himself as far as possible from the college. But the arrangement with Father Martin, originally intended to be temporary to cover the unexpected departure of the lecturer in pastoral theology, had continued by mutual consent to the satisfaction of both parties. Father Sebastian had shown no inhibition or embarrassment in occupying his predecessor's stall in church, taking over and reorganizing his office and sitting in his place at head of table, nor in introducing the changes he had carefully planned. Father Martin, unresentful and a little amused, perfectly understood. It would never have occurred to Father Sebastian that any predecessor could be a threat either to his authority or to his innovations. He neither confided in

Father Martin nor consulted him. If he wanted information about administrative details, he got it from the files or from his secretary. The most confident of men, he could probably have accommodated the Archbishop of Canterbury on his staff in a junior capacity without difficulty.

The relationship between him and Father Martin was one of trust and respect and, on Father Martin's part, of affection. As he had always found difficulty during his own stewardship in believing that he was in fact Warden, he accepted his successor with goodwill and some relief. And if he sometimes hankered a little wistfully for a warmer relationship, it was not one he could envisage. But now, seated by invitation in his customary chair by the fireplace and watching Father Sebastian's unusual restlessness, he was uneasily aware that something was needed from him – reassurance, advice or just the mutual sympathy of shared anxiety. He sat very still and, closing his eyes, murmured a brief prayer.

Father Sebastian stopped his pacing and said, 'Mrs Crampton left ten minutes ago. It was a painful interview.' He added, 'Painful for both of us.'

Father Martin said, 'It could not have been otherwise.'

He thought he detected in the Warden's voice a small peevish note of resentment that the Archdeacon had compounded his previous delinquencies by so inconsiderately getting himself murdered under their roof. The thought sparked off another even more disgracefully irreverent thought. What would Lady Macbeth have said to Duncan's widow had that lady come to Inverness Castle to view the body? 'A deplorable affair, madam, which my husband and I deeply regret. It was a most successful visit until then. We did all we could to make His Majesty comfortable.' Father Martin was amazed and shaken that an idea so perversely inappropriate could have come into his mind. He must, he thought, be getting light-headed.

Father Sebastian said, 'She insisted on being taken to the church to see where her husband died. Unwise, I thought, but Commander Dalgliesh gave in. She was adamant that she wanted him, not me, to accompany her. It was inappropriate but I thought it expedient not to protest. Of course it must mean that she saw the *Doom*. If Dalgliesh can trust her to keep quiet about the vandalism, why not trust my staff?'

Father Martin didn't like to say that Mrs Crampton wasn't a suspect and they were.

Father Sebastian, as if suddenly aware of his restlessness, came and sat opposite his colleague. 'I was unhappy about her driving home alone and suggested that Stephen Morby might accompany her. Of course it would have been inconvenient. He would have had to take the train back and then a taxi from Lowestoft. However, she preferred to be alone. I did ask if she would like to stay to lunch. She could have had it served quietly here or in my flat. The dining-room would hardly have been suitable.'

Father Martin silently agreed. It would have been an uncomfortable meal, with Mrs Crampton sitting among the suspects and being politely passed the potatoes, perhaps by her husband's murderer.

The Warden said, 'I'm afraid I failed her. One uses well-worn phrases on these occasions but they cease to make any sense, just a mutter of commonplace sounds with no reference to faith or meaning.'

Father Martin said, 'Whatever you said, Father, no one could have done it better. There are occasions that go beyond words.'

Mrs Crampton, he thought, would hardly have welcomed, or indeed needed, Father Sebastian's encouragement to Christian fortitude or his reminder of Christian hope.

Father Sebastian shifted uneasily in his chair then willed himself into stillness. 'I said nothing to Mrs Crampton about my altercation with her husband in the church yesterday afternoon. It would have caused her additional distress and could have done no possible good. I regret it deeply. It is distressing to know that the Archdeacon died with such anger in his heart. It was hardly a state of grace – for either of us.'

Father Martin said gently, 'We cannot know, Father, what spiritual state the Archdeacon was in when he died.'

His companion went on, 'I thought it a little insensitive of Dalgliesh to send his juniors to interview the priests. It would have been more appropriate had he spoken to us all himself. Naturally I co-operated, as I am sure did everyone else. I could wish that the police seemed more open to the possibility that someone outside the college is responsible, although I'm reluctant to believe that Inspector Yarwood had anything to do with it. Still, the sooner he is able to speak the better. And I'm naturally very anxious that the church should be reopened. The heart of the college hardly beats without it.'

Father Martin said, 'I don't suppose we shall be let back until the *Doom* has been cleaned, and perhaps that won't be possible. I mean, it may be needed in its present state as evidence.'

'That, of course, is ridiculous. Photographs have no doubt been taken and they should be sufficient. The cleaning does, however, present a difficulty. It will be a job for experts. The *Doom* is a national treasure. We could hardly let Pilbeam loose on it with a can of turpentine. And then there must be a service of rehallowing before the church can be used. I've been to the library to look at the canons, but they offer remarkably little guidance. Canon F15 deals with the profaning of churches but gives no direction for resanctification. There's the Roman rite, of course, and we could perhaps adapt that, but it is more complicated than seems appropriate. They envisage a procession led by a cross-bearer followed by the Bishop with mitre and pastoral staff, concelebrants, deacons and other ministers in proper liturgical vestitures processing before the people into the church.'

Father Martin said, 'I can't envisage the Bishop wishing to take part. You have, of course, been in touch with him, Father?'

'Naturally. He is coming over on Wednesday evening. He very considerately suggested that any time earlier might be inconvenient both for us and for the police. He has, of course, spoken to the trustees and I have little doubt what he will tell me formally when he arrives. St Anselm's will close at the end of this term. He is hoping that arrangements can be made to accommodate the ordinands in other theological colleges. It is expected that Cuddesdon and St Stephen's House will be able to help although not, of course, without difficulty. I have already spoken to the principals.'

Father Martin, outraged, cried out in protest but his old voice could produce only a humiliating quaver. 'But that's appalling. It gives us less than two months. What about the Pilbeams, Surtees, our part-time staff? Are people going to be thrown out of their cottages?'

'Of course not, Father.' There was a trace of impatience in Father Sebastian's voice. 'St Anselm's will close as a theological college at the end of this term but the resident staff will be kept on until the future of the buildings has been settled. That will apply also to the part-time staff. Paul Perronet has been on the telephone to me and will come over with the other trustees on Thursday. He's adamant that nothing of value should be removed at present either from the college or the church. Miss Arbuthnot's will was very clear as far as her intentions are concerned but undoubtedly the legal position will be complicated.'

Father Martin had been told the provisions of the will when he became Warden. He thought, but didn't say, we four priests will become rich men. How rich? he wondered. The thought horrified him. He found that his hands were shaking. Looking down at the veins like purple cords and the brown splotches which seemed more like the marks of a disease than the signs of old age, he felt his meagre store of strength ebbing away.

Looking at Father Sebastian he saw, with a sudden illuminating insight, a face pale and stoical but a mind already assessing its future, wonderfully impervious to the worst ravages of grief and anxiety. This time there could be no reprieve. Everything Father Sebastian had worked and planned for was going down in horror and scandal. He would survive but now, perhaps for the first time, he would have welcomed an assurance of it.

They sat opposite each other in silence. Father Martin longed to find the appropriate words but they wouldn't come. For fifteen years he hadn't once been asked for his advice, his reassurance, his sympathy or his help. Now, when they were needed, he found himself power-less. His failure went deeper than this moment. It seemed to encompass his whole priesthood. What had he given to his parishioners, to the ordinands or St Anselm's? There had been kindness, affection, tolerance and under-standing, but those were the common currency of all the well-intentioned. Had he, during the course of his ministry, changed a single life? He recalled the words of a woman overheard when he was leaving his last parish. 'Father Martin is a priest of whom no one ever speaks ill.' It seemed to him now the most damning of indictments.

After a moment he got up and Father Sebastian fol-lowed. He said, 'Would you like me, Father, to take a look at the Roman rite to see if it can be adapted for our use?'

Father Sebastian said, 'Thank you, Father, that would be helpful', and moved back to his chair behind the desk as Father Martin left the room and quietly closed the door behind him.

14

The first of the ordinands to be formally interviewed was Raphael Arbuthnot. Dalgliesh decided to see him with Kate. Arbuthnot took some time responding to the summons and it was ten minutes before he was shown into the interview room by Robbins.

Dalgliesh saw, with some surprise, that Raphael hadn't recovered himself; he looked as shocked and distressed as he had during the meeting in the library. Perhaps even this short lapse of time had brought home to him more forcibly the peril in which he stood. He moved as stiffly as an old man and refused Dalgliesh's invitation to sit. Instead he stood behind the chair, grasping the top with both hands, his knuckles as white as his face. Kate had the ridiculous notion that if she put out her hand to touch Raphael's skin or the curls of his hair, she would experience only unyielding stone. The contrast between the blond Hellenic head and the stark black of the clerical cassock looked both hierarchic and theatrically contrived.

Dalgliesh said, 'No one could have sat at dinner last night, as I did, without realizing that you disliked the Archdeacon. Why?'

It wasn't the opening that Arbuthnot had expected. Perhaps, thought Kate, he had mentally prepared himself for a more familiar academic gambit, innocuous preliminary questions about a candidate's personal history leading on to the more challenging inquisition. He stared fixedly at Dalgliesh and was silent.

It seemed impossible that any reply could come from those rigid lips, but when he spoke his voice was under control. 'I'd rather not say. Isn't it enough that I disliked him?' He paused, then said, 'It was stronger than that. I hated him. Hating him had become an obsession. I realize that now. Perhaps I was deflecting on to him the hatred I couldn't admit to feeling for someone or something else, a person, a place, an institution.'

He managed a rueful smile and said, 'If Father Sebastian were here he'd say I'm indulging my deplorable obsession with amateur psychology.'

Kate said, her voice surprisingly gentle, 'We do know about Father John's conviction.'

Was it his imagination, Dalgliesh wondered, that the tension in Raphael's hands relaxed a little? 'Of course. I'm being obtuse. I suppose you've checked on all of us. Poor Father John. The recording angel has nothing on the police computer. So you now know that Crampton was one of the chief prosecution witnesses. It was he, not the jury, who sent Father John to prison.'

Kate said, 'Juries don't send anyone to prison. The judge does that.' She added, as if afraid that Raphael was about to faint, 'Why don't you sit down, Mr Arbuthnot.'

After a moment of hesitation, he took the chair and made an obvious effort to relax. He said, 'People one hates ought not to get themselves murdered. It gives them an unfair advantage. I didn't kill him, but I feel as guilty as if I did.'

Dalgliesh said, 'The passage of Trollope you read at dinner yesterday, was that your choice?'

'Yes. We always choose what to read.'

Dalgliesh said, 'A very different archdeacon, another age. An ambitious man kneels beside his dying father and asks forgiveness for wishing him dead. It seemed to me that the Archdeacon took it personally.'

'He was intended to.' There was another silence, then Raphael said, 'I'd always wondered why he pursued Father John so vehemently. It isn't as if he was gay himself and suppressing it, terrified of exposure. Now I know he was vicariously purging his own guilt.'

Dalgliesh said, 'Guilt for what?'

'I think you had better ask Inspector Yarwood.'

Dalgliesh decided not to pursue that line of questioning for the moment. This wasn't the only question that he needed to ask Yarwood. Until the Inspector was fit to be interviewed he was groping in the half-light. He asked Raphael exactly what he had done after Compline was finished.

'First of all I went to my room. We're supposed to keep silence after Compline but the rule isn't invariably obeyed. Silence doesn't mean not speaking to each other. We don't act like Trappist monks, but we do usually go to our rooms. I read and worked on an essay until half-past ten. The wind was howling – well, you know, sir, you were here – and I decided to go into the house to see if Peter – that's Peter Buckhurst – was all right. He's recovering from glandular fever and he's far from well. I know he hates storms – not the lightning or thunder or heavy rain, just the howling of the wind. His mother died in the room next door to him in a night of high wind when he was seven and he's hated it ever since.'

'How did you enter the house?'

'The usual way. My room is N3 in the north cloister. I went through the cloakroom, across the hall and up the stairs to the second floor. There's a sick-room there at the back of the house and Peter has been sleeping in it for the last few weeks. It was obvious to me that he didn't want to be alone, so I said I'd stay there all night. There's a second bed in the sick-room so I slept there. I had already asked Father Sebastian's permission to leave college after Compline – I'd promised to attend the first Mass of a friend in a church outside Colchester – but I didn't like to leave Peter, so I decided to leave early this morning instead. The Mass isn't until ten-thirty so I knew I could make it.'

Dalgliesh asked, 'Mr Arbuthnot, why didn't you tell me this when we were in the library this morning? I asked if anyone had left his room after Compline.'

'Would you have spoken? It would have been pretty humiliating for Peter, wouldn't it, letting the whole college know that he's frightened of the wind?'

'How did you spend the evening together?'

'We talked, and then I read to him. A Saki short story, if you're interested.'

'Did you see anyone other than Peter Buckhurst after you entered the main building at about half-past ten?'

'Only Father Martin. He looked in on us at about eleven o'clock but he didn't stay. He was worried about Peter too.'

Kate asked, 'Was that because he knew Mr Buckhurst was frightened of high winds?'

'It's the kind of thing Father Martin gets to know. I don't think anyone else at college knew except the two of us.'

'Did you return to your own room at any time during the night?'

'No. There's a shower-room attached to the sick-bay if I wanted to shower. I didn't need pyjamas.'

Dalgliesh said, 'Mr Arbuthnot, are you absolutely certain that you locked the door to the house from the north cloister when you went in to your friend?'

'I'm absolutely sure. Mr Pilbeam usually checks the doors at about eleven when he locks the front door. He'll be able to confirm that it was locked.'

'And you didn't leave the sick-bay until this morning?'

'No. I was in the sick-bay all night. Peter and I put out our bedside lights at about midnight and settled down to sleep. I don't know about him, but I slept soundly. I woke just before six-thirty and saw that Peter was still asleep. I was on my way back to my room when I met Father Sebastian coming out of his office. He didn't seem surprised to see me and he didn't ask why I hadn't left. I realize now that he had other things on his mind. He just told me to ring round everyone, ordinands, staff and guests, and ask them to be in the library at seven-thirty. I remember I said, "What about Morning Prayer, Father?", and he replied, "Morning Prayer is cancelled".'

Dalgliesh asked, 'Did he give you any explanation for the summons?'

'No, none. It wasn't until I joined everyone else in the library at seven-thirty that I knew what had happened.'

'And there's nothing else you can tell us, nothing at all that could have any bearing on the Archdeacon's murder?'

There was a long silence during which Arbuthnot gazed down at the hands clasped in his lap. Then, as if he had reached a decision, he raised his eyes and looked intently at Dalgliesh. He said, 'You've been asking a lot of questions. I know that's your job. May I ask one now?'

Dalgliesh said, 'Certainly, although I can't promise to answer it.'

'It's this. It's obvious that you – the police, I mean – believe that someone who slept in college last night killed the Archdeacon. You must have some reason for believing that. I mean, isn't it far more likely that someone from outside broke into the church, perhaps to steal, and was surprised by Crampton? After all, this place isn't secure. He'd have no difficulty in getting into the courtyard. He probably wouldn't have much difficulty in breaking into the house and getting a key to the church. Anyone who's ever stayed here could know where the keys are kept. So I'm just wondering why you're concentrating on us – I mean, the priests and the ordinands.'

Dalgliesh said, 'We've an open mind on who committed this murder. More than that I can't tell you.'

Arbuthnot went on, 'You see, I've been thinking – well, of course, we all have. If anyone in college killed Crampton, it has to be me. No one else would or could. No one hated him as much and, even if they did, they aren't capable of murder. I'm wondering whether I could have done it without knowing. Perhaps I got up in the night and went back to my room, then saw him entering the church. Isn't it possible I could have gone after him, quarrelled violently with him and killed him?'

Dalgliesh's voice was calmly uninquisitive, 'Why should you think that?'

'Because it's at least possible. If this is what you call

329

an inside job, then who else could it have been? And there's one piece of evidence supporting it. When I went back to my room this morning after I'd phoned everyone to come to the library, I knew that someone had entered it during the night. There was a broken twig inside the door. Unless someone's removed it, it will still be there. Now you've closed the north cloister, I couldn't go back to check. I suppose it's evidence of a kind, but evidence of what?'

Dalgliesh asked, 'Are you sure that the twig wasn't in your room when you left after Compline to go and check on Peter Buckhurst?'

'I'm sure it wasn't. I'd have noticed it. I couldn't have missed it. Someone re-entered that room after I left to see Peter. I must have gone back sometime in the night. Who else could it have been at that hour and in a storm?'

Dalgliesh said, 'Have you ever in your life suffered from temporary amnesia?'

'No, never.'

'And you're telling me the truth, that you say you have no recollection of killing the Archdeacon?'

'Yes, I swear it.'

'All I can tell you is that whoever committed this murder can be in no doubt what he or she did last night.'

'You mean that I would have woken this morning with blood on my hands – literally on my hands?'

'I mean no more than I've said. I think that's all for now. If you later remember anything new, please tell us at once.'

The dismissal was summary and, Kate could see, unexpected. Still keeping his eyes on Dalgliesh, Arbuthnot murmured, 'Thank you,' and left.

They waited until the front door had closed behind him. Dalgliesh said, 'Well, which is it Kate, a consummate actor or a worried and innocent young man?'

'I'd say he's a pretty good actor. With looks like that you probably have to be. I know that doesn't make him guilty. It's a clever story though, isn't it? He more or less confesses to murder in the hope that he'll learn exactly how much we know. And his night with Buckhurst doesn't give him an alibi; he could easily have crept out when the boy was asleep, taken the keys to the church and rung the Archdeacon. We know from Miss Betterton that he's good at imitating voices; he could have pretended to be any of the priests and if he was seen in the house, well no one would question his right to be there. Even if Peter Buckhurst woke up and found him gone, there's a good chance he wouldn't betray his friend. Much easier to make himself believe that the spare bed wasn't empty.'

Dalgliesh said, 'We'd better question him next. You and Piers can do that. But if Arbuthnot took the key, why not put it back when he returned to the house? A strong probability is that whoever killed Crampton didn't go back into college unless, of course, that's exactly what we're intended to believe. If Raphael did kill the Archdeacon – and until we have spoken to Yarwood he remains the chief suspect – his cleverest ploy would be to throw the key away. Did you notice that he didn't once mention Yarwood as a possible suspect? He's not stupid, he must realize the possible significance of Yarwood's disappearance. He can't be naïve enough to assume that no police officer is ever capable of murder.'

Kate said, 'And the twig inside his room?'

'He says it's still there, and no doubt it is. The question is, how did it get there and when? It means that the SOCOs will have to extend the search area to Arbuthnot's rooms. If he's telling the truth – and it's an odd story – then the twig could be important. But this murder was carefully planned. If Arbuthnot had murder in mind, why complicate things by going to Peter Buckhurst's room? If his friend had been seriously distressed by the storm, Arbuthnot could hardly leave him. And he couldn't rely on the boy falling asleep, even at midnight.'

'But if he was hoping to fabricate an alibi, Peter Buckhurst was probably his only chance. After all, a sick and frightened young man would be easy to deceive about the time. If Arbuthnot planned the murder for midnight, for example, he could easily murmur to Buckhurst when they settled down to sleep that it was after twelve o'clock.'

'Which would only be helpful to him, Kate, if the pathologist could tell us more or less precisely when Crampton was killed. Arbuthnot hasn't an alibi, but that goes for everyone in college.'

'Including Yarwood.'

'And he may hold the key to the whole business. We have to press on but, until he's fit enough to be interviewed, we could be missing vital evidence.'

Kate asked, 'You don't see him as a suspect, sir?'

'At present he has to be, but he's an unlikely one. I can't see a man in such a precarious mental state planning and executing such a complicated crime. If finding Crampton so unexpectedly at St Anselm's had roused him to a murderous rage he could have struck him down in his bed.'

'But that goes for all the suspects, sir.'

'Exactly. We get back to the central question. Why was the murder planned in this way?'

Nobby Clark and the photographer were at the door. Clark's face assumed a look of solemn reverence as if he were entering a church. It was a sure sign that he had good news. Coming over to the table, he laid out Polaroids of fingerprints: the index to the little finger of the right hand, and beside them a palm print, again of the right hand, this time showing the side of the thumb and four clear prints of the fingers. He laid a standard fingerprint form beside them.

He said, 'Dr Stannard, sir. You couldn't hope for anything clearer. The palm print's on the stone wall to the right of the *Doom*, the other print's on the seat of the second box pew. We can take a palm print, sir, but it's hardly necessary with what we've got. No point in sending it off to HQ for verification. I've seldom seen clearer prints. They're Dr Stannard's, all right.'

15

Piers said, 'If Stannard is Cain, this will be our shortest investigation to date. Back to the smoke. Pity. I was looking forward to dinner at the Crown and a pre-breakfast walk on the beach.'

Dalgliesh was standing at the east window looking out over the headland to the sea. Turning, he said, 'I shouldn't give up hope of it.'

They had pulled out the desk from under the window and placed it in the middle of the room with the two upright chairs behind it. Stannard would sit in the low armchair now brought forward to face the desk. He would be physically the most comfortable but psychologically disadvantaged.

They waited in silence. Dalgliesh showed no inclination to talk and Piers had worked with him long enough to know when to keep quiet. Robbins must be having difficulty in finding Stannard. It was nearly five minutes before they heard the front door opening.

Robbins said, 'Dr Stannard, sir,' and settled himself unobtrusively in the corner, notebook in hand.

Stannard came in briskly, responding curtly to Dalgliesh's 'Good morning', and looked round as if wondering where he was expected to sit.

Piers said, 'This chair, Dr Stannard.'

Stannard looked with deliberate intentness round the room as if deploring its inadequacies, then sat, leaned back, appeared to decide that the assumption of ease was inappropriate, and resettled himself on the edge of the chair, legs clamped together, hands in his jacket pocket. His gaze, fixed on Dalgliesh, was inquiring rather than belligerent, but Piers sensed his resentment, and something stronger which he diagnosed as fear.

No one is at his best when involved in an investigation of murder; even reasonable and public-spirited witnesses, fortified by innocence, can come to resent the intrusion of police probing, and no one faces it with an entirely clear conscience. Minor and unrelated ancient delinquencies float to the surface of the mind like scum. Even so, Piers found Stannard singularly unprepossessing. It wasn't, he decided, only his prejudice against drooping moustaches; he just didn't like the man. Stannard's face, a thin over-long nose and close-set eyes, had settled into deeply-cleft lines of discontent. This was the face of a man who had never quite achieved what he felt was his due. What, Piers wondered, had gone wrong? The upper-second degree instead of the expected first? A lectureship at an ex-polytechnic university instead of Oxbridge? Less power, less money, less sex than he felt he deserved? Probably not too little sex; women unaccountably seemed attracted to this Che Guevara amateur revolutionary type. Hadn't he at Oxford lost his Rosie to just such a sour-faced wanker? Perhaps, he admitted, that was the cause of his prejudice. He was too experienced not to keep it under control, but even to admit to it gave him a perverted satisfaction.

He had worked with Dalgliesh long enough to know how this scene would be played. He would ask most of the questions; AD would come in when and as he chose.

It was never what the witness expected. Piers wondered whether Dalgliesh knew how intimidating was his dark silent watchful presence.

He introduced himself then began asking the usual preliminary questions in an even voice. Name, address, date of birth, occupation, marital state. Stannard's replies were short. At the end he said, 'I don't see what relevance my marital state has to all this. Actually I have a partner. Female.'

Without replying, Piers asked, 'And you arrived when, sir?'

'Friday night for a long weekend. I'm due to leave before dinner tonight. I presume there's no reason why I shouldn't?'

'Are you a regular visitor, sir?'

'Fairly. During the last eighteen months or so the occasional weekends.'

'Could you be more specific?'

'About half a dozen visits I suppose.'

'When were you last here?'

'A month ago. I forget the exact date. Then I arrived Friday night and stayed until Sunday. Compared with this weekend it was uneventful.'

Dalgliesh interposed for the first time. 'Why do you visit, Dr Stannard?'

Stannard opened his mouth, then hesitated. Piers wondered whether he had been about to reply, 'Why shouldn't I?' and had thought better of it. The answer, when it did come, sounded as if it had been carefully prepared.

'I'm researching a book on the family life of the early Tractarians covering both their childhood and youth, their later marriages, if any, and family life. The intention is to explore early experience with religious development and sexuality. As this is an Anglo-Catholic institution the library is particularly useful, and I have an entry to it. My grandfather was Samuel Stannard, a partner in the firm of Stannard, Fox and Perronet in Norwich. They have represented St Anselm's since its foundation and the Arbuthnot family before that. Coming here I combine research with an agreeable weekend break.'

Piers asked, 'How far has research progressed?'

'It's at an early stage. I don't get much free time. Contrary to popular belief, academics are overworked.'

'But you have papers with you, evidence of work done so far?'

'No. My papers are in college.'

Piers said, 'These visits – I would have thought you had exhausted the possibilities of the library here. What about other libraries? The Bodleian?'

Stannard said sourly, 'There are libraries other than the Bodleian.'

'True. There's Pusey House at Oxford. I believe they have a remarkable Tractarian collection. The librarian there should be able to help.' He turned to Dalgliesh. 'And there's London, of course. Is the Dr Williams Library in Bloomsbury still in existence, sir?'

Before Dalgliesh could reply, if he had intended to, Stannard broke out, 'What the hell business is it of yours where I choose to do my research? And if you're trying to show that, occasionally, the Met recruits educated officers, forget it. I'm not impressed.'

Piers said, 'Just trying to be helpful. So you've visited here some half-dozen times in the last eighteen months to work in the library and enjoy a recuperative weekend. Has Archdeacon Crampton been here on any of those previous occasions?'

'No. I never met him until this weekend. He didn't arrive until Saturday. I don't know when exactly, but the first I saw of him was at tea. Tea was laid out in the students' sitting-room and the room was pretty full when I arrived at four. Someone – I think it was Raphael Arbuthnot – introduced me to the people I hadn't met but I didn't feel inclined to chat so I took a cup of tea and a couple of sandwiches and went to the library. That old fool Father Peregrine took his head out of his book long enough to tell me that food and drink weren't allowed in the library. I went to my room. I saw the Archdeacon next at dinner. After dinner I worked in the library until they all went to Compline. I'm an atheist so I didn't join them.'

'And you learned of the murder when?'

'Just before seven when Raphael Arbuthnot rang to say that a general meeting had been called and that we were to assemble in the library at seven-thirty. I didn't much care for being spoken to as if I were back at school, but I thought I might as well see what it was all about. As far as the murder is concerned, I know less than you.'

Piers asked, 'Have you ever attended any of the services here?'

'No I haven't. I came here for the library and for a quiet weekend, not to attend services. It doesn't seem to worry the priests so I don't see why it should concern you.'

Piers said, 'Oh but it does, Mr Stannard, it does. Are

you telling us that you have never in fact been in the church?'

'No, I'm not saying that. Don't put words into my mouth. I may have looked in out of curiosity on one of the visits. I've certainly seen the inside, including the *Doom*, which has some interest for me. I'm saying I have never attended a service.'

Without looking up from the paper before him, Dalgliesh asked, 'When were you last in the church, Dr Stannard?'

'I can't remember. Why should I? Not this weekend anyway.'

'And when during this weekend did you last see Archdeacon Crampton?'

'After church. I heard some of them coming back about quarter-past ten. I was in the students' sitting-room watching a video. There was nothing worth seeing on television and they have a small collection of videos. I put on *Four Weddings and a Funeral*. I'd seen it before, but I thought it was worth a second viewing. Crampton looked in briefly but I wasn't exactly welcoming, so he made off.'

Piers said, 'So you must have been the last person, or one of the last people, to see him alive.'

'Which I suppose you regard as suspicious. I wasn't the last person to see him alive; his murderer was. I didn't kill him. Look, how often do I have to say it? I never knew the man. I'd no quarrel with him and I didn't go near the church yesterday evening. I was in bed by eleven-thirty. After the video finished I went out by the door into the south cloister and to my room. The gale was at its height by then and it wasn't a night for taking a last breath of sea air. I went straight to my set. It's number one in the south cloister.'

'Was there a light in the church?'

'Not that I noticed. Come to think of it, I didn't see any lights from the ordinands' rooms or the guest suites. There was the usual rather dim light in both cloisters.'

Piers said, 'You'll understand that we need to get as complete a picture as possible of what happened in the hours before the Archdeacon was killed. Did you hear or notice anything which could be significant?'

Stannard gave a mirthless laugh. 'I imagine a hell of a lot was happening, but I can't see into people's minds. I did get the impression that the Archdeacon wasn't exactly welcome, but no one made murderous threats to him in my hearing.'

'Did you speak to him at all after that introduction at tea?'

'Only to ask him to pass the butter at dinner. He passed it. I'm not good at small talk so I concentrated on the food and wine which were superior to the company. Not exactly a cheerful meal. It wasn't the usual happy all-boys-together-under-God – or under Sebastian Morell, which means the same thing. But your boss was there. He'll tell you about dinner.'

Piers said, 'The Commander knows what he saw and heard. We're asking you.'

'I've told you, not a cheerful meal. The ordinands seemed subdued, Father Sebastian presided with icy courtesy and some people had difficulty in keeping their eyes off Emma Lavenham, for which I can't say I blame them. Raphael Arbuthnot read a passage from Trollope – not a novelist I know but it seemed pretty innocuous to me. Not to the Archdeacon, however. And if Arbuthnot wanted to embarrass him he chose the right time. It's difficult to pretend you're enjoying your meal when your hands are shaking and you look as if you are about to sick it up over the plate. After dinner they all beetled off to church and that was the last I saw of any of them until Crampton looked in on me when I was watching the video.'

'And you saw or heard nothing suspicious during the night?'

'You asked that when we were together in the library. If I'd seen or heard anything suspicious, I'd have come forward before now.'

It was Piers who asked the question this time: 'And you haven't set foot in the church during this visit, either for a service or at any other time?'

'How many times have I got to keep telling you? The answer is no. No. No. No.'

Dalgliesh looked up and met Stannard's eyes. 'Then how do you explain the fact that your fresh fingerprints are on the wall next to the *Doom* and on the seat of the second box pew? The dust under the pew has been disturbed. It is highly likely the forensic scientists will find some traces of it on your jacket. Is that where you were hiding when the Archdeacon came into the church?'

And now Piers saw real terror. As always it unnerved him. He felt no triumph, only shame. It was one thing to put a suspect at a disadvantage, another to witness this transformation of a man into a terrified animal. Stannard seemed physically to shrink, a thin under-nourished child in a chair too large for him. His hands were still in his pockets. Now he tried to wrap them round his body. The thin tweed stretched and Piers thought he heard the rip of the lining seam.

Dalgliesh said quietly, 'The evidence is incontrovertible. You've been lying since you came into this room. If you didn't murder Archdeacon Crampton you would be wise to tell the truth now, all the truth.'

Stannard didn't reply. He had taken his hands from his pockets and now clasped them in his lap. With his head bent above them he looked incongruously like a man at prayer. He appeared to be thinking and they waited in silence. When at last he lifted his head and spoke, it was apparent that he had mastered the extremity of fear and was ready to fight back. Piers heard in his voice a mixture of obstinacy and arrogance.

'I didn't kill Crampton and you can't prove that I did. All right, I lied about not visiting the church. That was natural. I knew that if I told the truth you'd immediately seize on me as the prime suspect. It's all very convenient for you, isn't it? The last thing you want is to pin this on anyone at St Anselm's. I'm tailor-made to be fitted up, those priests are sacrosanct. Well, I didn't do it.'

Piers said, 'Then why were you in the church? You could hardly expect us to believe you went there to pray.'

Stannard didn't reply. He seemed to be steeling himself for the inevitable explanation or perhaps selecting the most convincing and appropriate words. When he spoke he looked fixedly at the far wall, carefully avoiding Dalgliesh's eyes. His voice was controlled but with a barely concealed note of petulant self-justification.

'All right, I accept that you have a right to an explanation and that I have a duty to provide it. It's perfectly innocent and nothing to do with Crampton's death. That being so, I would be grateful for your assurance that this interview is confidential.'

Dalgliesh said, 'You know we can't give you that.'

'Look, I've told you, it had nothing to do with Crampton's death. I only met him for the first time on Saturday. I'd never seen him before. I had no quarrel with him and no reason to wish him dead. I dislike violence. I'm a pacifist and not just by political conviction.'

Dalgliesh said, 'Dr Stannard, will you please answer my question. You were hiding in the church. Why?'

'I'm trying to tell you. I was looking for something. It's a document usually referred to by the few in the know as the St Anselm papyrus. It's reputed to be an order ostensibly signed by Pontius Pilate to the Captain of the Guard ordering the removal of the crucified body of a political troublemaker. Naturally you can see its importance. It was given to the founder of St Anselm's, Miss Arbuthnot, by her brother and has been in the custody of the Warden ever since. The story is that the document is a fake, but since no one is allowed to see it or submit it to scientific examination, the question is open. Obviously the document is of interest to any genuine scholar.'

Piers said, 'Like yourself, for example? I didn't realize you were an expert in pre-Byzantine manuscripts. Aren't you a sociologist?'

'That doesn't prevent me from having an interest in church history.'

Piers went on, 'So, knowing that you were unlikely to be given a sight of the document, you decided to steal it.'

Stannard gave Piers a look of concentrated malevolence. He said with heavy irony, 'I believe the legal definition of theft is taking with the intention of permanently depriving the owner of possession. You're a police officer, I should have thought that you'd have known that.'

Dalgliesh said, 'Dr Stannard, your rudeness may be natural to you, or you may find it a pleasurable if childish release of tension, but it is inadvisable to indulge it when involved in a police investigation of murder. So, you went to the church. Why did you think the papyrus was hidden in the church?'

'It seemed the natural place. I'd been going through the books in the library – at least as far as possible with Father Peregrine permanently there and noticing everything while pretending to notice nothing. I thought it was time to turn attention elsewhere. It occurred to me that the document could have been hidden behind the *Doom*. I went to the church on Saturday afternoon. The college is always quiet on Saturdays after luncheon.'

'How did you get into the church?'

'I had keys. I was here just after Easter when most of the ordinands were away and Miss Ramsey was on leave. I borrowed the church keys, a Chubb and a Yale, from the outer office and got them cut in Lowestoft. They weren't missed in the couple of hours it took. If they had been I planned to say that I'd found them lying in the south cloister. Anyone could have dropped them.'

'You thought of everything. Where are these keys now?'

'After Sebastian Morell's bombshell in the library this

morning I decided they weren't exactly the kind of thing I'd like to have found on me. If you must know, I chucked them away. To be more accurate, I wiped them of fingerprints and buried them under a clump of grass on the edge of the cliff.'

Piers said, 'Would you be able to find them again?'

'Probably. It might take a bit of time, but I know where I buried them within, say, ten yards.'

Dalgliesh said, 'Then you'd better find them. Sergeant Robbins will go with you.'

Piers asked, 'And what did you propose doing with the St Anselm papyrus if you found it?'

'Copying it. Writing an article about it for the broadsheets and in the academic press. I proposed bringing it where any document of that importance ought to be: in the public domain.'

Piers said, 'For cash, for academic glory, or for both?'

Stannard's look at him was positively venomous. 'If I'd written a book, as I had in mind, obviously it would make money.'

'Money, fame, academic prestige, your picture in the broadsheets. People have murdered for less.'

Before Stannard could expostulate, Dalgliesh said, 'I take it that you didn't find the papyrus.'

'No. I took a long wooden paper-knife with me hoping to dislodge whatever might be hidden between the *Doom* and the church wall. I was standing on one of the chairs to reach up when I heard someone coming into the church. I quickly replaced the chair and hid. Apparently you already know where.'

Piers said, 'The second box pew. Schoolboys' games. A bit humiliating, wasn't it? Couldn't you just have sunk to your knees? No, perhaps a pretence at prayer wouldn't have been convincing.'

'And confess that I'd got keys to the church? Oddly enough, that didn't seem to be an option.' He turned to Dalgliesh. 'But I can prove I'm telling the truth. I didn't watch to see who was coming in, but when they moved up the central aisle to the nave, I heard them clearly. It was Morell and the Archdeacon. They were arguing over the future of St Anselm's. I could probably reproduce most of the conversation. I've got a good memory for speech and they weren't bothering to keep their voices down. If you're looking for someone with a grudge against the Archdeacon, you don't need to look far. One of the things he was threatening was to get the valuable altar-piece moved out of the church.'

Piers asked, in a tone which could have been mistaken for genuine interest, 'What explanation were you proposing to give if they had happened to look under the seat of the pew and found you? I mean, you've obviously thought things through very thoroughly. Presumably you had some explanation ready?'

Stannard treated the inquiry as he might have an unintelligent intervention from a not very promising pupil. 'The suggestion is ridiculous. Why should they have searched the pew? Even if they had looked in the pew, why should they have bothered to kneel down and search under the seat? If they had, obviously I should have been in an embarrassing position.'

Dalgliesh said, 'You're in an embarrassing position now, Dr Stannard. You admit to one unsuccessful attempt to search the church. How can we be sure that you didn't return again late on Saturday night?'

'I give you my word that I didn't. What else can I say?'
Then he added truculently, 'And you can't prove that I
did.'

Piers said, 'You said you used a wooden paper-knife
to prod behind the *Doom*. Are you sure that's all you
used? Didn't you go into the kitchen at St Anselm's that
night while the community were at Compline and take
a carving knife?'

And now Stannard's careful nonchalance, the barely
concealed truculence and arrogance, gave way to frank
terror. The skin round the moist over-red mouth was a
white penumbra and the cheekbones stood out scarred
with red lines against skin which was drained into an
unhealthy greenish-grey.

He turned his whole body to Dalgliesh with a vehemence which nearly overturned the chair. 'My God,
Dalgliesh, you've got to believe me! I didn't go into the
kitchen. I couldn't stick a knife into anyone, not even an
animal. I couldn't slit the throat of a cat. It's ludicrous!
It's appalling to suggest it. I was in the church only
once, I swear it, and all I had with me was a wooden
paper-knife. I can show it to you. I'll get it now.'

He half rose from his chair and gazed with desperate
appeal from one set face to the other. No one spoke.
Then he said with a small surge of hope and triumph,
'There's something else. I think I can prove I didn't go
back. I rang my girlfriend in New York at eleven-thirty
our time. The relationship has hit a sticky patch and we
have been speaking by phone nearly every day. I used
my mobile and I can give you her number. I wouldn't
spend a half-hour speaking to her if I was planning to
murder the Archdeacon.'

'No,' said Piers. 'Not if the murder was planned.'

But gazing into Stannard's terrified eyes, Dalgliesh knew that here was one suspect who could almost certainly be eliminated. Stannard had no idea how the Archdeacon had died.

Stannard said, 'I'm due back at university on Monday morning. I was planning to leave tonight. Pilbeam was going to drive me to Ipswich. You can't keep me here, I've done nothing wrong.'

Getting no response, he added in a voice half-propitiatory, half-angry: 'Look, I've got my passport with me. I always carry it. I don't drive, so it's useful for identification. I suppose if I gave it up temporarily there's no objection to letting me go?'

Dalgliesh said, 'Inspector Tarrant will take charge of it and give you a receipt. This isn't the end of the matter, but you are free to go.'

'And I suppose you're going to tell Sebastian Morell what happened.'

'No,' said Dalgliesh. 'You are.'

16

Dalgliesh, Father Sebastian and Father Martin met in Father Sebastian's office. Father Sebastian had remembered almost word for word the conversation between him and the Archdeacon in the church. He spoke the dialogue as if reciting something learnt by rote but Dalgliesh didn't miss the note of self-disgust in his voice. At the end the Warden was silent, giving no explanation and offering no extenuation. During the recital Father Martin sat quietly in a fireside chair with his head bowed, as still and attentive as if he were hearing a confession.

There was a pause. Dalgliesh said, 'Thank you, Father. That agrees with the account given by Dr Stannard.'

Father Sebastian said, 'Forgive me if I'm intruding on your field of responsibility, but the fact that Stannard was hidden in the church on Saturday afternoon doesn't mean that he didn't return late that night. Do I take it that you have exonerated him from the inquiry?'

Dalgliesh had no intention of revealing that Stannard had been ignorant of how the Archdeacon had died. He was wondering whether Father Sebastian had forgotten the significance of the missing key, when the Warden said, 'Obviously having made a copy of the key, he didn't need to take one from the office. But surely he could have done that simply to throw suspicion elsewhere.'

Dalgliesh said, 'That would be to assume, of course,

that the murder was planned in advance and was not an impulse of the moment. Stannard isn't exonerated – at present no one is – but I've told him that he can leave and I imagine that you'll be glad to see the last of him.'

'Very glad. We were beginning to suspect that his explanation for being with us, his research into the domestic life of the early Tractarians, was a cover for another interest. Father Peregrine in particular was suspicious. But Stannard's grandfather was a senior partner in the firm of solicitors who had dealt with the college since the nineteenth century. He did a great deal for us and we were loath to disoblige his grandson. Perhaps the Archdeacon was right; we are too apt to be in thrall to our past. My meeting with Stannard was not comfortable. His attitude was a mixture of bluster and sophistry. He offered a not unusual excuse for cupidity and dishonesty: the sanctity of historical research.'

Father Martin hadn't spoken during the whole of the interview. He and Dalgliesh left the outer office in silence. Once outside he stopped short and asked, 'Would you like to see the Anselm papyrus?'

'Yes, very much.'

'I keep it in my sitting-room.'

They climbed the circular staircase to the tower. The view was spectacular but the room wasn't comfortable. It gave the impression of being furnished with odd pieces too old to be on public view but too good to throw away. Such an expedient jumble can produce an atmosphere of cheerful intimacy, but here it was depressing. Dalgliesh doubted whether Father Martin even noticed.

On the wall which faced north there was a small religious print in a brown leather frame. It was difficult to see clearly, but at first sight it had little artistic merit and the colours were so weak that it was difficult to make out even the central figure of the Virgin and Child. Father Martin took it down and slid off the top of the frame. He drew out the print. Beneath it were two panes of glass, and between them what looked like a sheet of thick cardboard, cracked and broken at the edges and covered with rows of scratched and spiky black lettering. Father Martin didn't carry it over to the window and Dalgliesh had difficulty in deciphering any of the Latin except for the superscription. There seemed to be a round circular mark in the right-hand corner where the papyrus had broken away. He could clearly see the criss-cross of the compounded reeds from which it was made.

Father Martin said, 'It has only been examined once, and that soon after Miss Arbuthnot received it. There seems no doubt that the papyrus itself is old, almost certainly dating from the first century AD. Her brother Edwin would have had no difficulty in getting hold of it. He was, as I expect you know, an Egyptologist.'

Dalgliesh said, 'But why did he hand it over to his sister? It seems a curious thing to have done whatever its provenance. If it was faked to discredit her religion, why keep it secret? If he thought it was genuine, wasn't that an even better reason for making it public?'

Father Martin said, 'That's one of the chief reasons why we've always regarded it as a fake. Why part with it when, if genuine, he would have got fame and prestige from its discovery? He may, of course, have wanted his sister to destroy it. He had probably kept photographs and, had she done so, could have accused the college of deliberately destroying a papyrus of incomparable importance. She was probably wise to act as she did. His motives are less explicable.'

Dalgliesh said, 'There's also the question of why Pilate would bother to put the command in writing. Surely a word in the right ear would have been the normal way.'

'Not necessarily. I don't have the same difficulty with that.'

Dalgliesh said, 'But the matter could now be settled one way or the other, if that's what you wish. Even if the papyrus dates back to the time of Christ, the ink could be carbon-dated. It's possible now to know the truth.'

Father Martin, with great care, was putting the print and the frame together again. Finally he hung the picture on the wall and stood back assessing that he had replaced it evenly. He said, 'You believe then, Adam, that the truth can never hurt.'

'I wouldn't say that. But I believe we have to search for it, however unwelcome it may be when we find it.'

'That's your job, a searching for truth. You never get the whole truth, of course. How could you? You're a very clever man but what you do doesn't result in justice. There's the justice of men and the justice of God.'

Dalgliesh said, 'I'm not that arrogant, Father. I limit my ambition to the justice of men, or as close to it as I can get. And even that isn't in my hands. It's my job to make an arrest. The jury decide on guilt or innocence; the judge sentences.'

'And the result is justice?'

'Not always. Perhaps even not often. But in an imperfect world it may be as close to it as we can get.'

Father Martin said, 'I'm not denying the importance

of truth. How could I? I'm simply saying that the search for it can be dangerous, and so can the truth when it's discovered. You suggest that we should have the Anselm papyrus examined, the truth established by carbon dating. But that wouldn't stop the controversy. People would argue that the papyrus is so convincing that it must be a copy of an earlier and genuine one. Others would choose not to believe the experts. We would face years of damaging controversy. There would always be something mysterious about the papyrus. We don't want to set up another Turin Shroud.'

There was a question which Dalgliesh wanted to ask but he hesitated, aware of its presumption, aware too that once spoken it would be answered honestly and perhaps with pain. 'Father, if the papyrus were examined and it were possible to know with almost complete certainty that it was genuine, would that make a difference to your faith?'

Father Martin smiled. He said, 'My son, for one who every hour of his life has the assurance of the living presence of Christ, why should I worry about what happened to earthly bones?'

In the office below, Father Sebastian had asked Emma to come and see him. Sitting her in a chair, he said, 'I expect you wish to go back to Cambridge as soon as possible. I've spoken to Mr Dalgliesh and he says that he has no objection. I understand that at present he has no power to keep anyone here who wishes to leave provided the police know how to contact them. There's no question, of course, of any of the priests or ordinands leaving.'

Irritation amounting to outrage made Emma's voice sharper than she realized. 'You mean that you and Mr

Dalgliesh have been discussing what I should or should not do! Father, isn't that for you and me to decide?'

Father Sebastian bent his head for a moment, then looked her in the eyes. 'I'm sorry, Emma, I've expressed myself clumsily. It wasn't like that. I rather assumed that you would wish to leave.'

'But why? Why should you assume that?'

'My child, there's a murderer among us. We have to face that. I should be easier in my mind if you were not here. I know that we have no reason to suppose that any of us is in danger at St Anselm's but it can't be a very happy or peaceful place for you, for anyone.'

Emma's voice was more gentle. 'That doesn't mean I want to leave it. You said that the college should continue with its daily life as far as possible. I thought that meant I would stay and give my usual three seminars. I don't see what that has got to do with the police.'

'Nothing, Emma. I spoke to Dalgliesh because I knew you and I would have to have this discussion. Before doing so I thought I ought to find out whether any of us is in fact free to leave. It would have been pointless to discuss your wishes until I'd ascertained that. You must forgive my tactlessness. We are all to some extent the prisoners of our upbringing. I'm afraid my instinct is to thrust women and children into the lifeboats.' He smiled, then said, 'It's a habit my wife used to complain of.'

Emma asked, 'What about Mrs Pilbeam and Karen Surtees? Are they leaving?'

He hesitated and gave a rueful smile. Emma was even able to laugh. 'Oh Father, you aren't going to tell me that they are both all right because they have a man to protect them!'

'No, I wasn't proposing to aggravate my offence. Miss Surtees has told the police that she intends to remain with her brother until an arrest is made. She may be here some time. I take it that it will be she who will be doing the protecting. I have suggested to the Pilbeams that Mrs Pilbeam should visit one of her married sons but she asked with some asperity who in that case would be doing the cooking.'

Emma was struck with an uncomfortable thought. She said, 'I'm sorry I was so sharp and perhaps I'm being selfish. If it would be easier for you – for everyone – if I left, then of course I'll go. I didn't mean to be a bother, or to increase your anxieties. I was just thinking of what I wanted.'

'Then please stay. Your presence, particularly for the next three days, may add to my anxiety, but it will immeasurably add to our comfort and peace. You have always been good for this place, Emma. You are good for it now.'

Again their eyes met and she had no doubt of what she saw in his: pleasure and relief. She looked away, aware that he might discern in her eyes a less acceptable emotion: pity. She thought, he's not young and this is terrible for him, perhaps the end of everything he's worked for and loved.

17

Lunch at St Anselm's was a simpler meal than dinner, consisting generally of soup followed by a variety of salads with cold meats and a hot vegetarian dish. Like dinner, it was eaten partly in silence. Today the silence was particularly welcome to Emma and, she suspected, to everyone present. When the community was together silence seemed the only possible response to a tragedy that in its bizarre horror was as much beyond speech as it was beyond comprehension. And silence at St Anselm's was always a benison, more positive than the mere absence of speech; now it invested the meal with a brief illusion of normality. Little was eaten, however, and even the soup bowls were pushed aside half empty while Mrs Pilbeam, white-faced, moved among them like an automaton.

Emma had planned to return to Ambrose to work but knew that concentration would be impossible. On an impulse which at first she found difficult to explain, she decided to see if George Gregory was in St Luke's Cottage. He wasn't always resident in college when she visited, but when he was they were easy in each other's company without ever being intimate. But now she needed to talk to someone who was in St Anselm's but not of it, someone with whom she need not weigh every word. It would be a relief to be able to discuss the murder with someone she suspected would find it more intriguing than personally distressing.

Gregory was at home. The door of St Luke's Cottage stood open and even as she approached she could hear that he was listening to Handel. She recognized the tape as one she owned herself, the counter-tenor James Bowman singing *Ombra Mai Fu*. The voice of exquisite beauty and clarity swelled out over the headland. She waited until the music ended and even as she lifted her hand to the knocker he called out for her to come in. She passed through his ordered book-lined study and into the glass extension overlooking the headland. He was drinking coffee and the rich smell of it filled the room. She hadn't waited for coffee in college, but when he offered to fetch a second cup she accepted. He placed a small table beside the low wicker chair and she leaned back, surprisingly glad to be there.

She had come with no clear ideas, but there was something she needed to say. She watched him as he poured the coffee. The goatee beard gave a slightly sinister Mephistophelean look to a face which she had always thought more handsome than attractive. He had a high sloping forehead from which the fair hair sprang back in waves so regular that they looked as if they had been produced by heated rollers. Under thin lids his eyes regarded the world with an amused or ironic contempt. He looked after himself. She knew that he ran daily and swam, except in the coldest months of the year. As he handed her the cup she saw again the deformity which he never made any attempt to conceal. The top half of the third finger on his left hand had been chopped off in adolescence in an accident with an axe. He had explained the circumstances to her at their first meeting and she had realized that he needed to emphasize that it had been an accident and his own fault, not a birth defect. It had surprised her that he should so obviously resent and feel it necessary to explain a deformity that could hardly inconvenience him. It was, she thought, a measure of his self-regard.

Now she said, 'There's something I want to consult you about – no, that's the wrong word – something I need to talk over.'

'I'm flattered, but why me? Wouldn't one of the priests be more appropriate?'

'I can't worry Father Martin with it and I know what Father Sebastian would say – at least I think I know, although he can be surprising.'

Gregory said, 'But if it's a moral question, they're supposed to be the experts.'

'I suppose it is a moral question – at least, it's an ethical question – but I'm not sure I want an expert. How far do you think we ought to co-operate with the police? How much should we tell them?'

'That's the question, is it?'

'That's the question.'

He said, 'We may as well be specific. I suppose you do want Crampton's murderer caught? You haven't any problem with that? You don't feel that in certain circumstances murder ought to be condoned?'

'No, I never feel that. I want all murderers caught. I'm not sure I know what ought to happen to them afterwards, but even if one feels empathy for them – perhaps even sympathy – I still want them caught.'

'But you don't want to take too active a part in the catching?'

'I don't want to hurt the innocent.'

'Ah,' he said, 'but you can't help it. Dalgliesh can't help it. That's what a murder investigation always does, it hurts the innocent. Which particular innocent have you in mind?'

'I'd rather not say.'

There was a silence, then she said, 'I don't know why I'm bothering you with this. I suppose I needed to talk to someone who isn't really part of the college.'

He said, 'You're talking to me because I'm not important to you. You're not attracted to me sexually. You're content to be here because nothing we say to each other will change the relationship between us; there's nothing to be changed. You think I'm intelligent, honest, unshockable and that you can trust me. All that is true. And, incidentally, you don't believe I murdered Crampton. You're perfectly right, I didn't. He made virtually no impact on me when he was alive and he makes even less now he's dead. I admit to a natural curiosity about who killed him, but that's as far as it goes. And I should like to know how he died, but you're not going to tell me and I shan't invite a rebuff by asking. But, of course, I'm involved. We all are. Dalgliesh hasn't sent for me yet, but I don't deceive myself that it's because I'm low on his list of suspects.'

'So what will you say when he does?'

'I shall answer his questions honestly. I shan't lie. If I'm asked for an opinion I shall give it with extreme care. I shan't theorize and I shan't volunteer information I'm not asked for. I certainly shan't attempt to do the police's work for them; they're paid enough, God knows. And I'll remember that I can always add to what I've told them, but words once spoken can't be recalled. That's

359

what I plan to do. When Dalgliesh or his minions condescend to call I'll probably be too arrogant or too inquisitive to take my own advice. Is that helpful?'

Emma said, 'So you're saying, don't lie but don't tell them more than you need. Wait until you're asked and then answer truthfully.'

'More or less.'

She asked a question that she had wanted to ask since their first meeting. It was odd that today seemed the right time. 'You're not in sympathy with St Anselm's, are you? Is that because you're not a believer yourself or because you don't think they are either?'

'Oh they believe all right. It's just that what they believe has become irrelevant. I don't mean the moral teaching; the Judaeo-Christian heritage has created Western civilization and we should be grateful to it. But the Church they serve is dying. When I look at the *Doom* I try to have some understanding of what it meant to fifteenth-century men and women. If life is hard and short and full of pain you need the hope of Heaven; if there is no effective law, you need the deterrent of Hell. The Church gave them comfort and light and pictures and stories and the hope of everlasting life. The twenty-first century has other compensations. Football for one. There you have ritual, colour, drama, the sense of belonging; football has its high priests, even its martyrs. And then there's shopping, art and music, travel, alcohol, drugs. We all have our own resources for staving off those two horrors of human life, boredom and the knowledge that we die. And now – God help us – there's the Internet. Pornography at the touch of a few keys. If you want to find a paedophile ring or discover how to make a bomb to blow up people you disagree with, it's all there for you. Plus, of course, a bottomless mine of other information, some of it even accurate.'

Emma said, 'But when all these things fail, even the music, the poetry, the art?'

'Then, my dear, I shall turn to science. If my end promises to be unpleasant, I shall rely on morphine and the compassion of my doctor. Or perhaps I shall swim out to sea and take my last look at the sky.'

Emma asked, 'Why do you stay here? Why did you take this job in the first place?'

'Because I enjoy teaching Ancient Greek to intelligent young men. Why are you an academic?'

'Because I enjoy teaching English literature to intelligent young men and women. That's a partial answer. I do sometimes wonder where exactly I'm going. It would be good to do original creative work rather than analyse the creativity of others.'

'Caught up in the thicket of the academic jungle? I've taken good care to avoid all that. This place suits me admirably. I've enough private money to ensure that I don't need to work full-time. I've a life in London – not one the fathers here would approve of – but I like the stimulus of contrast. I also need peace, peace to write and peace to think. I get it here. I'm never troubled with visitors. I fend people off with the excuse that I've only one bedroom. I can eat in college when I feel like it and be assured of excellent food, wines which are always drinkable and occasionally memorable, and conversation which is often stimulating and seldom boring. I enjoy solitary walking and the desolation of this coast suits me. I get free accommodation and my keep and the college pays a derisory stipend for teaching of a standard which they would otherwise find it difficult to attract or to afford. This murderer will put a stop to all that. I'm beginning seriously to resent him.'

'What is so horrible is the knowledge that it could be someone here, someone we know.'

'An inside job, as our dear police would say. It has to be, hasn't it? Come on Emma, you're not a coward. Face the truth. What thief is going to drive in the dark and on a stormy night to a remote church which he could hardly have expected to find open in the hope of breaking into the offerings box and collecting a few dud coins? And the circle of suspects isn't exactly large. You're out, my dear. Of course arriving first on the scene is always suspicious in detective fiction – to which, I may say, the priests here are addicted – but I think you can take it that you're in the clear. That leaves the four ordinands who were in college last night, and seven others: the Pilbeams, Surtees and his sister, Yarwood, Stannard and myself. I suppose even Dalgliesh doesn't seriously suspect any of our fathers-in-God, although he's probably keeping them in mind, particularly if he remembers his Pascal. "Men never do evil so completely and cheerfully as when they do it from religious conviction."'

Emma didn't want to discuss the priests. She said quietly, 'Surely we can eliminate the Pilbeams?'

'Unlikely murderers I admit, but then so are we all. But it would distress me to think of so good a cook serving a life sentence. All right, delete the Pilbeams.'

Emma was about to say that the four ordinands could surely be eliminated too, but something held her back. She was afraid of what she might hear. Instead she said,

'And surely you're not a suspect? You had no reason to hate the Archdeacon. In fact his murder could settle the question of closing St Anselm's. Isn't that the last thing you want?'

'It was coming anyway. The marvel is that the place has lasted so long. But you're right, I had no reason to wish Crampton dead. If I were capable of killing anyone – which I'm not except in self-defence – it would more probably be Sebastian Morell.'

'Father Sebastian? Why?'

'An old grudge. He stopped me becoming a Fellow of All Souls. It isn't important now but it mattered at the time. Oh dear me yes, it certainly mattered. He had just written a vicious review of my latest book with a barely concealed hint that I'd been guilty of plagiarism. I hadn't. It was one of those unlikely coincidences of phrases and ideas which can occur. But the scandal didn't help.'

'How horrible.'

'Not really. It happens, you must know that. It's every writer's nightmare.'

'But why did he give you this job? He can't have forgotten.'

'He's never mentioned it. It's possible that he has forgotten. It was important to me at the time, but evidently not important to him. Even if he remembered when I applied for the job, I doubt whether it would have worried him, not when it came to getting an excellent teacher for St Anselm's and getting him cheap.'

Emma didn't reply. Looking down on her bent head, Gregory said, 'Have some more coffee, then you can tell me the latest Cambridge gossip.'

18

When Dalgliesh rang to ask George Gregory to come to St Matthew's Cottage, Gregory said, 'I had hoped that I might be interviewed here. I'm expecting a phone call from my agent and she has this number. I have an intense dislike of mobile telephones.'

A business call on a Sunday seemed to Dalgliesh unlikely. As if sensing his scepticism, Gregory added, 'I'm supposed to meet her for lunch in London tomorrow, at the Ivy. I'd rather assumed that this won't now be possible, or if possible not convenient. I've tried to reach her but without success. I've left a message on her answerphone asking her to ring me. Obviously, if I can't be sure of getting a message to her today or early tomorrow, I'll have to go to London. I take it there's no objection.'

Dalgliesh said, 'I can see none at present. I would prefer everyone at St Anselm's to remain here at least until the first part of the investigation is over.'

'I've no wish to run away, I assure you. Quite the reverse. It's not every day one experiences vicariously the excitement of murder.'

Dalgliesh said, 'I don't think Miss Lavenham shares your pleasure in the experience.'

'Of course not, poor girl. But then she's seen the body. Without that visual impact of horror murder is surely an atavistic *frisson*, more Agatha Christie than real. I know that imagined terror is supposed to be more potent than reality, but I can't believe that's true of murder. Surely no one who actually sees a murdered body can ever erase it from the mind. You'll come over then? Thank you.'

Gregory's comment had been brutally insensitive but he hadn't been altogether wrong. It had been as a raw detective recently appointed to the CID and kneeling beside the body of that first never-to-be-forgotten victim that Dalgliesh had first experienced, in a rush of shock, outrage and pity, murder's destructive power. He wondered how Emma Lavenham was coping, whether there was something he could or ought to do to help her. Probably not. She may well see any attempt either as an intrusion or condescension. There was no one at St Anselm's to whom she could talk freely about what she had seen in the church except Father Martin and he, poor man, was more likely to need comfort and support than to be able to give it. She could, of course, leave and take her secret with her, but she wasn't a woman to run away. Why, without knowing her, was he so sure of that? Resolutely he put the problem of Emma temporarily out of mind and applied himself to the task in hand.

He was happy enough to see Gregory in St Luke's Cottage. He had no intention of interviewing the ordinands in their own rooms or at their convenience; it was appropriate, expedient and time-saving that they should come to him. But on his own ground Gregory would be more at ease, and suspects at ease were more likely to let down their guard. He could learn far more about his witness from an unobtrusive scrutiny of his rooms than from a dozen direct questions. Books, pictures, the arrangement of artefacts sometimes provided more revealing testimony than words.

As Dalgliesh and Kate followed Gregory into the left-hand sitting-room, he was struck again by the individuality of the three occupied cottages, from the Pilbeams' cheerful domestic comfort, Surtees's carefully-ordered workroom with its smell of wood, turpentine and animal food, to this, obviously the living space of an academic and one almost obsessively tidy. The cottage had been adapted to serve Gregory's two dominant interests, classical literature and music. The whole of the front room had been fitted with bookshelves from floor to ceiling, except above the ornate Victorian fireplace, where he had hung a print of Piranesi's *Arch of Constantine*. It was clearly important to Gregory that the height of the shelves should be designed to accommodate precisely the size of the books – a foible which Dalgliesh shared – and the impression was of a room clad in the ordered richness of softly-gleaming gold and brown leather. A plain oak desk holding a computer and a functional office chair stood beneath the window, which was uncurtained but fitted with a slatted wooden blind.

They passed through an open doorway into the extension. This was chiefly of glass and stretched the whole length of the cottage. This was Gregory's sitting-room, furnished with light but comfortable wicker chairs and a sofa, a drinks table and a larger circular table at the far end piled high with books and magazines. Even these were orderly, arranged, it would seem, according to size. The glass roof and sides were fitted with sun blinds which in the summer, Dalgliesh thought, would be essential. Even now the south-facing room was comfortably warm. Outside stretched the bleak scrub-land and a distant view of the tree-tops round the mere and, to the east, the great grey sweep of the North Sea.

The low chairs were not conducive to a police interrogation but no other seating was available. Gregory's chair faced south and he leaned back against the headrest and stretched out his long legs like a clubman perfectly at ease.

Dalgliesh began with questions to which he already knew the answers from his perusal of the personal files. Gregory's had been far less informative than those of the ordinands. The first document, a letter from Keble College, Oxford, had made plain by what means he had come to St Anselm's. Dalgliesh, who had almost total recall of the written word, had no difficulty in remembering it.

Now that Bradley has finally retired (and how on earth did you persuade him?), rumour has it that you are looking for a replacement. I wonder if you have thought of George Gregory? I understand he is busy at present on a new translation of Euripides and is looking for a part-time post, preferably in the country, where he can get on with this major work in peace. Academically, of course, you could not do better and he is a fine teacher. It's the usual story of the scholar who never quite fulfils his potential. He is not the easiest of men, but I think that he might suit you. He had a word with me when he dined here last Friday. I made no promise but said I would find out how you are placed. I gather that money is a consideration, but not the main one. It's the privacy and the peace he's really after.

Now Dalgliesh said, 'You came here in 1995 and by invitation.'

'You could say I was head-hunted. The college wanted an experienced teacher with Classical Greek and some Hebrew. I wanted a part-time teaching job, preferably in the country with accommodation. I have a house in Oxford but it's let at present. The tenant is responsible and the rent high. It's not an arrangement I want to upset. Father Martin would have called our coming together providential; Father Sebastian saw it as one more example of his power to order events to his and the college's advantage. I can't speak for St Anselm's but I don't think either party has regretted the arrangement.'

'When did you first meet Archdeacon Crampton?'

'On his first visit about three months ago when he was appointed as a trustee. I can't remember the exact date. He came again two weeks ago and then yesterday. On the second occasion he went to some trouble to seek me out and inquire on what terms precisely I thought I was employed here. I got the impression that if not discouraged he would begin to catechize me about my religious convictions, if any. I referred him to Sebastian Morell on the first matter and was sufficiently disobliging on the second to send him off to seek out easier victims – Surtees, I suspect.'

'And this visit?'

'I didn't see him until dinner yesterday. Not a particularly festive occasion, but you were there yourself, so you saw and heard as much as I did, probably more. After dinner I left without waiting for coffee and came back here.'

'And the rest of the night, Mr Gregory?'

'Spent in this cottage. Some reading, some revision, marking half a dozen students' essays. Then music, Wagner last night, and bed. And to save you the trouble of asking, I didn't leave the cottage at any time during the night. I saw no one and I heard nothing except the storm.'

'And you learned of the Archdeacon's murder when?'

'When Raphael Arbuthnot rang at about quarter to seven to say that Father Sebastian had called an emergency meeting of all residents in the library at seven-thirty. He gave no explanation and it wasn't until we all congregated as instructed that I learned of the murder.'

'What was your reaction to the news?'

'Complicated. Mostly, I suppose, initial shock and disbelief. I didn't know the man so I had no reason to feel personal grief or regret. That charade in the library was extraordinary, wasn't it? Trust Morell to set up something like that. I take it that it was his idea. There we all stood and sat like members of a dysfunctional family waiting for the will to be read. I've said that my first reaction was one of shock and, of course, it was. But it was shock I felt, not surprise. When I came into the library and saw Emma Lavenham's face I realized that this was serious. I think I knew, even before Morell spoke, what he was going to tell us.'

'You knew that Archdeacon Crampton wasn't exactly a welcome visitor at St Anselm's?'

'I try to distance myself from college politics; small and remote institutions like this can become hotbeds of gossip and innuendo. But I'm not exactly blind and deaf. I think most of us know that the future of St Anselm's is uncertain and that Archdeacon Crampton was determined that it should close sooner rather than later.'

'Would the closure inconvenience you?'

'I won't welcome it, but I saw it as a probability soon after I arrived. But considering the speed with which the Church of England moves, I thought I was safe for at least another ten years. I shall regret losing the cottage, particularly as I paid for the extension. I find this place congenial for my work and I'll be sorry to leave it. There's a chance, of course, that I may not have to. I don't know what the Church will do with the building but it won't be an easy property to sell. It's possible I may be able to buy the cottage. It's early days to be giving it much thought and I don't even know whether it belongs to the Church Commissioners or to the diocese. That world is alien to me.'

So either Gregory was unaware of the terms of Miss Arbuthnot's will or was taking care to conceal his knowledge. There seemed nothing more to be learned for the present, and Gregory began to edge himself out of his armchair.

But Dalgliesh hadn't finished. He said, 'Was Ronald Treeves one of your pupils?'

'Of course. I teach Classical Greek and Hebrew to all the ordinands except those who read Greats. Treeves's degree was in Geography; that meant he was taking the three-year course here and starting Greek from scratch. Of course, I was forgetting. You came here originally to look into that death. It seems comparatively unimportant now, doesn't it? Anyway, it always was unimportant, as a putative murder, I mean. The more logical verdict would have been suicide.'

'Was that your view when you saw the body?'

'It was a view I formed as soon as I had time to think calmly. It was the folded clothes that convinced me. A young man proposing to climb a cliff doesn't arrange his cloak and cassock with such ritual care. He came here for some private tuition on the Friday evening before Compline and seemed much as usual; that means he wasn't particularly cheerful, but then he never was. I can't remember that we had any conversation except that which related to the translation he had worked on. I left for London immediately afterwards and stayed the night at my club. It was as I was driving back on Saturday afternoon that I was stopped by Mrs Munroe.'

Kate asked, 'What was he like?'

'Ronald Treeves? Stolid, hard-working, intelligent – but not perhaps quite as clever as he thought, insecure, remarkably intolerant for a young man. I think Papa played a dominant part in his life. I suppose that could have accounted for his choice of job; if you can't succeed in Papa's field you can be as disobliging in your choice as possible. But we never discussed his private life. I make it my rule not to get involved with the ordinands. That way lies disaster, particularly in a small college like this. I'm here to teach them Greek and Hebrew, not to delve into their psyches. When I say that I need privacy, that includes privacy from the pressure of human person- ality. By the way, when are you expecting the news of this murder to break, publicly I mean? I suppose we can expect the usual influx of the media.'

Dalgliesh said, 'Obviously it can't be kept secret indefinitely. I'm discussing with Father Sebastian how the public relations branch can help. When there's any- thing to say, we'll hold a press conference.'

'And there's no objection to my leaving for London today?'

'I have no power to prevent you.'

Gregory got slowly to his feet. 'All the same, I think I'll cancel tomorrow's luncheon. I've a feeling there will be more to interest me here than in a tedious discussion of my publisher's delinquencies and the minutiae of my new contract. I suppose you would prefer me not to explain why I'm cancelling.'

'It would be helpful at the moment.'

Gregory was moving to the door. 'A pity. I'd rather enjoy explaining that I can't come to London because I'm a suspect in a murder inquiry. Goodbye, Commander. If you need me again you know where to find me.'

19

The squad ended the day as they had begun it, conferring together in St Matthew's Cottage. But now they were in the more comfortable of the two rooms, sitting on the sofa and in the armchairs and drinking the last coffee of the day. It was time to assess progress. The time and place of the telephone call to Mrs Crampton had been checked. It had been made from the instrument with the honesty box beside it mounted on the wall in the corridor outside Mrs Pilbeam's sitting-room. The call had been made at nine twenty-eight. This was one more piece of evidence, and an important one. It proved what they had suspected from the first: that the killer was in St Anselm's.

Piers had followed up the discovery. He said, 'If we're right and the caller later rang the Archdeacon's mobile, then everyone who attended Compline is in the clear. That leaves us with Surtees and his sister, Gregory, Inspector Yarwood, the Pilbeams and Emma Lavenham. I don't suppose any of us see Dr Lavenham as a serious suspect and we're discounting Stannard.'

Dalgliesh said, 'Not entirely. We've no power to hold him and I'm pretty certain he has no idea how Crampton died. That doesn't necessarily mean he wasn't implicated. He's out of St Anselm's but not out of mind.'

Piers said, 'There's one thing, though. Arbuthnot only just arrived in the sacristy in time for the service. I got that bit of information from Father Sebastian who had no idea, of course, of its importance. Robbins and I have checked, sir. Both of us could run from the door into the south cloister and across the courtyard in ten seconds. He'd just have had time to make the call and get to the church by nine-thirty.'

Kate said, 'It'd be risky, wouldn't it? Anyone could have seen him.'

'In the dark? And with the dim lights in the cloister? And who was there to see him? They were in church. It wasn't much of a risk.'

Robbins said, 'I wonder if it would be premature, sir, to exclude everyone in church. Suppose Cain had an accomplice. There's nothing to show that this was a one-man crime. Anyone who was actually in the church before nine twenty-eight couldn't have made the call but that doesn't mean one of them wasn't implicated in the murder.'

Piers said, 'A conspiracy? Well it could be. There were enough of them here who hated him. A one-man and one-woman crime maybe. When Kate and I interviewed the Surteeses it was pretty obvious that they were hiding something. Eric was frankly terrified.'

The only suspect who had produced anything of interest had been Karen Surtees. She had claimed that neither she nor her brother had left St John's Cottage at any time during the evening. They had watched television until eleven and then had gone to bed. Asked by Kate whether either of them could have left the cottage without the other knowing, she had said, 'That's a pretty crude way of asking whether either of us went out in a storm to murder the Archdeacon. Well, we didn't. And if you think Eric could have left the cottage without my knowing, the answer is no. We slept in the same bed, if you must know. I'm actually his half-sister and, even if I weren't, you're investigating murder, not incest, and it's none of your business anyway.'

Dalgliesh said, 'And you were both convinced she was telling the truth?'

Kate said, 'One look at her brother's face showed us that. I don't know whether she'd told him what she proposed to say, but he didn't like it. And it's odd, isn't it, that she bothered to tell us that? She could perfectly well have said that the storm kept them both awake for most of the night and provided an alibi that way. OK, I think she's a woman who likes to shock, but that doesn't seem reason enough for telling us about the incest – if that's what it is.'

Piers said, 'It shows she was damned anxious to provide an alibi though, doesn't it? It's almost as if the two of them are thinking ahead, telling the truth now because in the end they might have to rely on it in court.'

A twig had been found in Raphael Arbuthnot's set in the north cloister but the SOCOs had discovered nothing else of interest. During the day Dalgliesh had become confirmed in his initial view of its importance. If he were right in his theory, the twig was indeed a vital clue, but he judged that to voice his suspicions now would be premature.

They discussed the results of the individual interviews. Except for Raphael, everyone in college or in the cottages claimed to have been virtuously in bed by eleven-thirty and, although occasionally disturbed by the force of the wind, had seen or heard nothing unusual during the night. Father Sebastian had been co-operative but cool.

It was only with difficulty that he had concealed his dislike of being interviewed by subordinates and he had begun by saying that he could spare only a short time as he was expecting Mrs Crampton to arrive. A short time was all that was necessary. The Warden's story was that he had worked on an article he was contributing to a theological journal until eleven and had been in bed by eleven-thirty after his usual nightcap of whisky. Father John Betterton and his sister had read until half past ten, after which Miss Betterton had brewed cocoa for them both. The Pilbeams had watched television and had fortified themselves against a stormy night with copious cups of tea.

By eight o'clock it was time to end for the day. The SOCOs had long departed to their hotel and now Kate, Piers and Robbins said their good-nights. Tomorrow Kate and Robbins would drive to Ashcombe House to see what, if anything, could be learned about Margaret Munroe's time there. Dalgliesh locked up the papers he needed to keep private in his briefcase and walked across the headland into the western court to Jerome.

The telephone rang. It was Mrs Pilbeam. Father Sebastian had suggested that Commander Dalgliesh might like to have dinner in his set. It would save him the journey to Southwold. It would only be soup followed by salad and cold meat and some fruit but, if that was enough, Pilbeam would be happy to bring it over. Glad to be spared the car journey, Dalgliesh thanked her and said that the meal would be very welcome. It arrived within ten minutes, carried by Pilbeam. Dalgliesh suspected that he was unwilling for his wife to walk even the short distance across the courtyard after dark. Now, with surprising dexterity, he drew the desk a little away from the wall, laid the table and set out the meal.

Pilbeam said, 'If you just leave the tray outside, sir, I'll fetch it in about an hour.'

The thermos contained minestrone soup thick with vegetables and pasta and was obviously home-made. Mrs Pilbeam had provided a bowl of grated Parmesan cheese and there were hot rolls, wrapped in a napkin, and butter. Under the cover was a plate of salad and excellent ham. Someone, perhaps Father Sebastian, had supplied a bottle of claret although not a wineglass, but Dalgliesh, unwilling to drink alone, put it in the cupboard and after the meal brewed himself coffee. He placed the tray outside and, minutes later, heard Pilbeam's heavy tread on the stones of the cloister. He opened the door to say thank you and good-night.

He found himself in that discouraging state of physical tiredness and mental stimulation which is fatal to sleep. The silence was eerie, and when he went to the window he saw the college as a black silhouette, chimneys, tower and cupola an unbroken mass against a paler sky. The blue and white police tape was still looped around the columns of the north cloister, which was now almost clear of leaves. In the glow from the light above the south cloister door, the cobbles of the courtyard glistened and the fuchsia looked as unnaturally bright and incongruous as a splash of red paint flung against the stone wall.

He settled down to read but the peace around him found no echo within. What was it, he wondered, about this place which made him feel that his life was under judgement? He thought about the long years of self-imposed solitude since his wife's death. Hadn't he used his job to avoid the commitment of love, to keep inviolate more than that high uncluttered flat above the Thames which, when he returned to it at night, looked exactly the same as it had when he left it in the morning? To be a detached observer of life was not without dignity; to have a job which preserved your own privacy while providing you with the excuse – indeed the duty – to invade the privacy of others had its advantages for a writer. But wasn't there something ignoble about it? If you stood apart long enough, weren't you in danger of stifling, perhaps even losing, that quickening spirit which the priests here would call the soul? Six lines of verse came into his mind and he took a page of paper, ripped it in half, and wrote them down:

Epitaph for a Dead Poet
Buried at last who was so wise,
Six foot by three in clay he lies.
Where no hands reach, where no lips move,
Where no voice importunes his love.
How odd he cannot know nor see
This last fine self-sufficiency.

After a second he scribbled beneath it 'With apologies to Marvell'. He thought back to the days when his poetry had come as easily as had this light ironic verse. Now it was a more cerebral, a more calculated choice and arrangement of words. Was there anything in his life that was spontaneous?

He told himself that this introspection was becoming morbid. To shake it off he had to get out of St Anselm's.

What he needed before bed was a brisk walk. He closed the door to Jerome, passed Ambrose from which no lights were visible behind the tightly-drawn curtains and, unlocking the iron gate, turned resolutely south, making his way towards the sea.

20

It was Miss Arbuthnot who had decreed that there should be no locks on the doors of the ordinands' rooms. Emma wondered what she had feared they might do if not always at risk of interruption. Had there been, perhaps, an unacknowledged fear of sexuality? Perhaps as a consequence, no locks had been fitted in the visitors' sets. The locked iron gate by the church gave all the night-time security considered necessary; behind that elegantly designed barrier what was there to fear? Because there was no tradition of locks and bolts, none were available in college to be fitted and Pilbeam had been too busy all day to go to Lowestoft to buy them, even if he could have found a shop open on a Sunday. Father Sebastian had asked Emma whether she would be more comfortable in the main building. Emma, unwilling to betray nervousness, had assured the Warden that she would be perfectly all right. Father Sebastian hadn't asked her again and, when she returned to the set after Compline to discover that locks hadn't been fitted, she was too proud to seek him out, confess her fear and say that she had changed her mind.

She undressed and put on her dressing-gown, then settled down at her laptop and resolutely tried to work. But she was too tired. Thoughts and words came in a jumble overlaid by the events of the day. It had been late in the morning before Robbins had sought her out and asked her to come to the interview room. There Dalgliesh, with Inspector Miskin on his left, had taken her briefly through the events of the previous night. Emma had explained how she had been woken by the wind and had heard the clear note of the bell. She couldn't explain why she had put on her dressing-gown and gone down to investigate. It now seemed rash and stupid. She thought she must have been half-asleep or perhaps the single chime heard through the wind had woken a semi-conscious memory of the insistent bells of childhood and adolescence, a call to be sharply obeyed, not questioned.

But she had been fully awake when she had pushed open the church door and seen between the pillars the brightly lit *Doom* and the two figures, the one prone and the other collapsed over him in an attitude of pity or despair. Dalgliesh hadn't asked her to describe the scene in detail. Why should he, she thought; he'd been there. He didn't express sympathy or concern for what she had gone through, but then it wasn't she who was bereaved. The questions were clear and simple. It wasn't, she thought, that he had been trying to spare her; if there had been anything he wanted to know, he would have asked, whatever her distress. When Sergeant Robbins had first shown her into the interview room and Commander Dalgliesh had risen from his chair and invited her to sit, she had told herself: I'm not facing the man who wrote *A Case to Answer and Other Poems*, I'm facing a policeman. In this they could never be allies. There were people she loved and wanted to protect; he had no allegiance except to the truth. And at the end had come the question she had dreaded.

'Did Father Martin speak when you went up to him?'

She had paused before replying. 'Yes, just a few words.'

'What were they, Dr Lavenham?'

She didn't reply. She wouldn't lie, but even to recall the words now seemed an act of treachery.

The silence lengthened, then he said, 'Dr Lavenham, you saw the body. You saw what had been done to the Archdeacon. He was a tall, strong man. Father Martin is nearly eighty years old and becoming feeble. The brass candlestick, if it proves to be the weapon, would take some strength to wield. Do you really believe Father Martin could have done it?'

She had cried out vehemently, 'Of course not! He's incapable of cruelty. He's kind and loving and good, the best man I know. I never thought that. No one could.'

Commander Dalgliesh had said quietly, 'Then why do you suppose I do?'

He asked the question again. Emma looked him in the eyes. 'He said, "Oh God, what have we done, what have we done?" '

'And what do you suppose – thinking about it later – he meant by that?'

She had thought about it later. They had not been words to forget. Nothing about that scene would ever be forgotten. She kept her eyes on her interrogator.

'I think he meant that the Archdeacon would still be alive if he hadn't come to St Anselm's. Perhaps he wouldn't have been murdered if his killer hadn't known how strongly he was disliked here. That dislike could have contributed to his death. The college can't be guiltless.'

'Yes,' he had said more gently, 'that's what Father Martin has told me he meant.'

She looked at her watch. It was twenty past eleven. Knowing that it would be impossible to work, she went up to her bed. Because the set of rooms was at the end of the row, the bedroom had two windows, one of which looked out over the south wall of the church. She drew the curtains before getting into bed and tried resolutely to forget the unlocked door. She shut her eyes, only to find images of death bubbling like blood on her retina, reality made more terrible by imagination. She saw again the viscous pool of spilt blood, but now there lay above it like grey vomit a spatter of his brains. The grotesque images of the damned and grinning devils jerked into life and animated their obscene gestures. When she opened her eyes in the hope of banishing horror, the darkness of the bedroom pressed upon her. Even the air smelt of death.

She got out of bed and, unlatching the window facing the scrubland, pushed it open. There came a blessed rush of air and she gazed out over the vast silence and a sky pricked with stars.

She went back to bed, but sleep wouldn't come. Her legs were juddering with tiredness but fear was stronger than exhaustion. At last she got up and went downstairs. To watch in darkness that unlocked door was less traumatic than to imagine it opening slowly, to be in the sitting-room was better than lying helpless, waiting to hear those purposeful footsteps on the stairs. She wondered whether to ram a chair under the door handle, but couldn't bring herself to an action that seemed both demeaning and ineffectual. She despised herself for cowardice, telling herself that no one intended her harm. But then the images of cracked bones came back into her

383

mind. Someone on the headland, perhaps someone in the college, had taken a brass candlestick and smashed the Archdeacon's skull, striking again and again in a frenzy of bloodlust and hatred. Could that have been the action of someone sane? Was anyone at St Anselm's safe?

It was then that she heard the rasp of the iron gate opening, the click as it was shut. Footsteps were passing. They were confident but quiet, there was nothing furtive about this tread. Carefully she opened her door and glanced out, her heart thumping. Commander Dalgliesh was opening the door of Jerome. She must have made some sound because he turned and came over to her and she opened the door to him. The relief of seeing him, of seeing any human being, was overwhelming. She knew that it must show in her face.

He said, 'Are you all right?'

She managed a smile. 'Not very at present, but I shall be. I was finding it difficult to sleep.'

He said, 'I thought you would have moved to the main house. Didn't Father Sebastian suggest it?'

'He did offer but I thought I'd be all right here.'

He looked across at the church. He said, 'This isn't a good set for you. Would you like to change with me? I think you'd find it more comfortable.'

She found it difficult to conceal her relief. 'But wouldn't that be a bother?'

'Not in the slightest. We could move most of our things tomorrow. All you need now are bedclothes. I'm afraid your under-sheet may not fit my bed. Mine's a double.'

She said, 'Shall we just change our pillows and duvets?'

'Good idea.'

384

Carrying them into Jerome, she saw that he had already brought his own pillows and duvet downstairs and had lain them on one of the armchairs. Beside them was a canvas and leather grip. Perhaps he had put together the things he needed for the night and next day.

Going over to the cupboard, he said, 'The college has provided the usual innocuous drinks for us, and there's half a pint of milk in the fridge. Would you like cocoa or Ovaltine? Or, if you prefer, I've a bottle of claret.'

'I'd like some wine, please.'

He shifted the duvet for her and she sat down. He took a bottle, a corkscrew and two tumblers from the small cupboard.

'Obviously the college doesn't expect its guests to be drinking wine. We have the choice of tumblers or mugs.'

'A tumbler is fine. But it means opening a new bottle.'

'The best time to open it, when it's needed.'

She was surprised how much at ease she felt with him. That's all I needed, she told herself, someone else to be here. They didn't talk for long, only until a single glass of wine had been finished. They drank slowly. He spoke of coming to the college as a boy, of the fathers, their cassocks hitched up, bowling to him on a pitch behind the west gate; cycling into Lowestoft to buy fish; the pleasure of solitary reading in the library at night. He asked about the syllabus for her class at St Anselm's, how she chose the poets to study, what kind of response she got from the ordinands. The murder wasn't mentioned. Their talk wasn't desultory but neither was it forced. She liked the sound of his voice. She had the sensation that part of her mind was detached, floating above them and being soothed by this low male and female contrapuntal sound.

When she got up and said good-night, he rose at once and said with a formality he hadn't so far shown, 'I shall be spending the night in this armchair unless you object. If Inspector Miskin had been here I'd have asked her to stay. As she isn't, I'll take her place – unless you'd rather I didn't.'

She recognized that he was trying to make it easy for her, that he didn't want to impose, but that he knew how much she dreaded being alone. She said, 'But won't that be a terrible nuisance? You'll have an uncomfortable night.'

'I shall be very comfortable. I'm used to sleeping in armchairs.'

The bedroom in Jerome was almost identical to the one next door. The bedside lamp was switched on and she saw that he had not taken his books. He had been reading – or surely it must have been rereading – *Beowulf*. There was an old and faded Penguin paperback, David Cecil's *Early Victorian Novelists* with a photograph of the writer, looking ridiculously young, and on the back the price in old money. So, like her, she thought, he enjoyed picking up books in second-hand shops. The third book was *Mansfield Park*. She wondered whether to take them down to him, but was reluctant to intrude now that they had said their good-nights.

It was strange to be lying on his sheet. She hoped that he didn't despise her for her cowardice. The relief of knowing that he was downstairs was immense. She closed her eyes on darkness, not on the dancing images of death, and in minutes she was asleep.

She awoke after a dreamless night and saw from her watch that it was seven o'clock. The set was very quiet and when she went downstairs she saw that he had already left, taking the duvet and pillow with him. He had opened the window as if anxious that not even the faintest trace of his breath should remain. She knew that he would tell no one where he had spent the night.

BOOK THREE

Voices from the Past

I

Ruby Pilbeam needed no alarm clock. For eighteen years she had woken, winter and summer, at six o'clock. She did so on Monday morning, stretching out her hand to switch on the bedside light. Immediately Reg stirred, pushed back the bedclothes and began to edge out of the bed. There came to Ruby the warm smell of his body, bringing as always its familiar comfort. She wondered if he had been asleep or just lying still, waiting for her to move. Neither had slept except for brief periods of restless half-slumber, and at three o'clock they had got up and gone down to the kitchen to drink tea and wait for the morning. Then exhaustion had mercifully taken over from shock and horror and at four o'clock they had gone back to bed. They had then slept fitfully, but they had slept.

Both had been busy all Sunday, and only the ceaseless purposeful activity had given that dreadful day any semblance of normality. Last night, huddled together at the kitchen table, they had talked about the murder, whispering as if those small comfortable rooms of St Mark's Cottage were crammed with secret listeners. The talk had been guarded with suspicions unvoiced, broken sentences and periods of unhappy silence. Even to say that it was absurd to suggest that anyone at St Anselm's could be the murderer was to associate place and deed in treasonable proximity; to speak a name even in exoneration was to admit the thought that someone resident in college could have perpetrated such evil.

But they had arrived at two possible theories, the more comforting because they induced belief. Together before returning to bed they had mentally rehearsed the stories like a mantra. Someone had stolen the keys to the church, someone who had visited St Anselm's, perhaps months earlier and knew where they were kept and that Miss Ramsey's office was never locked. The same person had made an assignation with Archdeacon Crampton before he arrived on Saturday. Why meet in the church? What better place? They couldn't meet in the guest set without risk and there was nowhere private on the headland. Perhaps the Archdeacon had himself taken the keys and unlocked the church ready for his visitor. Then the arrival, the quarrel, the murderous rage. Perhaps the visitor had planned murder, had come with a weapon, a gun, a cosh, a knife. They hadn't been told how the Archdeacon had died, but both privately visualized the flash and thrust of a knife blade. And then the escape, a climb over the iron gate, leaving as he had entered. The second theory was even more plausible, adding weight to reassurance. The Archdeacon borrowed the keys and had gone to the church for purposes of his own. The intruder was a thief seeking to steal the altar picture or the silver. The Archdeacon had surprised him and the thief, in terror, had struck. This explanation once tacitly accepted as rational, neither Ruby nor her husband spoke again that night of the murder.

Usually Ruby went alone to the college. Breakfast wasn't until eight o'clock following the seven-thirty Mass, but Ruby liked to get started with planning her day. Father Sebastian breakfasted in his own sitting-room and there was his table to be laid ready for his invariable first meal of fresh orange juice, coffee and two wholemeal slices of toast with Ruby's home-made marmalade. At eight-thirty Mrs Bardwell and Mrs Stacey, her daily domestic helpers, would arrive from Reydon, driven by Mrs Bardwell in her old Ford. But not today. Father Sebastian had telephoned them both and asked them to delay their return for a couple of days. Ruby wondered what explanation he had given, but hadn't liked to ask. It meant more work for her and Reg, but Ruby was glad to be spared their avid curiosity, their speculations, their inevitable exclamations of horror. It occurred to her that murder might even be enjoyable for people who didn't know the victim and weren't under suspicion. Elsie Bardwell would certainly make the most of it.

Usually Reg came over to the house later than six-thirty, but today they left St Mark's Cottage together. He gave no explanation but she knew why it was. St Anselm's was no longer a safe and holy place. He shone the beam of his strong torch along the beaten-grass path to the iron gate leading to the west court. The faint haze of first light was creeping over the scrubland, but it seemed to her that she walked in an impenetrable darkness. Reg shone his torch on the gate to find the keyhole. Beyond the gate the row of dim lights in the cloisters illuminated the slender pillars and cast shadows over the stone paths. The north cloister was still taped and half its length was now free of leaves. The trunk of the horse-chestnut rose black and still from the welter of fallen leaves. When the beams of the torch briefly passed over the fuchsia on the east wall its red flowers glistened like drops of blood. In the corridor which separated her sitting-room from the kitchen, Ruby put out her hand to switch on the light. But the darkness wasn't total. Ahead the corridor was lit by a beam of light from the open cellar door.

She said, 'That's funny, Reg. The cellar door's open. Someone's up early. Or didn't you see that it was shut last night?

He said, 'It was shut last night. D'you think I'd have left it open?'

They moved to the head of the stone stairs. They were brightly lit by powerful overhead lights and fitted with a strong wooden handrail on each side. At the bottom of the steps, clearly seen in the glare from the light, was the sprawled body of a woman.

Ruby gave a sharp protesting cry. 'Oh God, Reg! It's Miss Betterton.'

Reg pushed Ruby aside. He said, 'Stay here, lass,' and she heard the clatter of his shoes on the stone. She hesitated only for a few seconds, then followed him down, clutching with both hands at the left handrail and together they knelt by the body.

She was lying on her back, her head towards the bottom step. There was a single gash to her forehead, but only an oozing of dried blood and serum. She was wearing a faded dressing-gown in paisley wool and under it a white cotton night-dress. Her thin grey hair stuck out from the side of her head in a plait, the wispy end held together by a twisted rubber band. Her eyes, fixed on the top of the stairs, were open and lifeless.

Ruby whispered, 'Oh dear God, no! You poor soul, you poor soul.'

She put an arm across the body in an instinctive gesture which she knew at once was futile. She could smell in the hair and from the dressing-gown the sour smell of unkempt old age and wondered that this should remain of Miss Betterton when all else had gone. Choked with a hopeless pity she withdrew her arm. Miss Betterton would not have wanted her touch in life; why impose it on her in death?

Reg straightened up. He said, 'She's dead. Dead and cold. Looks like she broke her neck. There's nowt anyone can do for her. You'd better go for Father Sebastian.'

The task of waking Father Sebastian, of finding words to speak and the strength to speak them, horrified Ruby. She would much rather that Reg broke the news, but that would mean she would have to stay alone by the body and this prospect was even more frightening. For the first time fear took over from pity. The recesses of the cellar stretched away, great areas of blackness in which imagined horrors lurked. She was not an over-imaginative woman, but now it seemed that the familiar world of routine, of conscientious work, of fellowship and of love was dissolving about her. She knew that Reg only had to stretch out a hand and the cellar, with its whitewashed walls and labelled racks of wine bottles, would become as familiar and harmless as it was when she and Father Sebastian went down to bring up the bottles for dinner. But Reg didn't stretch out his hand. Everything must be left as it was.

Every step seemed mountainous as she climbed the stairs on legs that had suddenly become almost too weak to support her. She switched on all the lights in the hall and stood for a moment gathering her strength before making her way up the two flights to Father Sebastian's flat. Her knock was at first too tentative and she had to bang on the door before it was opened with disconcerting suddenness and Father Sebastian faced her. She had never seen him before in his dressing-gown and for a moment, disorientated by shock, thought that she was facing a stranger. The sight of her must have shocked him too, for he put out a hand to steady her and drew her into the room.

She said, 'It's Miss Betterton, Father. Reg and I found her at the bottom of the cellar stairs. I'm afraid she's dead.'

She was surprised that her voice sounded so steady. Without speaking, Father Sebastian closed his door and hurried with her down the stairs, his hand supporting her arm. At the top of the cellar steps, Ruby waited and watched while he went down and said a few words to Reg, then knelt by the body.

After a moment he got to his feet. He spoke to Reg, his voice, as usual, calm, authoritative. 'This has been a shock for you both. I think it would be best if you went on quietly with your usual routine. Commander Dalgliesh and I will do what is necessary. It is only work and prayer that will get us through this terrible time.'

Reg climbed the steps to join her and together, without speaking, they went into the kitchen.

Ruby said, 'I suppose they'll be wanting breakfast as usual.'

'Of course they will, love. They can't face the day on empty stomachs. You heard what Father Sebastian said, we're to go on quietly with our usual routine.'

Ruby turned piteous eyes on him. 'It was an accident, wasn't it?'

'Of course it was. It could have happened any time. Poor Father John. This will be terrible for him.'

But Ruby wondered. It would be a shock, of course, sudden death always was. But there was no denying that Miss Betterton couldn't have been easy to live with. She reached for her white overall and began with a sad heart to prepare breakfast.

Father Sebastian went to his office and rang Dalgliesh in Jerome. His call was answered so quickly that it was obvious that the Commander was already up. He gave the news and, five minutes later, they stood together beside the body. Father Sebastian watched as Dalgliesh bent down, touched Miss Betterton's face with practised hands, then stood up and looked down in silent contemplation.

Father Sebastian said, 'Father John must be told, of course. That is my responsibility. I imagine that he's still asleep but I must see him before he comes down to the oratory for Morning Prayer. This will hit him hard. She wasn't an easy woman, but she was his only relation and they were close.' But he made no move to leave. Instead he asked, 'Have you any idea when this happened?'

Dalgliesh said, 'From the rigor mortis I would assume she has been dead about seven hours. The pathologist may be able to tell us more. It's never possible to be precise from a superficial examination. There will, of course, have to be a post-mortem.'

Father Sebastian said, 'She died after Compline, then, probably as late as midnight. Even so, she must have crossed the hall very quietly. But then she was always quiet. She moved like a grey shadow.' He paused, and added, 'I don't want her brother to see her here, not like this. Surely we could carry her to her room. She wasn't a religious woman, I know. We must respect her sensibilities. She wouldn't want to lie in the church even if it were open, nor, I think, in the oratory.'

'She must stay where she is, Father, until the pathologist has examined her. We have to treat this as a suspicious death.'

'But at least we can cover her up. I'll find a sheet.'

'Yes,' said Dalgliesh, 'we can certainly cover her.' As Father Sebastian turned to the stairs, he asked, 'Have you any idea what she was doing here, Father?'

Father Sebastian turned back and hesitated, then he said, 'I'm afraid I have. Miss Betterton helped herself to a bottle of wine on a fairly regular basis. All the priests knew about it and I imagine that the ordinands, perhaps even the staff, may have guessed. She never took more than one bottle about twice a week and it was never the best wine. Naturally I discussed the problem with Father John as tactfully as I could. I decided to take no action unless matters got out of hand. Father John regularly paid the price of the wine, at least of those bottles he discovered. Of course we realized the danger the steep steps posed for an elderly woman. That's why we had the stairs so brightly lit and replaced the rope with the wooden rails.'

Dalgliesh said, 'So finding you had a regular pilferer in the community, you provided a secure banister rail to facilitate the pilfering and to prevent her from breaking her neck.'

'Do you have difficulty with that, Commander?'

'No, given your priorities I don't suppose I do.'

He watched as Father Sebastian made his way, firmly

walking up the steps, and disappeared, closing the door behind him. That she had broken her neck a superficial examination made clear enough. She was wearing a pair of tight-fitting leather slippers and he had noticed that the sole of the right foot had curled away from the upper. The stairs were brightly lit and the light switch was at least two feet from the first step. Since the light had presumably been on when she fell, she could hardly have stumbled in darkness. But if she had tripped on the first step, surely she would have been found tumbled on the stairs either face downwards or on her back? On the third stair from the bottom he had detected what looked like a small smear of blood. From the position of the body it looked as if she had been hurled through the air, had struck her head on the stone step and somersaulted over. Surely it would be difficult for her to be flung with such force unless she had actually run with speed towards the steps. That, of course, was ridiculous. But what if she had been pushed? He felt a depressing and almost overwhelming sense of impotence. If this were murder, given that flapping sole, how could he ever hope to prove it? The death of Margaret Munroe was officially from natural causes. Her body had been cremated, her ashes buried or scattered on the earth. How expedient had this present death been for the murderer of Archdeacon Crampton?

But for now the experts in death would take over. Mark Ayling would be called to what might well be a second scene of crime, assessing the time of death, prowling round the body like a predator. Nobby Clark and his team would crawl over the cellar looking for clues they would be most unlikely to find. If there was something that Agatha Betterton had seen or heard, some knowledge which she had unwisely communicated to the wrong person, he was unlikely to learn it now.

He waited until Father Sebastian returned with a sheet which he laid reverently over the body, then the two of them climbed the cellar steps. Father Sebastian turned out the light and, stretching up, shot the bolt at the top of the cellar door.

Mark Ayling arrived with his usual promptness and more than his usual noise. Clattering through the hall with Dalgliesh, he said, 'I hoped to bring the PM report on Archdeacon Crampton with me but it's still being typed. Nothing in it to surprise you. Death from multiple blows to the head inflicted by a heavy weapon with a sharp edge, i.e. the brass candlestick. Almost certainly killed by the second blow. Otherwise a healthy middle-aged male who could have looked forward to drawing his pension.'

He put on thin latex gloves before cautiously descending the cellar steps, but he didn't this time wait to don his working overalls and his examination of the body, although not perfunctory, took little time.

At the end, getting to his feet, he said, 'Dead about six hours. Cause of death: a broken neck. Well, you didn't need to call me over to know that. The picture seems clear enough. She fell with force down the steps, struck her forehead on the third step from the bottom and was flung on to her back. I suppose you're asking yourself the usual question: did she fall or was she pushed?'

'I thought of asking you.'

'On the face of it I'd say she was pushed, but you need something more definite than a first impression. I wouldn't be prepared to swear to it in court. The steepness of the stairs is the problem. Could have been designed to kill old ladies. Given that slope, it's perfectly possible that she didn't actually touch the stairs until she struck her head near the bottom. I'd have to say that accidental death is at least as likely as murder. Why the suspicion, by the way? D'you think she saw something on Saturday night? And why was she going to the cellar anyway?'

Dalgliesh said cautiously, 'She had a habit of wandering at night.'

'After the wine, was she?'

Dalgliesh didn't reply. The pathologist clicked shut his case. He said, 'I'll send an ambulance for her and get her on the table as soon as possible, but I doubt I'll tell you anything you don't know. Death seems to follow you about, doesn't it? I take a job as locum pathologist while Colby Brooksbank is in New York getting his son married and I'm called out to more violent deaths than I usually autopsy in six months. Have you heard from the Coroner's office yet about the date for the Crampton inquest?'

'Not yet.'

'You will. He's already been on to me.'

He took a last look at the body and said with surprising gentleness, 'Poor lady. But at least it was quick. Two seconds of terror and then nothing. She'd have preferred to die in her bed – but then, wouldn't we all?'

2

Dalgliesh had seen no need to cancel his instruction to Kate to visit Ashcombe House and by nine o'clock she and Robbins were on their way. It was a morning of penetrating chill. The first light had spread itself, pink as diluted blood, over the grey waste of sea. A fine drizzle was falling and the air tasted sour. As the windscreen wipers smeared then cleared the glass, Kate saw a landscape drained of colour in which even the far fields of sugar beet had lost their green brightness. She had to fight down her slight resentment at being chosen for what she privately thought could be a waste of time. AD seldom admitted to a hunch, but she knew from her own experience that a detective's strong hunch usually has its roots in reality; a word, a look, a coincidence, something apparently insignificant or unrelated to the main inquiry which takes root in the subconscious and gives rise to that small shoot of unease. Often in the end it withers into inconsequence, but sometimes it provides the vital clue and only the foolish ignore it. She disliked leaving the scene of the crime with Piers in possession, but there were compensations. She was driving AD's Jaguar and that was a satisfaction apart from her pleasure in the car.

And she wasn't altogether sorry to have a respite from St Anselm's. She had seldom been part of a murder inquiry in which she had physically and psychologically felt less at home. The college was too masculine, too self-contained, even too claustrophobic for comfort. The priests and ordinands had been unfailingly polite but it was a courtesy which jarred. They saw her primarily as a woman, not as a police officer; she had thought that that battle had been won. She felt too that they were in possession of some secret knowledge, some esoteric source of authority which subtly diminished her own. She wondered whether AD and Piers felt the same. Probably not, but then they were men and St Anselm's, despite its apparent gentleness, was an almost defiantly masculine world. Furthermore it was an academic world, and there too AD and Piers would feel at home. Some of her old social and educational insecurities returned. She thought that she had come to terms with them, if not entirely conquered them. It was humiliating that fewer than a dozen black-cassocked men could revive those old uncertainties. It was with a positive sense of relief that she turned westwards from the cliff-top track and the pulse of the sea gradually faded. It had beaten for too long in her ears.

She would have preferred to have had Piers with her. At least they could have discussed the case on terms of equality, sparred and argued, and been more open than she could be with a junior officer. And she was beginning to find Sergeant Robbins irritating; she had always felt him almost too good to be true. She glanced at his boyish clear-cut profile, at the grey eyes gazing steadily ahead, and wondered again what had led him to choose the police. If he had seen the job as a vocation, well so had she. She had needed a job in which she could feel useful, where the lack of a university degree wouldn't be seen as a disadvantage, a job which provided stimulus, excitement and variety. For her the police service had been a means of putting behind her for ever the squalor and poverty of her childhood, the stink of those urine-soaked stairs at Ellison Fairweather Buildings. The service had given her much, including the flat overlooking the Thames which she could still hardly believe she had achieved. In return she had given it a loyalty and devotion that sometimes surprised even herself. For Robbins, in his spare time a lay preacher, it was probably a vocation to serve his Nonconformist God. She wondered whether what he believed was different from what Father Sebastian believed, and if so, how different and why, but judged the time was not propitious for a theological discussion. What would be the point? In her class at school there had been thirteen different nationalities and almost as many religions. For her, none had been possessed of a coherent philosophy. She told herself that she could live her life without God; she was not sure she could live it without her job.

The hospice was in a village south-east of Norwich. Kate said, 'We don't want to get tangled with the city. Watch out for the Bramerton turning on the right.'

Five minutes later they had left the A146 and were driving more slowly between denuded hedges behind which clusters of red-roofed bungalows and identical houses proclaimed the spread of suburbia over the green fields.

Robbins said quietly, 'My mum died in a hospice two years ago. The usual thing. Cancer.'

'I'm sorry. This visit isn't going to be easy for you.'

'I'm all right. They were wonderful to Mum in the hospice. To us as well.'

Keeping her eyes on the road, Kate said, 'Still, it's bound to bring back painful memories.'

'It's what Mum suffered before she went into the hospice that's painful.' There was another longer pause, then he said, 'Henry James called death "that distinguished thing".'

Oh God, thought Kate, first AD and his poetry, then Piers who knows about Richard Hooker, and now Robbins who reads Henry James! Why can't they send me a sergeant whose idea of a literary challenge is reading Jeffrey Archer?

She said, 'I had a boyfriend, a librarian who tried to get me to enjoy Henry James. By the time I'd got to the end of a sentence I'd forgotten how it began. Remember that criticism, some writers bite off more than they can chew. Henry James chews more than he's bitten off?'

Robbins said, 'I've only read *The Turn of the Screw*. That was after I'd seen the TV film. I came across that quote about death somewhere and it stuck.'

'Sounds good but it isn't true. Death is like birth, painful, messy and undignified. Most of the time anyway.' She thought, perhaps it's just as well. Reminds us that we're animals. Maybe we'd do better if we tried to behave more like good animals and less like gods.

There was a longer pause, then Robbins said quietly, 'Mum's death wasn't without dignity.'

Well, thought Kate, she was one of the lucky ones.

They found the hospice without difficulty. It was in the grounds of a solid red brick house on the outskirts of the village. A large sign directed them down a driveway to the right of the house and to a car park. Behind it stretched the hospice, a single-storey modern building fronted with a lawn in which two circular beds planted with a variety of low evergreen shrubs and heathers made a brave show of green, purple and gold.

Inside the reception area the immediate impression was of light, flowers and busyness. Two people were already at the reception desk, a woman making arrangements to take her husband out for a drive next day, and a clergyman patiently waiting. A baby was wheeled past, her round bald head ludicrously encircled with a red ribbon adorned with a huge bow in the centre. She turned on Kate her bland incurious gaze. A young girl, obviously with her mother, came in carrying a puppy. The child called out, 'We're bringing Trixie to see Granny', and laughed as the puppy slobbered over her ear. A young nurse in a pink overall with a name badge crossed the hall quietly supporting an emaciated man. Visitors came in with flowers and bags, calling out a cheerful greeting. Kate had expected an atmosphere of reverent calm, but not this sense of purposeful activity, of a stark functional building given life by the coming and going of people who felt at home in it.

When the grey-haired non-uniformed woman at the reception desk turned to them, she glanced at Kate's identification as if the arrival of two officers from the Metropolitan Police Force was a common occurrence. She said, 'You rang earlier, didn't you? Matron – Miss Whetstone – is expecting you. Her office is straight ahead.'

Miss Whetstone was waiting at the door. Either she was used to her visitors arriving promptly, or had exceptionally keen ears to catch their coming. She ushered them into a room, the walls of which were three-quarters glass. It was situated at the hub of the hospital and gave a view of two corridors stretching north and south. The easterly window looked out over a garden which seemed to Kate more institutional than the hospice itself. She saw a carefully-tended lawn with wooden benches at regular intervals round the stone paths and carefully-spaced beds in which the fading buds of tightly-furled roses gave smudges of colour among the denuded bushes.

Miss Whetstone waved them to a couple of chairs, seated herself behind the desk and gave them the encouraging smile of a schoolteacher welcoming not particularly promising new pupils. She was a short, heavily-bosomed woman with strong grey hair cut in a fringe above eyes that Kate suspected missed little, but which judged with determined charity. She was wearing a uniform dress in pale blue with a silver buckled belt and with the hospital badge pinned to her chest. Despite the atmosphere of institutional informality, Ashcombe House obviously believed in the status and virtues of the old-fashioned matron.

Kate said, 'We're looking into the death of a student at St Anselm's Theological College. The body was found by Mrs Margaret Munroe, who used to work here before she took the job at St Anselm's. There's no suggestion whatever that she was concerned in the young man's death, but she did leave a diary with a detailed account of how she found the body. A later entry mentions that the tragedy caused her to remember something which happened in her life twelve years ago. Apparently it was an event which, when she recalled it, caused her concern. We'd like to find out what it was. As she was nursing

407

here twelve years ago, there was a possibility it was something which happened here, someone she met, a patient she nursed. We're wondering whether your records would help. Or perhaps there's someone on the staff who knew her that we could talk to.'

On the journey Kate had mentally rehearsed what she would say, selecting, rejecting and assessing each word and sentence. It had been as much for her own clarification as for Miss Whetstone's. Before setting out she had been on the point of asking AD what exactly she was looking for, but hadn't wanted to betray confusion, ignorance or reluctance for the job.

As if sensing what she had felt, Adam Dalgliesh had said, 'Something important happened twelve years ago. Twelve years ago Margaret Munroe was nursing at Ashcombe House hospice. Twelve years ago, on 30 April 1988, Clara Arbuthnot died in the hospice. The facts may or may not be connected. It's a fishing trip rather than a specific enquiry.'

Kate had said, 'I can see that there could be a link between Ronald Treeves's death, however that happened, and Mrs Munroe's. I'm still not clear how all this connects with the Archdeacon's murder.'

'Nor am I, Kate, but I have a feeling that these three deaths – Ronald Treeves's, Margaret Munroe's and Crampton's – are connected. Not directly perhaps, but in some way. It's also possible that Margaret Munroe was murdered. If she was, then her death and Crampton's are almost certainly linked. I can't believe we've two murderers loose in St Anselm's.'

The argument had held a certain credibility at the time. Now, her small prepared speech ended, her doubts returned. Had she over-rehearsed the spiel? Would it have been better to rely on the inspiration of the moment? They weren't helped by Miss Whetstone's clear and sceptical gaze.

She said, 'Let me be sure I've understood you, Inspector. Margaret Munroe has recently died of a heart attack leaving a diary which refers to an event of importance in her life which happened twelve years ago. In connection with some unspecified enquiry you're anxious to know what this was. Since she worked here twelve years ago you're suggesting it could be something to do with the hospice. You're hoping that our records might help or that there might be someone still in post who knew her and would remember incidents of twelve years ago.'

Kate said, 'It's a long shot, I know. But the entry was made in the diary and we have to follow it up.'

'In connection with a boy who was found dead. Was that death foul play?'

'There's no suggestion of that, Miss Whetstone.'

'But there has been a recent murder at St Anselm's, surely. News gets about in the country. Archdeacon Crampton was done to death. Is this visit concerned with that inquiry?'

'We have no reason to suppose it is. Our interest in the diary began before the Archdeacon was murdered.'

'I see. Well, we all have a duty to help the police and I have no objection to looking at Mrs Munroe's file and passing on any information that might help you, provided I think that she wouldn't object if she were still with us. I can't believe the file will yield anything useful. Significant events happen frequently at Ashcombe House, including bereavement and death.'

Kate said, 'According to our information a patient died, a Miss Clara Arbuthnot, a month before Mrs Munroe took up her post here. We are anxious to check the dates. We'd like to know if there was a chance that the two women did meet.'

'That seems highly unlikely unless they met outside Ashcombe House. However, I can check the dates for you. All our records are now, of course, on computer, but we haven't gone back as far as twelve years. We only keep the staff records in case prospective employers ask us for a reference. Both these files are in the main house. There may be information on Miss Arbuthnot's medical record that I regard as confidential. You'll understand I can't pass that on.'

Kate said, 'It would be helpful if we could see both files, Mrs Munroe's record of employment and Miss Arbuthnot's medical record.'

'I don't think I could allow that. Of course this situation is unusual. I've never been faced with this kind of request before. You have hardly been forthcoming about your interest either in Mrs Munroe or in Miss Arbuthnot. I think I should have a word with Mrs Barton – she's our chairman – before we go any further.'

Before Kate had decided how to respond, Robbins said, 'If all this sounds vague it's because we don't ourselves know what we're looking for. We only know that something important happened in Mrs Munroe's life twelve years ago. She seems to have been a lady with few interests outside her job and it's possible that it was something to do with Ashcombe House. Couldn't you have a look at the two files to check we've got the dates right? If there's nothing on Mrs Munroe's file that seems to you significant, then I'm afraid we've been wasting your time. If there is something, then you could consult Mrs Barton before deciding whether it would be right to reveal it.'

Miss Whetstone looked at him steadily for a moment. 'That seems sensible. I'll see if I can lay hands on the records. It may take a little time.'

At that moment the door was opened and a nurse put her head round. 'The ambulance has just arrived, Miss Whetstone, with Mrs Wilson. Her daughters are with her.'

Miss Whetstone's face immediately brightened into happy expectancy. She might have been welcoming a fellow-guest into a prestigious hotel.

'Good. Good. I'll come. I'll come now. We're putting her in with Helen, aren't we? I think she'll be more comfortable with someone her own age.' She turned to Kate. 'I'll be busy for a little time. Do you want to come back or wait?'

Kate felt that their physical presence in her office offered the best hope of getting the information quickly. She said, 'We'll wait if we may, please', but after hearing the first two words Miss Whetstone was out of the door.

Kate said, 'Thank you, Sergeant. That was helpful.'

She strode over to the window and stood quietly watching the comings and goings in the corridor. Glancing at Robbins she saw that his face was white and set in a mask of endurance. She thought she could detect a bead of moisture at the corner of his eye and quickly looked away. She thought, I'm not as good or as kind as I used to be two years ago. What's happening to me? AD was right when I spoke to him. If I can't give this job what it needs, and that includes humanity, maybe I'd be better leaving. Thinking of Dalgliesh, she wished with a sudden intensity that he were there. She smiled, remembering how in such a situation he could never resist the lure of words. It sometimes seemed to her that his reading was an obsession. He would be too scrupulous to study the papers left on the desk unless they were relevant to the inquiry, but he would certainly be moving over to study the numerous notices on the large cork board which obscured part of the window.

Neither she nor Robbins spoke and they remained standing as they had been when Miss Whetstone got up from her chair. They were not kept waiting long. It was just under a quarter of an hour when she returned with two folders and again seated herself at her desk and laid them before her.

'Do sit down, please,' she said.

Kate felt like a candidate at an interview awaiting the humiliating exposure of an unimpressive record.

Miss Whetstone had obviously studied the files before returning. She said, 'I'm afraid there's nothing here to help you. Margaret Munroe came to us on 1 June 1988 and left on 30 April 1994. She was suffering from a deteriorating condition of the heart and was strongly recommended by her doctor to seek less demanding work. She went, as you know, to St Anselm's mainly to look after the linen and to undertake such minor nursing tasks as might be expected in a small college consisting mostly of healthy young men. There's little on her record except the usual applications for annual leave, medical certificates and an annual confidential report. I arrived six months after she left, so have no personal knowledge of her, but she seems to have been a conscientious and sympathetic if unimaginative nurse. The lack of imagination may have been a virtue; the lack of sentimentality certainly was. No one here is ever helped by over-emotionalism.'

Kate said, 'And Miss Arbuthnot?'

'Clara Arbuthnot died a month before Margaret Munroe came to us. She can't, therefore, have been nursed by Mrs Munroe and if they did meet, it wasn't here as patient and nurse.'

Kate asked, 'Did Miss Arbuthnot die alone?'

'No patient dies alone here, Inspector. Certainly she had no relations, but a priest, a Revd Hubert Johnson, saw her at her request before she died.'

Kate said, 'Would it be possible to speak to him, Miss Whetstone?'

Miss Whetstone said drily, 'That, I'm afraid, is beyond the capacity even of the Metropolitan Police. He was a patient here at the time, receiving a temporary period of care, and died here two years later.'

'So there's no one now who has any personal memory of Mrs Munroe's life twelve years ago?'

'Shirley Legge is our longest-serving staff member. We don't have a high turnover but the work does make very special demands and we take the view that it's probably wise for nurses to have a change from terminal cases from time to time. I think she's the only nurse who was here twelve years ago although I would have to check. Frankly, Inspector, I haven't the time. You could certainly have a word with Mrs Legge. I think she's on duty.'

Kate said, 'I'm afraid we're being something of a

nuisance but it would be helpful to see her. Thank you.'

Again Miss Whetstone disappeared leaving the two records on her desk. Kate's first impulse was to take a look at them, but something stopped her. Partly it was her belief that Miss Whetstone had been honest with them and that there was nothing more to be learned, and partly a realization that their every movement was visible through the glass partition. Why antagonize Miss Whetstone now? It wouldn't help the inquiry.

The Matron returned five minutes later with a sharp-featured middle-aged woman whom she introduced as Mrs Shirley Legge. Mrs Legge wasted no time.

'Matron says you're asking about Margaret Munroe. Afraid I can't help you. I did know her but not all that well. She didn't go in for close friendships. I remember she was a widow and had this son who'd won a scholarship to some public school or other, I can't remember which. He was keen on going into the Army and I think they were paying for him at university before he took a commission. Something like that anyway. I'm sorry to hear she's dead. I think there were only the two of them so it'll be tough on the son.'

Kate said, 'The son died before her. Killed in Northern Ireland.'

'That would have been hard for her. I don't suppose she cared much about dying herself after that happened. The boy was her life. Sorry I can't be more helpful. If anything important did happen to her while she was here, she didn't tell me. You could try Mildred Fawcett.' She turned to Miss Whetstone. 'You remember Mildred, Miss Whetstone? She retired shortly after you arrived. She knew Margaret Munroe. I think they trained

414

together at the old Westminster Hospital. Might be worth having a word.'

Kate said, 'Miss Whetstone, are you likely to have her address on record?'

It was Shirley Legge who answered. 'No need to bother. I can tell you that. We still exchange Christmas cards. And she's got the kind of address that sticks in the memory. It's a cottage just outside Medgrave off the A146, Clippety-Clop Cottage. I think there used to be farm horses stabled nearby.'

So here at last they had struck lucky. Mildred Fawcett might well have retired to a cottage in Cornwall or to the North-East. Instead Clippety-Clop Cottage was directly on their road to St Anselm's. Kate thanked Miss Whetstone and Shirley Legge for their help and asked if they could have a look at the local telephone directory. Here again they were lucky. Miss Fawcett's number was listed.

A wooden box on the counter of the reception desk was labelled 'Flowers Fund' and Kate folded and slipped in a five-pound note. She doubted whether this was legitimate expenditure of police funds, and she wasn't sure whether the gesture had been one of generosity or a small superstitious offering to fate.

3

Back in the car, their seat-belts fastened, Kate rang Clippety-Clop Cottage but got no reply. She said, 'I'd better report on progress – or the lack of it.'

The conversation was brief. Putting down the telephone, she said, 'We see Mildred Fawcett as planned, if we can reach her. Then he wants us back as quickly as possible. The pathologist has just left.'

'Did AD say how it happened? Was it an accident?'

'Too early to tell, but that's what it looks like. And if it wasn't, how the hell can we prove it?'

Robbins said, 'The fourth death.'

'All right, Sergeant, I can count.'

She drove carefully out of the drive but once on the road increased her speed. Miss Betterton's death was unsettling in more ways than its initial impact of shock. Kate wasn't unusual in needing to feel that the police, once on the job, were in command. An investigation might go well or ill, but it was they who questioned, probed, dissected, assessed, decided on strategy and held the cords of control. But there was something about the Crampton murder, an anxiety subtle and unvoiced, which had lain at the back of her mind almost from the beginning but which until now she hadn't faced. It was the realization that the power might lie elsewhere, that despite Dalgliesh's intelligence and experience there was another mind at work equally intelligent and with a different experience. She feared that the control, which once lost could never be regained, might already have slipped from their hands. She was impatient to be back at St Anselm's as soon as possible. In the meantime it was pointless to speculate; so far their journey had produced nothing that was new.

She said, 'Sorry I was so short. There's no point in discussing it until we have more facts. For now we concentrate on finishing the job in hand.'

Robbins said, 'If we're on a wild goose chase, at least they're flying in the right direction.'

Once they approached Medgrave, Kate slowed down almost to a crawl; more time would be lost by missing the cottage than by driving slowly. She said, 'You look to the left, I'll take the right. We could always ask but I'd rather not. I don't want to advertise our visit.'

It wasn't necessary to ask. As they approached the village she saw a neat brick and tile cottage standing some forty feet back from the green verge on a slight rise of the road. A white board on the gate bore the name in carefully painted bold black letters, CLIPPETY-CLOP COTTAGE. It had a central porch with the date, 1893, carved in stone above it and two identical bow windows on the ground floor with a line of three above. The paintwork was a shiny white, the window-panes glittered and the flagstones leading to the front door were free of weeds. The immediate impression was of order and comfort. There was room to park on the verge and they moved up the path to an iron knocker in the shape of a horseshoe. There was no reply.

Kate said, 'Probably out, but it's worth going round the back.'

The early drizzle had ceased and although the air was still sharp the day had lightened and there were threads of barely discernible blue in the eastern sky. A stone path to the left of the house led to an unlocked gate and into the garden. Kate, born and bred in the inner city, knew little of gardening, but she could see at once that an enthusiast had been at work. The spacing of the trees and shrubs, the careful design of the beds and the neat vegetable patch at the end showed that Miss Fawcett was an expert. The slight rise of the ground meant too that she had a view. The autumn landscape stretched untrammelled in all its varied greens, golds and browns under the wide East Anglian sky.

A woman, hoe in hand, bending over one of the beds, rose as they approached and came towards them. She was tall and gypsy-like, with a brown face, deeply wrinkled, and black hair hardly touched with grey combed tightly back and fastened at the nape of her neck. She was wearing a long woollen skirt with an apron of sacking over it with a wide central pocket, heavy shoes and gardening gloves. She seemed neither surprised nor disconcerted to see them.

Kate introduced herself and Sergeant Robbins, showed her identification and repeated the essentials of what she had previously said to Miss Whetstone. She added, 'They weren't able to help at the hospice, but Mrs Shirley Legge said that you were there twelve years ago and knew Mrs Munroe. We found your number and did try to telephone, but there was no reply.'

'I expect I was at the bottom of the garden. Friends tell me I should have a mobile, but that's the last thing I want. They're an abomination. I've given up travelling by train until they introduce mobile-free compartments.'

Unlike Miss Whetstone, she asked no questions. One might imagine, thought Kate, that visits from two officers of the Metropolitan Police were a regular occurrence. She gazed at Kate steadily, then said, 'You'd better come in and I'll see if I can help.'

They were led through a brick-floored pantry with a deep stone sink under the window and fitted bookshelves and cupboards along the opposite wall. There was a smell of moist earth and apples, with a trace of paraffin. The room was obviously used partly as a tool-shed and storeroom. Kate's eyes took in a box of apples, on the shelf, onions threaded on a string, swathes of twine, buckets, a curled garden hose on a hook and a rack of garden tools, all clean. Miss Fawcett took off her apron and shoes and preceded them bare-footed into the sitting-room.

It spoke to Kate of a self-contained and solitary life. There was one high-backed armchair in front of the fire with an angled lamp on a table to the left, and another table on the right holding a pile of books. A round table in front of the window was set for one person and the remaining three chairs had been pushed back against the wall. A large ginger cat was curled, plump as a cushion, on a low button-backed chair. At their entry he raised a ferocious head, gazed fixedly at them then, affronted, descended from the chair and lumbered out to the pantry. They heard the click of a cat-flap. Kate thought she had never seen an uglier cat.

Miss Fawcett pulled out two straight-backed chairs, then went to a cupboard fitted in the alcove to the left of the fireplace. She said, 'I don't know whether I can help you, but if something important did happen to Margaret Munroe when we were both nursing at the hospice, I probably mentioned it in my diary. My father insisted that we keep diaries as children and the habit has stuck. It's rather like insisting on prayers before bed; once begun in childhood, there's an obligation to conscience to keep going, however disagreeable. You said twelve years ago. That would bring us to 1988.'

She settled down in the chair before the fire and picked up what looked like a child's exercise book.

Kate said, 'Do you remember whether you nursed a Miss Clara Arbuthnot when you worked at Ashcombe House?'

If Miss Fawcett thought the sudden mention of Clara Arbuthnot odd she didn't say so. She said, 'I remember Miss Arbuthnot. I was the nurse chiefly responsible for her care from the day of her admission until she died five weeks later.'

She took her spectacle-case from her skirt pocket and turned over the pages of the diary. It took a little time to find the right week; as Kate had feared, Miss Fawcett's interest was caught by other entries. Kate wondered if she was being deliberately slow. After a minute she sat silently reading, then pressed both hands over the entry. Once again Kate experienced her keen intelligent gaze.

She said, 'There's a mention here both of Clara Arbuthnot and Margaret Munroe. I find myself in some difficulty. I promised secrecy at the time and I see no reason now to break my word.'

Kate thought before speaking, then she said, 'The information you have there may be crucial to us for other reasons than an ordinand's apparent suicide. It really is important that we know what you have written, and know as soon as possible. Clara Arbuthnot and Margaret Munroe are both dead. Do you think they would wish you to remain silent if it's a matter of helping justice?'

Miss Fawcett got to her feet. She said, 'Will you please take a walk in the garden for a few minutes. I'll knock on the window when I want you back. I need to think about this on my own.'

They left her still standing. Outside they walked shoulder to shoulder to the far end of the garden and stayed looking out over the scarred fields. Kate was tormented with impatience. She said, 'That diary was only a few feet away. All I needed was a quick glance. And what do we do if she won't say anything more? OK, there's always a subpoena if the case goes to court, but how do we know that the diary's relevant? It's probably an entry describing how she and Munroe went to Frinton and had sex under the pier.'

Robbins said, 'There isn't a pier at Frinton.'

'And Miss Arbuthnot was dying. Oh well, we'd better stroll back. I don't want to miss the knock on the window.'

When it came they went back into the sitting-room quietly, anxious not to betray impatience.

Miss Fawcett said, 'I have your word that the information you seek is necessary to your present investigation and that, if it proves irrelevant, no note will be taken of what I say.'

Kate said, 'We can't tell, Miss Fawcett, whether it will be relevant or not. If it is, then of course it will have to come out, possibly even in evidence. I can't give any assurances, I can only ask you to help.'

Miss Fawcett said, 'Thank you for your honesty. As it happens you are fortunate. My grandfather was a chief constable and I am one of that generation – sadly decreasing – who still trust the police. I'm prepared to tell you what I know, and also to hand over the diary, if the information is useful.'

Kate judged that further argument was unnecessary and might be counter-productive. She simply said 'thank you', and waited.

Miss Fawcett said, 'I've been thinking while you were in the garden. You told me that this visit arises from the death of a student at St Anselm's College. You also said that there was no suggestion that Margaret Munroe was involved in that death except when she found the body. But there has to be more to it than that, doesn't there? You wouldn't be here, a detective inspector and a sergeant, unless there was suspicion of foul play. This is a murder inquiry, isn't it?'

'Yes,' said Kate, 'it is. We are part of a team investigating the murder of Archdeacon Crampton at St Anselm's College. There may be absolutely no link with Mrs Munroe's diary entry, but it's something we have to check. I expect you know about the Archdeacon's death.'

'No,' said Miss Fawcett, 'I don't know. I very seldom buy a daily newspaper and I've no television. Murder makes a difference. There's an entry in my diary for 27 April 1988 and it does concern Mrs Munroe. My problem is that at the time we both promised secrecy.'

Kate said, 'Miss Fawcett, could I please see the entry?'

'I don't think it would be very illuminating if you did. I wrote down few of the details. But I remember more than I've recorded here. I think I have a duty to tell you, although I doubt whether it has anything to do with your inquiry, and I have your assurance that, if it isn't, the matter will be taken no further.'

Kate said, 'We can promise you that.'

Miss Fawcett sat stiffly upright, her palms pressed against the open pages of the diary as if to shield them from prying eyes. She said, 'In April 1988 I was nursing terminally ill patients at Ashcombe House. This, of course, you already know. One of my patients told me that she wished to marry before she died, but that her intention and the ceremony were to be kept secret. She asked me to be a witness. I agreed. It wasn't my place to ask questions and I asked none. This was a wish expressed by a patient of whom I had become fond, and whom I knew had little time left to live. The surprise was that she had the strength for the ceremony. It was arranged by archbishop's licence and took place at midday on the twenty-seventh at the small church, St Osyth's at Clampstoke-Lacey, outside Norwich. The priest was The Revd Hubert Johnson whom my patient had met at the hospice. I didn't see the bridegroom until he arrived by car to collect the patient and myself, ostensibly for a country drive. Father Hubert was to find a second witness but failed to do so. I can't now remember what went wrong. As we were leaving the hospice I saw Margaret Munroe. She was just leaving after her interview with the matron for a nursing post. It was, in fact, at my suggestion that she had applied. I knew that I could rely on her absolute discretion. We trained together at the old Westminster Hospital in London although she was, of course, considerably younger than myself. I was a late entry to nursing after a brief academic career. My father was strongly opposed to my choice of profession and I had to wait until he died before I could apply for training. The wedding ceremony took place and the patient and I returned to the hospice. She seemed much happier and more at peace in those last days, but neither she nor I spoke again of the marriage. So much happened during my years at the hospice that I doubt whether I would have recalled it without this entry if I hadn't had an earlier enquiry. Seeing the written words, even without a name, brought it back with astonishing clarity. It was a beautiful day; I remember the graveyard at St Osyth's was yellow with daffodils and we came out of the porch into sunshine.'

Kate said, 'Was the patient Clara Arbuthnot?'

Miss Fawcett looked at her. 'Yes, it was.'

'And the bridegroom?'

'I've no idea. I can't recall his face or his name, and I doubt whether Margaret would've been able to help if she'd been alive.'

Kate said, 'But she would have signed the marriage certificate as a witness and surely names would have been mentioned.'

'I imagine they would. But there was no particular reason why she should remember. After all, at a church wedding only Christian names are used during the service.' She paused and then said, 'I have to confess that I haven't been entirely open with you. I wanted time to think, to consider how much, if anything, I should reveal. I had no need to consult the diary before answering your question. I had looked up that date before. On Thursday 12 October Margaret Munroe telephoned me from a callbox in Lowestoft. She asked me the name of the bride and I told her. I couldn't give her the name of the groom. It isn't recorded in my diary and, if I ever knew it, it's long since forgotten.'

Kate said, 'Is there anything at all you remember about the bridegroom? His age, what he looked like, how he spoke? Did he ever come again to the hospice?'

'No, not even when Clara was dying, and as far as I know he had no part in the cremation service. That was arranged by a firm of solicitors in Norwich. I never saw or heard from him again. There was one thing though. I noticed it when we stood before the altar and he was putting the ring on Clara's finger. The top part of the ring finger on his left hand was missing.'

Kate's surge of triumph and excitement was so exhilarating that she feared that it must show on her face. She didn't glance at Robbins. Keeping her voice steady, she asked: 'Did Miss Arbuthnot ever confide in you about the reason for the marriage? Is it possible, for example, that there was a child involved?'

'A child? She never spoke of having a child and as far as I recall there was no mention of a pregnancy on her medical records. No child ever visited her; but then, neither did the man she married.'

'So she told you nothing?'

'Only that she planned to marry, that the marriage must be kept absolutely secret, and that she needed my help. I gave it.'

'Is there anyone she might have confided in?'

'The priest who married her, Father Hubert Johnson, spent a great deal of time with her before she died. I remember that he gave her Holy Communion and heard her confession. I had to ensure that they weren't disturbed when he was with my patient. She must have told him everything, either as a friend or as a priest. But he was seriously ill himself at the time and died two years later.'

There was nothing more to be learned and after thanking Miss Fawcett for her help Kate and Robbins returned to the car. Miss Fawcett was watching them from the door of the cottage and Kate drove out of sight before finding a suitable place on the grass verge to bring the Jaguar to a stop. She took up the telephone and said with satisfaction, 'Something positive to report. We're getting somewhere at last.'

4

After lunch, as Father John did not appear, Emma went up and knocked at the door of his private apartment. She dreaded seeing him, but when he opened the door he looked very much as he always did. His face brightened and he welcomed her in.

She said, 'Father, I'm so sorry, so dreadfully sorry,' and held back her tears. She told herself she had come to speak words of comfort, not to add to his distress. But it was like comforting a child. She wanted to take him in her arms. He led her to the chair before the fire, the chair which she guessed was his sister's, and sat opposite her.

He said, 'I wonder if you would do something for me, Emma.'

'Of course. Anything, Father.'

'It's her clothes. I know they'll have to be sorted and given away. It seems very early to be thinking of that now, but I expect you'll be leaving us by the end of the week and I wondered whether you would do it. Mrs Pilbeam would help, I know. She's very kind, but I'd rather it were you. Perhaps tomorrow, if that's convenient.'

'Of course I will, Father. I'll do it after my afternoon seminar.'

He said, 'Everything she owned is in her bedroom. There should be some jewellery. If there is, will you take

427

it and sell it for me? I'd like the money to go to some charity concerned with helping prisoners. I think there must be one.'

Emma said, 'I'm sure there is, Father. I'll find out for you. But wouldn't you like to look at the jewellery first and decide if there's anything you'd like to keep?'

'No thank you, Emma. That's thoughtful, but I'd rather it all went.'

There was a silence, then he said, 'The police were here this morning, examining the flat and her room. Inspector Tarrant came with one of those search officers in white coats. He introduced him as Mr Clark.'

Emma's voice was sharp. 'Searched the flat for what?'

'They didn't say. They weren't here for long and they left everything very tidy. You wouldn't have known that they'd been here.' There was another pause, then he said, 'Inspector Tarrant asked me where I'd been and what I did last night between Compline and six o'clock.'

Emma cried, 'But that's intolerable!'

He smiled sadly. 'No, not really. They have to ask these questions. Inspector Tarrant was very tactful. He was only doing his duty.'

Emma reflected angrily that much of the world's grief was caused by people who claimed that they were only doing their duty.

Father John's quiet voice broke in. 'The pathologist was here, but I expect you heard him arrive.'

'The whole community must have heard him. It wasn't a discreet arrival.'

Father John smiled. 'No it wasn't, was it? He didn't stay long either. Commander Dalgliesh asked me if I wanted to be there when they took the body away, but

I said I'd rather stay here quietly by myself. After all, it wasn't Agatha they were taking away. She'd gone long ago.'

Gone long ago. What exactly, Emma wondered, did he mean? The three words clanged in her mind as sonorous as a funeral bell.

Getting up to go, she took his hand again and said, 'I'll see you tomorrow then, Father, when I come to parcel up the clothes. Are you sure there's nothing else I can do?'

He thanked her, then said, 'There is just one other thing. I hope I'm not imposing on your goodness, but will you please find Raphael. I haven't seen him since it happened but I'm afraid this will distress him greatly. He was always kind to her and I know that she loved him.'

She found Raphael standing on the edge of the cliff about a hundred yards from the college. When she reached him he sat down on the grass and she joined him and put out her hand.

Staring out to sea and without turning to her, he said, 'She was the only one here who cared for me.'

Emma cried, 'That isn't true, Raphael, you know it isn't!'

'I mean cared for *me*. Myself. Raphael. Not as the object of general benevolence. Not as a suitable candidate for the priesthood. Not as the last surviving Arbuthnot – even if I am a bastard. You must have been told. Dumped here as a baby in one of those straw baby carriers – squashy with a handle both sides. Leaving me in the rushes by the mere would have been more appropriate, but perhaps my mother thought I wouldn't be discovered there. At least she cared enough to dump me at the college where I'd be found. They didn't have much choice about taking me in. Still, it's given them twenty-five years of feeling benevolent, exercising the virtue of charity.'

'You know that isn't how they feel.'

'It's how I feel. I know I sound egotistical and self-pitying. I *am* egotistical and self-pitying. You don't have to tell me. I used to think everything would be all right if I could get you to marry me.'

'Raphael, that's ridiculous. When you're thinking clearly you know it is. Marriage isn't therapy.'

'But it would have been something definite. It would have anchored me.'

'Doesn't the Church anchor you?'

'It will once I'm priested. No going back then.'

Emma thought carefully for a moment, then said, 'You don't have to be ordained. It has to be your decision, no one else's. If you're not certain you shouldn't go ahead.'

'You sound like Gregory. If I mention the word vocation he tells me not to talk like a character in a Graham Greene novel. We'd better be going back.' He paused, then laughed. 'She was a terrible nuisance in some ways on those trips to London, but I never wished I was with anyone else.'

He got to his feet and began striding towards the college. Emma made no attempt to catch him up. Walking more slowly on the edge of the cliff, she felt a great sadness for Raphael, for Father John and for all the people she loved at St Anselm's.

She had reached the iron gate into the west court when she heard a voice calling and, turning, saw Karen Surtees walking briskly towards her across the scrubland.

They had seen each other on previous weekends when both had been in college, but had never spoken except to exchange an occasional good morning. Despite this, Emma had never felt that there was antagonism between them. She waited with some curiosity to know what would be said now. Karen glanced back towards St John's Cottage before speaking.

'Sorry to shout at you like that. I just wanted a word. What's all this about old Betterton being found dead in the cellar? Father Martin came over to tell us this morning, but he wasn't exactly forthcoming.'

There seemed no reason to conceal what little she knew. Emma said, 'I think she tripped on the top step.'

'Or was she pushed? Anyway, this is one death they can't try to pin on Eric or me – that is, if she died before midnight. We drove to Ipswich last night to see a film and have dinner. We wanted to get out of the place for an hour or so. I suppose you've no idea how the investigation is going? I mean, the Archdeacon's murder.'

Emma said, 'None at all. The police don't tell us anything.'

'Not even the handsome commander? No, I suppose he wouldn't. God, that man's sinister! I wish to hell he'd get a move on, I want to get back to London. Anyway, I'm staying on here with Eric until the end of the week. There's just one thing I wanted to ask you. You may not be able to help or you may not want to, but I can't think of anyone else to ask. Are you a churchgoer? Do you take communion?'

The question was so unexpected that Emma was for a moment disorientated. Karen said, almost impatiently, 'I mean in church, holy communion. Do you take it?'

'Yes, sometimes.'

'I'm wondering about the wafers they hand out. What happens? I mean, do you open your mouth and they pop them in or do you hold out your hands?'

The conversation was bizarre, but Emma answered, 'Some people open their mouths but in Anglican churches it's more usual to hold up your palms one over the other.'

'And I suppose the priest stands and watches you while you actually eat the wafer?'

'He might if he's speaking all the words in the Prayer Book service over you, but usually he passes along to the next communicant, and then there could be a short wait while either he or another priest comes with the chalice.' She asked, 'Why do you need to know?'

'No particular reason. It's something I'm curious about. I thought I might go to a service and I don't want to get it wrong and make a fool of myself. But don't you have to be confirmed? I mean, they'll probably turn me away.'

Emma said, 'I don't think that would happen. There'll be a Mass in the oratory tomorrow morning.' She added, not without a tinge of mischief, 'You could tell Father Sebastian you'd like to attend. He'll probably ask you a few questions. He might want you to go to confession first.'

'Confess to Father Sebastian! Are you mad? I think I'll wait for spiritual regeneration until I get back to London. By the way, how long are you thinking of staying?'

Emma said, 'I should go on Thursday but I'm able to take an extra day. I'll probably be here until the end of the week.'

'Well, good luck, and thanks for the information.'

She turned and with hunched shoulders walked briskly back to St John's Cottage.

Watching her go, Emma told herself that it was just as well Karen hadn't wanted to stay longer. It would have been tempting to have talked over the murder with another woman and one of her own age, tempting but perhaps unwise. Karen might have questioned her about finding the Archdeacon's body, asked questions which it would have been awkward to parry. Everyone else at St Anselm's had been scrupulous in their reticence, but somehow reticence wasn't a quality she associated with Karen Surtees. She walked on, puzzled. Of all the questions Karen might have wanted to ask, the one she had asked was the last that Emma would have expected.

5

It was one-fifteen and Kate and Robbins had returned. Dalgliesh saw that Kate, reporting precisely on their mission, was trying to keep the note of triumph and excitement out of her voice. She was always at her most detached and professional in moments of high success, but the enthusiasm was evident in her voice and in her eyes, and Dalgliesh welcomed it. Perhaps he was getting back the old Kate, the Kate for whom policing had been more than a job, more than an adequate salary and the prospect of promotion, more than a ladder out of the mire of the deprivation and squalor of her childhood. He had hoped to see that Kate again.

She had telephoned the news of the marriage as soon as she and Robbins had said their thank-yous and good-byes to Miss Fawcett. Dalgliesh had instructed Kate to get a copy of the marriage certificate and return to St Anselm's as soon as possible. A study of the map had shown that Clampstoke-Lacey was only fourteen miles away and it had seemed reasonable first to try the church.

But they had had no luck. St Osyth's was now part of a team ministry and there was at present an interregnum with a new priest temporarily taking the services. He was visiting one of the other churches and his young wife knew nothing of the whereabouts of the parish registers, indeed seemed hardly to know what they were, and could only suggest that they waited for her husband to return. She expected him before supper unless he was invited to have a meal with one of the parishioners. If this happened he would probably telephone, although sometimes he was so preoccupied with parish concerns he forgot. The slight note of peevish resentment that Kate detected in her voice suggested that this was not an unusual occurrence. The best plan now seemed to be to try the Register Office in Norwich and here they had more luck. A copy of the marriage certificate had been promptly produced.

In the meantime Dalgliesh had telephoned Paul Perronet in Norwich. There were two important questions to which he needed answers before they interviewed George Gregory. The first was the exact wording of Miss Arbuthnot's will. The second related to the provisions of an Act of Parliament and the date on which the legislation had come into force.

Kate and Robbins hadn't waited to get themselves lunch and now fell with eagerness upon the cheese rolls and coffee provided by Mrs Pilbeam.

Dalgliesh said, 'We can guess now how it was that Margaret Munroe recalled the wedding. She had been writing her diary, dwelling on the past, and two images came together; Gregory on the shore taking off his left glove and feeling for Ronald Treeves's pulse, and the page of bridal pictures in the *Sole Bay Weekly Gazette*. The fusion of death and life. Next day she telephoned Miss Fawcett, not from the cottage where she might have been disturbed, but from a telephone box in Lowestoft. She was given confirmation of what she must surely have suspected: the name of the bride. It was only then that she spoke to the person most concerned. There were only two people to whom those words could apply, George Gregory and Raphael Arbuthnot. And within hours of speaking and receiving reassurance, Margaret Munroe was dead.'

Refolding the copy of the marriage certificate, he said, 'We'll speak to Gregory in his cottage, not here. I'd like you to come with me, Kate. His car is here so if he's out he can't have gone far.'

Kate said, 'But the marriage doesn't give Gregory a motive for the Archdeacon's murder. It should have taken place twenty-five years ago. Raphael Arbuthnot can't inherit. The will says he has to be legitimate according to English law.'

'But that's exactly what the marriage makes him, legitimate according to English law.'

Gregory could only just have returned. He opened the door to them wearing a black long-sleeved track suit and with a towel round his neck. His hair hung damply and the cotton clung to his chest and arms.

Without standing aside to let them in, he said, 'I was just about to shower. Is this urgent?'

He was making them as unwelcome as importunate salesmen, and Dalgliesh for the first time saw in his eyes the challenge of an antagonism that he was making no attempt to conceal.

He said, 'It is urgent. May we come in?'

Leading them through the study into the rear extension, Gregory said, 'You have, Commander, something of the air of a man who feels that he is at last making progress. Some might say about time. Let us hope it doesn't all end in the Slough of Despond.'

He motioned them to a sofa and sat himself at his

desk, swivelling round the chair and stretching out his legs. He then began vigorously towelling his hair. Across the room Dalgliesh could smell his sweat.

Without taking the marriage certificate from his pocket, he said, 'You married Clara Arbuthnot on 27 April 1988 at St Osyth's church, Clampstoke-Lacey, Norfolk. Why didn't you tell me? Did you really believe that the circumstances of that marriage weren't relevant to the murder inquiry?'

For a couple of seconds Gregory was still and silent, but when he spoke his voice was calm and unworried. Dalgliesh wondered whether he had days ago braced himself for this encounter.

'I suppose by referring to the circumstances of the marriage you've understood the significance of the date. I didn't tell you because I didn't think it was any of your business. That's the first reason. The second is that I promised my wife that the marriage would remain a secret until I had informed our son – and, incidentally, Raphael is my son. The third is that I haven't yet told him and I judged that the right moment to do so had not yet come. However, it looks as if you're forcing my hand.'

Kate said, 'Does anyone at St Anselm's know?'

Gregory looked at her as if aware of her for the first time, and deploring what he saw. 'No one. Obviously they will have to know and equally obviously they will blame me for keeping Raphael in the dark for so long. And them too, of course. Human nature being what it is, they'll probably find that more difficult to forgive. I can't see myself occupying this cottage for much longer. As I only took this job to get to know my son, and as St Anselm's is doomed to close, that won't now matter.

But I could wish to conclude this episode in my life more agreeably and in my own time.'

Kate asked, 'Why the secrecy? Even the staff at the hospice were kept in the dark. Why bother to marry if no one was ever to be told?'

'I thought I'd explained that. Raphael was to be told, but when I judged the moment to be right. I could hardly envisage being caught up in a murder investigation and have the police ferreting about in my private life. The moment still isn't right, but I suppose you'll have the satisfaction of telling him now.'

'No,' said Dalgliesh. 'That's your responsibility, not ours.'

The two men looked at each other, then Gregory said, 'I suppose you have some right to an explanation, or as close to one as I can get. You should know better than most men that our motives are rarely as uncomplicated and never as pure as they seem. We met at Oxford when I was her supervisor. She was an astonishingly attractive eighteen-year-old and when she made it plain that she wanted an affair, I wasn't the man to resist. It was a humiliating disaster. I hadn't realized that she was confused about her sexuality and was deliberately using me as an experiment. She was unfortunate in her choice. No doubt I could have been more sensitive and imaginative, but I've never seen the sexual act as an exercise in acrobatic ingenuity. I was too young and perhaps too conceited to take sexual failure philosophically and this was a spectacular failure. One can deal with most things but not with frank disgust. I'm afraid I wasn't very kind. She didn't tell me that she was pregnant until it was too late for an abortion. I think she'd tried to persuade herself that none of it was happening. She was not a sensible woman. Raphael inherits his looks but not his intelligence from his mother. There was no question of marriage; the idea of that commitment has horrified me all my life, and she made her hatred of me abundantly plain. She told me nothing about the birth, but did write later to say that a boy had been born and that she'd left him at St Anselm's. After that she went abroad with a woman companion and we never met again.

'I didn't keep in touch with her but she must have made it her business to know where I was. In early April 1988 she wrote to say that she was dying and asked me to visit her in Ashcombe House hospice outside Norwich. It was then that she asked me to marry her. The explanation she gave was that it was for the sake of her son. She had also, I believe, found God. It has been a tendency of the Arbuthnots to find God, usually at the time most inconvenient for their family.'

Kate asked again, 'So why the secrecy?'

'She insisted on it. I made the necessary arrangements and merely called at the hospice asking to take her for a drive. The nurse who had mainly looked after her was in on the secret and was the chief witness. There was some problem, I remember, about the second witness but a woman visiting the hospice for an interview agreed to help. The priest was a fellow-sufferer whom Clara had met at the hospice and who occasionally attended for what I think they call respite care. St Osyth's at Clampstoke-Lacey was his church. He obtained for us an archbishop's licence so no banns were necessary. We went through the prescribed form of words and then I drove Clara back to the hospice. Clara wished me to keep the marriage certificate and I still have it. She died three days later. The woman who'd nursed her wrote that she had died without pain and that the marriage had given her peace at the last. I'm glad that it made a difference to one of our lives; it had absolutely no effect on mine. She had asked me to break the news to Raphael when I judged the moment was right.'

Kate said, 'And you waited twelve years. Did you ever intend to tell him?'

'Not necessarily. I certainly didn't intend to burden myself with an adolescent son or to burden him with a father. I'd done nothing for him, taken no part in his upbringing. It seemed ignoble suddenly to present myself as if my purpose were to look him over and see if he were a son worth acknowledging.'

Dalgliesh said, 'Isn't that, in effect, what you did?'

'I plead guilty. I discovered in myself a certain curiosity, or perhaps it was the urging of those insistent genes. Parenthood is, after all, our only chance of vicarious immortality. I made discreet and anonymous enquiries and discovered that he went abroad for two years after university, then came back here and announced his intention of becoming a priest. As he hadn't read theology he had to undertake a three-year course. Six years ago I came here as a guest for a week. I later learned that there was a vacancy for a part-time teacher of Ancient Greek and applied for the post.'

Dalgliesh said, 'You know that St Anselm's is almost certainly scheduled to be closed. After the death of Ronald Treeves and the murder of the Archdeacon that closure is likely to be sooner rather than later. You do realize that you have a motive for Crampton's murder?

Both you and Raphael. Your wedding took place after the coming into force of the Legitimacy Act of 1976 which legitimized your son. Section Two of the Act provides that, where the parents of an illegitimate person marry one another and the father is domiciled in England or Wales, the person is rendered legitimate from the date of the marriage. I've checked on the exact wording of Miss Agnes Arbuthnot's will. If the college closes, everything it contains originally given by her is to be shared between the descendants of her father, either in the male or female line, provided they are practising members of the Church of England and are legitimate in English law. Raphael Arbuthnot is the sole heir. Are you going to tell me that you didn't know that?'

For the first time Gregory showed signs that he was losing his careful mask of ironic detachment. His voice was peremptory. 'The boy doesn't know. I can see that this gives you a convenient motive for making me your chief suspect. Even your ingenuity can't produce a motive for Raphael.'

There were, of course, other motives than gain, but Dalgliesh didn't pursue them.

Kate said, 'We've only your word for it that he doesn't know he's the heir.'

Gregory got to his feet and towered over her. 'Then send for him and I'll tell him here and now.'

Dalgliesh intervened. 'Is that either wise or kind?'

'I don't bloody well care whether it is or it isn't! I'm not having Raphael accused of murder. Send for him and I'll tell him myself. But first I'm going to shower. I've no intention of presenting myself as his father stinking of sweat.'

He disappeared into the body of the house and they heard his footsteps on the stairs.

Dalgliesh said to Kate, 'Go to Nobby Clark and tell him we need an exhibit bag. I want that track suit. And ask Raphael to come here in five minutes' time.'

Kate said, 'Is it really necessary, sir?'

'For his sake, yes it is. Gregory is perfectly right; the only way to convince us that Raphael Arbuthnot is ignorant of his parentage is for us to be here when he's told.'

She was back with the exhibit bag within minutes. Gregory was still in the shower.

Kate said, 'I've seen Raphael. He'll be along in five minutes.'

They waited in silence. Dalgliesh glanced round at the ordered room and at the office seen through the open door; the computer on the desk facing the wall, the bank of grey filing cabinets, the bookcases with the leather tomes meticulously arranged. Nothing here was superfluous, nothing for ornament or show. It was the sanctum of a man whose interests were intellectual and who liked his life comfortable and uncluttered. Dalgliesh thought wryly that it was about to be cluttered now.

They heard the door open and Raphael came through the outer room and into the extension. Within seconds he was followed by Gregory, now wearing trousers and a navy blue freshly-ironed shirt, but with his hair still tousled. He said, 'Perhaps we'd better all sit down.'

They did so. Raphael, puzzled, glanced from Gregory to Dalgliesh but didn't speak.

Gregory looked across at his son. He said, 'There's something I have to tell you. This moment isn't of my choosing, but the police have taken more interest in my private concerns than I expected, so there's no choice. I married your mother on 27 April 1988. This was a ceremony you may feel should more appropriately have taken place twenty-six years ago. There's no way to say this without sounding melodramatic. I'm your father, Raphael.'

Raphael fixed his eyes on Gregory. He said, 'I don't believe it. It isn't true.'

It was the usual commonplace response to shocking and unwelcome news. He said again more loudly, 'I don't believe it', but his face showed a different reality. The colour drained from his brow, cheeks and neck in a steadily retreating line, so visible that it looked as if the normal surge of the blood had been reversed. He got to his feet and stood very still, looking from Dalgliesh to Kate as if desperately seeking a denial. Even the muscles of his face seemed momentarily to sag, the incipient lines to deepen. And for a brief moment Dalgliesh saw for the first time a trace of resemblance to his father. He had hardly time to recognize it before it was gone.

Gregory said, 'Don't be tedious, Raphael. Surely we can play this scene without recourse to Mrs Henry Wood. I've always disliked Victorian melodrama. Is this the kind of thing I'd joke about? Commander Dalgliesh has a copy of the marriage certificate.'

'That doesn't mean you're my father.'

'Your mother only had sex with one man in the whole of her life. I was he. I acknowledged my responsibility in a letter to your mother. For some reason she required that small admission of folly. After our wedding she gave me the correspondence between us. And then, of course,

443

there is the DNA. The facts are unlikely to be challenged.' He paused, then said, 'I'm sorry you find the news so repugnant.'

Raphael's voice was so cold that it was almost unrecognizable. 'And what happened? The usual story, I suppose. You fucked her, got her pregnant, decided you didn't care for the idea either of marriage or parenthood, and opted out?'

'Not precisely. Neither of us wanted a child and there was no possibility of marriage. I was the elder and I suppose the more to blame. Your mother was only eighteen. Doesn't your religion rest on an act of cosmic forgiveness? So why not forgive her? You were better off with those priests than you would have been with either of us.'

There was a long silence, then Raphael said, 'I would have been heir to St Anselm's.'

Gregory looked at Dalgliesh, who said, 'You are the heir, unless there's some legal quibble which I've overlooked. I've checked with the solicitors. Agnes Arbuthnot wrote in her will that if the college closed, all she had bequeathed to it should go to the legitimate heirs of her father, either in the male or female line, providing they were communicant members of the Church of England. She didn't write "born in wedlock", she wrote "legitimate in English law". Your parents married after the provisions of the 1976 Legitimacy Act came into force. That makes you legitimate.'

Raphael walked over to the southern window and stood silently looking out over the headland. He said, 'I'll get used to it, I expect. I got used to having a mother who dumped me like a bundle of unwanted clothes in a charity shop. I got used to not knowing the name of my father or even if he were alive. I got used to being brought up in a theological college when my contemporaries had a home. I'll get used to this. At present all I want is never to have to see you again.'

Dalgliesh wondered if Gregory had detected in his son's voice the quickly controlled quaver of emotion.

Gregory said, 'No doubt that can be arranged, but not now. I imagine Commander Dalgliesh wants me to stay here. This exciting new information has given me a motive. You too, of course.'

Raphael turned on him. 'Did you kill him?'

'No, did you?'

'God, this is ridiculous!' He turned to Dalgliesh. 'I thought it was your job to investigate murder, not muck up people's lives.'

'I'm afraid the two very often go together.'

Dalgliesh glanced at Kate, and together they walked towards the door.

Gregory said, 'Obviously Sebastian Morell will have to be told. I'd prefer that you left that to me or to Raphael.' He turned to his son. 'Is that all right by you?'

Raphael said, 'I'll say nothing. Tell him whenever you like. It's a matter of supreme indifference to me. Ten minutes ago I didn't have a father. I haven't got one now.'

Dalgliesh asked Gregory, 'How long do you propose to wait? It can't be indefinite.'

'It won't be, although, after twelve years, a week or so hardly seems significant. I'd prefer to say nothing until your investigation is complete, assuming that it ever is. But that's hardly practical. I'll tell him at the end of the week. I think I might be allowed to choose my own time and place.'

Raphael had already left the cottage, and through the great panes of glass, smudged by the sea mists, they could see him striding over the headland towards the sea. Looking after him, Kate said, 'Will he be all right? Shouldn't someone go after him?'

Gregory said, 'He'll survive. He's not Ronald Treeves. For all his self-pity, Raphael has been indulged all his life. My son is fortified by a core of healthy self-regard.'

When Nobby Clark was summoned to take possession of his track suit he made no difficulty about handing it over and watched with sardonic amusement as it was placed in a plastic bag and labelled before seeing Dalgliesh, Kate and Clark out of the cottage as formally as if he were saying goodbye to esteemed guests.

They made their way towards St Matthew's. Kate said, 'It's a motive. I suppose Gregory has to be our chief suspect, but it doesn't really make sense, does it? I mean, it's obvious this place is going to be closed down. Raphael would have inherited anyway in the end. There wasn't any hurry.'

Dalgliesh said, 'But there was. Think about it, Kate.'

He gave no explanation and Kate knew better than to ask.

They had reached St Matthew's Cottage when Piers appeared at the door. He said, 'I was just going to ring you, sir. We've had a call from the hospital. Inspector Yarwood is well enough to be interviewed. They suggest we leave it until tomorrow morning when he'll be more rested.'

6

All hospitals, thought Dalgliesh, whatever their situation or architecture, are essentially alike; the same smell, the same paint, the same notices directing visitors to wards and departments, the same inoffensive pictures in the corridors chosen to reassure not to challenge, the same visitors with their flowers and packages making their confident way to familiar bedsides, the same staff in a variety of uniforms and half-uniforms, moving purposefully in their natural habitat, the same tired resolute faces. How many hospitals had he visited since his days as a detective constable, keeping watch over prisoners or witnesses, taking deathbed statements, questioning medical staff with more immediate things on their minds than his preoccupations?

As they approached the ward, Piers said, 'I try to keep out of these places. They give you infections that they can't cure and if your own visitors don't exhaust you to death, other patients' visitors will. You can never get enough sleep and the food's inedible.'

Looking at him, Dalgliesh suspected that the words hid a deeper repugnance, amounting almost to a phobia. He said, 'Doctors are like the police. You don't think about them until you need them, and then you expect them to work miracles. I'd like you to stay outside while I speak to Yarwood, at least initially. If I need a witness I'll call you in. I'll have to take this gently.'

A houseman, looking ridiculously young and with the customary stethoscope round his neck, confirmed that Inspector Yarwood was fit now to be interviewed and directed them to a small side-ward. Outside a uniformed police constable was keeping watch. He got up smartly as they approached and stood to attention.

Dalgliesh said, 'DC Lane, isn't it? I don't think you'll be needed once it's known that I've spoken to Inspector Yarwood. You'll be glad to get away, I expect.'

'Yes sir. We are pretty short-staffed.'

Who isn't? thought Dalgliesh.

Yarwood's bed was positioned to give him a view of the window and over the regulated roofs of suburbia. One leg suspended on a pulley was in traction. After their encounter in Lowestoft, they had met only once and briefly at St Anselm's. He had been struck then by the look of weary acceptance in the man's face. Now he seemed bodily to have shrunk and the weariness to have deepened into defeat. Dalgliesh thought, hospitals take over more than the body; no one exerts power from these narrow functional beds. Yarwood was diminished in spirit as in size and the darkened eyes turned on Dalgliesh held a look of puzzled shame that malignant fate should have laid him so low.

It was impossible to avoid the first banal question as they shook hands.

'How are you feeling now?'

Yarwood avoided a direct answer. 'If Pilbeam and the lad hadn't found me when they did I'd have been a goner. An end of feeling. An end to claustrophobia. Better for Sharon, better for the kids, better for me. Sorry to sound such a wimp. In that ditch, before I became

448

unconscious, there was no pain, no worry, just peace. It wouldn't have been a bad way to go. The truth is, Mr Dalgliesh, I wish they'd left me there.'

'I don't. We've had enough deaths at St Anselm's.' He didn't say that now there had been another.

Yarwood stared out over the roof-tops. 'No more trying to cope, and no more feeling such a bloody failure.'

Searching for the words of comfort which he knew he couldn't find, Dalgliesh said, 'You have to tell yourself that, whatever hell you're in at present, it won't last for ever. Nothing ever does.'

'But it could get worse. Difficult to believe, but it could.'

'Only if you let it.'

There was a pause, then Yarwood said with an obvious effort, 'Point taken. Sorry I let you down. What happened exactly? I know that Crampton's been murdered, but nothing else. You've managed so far to keep the details out of the national papers and the local radio only gave the bare facts. What happened? I suppose you came for me after you discovered the body and found I'd gone. Just what you needed, a murderer on the loose and the one man you could look to for a spot of professional help doing his best to qualify as a suspect. It's odd, but I just can't work up any interest in it, I just can't make myself care. Me, who used to be branded an over-zealous officer. I didn't kill him, by the way.'

'I didn't think you did. Crampton was found in the church and the facts so far suggest he was lured there. If you'd wanted a bloody encounter, you'd only have had to go next door.'

'But that's true of everyone in college.'

449

'The killer wanted to incriminate St Anselm's. The Archdeacon was intended as the chief but not the only victim. I don't think you feel like that.'

There was a pause. Yarwood shut his eyes then shifted his head restlessly on the pillow. He said, 'No, I don't feel like that. I love that place. And now I've spoilt that too.'

'It's not so easy to spoil St Anselm's. How did you meet the Fathers?'

'It was about three years ago. I was a sergeant then, new to the Suffolk force. Father Peregrine had backed into a lorry on the Lowestoft road. No one was hurt, but I had to interview him. He's too absent-minded to be a safe driver and I managed to persuade him to stop. I think the Fathers were grateful. Anyway they never seemed to mind when I started turning up. I don't know what it was about the place but I felt different when I was there. When Sharon left me I began driving over for Sunday morning Mass. I'm not religious and I really hadn't a clue what was going on. It didn't seem to matter. I just liked being there. The Fathers have been kind to me. They don't pry, they don't invite confidences, they just accept. I've had it all, doctors, psychiatrists, counsellors, the lot. St Anselm's was different. No, I wouldn't harm them. There's a police constable outside this room though, isn't there? I'm not stupid. A bit crazy, but not stupid. It's my leg that got broken, not my head.'

'He's there for your protection. I'd no way of knowing what you'd seen, what evidence you might be able to give. Someone could have wanted you out of the way.'

'A bit far-fetched, isn't it?'

'I preferred not to risk it. Can you remember what happened on Saturday night?'

'Yes, until I actually lost consciousness in the ditch. The walk against the wind is a bit hazy – it seems to have lasted a shorter time than it did – but I remember the rest of it. Most of it, anyway.'

'Let's start from the beginning. What time did you leave your room?'

'About five past twelve. The storm woke me. I'd been dozing but not sleeping soundly. I switched on my light and looked at my watch. You know how it is when you're having a bad night. You lie there hoping that it's later than you think, that it'll soon be morning. And then the panic struck. I tried to fight it. I lay there sweating, rigid with terror. I had to get out, out of the room, out of Gregory, away from St Anselm's. It would've been the same wherever I was. I must have put on a coat over my pyjamas and my shoes without waiting to put on socks. I can't remember that bit. The wind didn't worry me much. In a way I think it helped. I'd have walked out even into a blizzard and twenty feet of snow. God, I wish I had.'

'How did you leave?'

'By the iron gate between the church and Ambrose. I've got a key – all the visitors are given one. But you know that.'

Dalgliesh said, 'We found the gate locked. Do you remember locking it after you?'

'I must have done, mustn't I? It's the sort of thing I'd do automatically.'

'Did you see anyone near the church?'

'No one. The courtyard was empty.'

'And you didn't hear anything, see any lights? See the door of the church open, for example?'

'I heard nothing but the wind and I don't think there

was a light in the church. If there was I didn't see it. I think I'd have noticed if the door had been wide open, but not if it had just been ajar. I did see someone, but not near the church. It was earlier, just when I was passing the front door of Ambrose. It was Eric Surtees, but he was nowhere near the church. He was in the north cloister letting himself into the house.'

'Didn't that strike you as strange?'

'Not really. I can't describe what I felt at that moment. Breathing in that great rushing air, the sense of being outside the walls. If I'd thought about Surtees at all, I suppose I'd have taken it for granted that he'd been called in to cope with some domestic emergency. He is the handyman, after all.'

'After midnight, in the middle of a storm?'

There was a silence between them. It was interesting, thought Dalgliesh, how his questioning, so far from worrying Yarwood, seemed to have lifted his spirits and deflected his mind, at least temporarily, from the weight of his own troubles.

Now Yarwood said, 'He's an unlikely murderer, isn't he? A gentle, unassuming, useful kind of chap. He had no reason to hate Crampton as far as I know. Anyway, he was letting himself into the house, not into the church. What was he doing if he wasn't on call?'

'Perhaps collecting the keys to the church. He'd know where to find them.'

'A bit foolhardy, wouldn't it be? And why the hurry? Wasn't he supposed to be painting the sacristy on Monday? I think I heard Pilbeam mention it. And if he'd wanted a key, why not take it earlier? He could move about the main building as he chose.'

'That would have been riskier. The ordinand who prepared the church for the service would have noticed that one set of keys was missing.'

'All right, I give you that, sir. But the same argument applies to Surtees as it does to me. If he'd wanted to pick a fight with Crampton he knew where to find him. He knew that the door of Augustine would be open.'

'You're sure it was Surtees? Sure enough to swear to it in court if necessary? It was after midnight and you were in a pretty bad state.'

'It was Surtees. I've seen him often enough. The lights in the cloisters are dim but I couldn't be mistaken. I'd maintain that in court under cross-examination, if that's what you're asking. Not that it would do much good. I can hear defending counsel's final address to the jury. Poor visibility. Figure seen only for a second or two. Witness a deeply disturbed man, crazy enough to walk out into a raging storm. And then, of course, the evidence that, unlike Surtees, I disliked Crampton.'

But now Yarwood was beginning to tire. His sudden spurt of interest in the murder inquiry seemed to have exhausted him. It was time to go, and with this new information Dalgliesh was anxious to leave. But first he must be sure there was nothing more to learn. He said, 'We'll need a statement, of course, but there's no great urgency. By the way, what do you think brought on your panic attack? The quarrel with Crampton after tea on Saturday?'

'You've heard about that? Well of course you would. I didn't expect to see him at St Anselm's and I imagine it was just as much of a shock for him. And I didn't start the row, he did. He just stood there spitting the old accusations at me. He was shaking with anger, like a man in some kind of fit. It goes back to the death of his wife. I was a detective-sergeant then and it was my first murder case.'

'Murder?'

'He killed his wife, Mr Dalgliesh. I was sure of it at the time and I'm sure now. OK, I was over-zealous, I made a cock-up of the whole inquiry. In the end he complained of harassment and I was reprimanded. It did my career no good. I doubt I'd have made inspector if I'd stayed with the Met. But I'm as sure now as I was then that he killed her and got away with it.'

'On what evidence?'

'There was a bottle of wine by her bed. She died from an overdose of aspirin and alcohol. The bottle had been wiped clean. I don't know how he got her to take a whole bottle of tablets but I'm damned sure he did. And he was lying, I know he was lying. He said he never went up to the bed. He did a bloody sight more than that.'

Dalgliesh said, 'He could have been lying about the bottle and about not approaching the bed. That doesn't make him a murderer. He could have found her dead and panicked. People behave oddly under stress.'

Yarwood reiterated obstinately, 'He killed her, Mr Dalgliesh. I saw it in his face and in his eyes. He was lying. That doesn't mean I took the opportunity to avenge her.'

'Is there anyone who might? Had she close relations, siblings, a former lover?'

'No one, Mr Dalgliesh. Just her parents and they didn't strike me as being particularly sympathetic. She never got justice, and nor did I. I'm not sorry Crampton's dead, but I didn't kill him. And I don't think I'll care over-much if you never discover who did.'

Dalgliesh said, 'But we shall. And you're a police officer. You can't really believe what you just said. I'll be in touch. Keep what you've told me to yourself. But you know all about discretion.'

'Do I? I suppose so. It's difficult to believe now that I'll ever get back on the job.'

He turned his face away in a gesture of deliberate rejection. But there was one final question Dalgliesh needed to ask. He said, 'Did you discuss your suspicions about the Archdeacon with anyone at St Anselm's?'

'No. It wasn't the kind of talk they'd have wanted to hear. Anyway, it was all in the past. I never expected to see the man again. They'll know now – that is if Raphael Arbuthnot bothers to tell them.'

'Raphael?'

'He was in the south cloister when Crampton tackled me. Raphael heard every word.'

7

They had driven to the hospital in Dalgliesh's Jaguar. Neither he nor Piers spoke while they buckled themselves into their seats and they had thrown off the eastern suburbs of the city before Dalgliesh briefly reported what he had learned.

Piers listened in silence, then said, 'I can't see Surtees as a killer, but if he did do it he wouldn't have been alone. His sister would've had a hand in it somehow. I can't believe anything happened at St John's Cottage on Saturday night that she didn't know about. But why should either of them want Crampton dead? OK, so they probably knew he was hell-bent on getting St Anselm's closed down at the first opportunity. That wouldn't have suited Surtees – he seems to have set himself up very nicely with his cottage and his pigs – but he wasn't going to stop closure by killing Crampton. And if he had a private quarrel with the man, why bother to set up an elaborate scheme to lure him into the church? He knew where Crampton was sleeping; he must have known too that the door was unlocked.'

Dalgliesh said, 'So did everyone in the college, including the visitors. Whoever killed Crampton wanted to make sure that we'd know it was an inside job. That much was apparent from the beginning. There's no obvious motive for either Surtees or his half-sister. If we're considering motive, George Gregory has to be prime suspect.'

None of that needed reiterating and Piers wished he'd kept his mouth shut. He had learnt that when AD was in one of his silent moods it was sensible to stay quiet, particularly if one had nothing original to contribute.

Back at St Matthew's Cottage, Dalgliesh decided to interview the two Surteeses with Kate. Five minutes later, escorted by Robbins, they arrived. Karen Surtees was shown into the waiting room and the door firmly closed.

It was apparent that Eric Surtees had been mucking out the piggery when Robbins arrived to summon him, and he brought into the interview room a strong but not disagreeable smell of earth and animal. He had taken time only to wash his hands and now sat with them lying side by side, knuckles clenched, in his lap. They were held with such controlled stillness that they seemed curiously at odds with the rest of his body, reminding Dalgliesh of two small animals curled in petrified fear. He would have had no time to consult his sister and his backward glance at the door as he came in betrayed his need for her presence and support. Now he sat in unnatural stillness; only his eyes moved from Dalgliesh to Kate and back again, then settled on Dalgliesh. Dalgliesh was experienced in recognizing fear and he didn't misinterpret. He knew that it was often the innocent who were the most obviously frightened; the guilty, once they had concocted their ingenious story, were eager to tell it, borne through their interrogation by a surge of hubris and bravado which could sweep before it any embarrassing manifestations of guilt or fear.

He wasted no time on formalities. He said, 'When my officers questioned you on Sunday you said that you hadn't left St John's Cottage during Saturday night. I shall now ask you again. Did you go either to the college or to the church after Compline on Saturday?'

Surtees gave a quick glance at the window as if it offered escape, before again willing himself to meet Dalgliesh's eyes. His voice sounded unnaturally high.

'No, of course not. Why should I?'

Dalgliesh said, 'Mr Surtees, you were seen by a witness entering St Anselm's from the north cloister just after midnight. There can be no doubt about the identification.'

'It wasn't me. It must have been someone else. Nobody could have seen me because I wasn't there. It's a lie.'

The confused denial must have sounded unconvincing even to Surtees's ears.

Dalgliesh said patiently, 'Mr Surtees, are you asking to be arrested for murder?'

Surtees seemed visibly to shrink. He looked little more than a boy. There was a long pause, then he said, 'All right, I did go back to the college. I woke up and saw a light in the church so I went to investigate.'

'At what time did you see this light?'

'At about midnight, like you said. I got up to go to the lavatory and that's when I saw it.'

Kate spoke for the first time.

'But the cottages are all built to the same plan. The bedrooms and bathrooms are at the back. In your cottage they face north-west. How could you have seen the church?'

Surtees licked his lips. He said, 'I was thirsty. I went down to get a cup of water and saw the light from the sitting-room. At least I thought I saw it. It was only faint. I thought I'd better investigate.'

Dalgliesh said, 'Didn't you think to wake your sister or telephone Mr Pilbeam or Father Sebastian? Surely that would be the natural thing to do.'

'I didn't want to disturb them.'

Kate said, 'Pretty courageous of you venturing out alone on a stormy night to confront a possible intruder. What were you planning to do when you got to the church?'

'I don't know. I wasn't thinking very clearly.'

Dalgliesh said, 'You're not thinking very clearly now, are you? However, go on. You say you went over to the church. What did you find?'

'I didn't go in. I couldn't because I hadn't got a key. The light was still on. I let myself into the house and fetched one of the keys from Miss Ramsey's office but when I returned to the north cloister the light in the church had gone out.' He was speaking more confidently now and the clenched hands visibly relaxed.

It was Kate who, after a brief glance at Dalgliesh, took over the questioning. 'So what did you do then?'

'I didn't do anything. I thought I must have been mistaken about the light.'

'But you seemed quite certain about it earlier, otherwise why venture out into the storm? First a light is on, and then mysteriously it's switched off. Didn't it occur to you to go into the church to investigate? That was your purpose, wasn't it, in leaving the cottage?'

Surtees mumbled, 'It didn't seem necessary, not when there wasn't a light any more. I told you, I thought I'd been mistaken.' He added, 'I did try the sacristy door

459

and it was locked so I knew that no one was in the church'.

'After the Archdeacon's body was found, one of the three sets of church keys was discovered to be missing. How many sets were in place when you took the keys?'

'I can't remember. I didn't notice. I was just anxious to get out of the office. I knew exactly where the church keys were on the key board and I just took the nearest pair.'

'And you didn't return them?'

'No. I didn't want to go into the house again.'

Dalgliesh interposed quietly, 'In that case, Mr Surtees, where are those keys now?'

Kate had seldom seen a suspect more broken by terror. The brave spirit of hope and confidence which had been apparent during the early part of the questioning drained away and Surtees slumped forward in the chair, his head bowed and his whole body shaking.

Dalgliesh said, 'I'm going to ask you once again. Did you go into the church on Saturday night?'

Surtees managed to sit upright and even to meet Dalgliesh's eyes. And now it seemed to Kate that terror was giving way to relief. He was about to tell the truth and was glad to put an end to the prolonged ordeal of lying. Now he and the police would be on the same side. They would approve of him, absolve him, tell him that they understood. She had seen it all so many times before.

Surtees said, 'All right, I did go into the church. But I didn't kill anybody, I swear I didn't. I couldn't! I swear before God that I never touched him. I was only there for less than a minute.'

Dalgliesh asked, 'Doing what?'

'I was getting something for Karen, something she needed. It was nothing to do with the Archdeacon. It's private between us.'

Kate said, 'Mr Surtees, you must know that that isn't good enough. Nothing is private in a murder investigation. Why did you go to the church on Saturday night?'

Surtees looked at Dalgliesh, as if willing him to understand. 'Karen needed another consecrated wafer. It had to be consecrated. She asked me to get one for her.'

'She asked you to steal for her?'

'She didn't see it like that.' There was a silence, then he said, 'Yes, I suppose so. But it wasn't her fault, it was mine. I didn't have to agree. I didn't want to do it, the Fathers have always been good to me, but it was important to Karen and in the end I said I'd go. She had to have it this weekend because she needs it on Friday. She just didn't think it was all that important. It was just a wafer to her. She wouldn't have asked me to steal something valuable.'

Dalgliesh said, 'But this was something valuable, wasn't it?'

Again there was a silence.

Dalgliesh said, 'Tell me what happened on Saturday night. Think back and think clearly. I want every detail.'

Surtees was calmer now. He seemed to be drawing himself up and the colour was again blotching his cheeks. He said, 'I waited until very late. I had to be sure they would all be asleep or at least in their rooms. And the storm was a help. I didn't think they'd be going for a walk. It was about a quarter to midnight when I started out.'

'Wearing?'

'Just my dark brown corduroys and a thick leather jacket. No light clothes. We thought it would be safer to wear dark clothes, but I wasn't disguised.'

'Did you wear gloves?'

'No. We – I didn't think it was necessary. I've only got thick gardening gloves and an old woollen pair. I'd have had to take them off to pick up the wafer, cope with the locks, and I didn't think it mattered not wearing gloves. No one would know there had been a theft. They wouldn't miss one wafer, they'd think they'd miscounted. That's what I argued. I've just got the two keys, one to the iron gate and the other to the door from the north cloister. Usually I don't need them during the day as the gate and the doors from both the cloisters are left open. I knew that the church keys were in Miss Ramsey's office. Sometimes at festivals like Easter I give them flowers or greenery. Father Sebastian would ask me to leave them in a bucket of water in the sacristy. There's always one of the students who's good at decorating the church. Sometimes Father Sebastian hands me the keys or he tells me to get them from the office, lock up carefully after me and return them. We're supposed to sign for the church keys if we take them but sometimes people don't bother.'

'They made it very easy for you, didn't they? But then, it isn't difficult to steal from people who trust you.'

There was a second when Dalgliesh was simultaneously aware of the note of contempt in his voice and of Kate's unspoken surprise. He told himself that this was too close to personal involvement.

Surtees said, with more confidence than he had shown

before, 'I wasn't going to hurt anyone, I couldn't hurt anyone. And even if I'd managed to steal the wafer, no one at the college would have been hurt. I don't think they'd even have known. It was just one wafer. It wouldn't have cost more than a penny.'

Dalgliesh said, 'So let's get back to what exactly happened on Saturday night. We'll leave out the excuses and justification. We'll stick to the facts, all the facts.'

'Well, as I said, it was about a quarter to twelve when I set out. The college was very dark and the wind was howling. There was only one light and that was in one of the guest-rooms and the curtains were drawn. I used my key to get into the college through the back door, then past the scullery and into the main part of the house. I had a torch with me so I didn't need to put on any of the lights, but there was one light burning beneath the statue of the Madonna and Child in the main hall. I had a story ready if anyone appeared. I was going to say that I thought I'd seen a light from inside the church and was coming to get the keys to investigate. I knew it would sound unconvincing but I wasn't really expecting to have to use it. I took the keys and went out again the way I'd come in, locking the door behind me. I put out the cloister lights and kept close to the wall. There wasn't any trouble with the mortice lock to the sacristy, it's always kept oiled and the key turned very easily. I pushed open the door very gently, lighting my way with the torch and turned off the alarm system.

'I was beginning to feel less frightened and more optimistic; it had all gone so easily. I knew where the wafers would be, of course, to the right of the altar in a kind of alcove with a red light shining above it. They keep consecrated wafers there in case one of the priests has to take them out to someone who is sick in the community, or sometimes they are taken to a communion service at one of the village churches where they don't have a priest. I had an envelope in my pocket and I was going to put the wafer inside. But when I pushed open the door into the church I saw there was someone there. It wasn't empty.'

Again he paused. Dalgliesh resisted temptation to comment or question. Surtees had his head bowed, his hands clasped in front of him. He looked as if remembering had suddenly become an effort.

He said, 'There was a light on at the north end of the church, the light over the *Doom*. And there was someone standing there, a figure in a brown cloak and hood.'

It was Kate who couldn't resist the question: 'Did you recognize him?'

'No. He was partly behind a pillar and the light was too dim. And the hood was up over his head.'

'Tall or short?'

'I think about average, not particularly tall. I can't really remember. And then, in the minute while I watched, the big south door opened and someone came in. I didn't recognize him either. I didn't really see him, I just heard him call out "Where are you?" and then I shut the door. I knew the whole thing was off. There was nothing for it but to lock up after me and go back to the cottage.'

Dalgliesh said, 'Are you absolutely certain that you recognized neither of the figures?'

'Quite certain. I never saw either face. I didn't really see the second man at all.'

'But you know it was a man?'

'Well, I heard the voice.'

Dalgliesh said, 'Who do you think it was?'

'Judging from the voice, I think it might have been the Archdeacon.'

'So he must have spoken quite loudly?'

Surtees flushed. He said unhappily, 'I suppose it must have been quite loud. It didn't seem so at the time. Of course the church was very quiet and the voice sort of echoed. I can't be certain it was the Archdeacon. It's just the impression I had at the time.'

It was apparent he could tell them nothing more certain about the identity of either figure. Dalgliesh asked him what he had done after leaving the church.

'I reset the alarm, locked the door behind me and went out through the courtyard past the south door of the church. I don't think it was open or even ajar. I can't remember seeing a light but I wasn't really noticing. I was just anxious to get away. I battled my way across the headland against the wind and told Karen what had happened. I was hoping I'd have a chance to return the keys some time on Sunday morning but when we were sent for to go to the library and were told about the murder, I knew it wouldn't be possible.'

'So what did you do with them?'

Surtees said miserably, 'I buried them in a corner of the pig pen.'

Dalgliesh said, 'When this interview is over, Sergeant Robbins will go with you to recover them.'

Surtees made to get up but Dalgliesh said, 'I said when the interview is over. It isn't over yet.'

The information they had just gained was the most

important they had been given so far, and he had to resist the temptation to follow it up at once. But first it was necessary to get what confirmation he could of Surtees's story.

8

Summoned by Kate, Karen Surtees came into the room with no apparent sign of nervousness, seated herself beside her half-brother without waiting for Dalgliesh's invitation, hitched her black shoulder-bag on to the back of the chair and turned immediately towards Surtees.

'You all right, Eric? No third degree?'

'Yes, I'm all right. I'm sorry, Karen. I've told them.' He said again, 'I'm sorry.'

'What for? You did your best. It wasn't your fault there was someone in the church. You tried. Just as well for the police that you did. I hope they're grateful.'

Surtees's eyes had brightened at the sight of her and there was an almost palpable sense of her fortifying strength passing through him as she briefly laid her hand on his. His words had been apologetic but there had been nothing servile in the look he gave her. Dalgliesh recognized the most dangerous of complications – love.

And now she turned her attention to him, fixing on him a concentrated and challenging gaze. Her eyes widened and he thought she was suppressing a secretive smile.

Dalgliesh said, 'Your brother has admitted that he was in the church on Saturday night.'

'Early Sunday morning. It was after midnight. And he's my half-brother – same dad, different mothers.'

Dalgliesh said, 'So you told my officers earlier. I've heard his story. I'd like to hear yours.'

'It will be much the same as Eric's. He's not much good at lying, as you've probably discovered. That can be inconvenient at times but it has its advantages. Well, it's no great deal. He hasn't done anything wrong and the idea that he could hurt anyone, let alone kill them, is ridiculous. He can't even kill his own pigs! I asked him to get me a consecrated wafer from the church. If you don't go in for these things, I can tell you that they're small white discs made, I imagine, of flour and water, about the size of a two-penny piece. Even if he'd managed to get one and been caught, I can't see the magistrates committing him to the Crown Court for sentence. Value – insignificant.'

Dalgliesh said, 'It depends on your scale of values. Why did you want it?'

'I don't see what that has to do with your present inquiry, but I don't mind telling you. I'm a freelance journalist and I'm writing an article on the Black Mass. It's been commissioned, by the way, and I've done most of the research. The people I've succeeded in infiltrating need a consecrated wafer and I promised to get one. And don't say that I could have bought a whole box of unconsecrated wafers for a quid or two. That was Eric's argument. This is genuine research and I needed the genuine article. You may not respect my job but I take it as seriously as you take yours. I'd promised to provide a consecrated wafer and that was what I was going to do. The research would have been a waste of time otherwise.'

'So you persuaded your half-brother to steal it for you.'

'Well, Father Sebastian wasn't going to give me one if I asked nicely, was he?'

'Your brother went alone?'

'Of course. No sense in my tagging along and adding to the risk. At a pinch he could justify being in the college. I couldn't.'

'But you did wait up for him?'

'It wasn't a question of waiting up. We'd never actually been to bed, at least not to sleep.'

'So you heard his account of what happened immediately he got back, not next morning?'

'He told me as soon as he got back. I was waiting and he told me.'

'Miss Surtees, this is very important. Please think back and try to remember exactly what you were told and in your brother's words.'

'I don't think I can remember the exact words but the sense was plain enough. He told me he'd had no problem in getting the key. He opened the sacristy door by the light of his torch and then the door leading into the church. It was then he saw the light over that oil painting opposite the main door, the *Doom*, isn't it? And a figure standing close to it wearing a cloak and hood. Then the main door opened and someone else came in. I asked him if he recognized either figure and he said he didn't. The one in the cloak had the hood up and his back to him and he only had a brief glimpse of the second man. He thought that the second figure called out "Where are you?" or something like that. The impression he got was that it could have been the Archdeacon.'

'And he didn't suggest to you at all who the other figure might have been?'

'No, but he wouldn't, would he? I mean, he didn't think there was anything sinister about seeing a cloaked

469

figure in the church. It mucked things up for us and it was odd at that time of night, but he naturally assumed that it was one of the priests or one of the students. I assumed the same. God knows what they were doing there after midnight. They could have been having their own Black Mass for all we cared. Obviously if Eric had known the Archdeacon was going to be murdered he'd have taken more notice. At least I suppose he would. What do you think you'd have done, Eric, faced with a murderer with a knife?'

Surtees looked at Dalgliesh as he replied. 'Run away, I suppose. I'd have raised the alarm, of course. The guest sets aren't locked so I'd probably have rushed into Jerome for your help. At the time I was just disappointed that I'd managed to get the key without being seen and it was beginning to seem so easy and now I'd have to go back and say I'd failed.'

There was nothing more to be learned from him at present and Dalgliesh told him that he could go, first warning them both that the information they had given must be kept absolutely secret. They had clearly put themselves in danger of the charge of obstructing the police if not something more serious. Sergeant Robbins would now go with Surtees to recover the keys which would be kept in police possession. Both gave the assurance demanded, Eric Surtees with as much formality as if taking a solemn oath, his sister ungraciously.

As Surtees finally got up to go his half-sister got up too, but Dalgliesh said, 'I'd like you to stay if you would, Miss Surtees. I've one or two further questions.'

As the door closed behind her half-brother, Dalgliesh said, 'When I first began talking to your brother, he said that you wanted him to get you another wafer. So this wasn't the first time. An earlier attempt had been made. What happened on the first occasion?'

She sat very still, but her voice was composed when she answered. 'Eric made a slip of the tongue. There was only this once.'

'I don't think so. Of course, I could get him back and ask him, and indeed I shall ask him. But it would be simpler if you explained to me now what happened on the previous occasion.'

She said defensively, 'It had nothing to do with this murder. It happened last term.'

'I must be the judge of what relates to this murder. Who stole the wafer for you the time before?'

'It wasn't stolen that time, not precisely. It was handed over to me.'

'Was it by Ronald Treeves?'

'Yes, it was, if you must know. Some of the wafers are consecrated and taken to churches round about where temporarily there isn't a priest and where there's to be Holy Communion. The wafers are consecrated and taken to the church by whoever is going to take or help with the service. That was Ronald's job that week and he took out one wafer for me. One wafer out of so many. It was a small thing to ask.'

Kate suddenly intervened. 'You must have known that it wasn't a small thing for him to do. How did you pay him? The obvious way?'

The girl flushed, but with anger not embarrassment. For a moment Dalgliesh thought she would flare into open antagonism; it would, he thought, have been justified. He said quietly, 'I'm sorry if you found that offensive. I'll rephrase it. How did you manage to persuade him?'

Her momentary outrage was over. Now she looked at him from narrowed calculating eyes, then visibly relaxed. He could identify the second when she realized that candour would be more prudent and perhaps more satisfying.

She said, 'All right, I persuaded him in the obvious way, and if you're thinking of handing out moral judgement you can forget it. Anyway, it's none of your business.' She glanced over at Kate and the look was frankly hostile. 'Or hers. And I don't see what relevance all this has to the Archdeacon's murder. They can't possibly be related.'

Dalgliesh said, 'The truth is that I can't be sure. They could be. If they aren't, none of this will be used. I'm not asking about the theft of the wafer out of prurient curiosity about your private life.'

She said, 'Look, I rather liked Ronald. OK, maybe it was more that I felt sorry for him. He wasn't exactly popular here. Papa too rich, too powerful, wrong business too. In armaments isn't he? Anyway, Ronald didn't really fit in. When I came down to stay with Eric we'd meet occasionally and walk along the cliffs to the mere. We'd talk. He told me things you wouldn't be able to get out of him in a million years, and nor would these priests, confession or no confession. And I did him a favour. He was twenty-three and a virgin. Look, he was desperate for sex – dying for it.'

Perhaps, thought Dalgliesh, he had died for it. He heard the continuing voice, 'Seducing him wasn't exactly a chore. Men make a fuss about seducing female virgins.

472

God knows why, exhausting and unrewarding I'd have thought, but the other way has its excitements. And if you want to know how we kept it from Eric, we didn't go to bed in the cottage, we made love in the bracken on the cliffs. He was a damn sight luckier to have me initiating him than going with a whore – which he'd tried once and then got so disgusted he couldn't see it through.' She paused, and as Dalgliesh didn't speak, went on more defensively. 'He was training to be a priest, wasn't he? What use would he be to other people if he hadn't lived? He used to go on about the grace of celibacy and I suppose celibacy is all right if that's your thing. But, believe me, it wasn't his. He was lucky to find me.'

Dalgliesh said, 'What happened to the wafer?'

'Oh God, that was bad luck! You'll hardly believe this. I lost it. I put it into a plain envelope and pushed it into my briefcase with other papers. That's the last I saw of it. It probably fell into the waste-paper basket when I pulled the papers out of the briefcase. Anyway, I haven't found it.'

'So you wanted him to get you another and this time he was less compliant.'

'You could put it like that. He must have been thinking things over in the vacation. You'd think I'd ruined his life instead of contributing to his sexual education.'

Dalgliesh said, 'And within a week he was dead.'

'Well, I'm not responsible for that. I didn't want him dead.'

'So you think it could have been murder?'

This time she gazed at him appalled, and he saw both surprise and terror in her eyes.

'Murder? Of course it wasn't murder! Who the hell

473

would want to murder him? It was accidental death. He started poking around in the cliffs and brought the sand down on himself. There was an inquest. You know what the verdict was.'

'When he refused to hand over a second consecrated wafer, did you attempt blackmail?'

'Of course not!'

'Did you even by implication suggest that he was now in your power, that you had information that could get him expelled from the college, ruining his chances of ever being ordained?'

'No!' she said vehemently. 'No, I didn't. What the hell would be the use? It would compromise Eric for one thing and, for another, those priests would believe him, not me. I wasn't in a position to blackmail him.'

'You think he realized that?'

'How the hell do I know what he thought? He was half crazy, that's all I know. Look, you're supposed to be investigating the murder of Crampton. Ronald's death had nothing to do with this case. How could it have?'

'I suggest you leave me to decide what has or has not to do with this case. What happened when Ronald Treeves came to St John's Cottage on the night before he died?'

She sat there in sullen silence. Dalgliesh said, 'You and your brother have already withheld information vital to this investigation. If we'd been told on Sunday morning what we've now learned, someone might have been under arrest. If neither you nor your brother had anything to do with Archdeacon Crampton's death, I suggest you answer my questions honestly and truthfully. What happened when Ronald Treeves came to St John's Cottage on that Friday night?'

'I was there already. I'd come down from London for the weekend. I didn't know he was going to call. And he had absolutely no right to walk into the cottage like he did. OK, we've got used to leaving doors open, but the cottage is supposed to be Eric's home. He came barging upstairs, and if you must know, found Eric and me in bed. He just stood in the doorway and stared. He looked crazy, absolutely crazy. And then he started spitting out ridiculous accusations. I can't really remember what he said. I suppose it could have been funny, but actually it was rather frightening. It was like being ranted at by a lunatic. No, that's the wrong word. It wasn't a rant. He didn't shout or scream, he hardly raised his voice. That's what made it rather terrifying. Eric and I were naked which put us at a bit of a disadvantage. We just sat up in bed and stared at him while that high voice went on and on. God, it was weird. D'you know, he'd actually thought I was going to marry him. Me, a parson's wife! He was mad. He looked crazy and he was crazy.'

She told it with a puzzled incredulity as if confiding to a friend over a drink in a bar.

Dalgliesh said, 'You seduced him and he thought you loved him. He gave you a consecrated wafer because you asked and he could refuse you nothing. He knew precisely what it was he had done. And then he saw that there never had been love, that he had been used. The next day he killed himself. Miss Surtees, do you in any way feel responsible for that death?'

She cried vehemently, 'No I don't! I never told him I loved him. It wasn't my fault if he thought I did. And I don't believe he killed himself. It was an accident. That's what the jury found and that's what I believe.'

Dalgliesh said quietly, 'I don't think it is, you know. I think you know very well what drove Ronald Treeves to his death.'

'Even if I do that doesn't make me responsible. And what the hell did he think he was doing, barging in like that and rushing upstairs as if he owned the place. And now I suppose you'll tell Father Sebastian and get Eric thrown out of the cottage.'

Dalgliesh said, 'No, I shall not tell Father Sebastian. You and your brother have put yourselves in considerable peril. I can't impress on you too strongly that what you've told me must remain secret. All of it.'

She said ungraciously, 'All right. We're not going to speak, why should we? And I don't see why I should feel guilty about Ronald or about the Archdeacon. We didn't kill him. But we thought you'd be ready enough to think we did if you got a chance. Those priests are sacrosanct, aren't they? I suggest you start looking at their motives instead of picking on us. And I didn't think it would matter, not telling you about Eric going to the church. I thought one of the students had killed the Archdeacon and he'd confess anyway. That's what they go in for, isn't it, confessions? I'm not going to be made to feel guilty. I'm not cruel and I'm not callous. I was sorry for Ronald. I didn't bully him into giving me that wafer. I asked him, and in the end he agreed. And I didn't have sex with him to get the wafer. OK, that was part of it, but it wasn't the whole. I did it because I was sorry for him and because I was bored, and maybe for other reasons which you wouldn't understand and would disapprove of if you did.'

There was nothing else to be said. She was frightened

but she was not ashamed. Nothing he could have said would have made her feel responsible for Ronald Treeves's death. He thought now of the desperation which had driven Treeves to that appalling end. He had been faced with the stark choice of staying on at St Anselm's with the constant threat of betrayal and the tormenting knowledge of what he'd done, or confessing to Father Sebastian with the almost certainty that he would have to return home to his father as a failure. Dalgliesh wondered what Father Sebastian would have said and done. Father Martin would, he thought, have shown mercy. He was less sure about Father Sebastian. But even if mercy had been shown, how could Treeves have stayed on with the humiliating knowledge that he was there on probation?

At last he let her go. He felt a profound pity and an anger which seemed directed against something deeper and less identifiable than Karen Surtees and her insensitivities. But what right had he to feel anger? She could claim her own kind of morality. If you promised to provide a consecrated wafer you didn't cheat. If you were an investigative journalist you took the job seriously, conscientious even in deceit. There had been no meeting of minds, there never could be. It was for her inconceivable that anyone would kill himself for a small disc of flour and water. For her the sex had been little more than a relief from boredom, the satisfying power of initiation, a new experience, the lightly taken exchange of pleasure. To take it more seriously led at best to jealousy, demands, recriminations and mess; at worst to a mouth choked with sand. And hadn't he in his solitary years separated his sexual life from commitment, even if he had been more fastidious and prudent in his choice of partner and more sensitive to the hurt of others? He wondered what he would say to Sir Alred; probably merely that an open verdict would have been more logical than one of accidental death but that there was no evidence of foul play. But there had been foul play.

He would keep Ronald's secret. The boy had left no suicide note. There was no way of knowing whether in those last seconds and too late, he might have changed his mind. If he had died because he couldn't bear his father to know the truth it wasn't for him, Dalgliesh, to reveal it now.

He became conscious of the prolonged silence and of Kate sitting beside him wondering why he didn't speak. He was aware of her contained impatience.

He said, 'Right. We're getting somewhere at last. We've found the missing key. That means that Cain did, after all, go back into the college and return the one he used. And now we find that brown cloak.'

Kate said, her voice echoing his thoughts, 'If it still exists to be found.'

9

Dalgliesh called Piers and Robbins into the interview room and put them in the picture. He said, 'You checked all the cloaks, brown and black?'

It was Kate who replied. 'Yes sir. Now that Treeves is dead there are nineteen students in residence and nineteen cloaks. Fifteen students are absent and all except one, who went home to celebrate his mother's birthday and wedding anniversary, have taken their cloaks. That means there should have been five in the cloakroom when we checked, and there were. They've all been examined pretty carefully and so have the cloaks of the priests.'

'Do the cloaks have name tabs? I didn't look when I first checked on them.'

It was Piers who replied. 'All of them. Apparently they're the only clothes that do. I suppose it's because they're identical except for size. There's no cloak in college without a name tab.'

They had no way at present of knowing whether the killer had actually worn the cloak during the murderous attack. It was possible even that there had been a third person waiting in the church when the Archdeacon arrived, someone whom Surtees hadn't glimpsed. But now that they knew that a cloak had been worn, and almost certainly by the killer, all five cloaks, although apparently clean, would have to be scientifically examined by the lab for minute traces of blood, hairs or fibres. But what about the twentieth cloak? Was it possible that it had been overlooked when Ronald Treeves's clothes were bundled up for return to his family after his death?

Dalgliesh thought back to the interview with Sir Alred at New Scotland Yard. Sir Alred's chauffeur had been sent with another driver to collect the Porsche and had taken the parcel of clothes back to London with him. But had it contained a cloak? He tried to force memory into recollection. There had been a mention, surely, of a suit, shoes and certainly a cassock, but had he mentioned a brown cloak?

He said to Kate, 'Get Sir Alred for me. He gave me a card with his home address and phone number before he left the Yard. You'll find it on the file. I imagine he's unlikely to be there at this time, but someone will be. Tell them I have to speak to him personally and that it's urgent.'

He had expected difficulty. Sir Alred wasn't a man to be readily accessible by telephone and there was always the possibility that he wasn't in the country. But they were lucky. The man who answered the telephone at his home, although reluctantly convinced of the urgency, gave the number of Sir Alred's Mayfair office. Here they were answered by the usual upper-class unaccommodating voice. Sir Alred was in a meeting. Dalgliesh said that he must be fetched. Could the Commander please wait? The delay was unlikely to be for more than three-quarters of an hour. Dalgliesh said that he was unable to wait even for three-quarters of a minute. The voice said, 'Will you hold on, please.'

Within less than a minute Sir Alred was on the phone. The strong authoritarian voice came over unworried but with a note of controlled impatience. 'Commander Dalgliesh? I was expecting to hear from you but hardly in the middle of a conference. If you've any news I'd rather hear it later. I take it this affair at St Anselm's is related to my son's death?'

Dalgliesh said, 'There's no evidence to suggest that at present. I'll get in touch with you about the inquest verdict as soon as I've completed my investigations. In the meantime murder has priority. I wanted to ask you about your son's clothes. I remember your telling me that they were returned to you. Were you present when the parcel was opened?'

'Not when it was opened but shortly afterwards. It isn't something I'd normally have taken an interest in but my housekeeper, who dealt with it, wanted to consult me. I told her to take the clothes to Oxfam but the suit was the same size as her son wore and she asked me whether I would be happy if she gave it to him. She was also worried about the cassock. She didn't think that would be any use to Oxfam and wondered if she ought to send it back. I told her that, as they'd got rid of it, they'd hardly be interested in seeing it returned and that she could dispose of it in any way that occurred to her. I think it was put into the dustbin. Is that all?'

'And the cloak, a brown cloak?'

'There was no cloak.'

'You can be sure of that, Sir Alred?'

'No, of course I can't. I didn't open the parcel. But if there had been a cloak it's likely Mrs Mellors would have mentioned it, asked me what I wanted done with it. As far as I remember she brought in the whole parcel to me. The clothes were still in the brown paper, the string partly wrapped round. I can see no reason why she should have removed the cloak. I take it that all this is relevant to your enquiries?'

'Very relevant, Sir Alred. Thank you for your help. Can I reach Mrs Mellors at your house?'

The voice had grown impatient. 'I've no idea. I don't control my servants' movements. She does live in so I imagine she can be contacted. Good day, Commander.'

They were fortunate, too, with the return call to the Holland Park house. The same male voice answered the telephone but said that he would put through the call to the housekeeper's flat.

Mrs Mellors, once assured that Dalgliesh had spoken to Sir Alred and was ringing with his approval, took this on trust and merely said that, yes, she had been the one to open the parcel of Mr Ronald's clothes when they were returned from St Anselm's and had made a list of the contents. There had been no brown cloak. Sir Alred had kindly given permission for her to take the suit. The rest of the items had been taken by one of the staff to the Oxfam shop at Notting Hill Gate. The cassock she had thrown away. She had thought that it was a pity to waste the material, but she couldn't imagine that anyone would want to wear it.

She added, somewhat surprisingly for a woman whose confident voice and intelligent responses had sounded rational, 'The cassock was found by his body, wasn't it? I'm not sure I would've liked to wear it. There was something rather sinister about it, I thought. I did wonder whether to cut off the buttons – they could have

482

come in useful – but I didn't like to touch it. To tell you the truth, I was glad to see it go into the bin.'

After he had thanked her and put down the receiver, Dalgliesh said, 'So what happened to the cloak and where is it now? The first step is to speak to the person who parcelled up the clothes. Father Martin told me that it was done by Father John Betterton.'

In front of the great stone fireplace in the library Emma was giving her second seminar. As with the first, she had little hope of distracting the thoughts of her small group of students from the other more grimly sober activities which were being carried on around them. Commander Dalgliesh hadn't yet given permission for the reopening and rehallowing services which Father Sebastian had planned. The scene of crime officers were still on the job, arriving each morning in a sinister little van which someone must have driven from London for their use, and which was parked outside the front entrance in defiance of Father Peregrine's objections. Commander Dalgliesh and his two detective inspectors still pursued their mysterious inquiries and the lights burned late at night in St Matthew's Cottage.

The students had been forbidden by Father Sebastian to discuss the murder; in his words, 'to connive in evil and aggravate distress by ill-informed and speculative gossip'. He could hardly have expected the prohibition to be observed and Emma wasn't sure that it had been helpful. Certainly the speculation was discreet and spasmodic rather than general or prolonged, but the fact that it had been forbidden only added guilt to the weight of anxiety and tension. Open discussion, she felt, would have been better. As Raphael said, 'Having the police in the house is like being invaded by mice; even when you don't see or hear them you know they're there.'

The death of Miss Betterton had added little to the weight of distress. It was no more than a second but softer blow on nerves already anaesthetized by horror. The community, having accepted that the death was accidental, tried to distance it from the horror of the Archdeacon's murder. Miss Betterton had been rarely seen by the ordinands and only Raphael genuinely mourned for her. But even he seemed to have gained some kind of balance since yesterday, a precarious equilibrium between withdrawal into his private world and flashes of hard acerbity. Since that moment of talk on the headland, Emma hadn't seen him alone. She was glad. He wasn't easy to be with.

There was the seminar room at the back of the house on the second floor, but Emma had chosen to use the library. She told herself that it was more convenient to have the books she might need for reference close at hand, but knew that there was a less rational explanation for her choice. The seminar room was too claustrophobic, in atmosphere if not in size. However frightening the presence of the police, it was more bearable to be at the heart of the house than closeted on the second floor, isolated from activity which it was less traumatic to hear than to imagine.

Last night she had slept, and slept well. Security locks to the guest sets had been fitted and the keys handed over. She was grateful to be sleeping in Jerome rather than next to the church with that dominant and obscurely threatening window, but only Henry Bloxham had mentioned the change. She had overheard him speaking to Stephen. 'I understand that Dalgliesh asked to change sets so that he can be next to the church. What is he expecting, the murderer to return to the scene of the crime? D'you think he sits up all night watching from the window?' No one had spoken of it to her.

Occasionally on her visits to St Anselm's one or more of the priests, if not otherwise occupied, would sit in at a seminar, always first asking her permission. They never spoke, nor did she ever feel that she was being assessed. Today the four ordinands were joined by Father John Betterton. As usual, Father Peregrine was silently at work at his desk at the far end of the library, seemingly impervious to their presence. A small fire had been lit in the grate, more for comfort than for additional heat, and they sat round it in low chairs, except for Peter Buckhurst; he had chosen a high-back and sat upright and silent, his pale hands resting on the text as if he were reading Braille.

This term Emma had planned that they should read and discuss the poetry of George Herbert. Today, rejecting the ease of familiarity for a more demanding poem, she had chosen *The Quidditie*. Henry had just finished reading aloud the last verse.

> It is no office, art, or news,
> Nor the Exchange, or busie Hall;
> But it is that which while I use
> I am with thee, and *Most take all*.

There was a silence, then Stephen Morby asked, 'What does "quidditie" mean?'

Emma said, 'What a thing is; its essence.'

'And the final words, "I am with thee, and most take all"? It sounds like a misprint, but it obviously isn't. I mean, we'd expect the word "must", not "most".'

Raphael said, 'The note in my edition says it refers to a card game. Winner takes all. So I suppose Herbert's saying that when he's writing poetry he holds the hand of God, the winning hand.'

Emma said, 'Herbert is fond of gaming puns. Remember *The Church Porch*? This could be a card game where you give up cards in order to obtain better ones. We mustn't forget Herbert's talking about his poetry. When he's writing it he has everything because he's one with God. His readers at the time would have known the card game he was referring to.'

Henry said, 'I wish I did. We should do some research, I suppose, and find how it was played. It shouldn't be difficult.'

Raphael protested. 'But pointless. I want the poem to lead me to the altar and silence, not to a reference book or a pack of cards.'

'Agreed. This is typical Herbert, isn't it? The mundane, even the frivolous, sanctified. But I'd still like to know.'

Emma's eyes were on her book and she was only aware that someone had come into the library when the four students simultaneously rose to their feet. Commander Dalgliesh stood in the doorway. If he was disconcerted to find that he had interrupted a seminar, he didn't show it, and his apology, made to Emma, sounded more conventional than heartfelt.

'I'm sorry, I didn't realize you were using the library. I'd like a word with Father John Betterton and was told I'd find him here.'

Father John, a little flustered, began to edge himself out of his low leather chair. Emma knew that she was blushing but, since there was no way of concealing the tell-tale flush, made herself meet Dalgliesh's dark unsmiling eyes. She didn't get up, and it seemed to her that the four ordinands had moved closer to her chair, like a cassock-clad bodyguard silently confronting an intruder.

Raphael's voice was ironic and over-loud. 'The words of Mercury are harsh after the songs of Apollo. The poet detective, just the man we need. We're grappling with a problem with George Herbert. Why not join us, Commander, and contribute your expertise?'

Dalgliesh regarded him for a few seconds in silence, then said, 'I'm sure Miss Lavenham has all the expertise necessary. Shall we go, Father?'

The door closed behind them and the four ordinands sat down. For Emma the episode had had an importance beyond the words spoken or the glances exchanged. She thought, the Commander doesn't like Raphael. He wasn't, she felt, a man who would ever let personal feelings intrude into his professional life. Almost certainly he wouldn't now. But she felt quietly sure that she hadn't misread that small spark of antagonism. What was odder was her own brief moment of pleasure at the thought.

II

Father Betterton trotted beside him across the hall, out
of the front door and round the south of the house to
the cottage, accommodating his short legs to Dalgliesh's
stride like an obedient child, his hands folded within his
black cloak. He seemed more embarrassed than worried.
Dalgliesh had wondered how he would react to police
questioning. In his experience anyone whose previous
encounters with the police had resulted in arrest was
never afterwards at ease with them. He had feared that
Father Betterton's trial and imprisonment, which surely
must have been for him an appallingly traumatic experience, might have left him unable to cope. Kate had
described how he had reacted with stoically controlled
revulsion to the taking of his prints but then, few potential suspects welcomed this official thieving of identity.
Apart from this, Father John had seemed less obviously
affected both by the murder and by the death of his sister
than were the rest of the community, preserving always
the same look of puzzled acceptance of a life which had
to be endured rather than possessed.

In the interview room he seated himself on the edge
of the chair with no sign that he was expecting an ordeal.
Dalgliesh asked, 'Were you responsible, Father, for packing up Ronald Treeves's clothes for return to his father?'

Now the faint impression of embarrassment was
replaced by an unmistakable guilty flush. 'Oh dear, I

think I may have done something foolish. You wanted to ask about the cloak, I expect.'

'Did you send it back, Father?'

'No. No, I'm afraid I didn't. It's rather difficult to explain.' He was still more embarrassed than frightened as he looked across at Kate. 'It would be easier if I could have your other officer here, Inspector Tarrant. You see, it's all rather embarrassing.'

That wasn't a request to which Dalgliesh would normally have agreed, but the circumstances were unusual. He said, 'As a police officer Inspector Miskin is used to embarrassing confidences. But if you would feel happier . . .'

'Oh yes indeed. Yes please, I should. I know it's foolish of me but it would be easier.'

At a nod from Dalgliesh, Kate slipped out. Piers was busy upstairs seated at the computer.

She said, 'Father Betterton has something to say unsuitable for my chaste female ears. AD wants you. It looks as if Treeves's cloak was never sent back to Dad. If so, why the hell weren't we told before? What's wrong with these people?'

Piers said, 'Nothing. It's just that they don't think like policemen.'

'They don't think like anyone I've ever met. Give me a good old-fashioned villain any day.'

Piers gave up his seat to her and went down to the interviewing room.

Dalgliesh said, 'So exactly what happened, Father?'

'I expect Father Sebastian told you that he asked me to bundle up the clothes. He thought – well, we thought – that it wouldn't be fair to ask one of the staff to do it.

490

The clothes of dead people are so personal to them, aren't they? It's always a distressing business. So I went to Ronald's room and got them together. He didn't have much, of course. The students aren't encouraged to bring too many possessions or clothes with them, only what is needed. I put the things together, but when I was folding the cloak I noticed that . . .' He hesitated, and then said, 'Well, I noticed that it was stained on the inside.'

'How was it stained, Father?'

'Well, it was obvious that he'd been lying on the cloak and making love.'

Piers said, 'It was a semen stain?'

'Yes. Yes it was. Quite a big one really. I felt I didn't want to send the cloak back to his father like that. Ronald wouldn't have wished me to and I knew – well, we all knew – that Sir Alred hadn't wanted him to come to St Anselm's, hadn't wanted him to be a priest. If he'd seen the cloak he could've made trouble for the college.'

'You mean a sexual scandal?'

'Yes, something like that. And it would have been so humiliating for poor Ronald. It was the last thing he would have wanted to happen. I wasn't very clear in my mind but it just seemed wrong to send the cloak back in the state it was in.'

'Why didn't you attempt to clean it?'

'Well I did think about that, but it wouldn't have been very easy. I was afraid that my sister would see me carrying it about and ask me what I was doing. And I'm not very good at washing things. And of course I didn't want to be seen doing it. The flat is small and we have – we had – very little privacy from each other. I just put the problem aside. I know it was silly, but I had to get the parcel ready for Sir Alred's chauffeur and I thought I would deal with it another time. And there was another problem – I didn't really want anyone here to know, I didn't want Father Sebastian to be told. You see, I knew who it was. I knew the woman he had been making love to.'

Piers said, 'So it was a woman?'

'Oh yes, it was a woman. I know I can tell you this in confidence.'

Dalgliesh said, 'If it has no bearing on the murder of the Archdeacon there's no reason why anyone but ourselves should know it. But I think I can help you. Was it Karen Surtees?'

Father Betterton's face showed his relief. 'Yes it was. Yes, I'm afraid that's right. It was Karen. You see I'm rather fond of bird-watching and I saw them through my binoculars. They were in the bracken together. Of course I didn't tell anyone. It's the kind of thing Father Sebastian would find it very difficult to overlook. And then there's Eric Surtees. He's a good man and he's happy here with us and his pigs. I didn't want to say anything that would upset the arrangement. And it didn't seem such a terrible thing to me. If they loved each other, if they were happy together . . . But of course I don't know how it was with them. I don't know anything about it really. But when one thinks of the cruelty and pride and selfishness which we often condone, well, I couldn't feel that what Ronald did was so very terrible. He wasn't really happy here, you know. He didn't fit in somehow and I don't think he was happy at home either. So perhaps he needed to find someone who would show him sympathy and kindness. Other people's lives are so mysterious, aren't they? We mustn't judge. We owe the dead our pity and understanding as well as the living. So I prayed about it and decided to say nothing. Only, of course, I was left with the problem of the cloak.'

Dalgliesh said, 'Father, we need to find it quickly. What did you do with it?'

'I rolled it up as tightly as I could and pushed it to the back of my wardrobe. I know it sounds foolish but it seemed sensible at the time. There didn't really seem any hurry about it. But the days passed and it became more difficult. Then on that Saturday I realized I must make some kind of decision. I waited until my sister was taking a walk. I took one of my handkerchiefs and held it under the hot tap and rubbed it well with soap and managed to clean the cloak quite effectively. I rubbed it dry with a towel and held it in front of the gas fire. Then I thought the best thing would be to take off the name tab so that people weren't reminded of Ronald's death. After that I went down and hung it in the cloakroom on one of the pegs. That way if any of the ordinands forgot their cloaks they could use it. I decided that after I'd done that I would explain to Father Sebastian that the cloak hadn't been sent off with the other clothes, without giving an explanation: I'd tell him I'd hung it in the cloakroom. I knew he'd just assume I'd been careless and forgotten about it. It really seemed the best way.'

Dalgliesh had learnt from experience that to hurry a witness was to invite disaster. Somehow be controlled his impatience. He said, 'And where is the cloak now, Father?'

'Isn't it on the peg where I hung it, the peg on the

extreme right? I hung it there just before Compline on Saturday. Isn't it still there? Of course, I couldn't check – not that I thought of it – because you've locked the cloakroom door.'

'When exactly did you hang it there?'

'As I've explained, just before Compline. I was one of the first to go into the church. There were very few of us with so many students away and their cloaks were hanging in a row. Of course, I didn't count them. I just hung Ronald's cloak where I've told you, on the last peg.'

'Father, did you at any time wear the cloak while it was in your possession?'

Father Betterton's puzzled eyes looked into his. 'Oh no, I wouldn't have done that. We've our own black cloaks. I wouldn't have needed to wear Ronald's.'

'Do the students normally wear their own cloaks only, or are they, as it were, communal?'

'Oh, they wear their own. I dare say sometimes they may get muddled but that wouldn't have happened that night. None of the ordinands wear their cloaks to Compline except in the bitterest winter. It's only a short walk to the church along the north cloister. And Ronald would never have lent his cloak to anyone else. He was very fussy about his belongings.'

Dalgliesh asked, 'Father, why didn't you tell me this earlier?'

Father John's puzzled eyes looked into his. 'You didn't ask me.'

'But didn't it occur to you when we examined all the cloaks and clothes for blood that we would need to know if any were missing?'

Father John said simply, 'No. And it wasn't missing, was it? It was on a peg in the cloakroom with the others.' Dalgliesh waited. Father John's mild confusion had deepened into distress. He looked from Dalgliesh to Piers and saw no comfort in their faces. He said, 'I hadn't thought about the details of your investigation, what you were doing or what it all might mean. I didn't want to and it didn't seem any of my business. All I've done is to try to answer honestly any questions you've put to me.'

It was, Dalgliesh had to admit, a complete vindication. Why should Father John have thought the cloak significant? Someone more knowledgeable in police procedure, more curious or interested, would have volunteered the information even if not expecting it to be particularly useful. Father John was none of these things, and even if it had occurred to him to speak, the protection of Ronald Treeves's pathetic secret would probably have seemed more important.

Now he said contritely, 'I'm sorry. Have I made things difficult for you? Is it important?'

And what, thought Dalgliesh, could he honestly answer to that. He said, 'What is important is the exact time you hung the cloak on the end peg. You're sure that it was just before Compline?'

'Oh yes, quite sure. It would have been nine-fifteen. I'm usually among the first into the church for Compline – I was going to mention the matter to Father Sebastian after the service, but he hurried away and I didn't get the chance. And next morning, when we all heard about the murder, it seemed such an unimportant thing to worry him with.'

Dalgliesh said, 'Thank you for being so helpful, Father.

What you've told us is important. It is even more important that you keep it private. I'd be grateful if you wouldn't mention this conversation to anyone.'

'Not even to Father Sebastian?'

'Not to anyone, please. When the investigation is over you'll be free to tell Father Sebastian as much as you choose. At present I don't want anyone here to know that Ronald Treeves's cloak is somewhere in college.'

'But it won't be somewhere, will it?' The guileless eyes looked at him. 'Isn't it still be on the peg?'

Dalgliesh said, 'It isn't on the peg now, Father, but I expect we'll find it.'

Gently he steered Father Betterton to the door. The priest seemed suddenly to have become a confused and worried old man. But at the door he gathered strength and turned to speak a few last words.

'Naturally I shan't tell anyone about this conversation. You've asked me not to do so and I won't. May I please also ask you to say nothing about Ronald Treeves's relationship with Karen.'

Dalgliesh said, 'If it is relevant to the death of Archdeacon Crampton it will have to come out. Murder is like that, Father. There's very little we can keep secret when a human being has been done to death. But it will only be revealed if and when it is necessary.'

Dalgliesh impressed on Father John again the importance of telling no one about the cloak and let him go. There was, he thought, one advantage of dealing with the priests and ordinands of St Anselm's: you could be reasonably certain that a promise, once given, would be kept.

12

Less than five minutes later the whole team, including the SOCOs, were behind the closed doors of St Matthew's Cottage. Dalgliesh reported the new development. He said, 'Right. So we begin the search. We need first to be clear about the three sets of keys. After the murder only one set was missing. During the night Surtees took a set and didn't return it. That set has been recovered from the pigsty. That means that Cain must have taken the second set and replaced it after the murder. Assuming that Cain was the figure wearing the cloak, this could be hidden anywhere, inside the college or out. It's not an easy thing to conceal but Cain had the whole headland and shore available and plenty of time between midnight and five-thirty. It could even have been burnt. There are plenty of ditches crossing the headland where a fire wouldn't be noticed, even if someone were abroad. All he would need would be some paraffin and a match.'

Piers said, 'I know what I'd have done with it, sir. I'd have fed it to the pigs. Those animals will eat anything, particularly if it's bloodstained, in which case we'll be lucky to find anything except perhaps the small brass chain at the back of the neck.'

Dalgliesh said, 'Then look for it. You and Robbins had better make a start with St John's Cottage. We've been given authority by Father Sebastian to go where we like, so no warrant is necessary. If any of the people in the cottages makes trouble, we may need a warrant. It's important no one knows what we're looking for. Where are the ordinands at present, does anyone know?'

Kate said, 'I think they're in the lecture room on the first floor. Father Sebastian is giving them a seminar on theology.'

'That should keep them occupied and out of the way. Mr Clark, will you and your team take the headland and the shore. I doubt whether Cain would have made his way through that storm to chuck the cloak into the sea, but there are plenty of hiding places on the headland. Kate and I will take the house.'

The group dispersed, the SOCOs turning seaward and Piers and Robbins making their way towards St John's Cottage. Dalgliesh and Kate went through the iron gate into the west courtyard. The north cloister was now free of leaves but nothing of interest had been discovered from the SOCOs' meticulous search except the small twig, its leaves still fresh, on the floor of Raphael's set.

Dalgliesh unlocked the door of the cloakroom. The air smelt unfresh. The five hooded cloaks hung on their pegs in a sad decrepitude as if they had been there for decades. Dalgliesh put on his search gloves and turned back the hood of each cloak. The name tabs were in place: Morby, Arbuthnot, Buckhurst, Bloxham, McCauley. They passed into the laundry-room. There were two high windows with a Formica-topped table beneath them and under it four plastic laundry baskets. To the left was a deep porcelain sink with a wooden draining-board each side, and a tumble-dryer. The four large washing machines were fixed to the right-hand wall. All the porthole doors were closed.

Kate stood in the doorway while Dalgliesh opened the first three doors. As he bent to the fourth, she saw him stiffen and went up to him. Behind the thick glass, blurred but identifiable, were the folds of a brown woollen garment. They had found the cloak.

On the top of the machine was a white postcard. Kate picked it up and silently passed it to Dalgliesh. The writing was black, the letters meticulously formed. *'This vehicle should not be parked in the forecourt. Kindly remove it to the rear of the building. P.G.'*

Dalgliesh said, 'Father Peregrine, and it looks as if he turned off the machine. There are only about three inches of water here.'

Kate said, 'Is it bloody?' and, bending, peered close.

'It's difficult to see, but the lab won't need much to get a match. Ring Piers and the SOCOs, will you Kate. Call off the search. I want this door removed, the water drained off and the cloak sent to the lab. I need hair samples from everyone at St Anselm's. Thank God for Father Peregrine. If a machine this size had gone full cycle I doubt whether we'd have got anything useful, either blood, fibres or hair. Piers and I will have a word with him.'

Kate said, 'Surely Cain was taking an extraordinary risk. It was crazy coming back, even crazier to set the machine going. It was only by chance we didn't find the cloak earlier.'

'He didn't mind if we did find it. He may even have wanted it found. All that mattered was that it couldn't be linked to him.'

'But he must have known that there was a risk that Father Peregrine would wake up and turn off the machine.'

'No, he didn't know, Kate. He was one of the people

here who never uses those machines. Remember Mrs Munroe's diary? George Gregory had his washing done by Ruby Pilbeam.'

Father Peregrine was sitting at his desk at the west end of the library, hardly visible behind a pile of volumes. No one else was present.

Dalgliesh said, 'Father, did you turn off one of the washing machines on the night of the murder?'

Father Peregrine lifted his head and appeared to take some seconds recognizing his visitors. He said, 'I'm sorry. It's Commander Dalgliesh, of course. Of what are we speaking?'

'Saturday night. The night Archdeacon Crampton was killed. I'm asking if you went into the laundry-room and turned off one of the machines.'

'Did I?'

Dalgliesh handed over the postcard. 'You wrote this, I presume. Those are your initials. This is your hand-writing.'

'Yes, that is my hand certainly. Dear me, it seems to be the wrong card.'

'What did the right one say, Father?'

'It said that ordinands should not use the washing machines after Compline. I go to bed early and sleep lightly. The machines are old and when they start up the noise is extremely disrupting. The defect, I understand, is in the water system rather than in the machines themselves, but the cause is immaterial. Ordinands are supposed to keep silence after Compline. It is not an appropriate time to do their personal laundry.'

'And did you hear the machine, Father? Did you place this note on it?'

'I must have done. But I expect I was half asleep at the time and it slipped my mind.'

Piers said, 'How could it have slipped your mind, Father? You weren't too sleepy to write the note, find a card and a pen.'

'Oh but I explained, Inspector. This is the wrong note. I have quite a number already written. They're in my room if you care to see.'

They followed him through the door that led into his cell-like room. There on the top of the crowded bookcase was a cardboard box containing some half-dozen cards. Dalgliesh rifled through them. *'This desk is for my use only. Ordinands should not leave their books here.'* *'Kindly replace the books on these shelves in their precise order.'* *'These machines should not be used after Compline. In future any machines working after ten o'clock will be turned off.'* *'This board is for official notices only, not for the exchange of trivia by ordinands.'* All bore the initials P.G.

Father Peregrine said, 'I'm afraid I was very sleepy. I picked up the wrong card.'

Dalgliesh said, 'You heard the machine start up some time in the night and went out to turn off the noise. Didn't you realize the importance of this when Inspector Miskin questioned you?'

'The young woman asked me whether I had heard anyone come in or leave the building, or whether I had gone out myself. I remember the words exactly. She told me I must be very precise in answering her questions. I was. I said no. Nothing was said to me about washing machines.'

Dalgliesh said, 'The doors of all the machines were closed. It's usual, surely, for them to be left open when not in use. Did you close them, Father?'

Father Peregrine said complacently, 'I can't remember but I expect I did. It would be a natural thing to do. Tidiness, you know. I dislike seeing them left open. There's no good reason for it.'

Father Peregrine's thoughts seemed to be on his desk and the work in hand. He led the way back into the library and they followed him. He settled himself down at the desk again, as if the interview were over.

Dalgliesh said with all the force he could command, 'Father, are you at all interested in helping me to catch this murderer?'

Father Peregrine, not in the least intimidated by Dalgliesh's six-foot-two inches towering over him, appeared to consider the question as a proposition rather than an accusation. He said, 'Murderers should be caught, certainly, but I don't really think I'm competent to help you, Commander. I have no experience of police investigation. I think you should call on Father Sebastian or Father John. They both read a great deal of detective fiction, and that probably gives them an insight. Father Sebastian lent me a volume once. I think it was by a Mr Hammond Innes. It was too clever for me, I'm afraid.'

Piers, speechless, raised his eyes to heaven and turned his back on the débâcle. Father Peregrine dropped his eyes to his book, but then showed signs of animation and looked up again.

'Just a thought. This murderer, having done his murdering, would surely want to make his getaway. I expect he had a getaway car ready outside the west gate. The expression is familiar to me. I can't believe, Commander, that he would think it a convenient time to do his personal laundry. The washing machine is a kipper.'

Piers muttered 'red herring', and took a step away from the desk as if he could bear no more.

Father Peregrine said, 'Kipper or red herring, the meaning is the same. Red herrings were, of course, the staple protein on this coast for many years. It's a curious word. I imagine the etymology is Middle English *kypre* from the Old English *cypera*. I'm surprised you don't use it in place of red herring. You could say that an investigation was "kippered" when its success was jeopardized by irrelevant and misleading information.' He paused, then added, 'Like my note, I'm afraid.'

Dalgliesh said, 'And you saw and heard nothing when you left your room?'

'As I have explained, Commander, I have no memory of having left my room. However, the evidence of my note and the fact that the machine was turned off seem incontrovertible. Certainly if anyone had entered my room to take the postcard I should have heard. I'm sorry not to be more helpful.'

Father Peregrine again turned his attention to his books and Dalgliesh and Piers left him to his work.

Outside the library, Piers said, 'I don't believe it. The man's mad. And he's supposed to be competent to teach postgraduates!'

'And does it brilliantly, so I'm told. I can believe it. He wakes, hears a noise he detests, pads out half-asleep and picks up what he thinks is his usual note, then fumbles back into bed. The difficulty is that he doesn't for one moment believe that anyone in St Anselm's is a murderer. He doesn't admit the possibility to his mind. It's the same with Father John and the brown cloak. Neither of them is trying to obstruct us, they are not being deliberately unhelpful. None of them thinks like a policeman and our questions seem an irrelevance. They refuse to accept even the possibility that someone at St Anselm's was responsible.'

Piers said, 'Then they're in for one hell of a shock. And Father Sebastian? Father Martin?'

'They've seen the body, Piers. They know where and how. The question is, do they know who?'

13

In the laundry-room the dripping cloak had been carefully lifted and placed in an open plastic bag. The water,
so faintly pink that the colour seemed more imagined
than real, was siphoned into bottles and labelled. Two
of Clark's team were dusting the machine for prints. It
seemed to Dalgliesh a pointless exercise; Gregory had
worn gloves in the church and was unlikely to have
taken them off before he returned to his cottage. But
the job had to be done; the defence would look for
any opportunity to question the efficiency of the
investigation.

Dalgliesh said, 'This confirms Gregory as prime suspect, but then he was from the time we knew about the
marriage. Where is he, by the way? Do we know?'

Kate said, 'He drove to Norwich this morning. He
told Mrs Pilbeam he'd be back by mid afternoon. She
cleans his cottage for him and she was there this
morning.'

'We'll question him as soon as he returns and this
time we use PACE. I want the interview recorded. Two
things are important. He mustn't know that Treeves's
cloak was left in college or that the washing machine
was turned off. Speak to Father John and Father Peregrine again, will you, Piers? Be tactful. Try to ensure that
the message gets through to Father Peregrine.'

Piers went out. Kate said, 'Couldn't we get Father

Sebastian to announce that the door to the north cloister is open and that students can use the laundry-room? We could then keep watch to see if Gregory comes for the cloak. He'll want to know if we've found it.'

'Ingenious, Kate, but it will prove nothing. He's not going to fall into that trap. If he does decide to come he'll bring some soiled washing with him. But why should he? He planned for the cloak to be found, one more piece of evidence to convince us that this was an inside job. All that concerns him is that we can't prove that he wore it on the night of the murder. Normally he'd have been safe. It was bad luck for him that Surtees went to the church on Saturday night. Without his evidence there would have been no proof that the murderer wore a cloak. Bad luck for him, too, that the machine was turned off. If the washing cycle had been completed any evidence would almost certainly have been destroyed.'

Kate said, 'He could still claim that Treeves had lent him the cloak some time previously.'

'But how likely is that? Treeves was a young man jealous of his possessions. Why would he lend anyone his cloak? But you're right. That will probably be part of his defence.'

Piers had returned. He said, 'Father John was in the library with Father Peregrine. I think they've both got the message. But we had better wait for Gregory and intercept him as soon as he arrives back.'

Kate asked, 'And if he wants a lawyer?'

Dalgliesh said, 'Then we'll have to wait until he gets one.'

But Gregory had no wish for a lawyer. An hour later

he seated himself at the table in the interview room with every appearance of calm.

He said, 'I think I know my rights and just how far you are permitted to go without incurring the expense of a lawyer. Those who would be any good I can't afford, and those I can afford wouldn't be any good. My solicitor, although perfectly competent when it comes to drawing up a will, would be an irritating encumbrance to us all. I didn't kill Crampton. Not only is violence repugnant to me, I had no reason to wish him dead.'

Dalgliesh had decided that he would leave the questioning to Kate and Piers. Both sat opposite Gregory, and Dalgliesh himself moved to the east-facing window. It was, he thought, a curious setting for a police interview. The barely furnished room, with the square table, the four upright chairs and the two armchairs, was just as they had first seen it. The one change was a brighter bulb in the single overhanging light over the table. Only in the kitchen, with its collection of mugs and the faint smell of sandwiches and coffee, and in the more comfortably furnished sitting-room opposite, where Mrs Pilbeam had actually provided a jug of flowers, were there any signs of their occupation. He wondered what a casual watcher would have made of the present scene, of this bare functional space, of the three men and one woman so obviously intent on their private business. It could only be an interrogation or a conspiracy and the rhythmic booming of the sea emphasized the atmosphere of secrecy and menace.

Kate switched on the machine and they went through the preliminaries. Gregory gave his name and address and the three police officers stated their names and ranks.

It was Piers who began the questioning. He said, 'Archdeacon Crampton was murdered at about midnight last Saturday. Where were you after ten o'clock that night?'

'I told you that earlier when you first questioned me. I was in my cottage, listening to Wagner. I didn't leave the cottage until I was summoned by telephone to attend Sebastian Morell's assembly in the library.'

'We have evidence that someone went to Raphael Arbuthnot's room that night. Was it you?'

'How could it be? I just told you I didn't leave my cottage.'

'On 27 April 1988 you married Clara Arbuthnot, and you have told us that Raphael is your son. Did you know at the time of the marriage that the ceremony would make him legitimate, the heir to St Anselm's?'

There was a slight pause. Dalgliesh thought, he doesn't know how we found out about the marriage. He's not sure how much we know.

Then Gregory said, 'I wasn't aware of it at the time. Later – and I can't remember when – it came to my knowledge that the 1976 Act had legitimized my son.'

'At the time of the marriage did you know the provisions of Miss Agnes Arbuthnot's will?'

There was no hesitation now. Dalgliesh was confident that Gregory would have made it his business to know, probably by research in London. But he wouldn't have done that under his own name and could be reasonably sure that this at least was evidence they wouldn't easily find. He said, 'No, I didn't know.'

'And your wife didn't tell you before or after the marriage?'

Again the slight hesitation, the flicker of the eyes. Then he decided to take a risk. 'No, she didn't. She was more concerned with saving her soul than with financial benefit to our son. And if these somewhat naïve questions are intended to stress that I had motive, may I point out that so did all four resident priests.'

Piers broke in, 'I thought you told us you were unaware of the provisions of the will.'

'I wasn't thinking of pecuniary advantage. I was thinking of the obvious dislike felt for the Archdeacon by virtually everyone in college. And if you're alleging that I killed the Archdeacon to ensure an inheritance for my son, may I point out that the college was scheduled to close. We all knew that our time here was limited.'

Kate said, 'Closure was inevitable, perhaps, but not immediate. Father Sebastian might well have negotiated a further year or two. Long enough for your son to complete his training and to be ordained. Was that what you wanted?'

'I'd have preferred another career for him. But this, I understand, is one of the smaller irritations of parenthood. Children seldom make sensible choices. As I have ignored Raphael for twenty-five years, I can hardly expect to have a say now in how he runs his life.'

Piers said, 'We have learned today that the Archdeacon's murderer almost certainly wore an ordinand's cloak. We have found a brown cloak in one of the washing machines in St Anselm's laundry-room. Did you put it there?'

'No I did not, nor do I know who did.'

'We also know that someone, probably a man, phoned Mrs Crampton at nine-twenty-eight on the night of the murder pretending to call from the diocesan office and asking for the number of the Archdeacon's mobile phone. Did you make that call?'

Gregory suppressed a faint smile. 'This is a surprisingly simplistic interrogation for what I understand is regarded as one of Scotland Yard's more prestigious squads. No, I did not make that call, nor do I know who did.'

'It was a time when the priests and the four ordinands in residence were due in church for Compline. Where were you?'

'In my cottage marking essays. And I wasn't the only man not to attend Compline. Yarwood, Stannard, Surtees and Pilbeam resisted the temptation to hear the Archdeacon preach, as did the three women. Are you sure it was a man who made that call?'

Kate said, 'The Archdeacon's murder wasn't the only tragedy that put St Anselm's future at risk. The death of Ronald Treeves didn't help. He was with you on the Friday evening. He died the next day. What happened that Friday?'

Gregory stared at her. The spasm of dislike and contempt in his face was as raw and explicit as if he had spat. Kate flushed. She went on, 'He'd been rejected and betrayed. He came to you for comfort and reassurance and you sent him away. Isn't that what happened?'

'He came to me for a lesson in New Testament Greek which I gave him. Shorter than usual, admittedly, but that was at his wish. Obviously you know about his stealing the consecrated wafer. I advised him to confess to Father Sebastian. It was the only possible advice and you would have given the same. He asked me if this would mean expulsion and I said, given Father Sebastian's peculiar view of reality, I thought it would. He wanted assurance but I couldn't honestly give it to him. Better to risk expulsion than fall into the hands of a blackmailer. He was the son of a rich man; he could have been paying that woman for years.'

'Have you any reason to suppose that Karen Surtees is a blackmailer? How well do you know her?'

'Well enough to know that she is an unscrupulous young woman who likes power. His secret would never have been safe with her.'

Kate said, 'So he went out and killed himself.'

'Unfortunately. That I could neither have foreseen nor prevented.'

Piers said, 'And then there was a second death. We've evidence that Mrs Munroe had discovered that you are Raphael's father. Did she confront you with this knowledge?'

There was another pause. He had placed his hands on the table and now sat regarding them. It was impossible to see his face, but Dalgliesh knew that the man had reached a point of decision. Again he was asking himself how much the police knew and with what certainty. Had Margaret Munroe spoken to someone else? Had she perhaps left a note?

The pause lasted for less than six seconds but seemed longer. Then he said, 'Yes, she came to see me. She had made some enquiry – she didn't say what – that confirmed her suspicions. Two things apparently worried her. The first was that I was deceiving Father Sebastian and working here under false pretences; more importantly, of course, was that Raphael ought to be told. None of it was her business, but I thought it wise to explain why I hadn't

511

married Raphael's mother when she was pregnant, and why I changed my mind. I said I was waiting to tell my son until I had reason to believe that the news wouldn't be too unwelcome to him. I wanted to choose my own time. She could be assured that I would speak before the end of term. On that undertaking – which incidentally she had absolutely no right to extract – she said she would keep the secret.'

Dalgliesh said, 'And that night she died.'

'Of a heart attack. If the trauma of the discovery and the effort it took to confront me proved fatal, then I'm sorry. I can't be held responsible for every death that takes place at St Anselm's. You will be accusing me next of pushing Agatha Betterton down the cellar steps.'

Kate said, 'And did you?'

This time he was clever at concealing his dislike. He said, 'I thought you were investigating the murder of Archdeacon Crampton, not attempting to cast me as a serial killer. Shouldn't we be concentrating on the one death which was undoubtedly murder?'

It was then Dalgliesh spoke. He said, 'We shall be requiring samples of hair from everyone who was in college last Saturday night. I take it you have no objection?'

'Not if the indignity is to be extended to all the other suspects. It's hardly a procedure needing a general anaesthetic.'

There was little point in prolonging the questioning. They went through the routine for ending the interview and Kate switched off the tape.

Gregory said, 'If you want your hairs, you'd better come for them now. I propose to work and have no intention of being interrupted.'

He strode off into the darkness.

Dalgliesh said, 'I want those samples taken tonight. Then I'm driving back to London. I'd like to be at the lab when the cloak is examined. We should get a result within a couple of days if they give it priority. You two and Robbins will remain here. I'll arrange with Father Sebastian for you to move into this cottage. I dare say he can provide sleeping bags or mattresses if there are no spare beds. I want a twenty-four hour watch kept on Gregory.'

Kate said, 'And if we get nothing from the cloak? Everything else we've got is circumstantial. Without forensic evidence we haven't got a case.'

She had only been stating the obvious and neither Dalgliesh nor Piers replied.

14

When his sister was alive, Father John seldom appeared at meals except for dinner, when all the community were expected to be present for what Father Sebastian obviously regarded as a unifying celebration of community life. But now, and a little unexpectedly, he arrived for Tuesday afternoon tea. With this latest death there had been no ceremonial calling together of the whole of the college; the news had been given to priests and ordinands individually by Father Sebastian with the minimum of fuss. The four ordinands had already visited Father John to express their condolences, and now they tried to show sympathy by replenishing his cup and bringing him sandwiches, scones and cake in succession from the refectory table. He sat near the door, a tranquil diminished little man, unflinchingly polite and occasionally smiling. After tea Emma suggested that she should begin looking through Miss Betterton's wardrobe and they went up to the flat together.

She had wondered how she could bundle up the clothes and had asked Mrs Pilbeam for a couple of strong plastic bags, one for items which might be welcomed by Oxfam or some other charity shop and the other for clothes destined to be thrown away. But the two black bags presented to her had looked so intimidatingly unsuitable for anything other than rubbish that she had decided to make a preliminary sorting of the wardrobe and then bag and remove the clothes at a time when Father John wasn't in the flat.

She left him sitting in the gloaming by the faint blue flames of his gas fire and went through to Miss Betterton's bedroom. A central pendant light with a dusty old-fashioned shade gave inadequate illumination, but an anglepoise lamp on the table by the single brass bed was fitted with a more powerful bulb and by directing the beam on the room she was able to see to begin her task. To the right of the bed was an upright chair and a bow-fronted chest of drawers. The only other furniture was an immense mahogany wardrobe decorated with carved scrolls which occupied the space between the two small windows. Emma opened the door and breathed in a musty smell overlaid with the scent of tweed, lavender and mothballs.

But the task of sorting and discarding proved less formidable than she had feared. Miss Betterton in her solitary life had managed with few clothes and it was difficult to believe she had purchased anything new in the last ten years. Emma drew from the wardrobe a heavy musquash coat with bare patches, two tweed suits which, with their over-padded shoulders and fitted jackets, looked as if they had last been worn in the 1930s, a motley collection of cardigans and long tweed skirts, and evening dresses in velvet and satin of excellent quality but archaic cut which it was difficult to believe a modern woman would wear except as fancy dress. The chest of drawers held shirts and underclothes, knickers washed but stained at the crotch, long-sleeved vests and rolled balls of thick stockings. There was little here that a charity shop would welcome.

She felt a sudden revulsion and a defensive pity on Miss Betterton's behalf that Inspector Tarrant and his colleague should have rummaged among these pathetic leavings. What had they expected to find – a letter, a diary, a confession? Medieval congregations, exposed Sunday after Sunday to the terrifying imagery of the *Doom*, prayed to be delivered from sudden death, fearing that they might go to their creator unshriven. Nowadays man, in his last moment, was more likely to regret the untidy desk, the unfulfilled intentions, the incriminating letters.

There was a surprising find in the bottom drawer. Carefully placed between brown paper was an RAF officer's tunic with wings above the left pocket, two rings on the sleeves and the ribbon of some gallantry award. With it was a squashed, rather battered cap. Moving the musquash coat she laid them together on the bed and contemplated them for a moment in baffled silence.

She found the jewellery in the top left-hand drawer of the chest of drawers in a small leather box. There wasn't much, and the cameo brooches, heavy gold rings and long pearl necklaces looked as if they were family heirlooms. It was difficult to assess their value, although some of the stones looked good, and she wondered how best she could deal with Father John's request to have the jewellery sold. Perhaps the best plan would be to take all the pieces to Cambridge and get a valuation from one of the city's jewellers. In the meantime keeping them safe would be a responsibility.

There was a false bottom to the box and, lifting it, she found a small envelope yellowed with age. She opened it and tipped out on to her palm a single ring. It was gold and, although the stones were small, they were prettily mounted, a central ruby in a cluster of diamonds. On impulse she slipped it on to the third finger of her left hand and recognized it for what it was: an engagement ring. If it had been given to Miss Betterton by the airman, he must have been killed; how else would she have come by his uniform? Emma had a vivid image of a single plane, Spitfire or Hurricane, spiralling out of control and trailing its long tongue of fire before plunging into the Channel. Or had he been a bomber pilot, shot down over some enemy target, joining in death those whom his bombs had killed? Had he and Agatha Betterton been lovers before he died?

Why was it, she wondered, so difficult to believe that the old had been young, with the strength and animal beauty of youth, had loved, been loved, laughed and been full of youth's unmeditated optimism? She pictured Miss Betterton on the few occasions when she had seen her, striding along the cliff path, woollen cap on head, chin forward, as if combating a more bitterly intractable enemy than the wind; passing Emma on the stairs with a brief nod of recognition or a sudden dart from her dark, disturbingly inquisitive eyes. Raphael had liked her, had been willing to spend time with her. But had that been genuine affection or the duty of kindness? And if this were indeed an engagement ring, why had she stopped wearing it? But perhaps that wasn't so difficult to understand. It represented something that was over and had to be folded away as she had folded away her lover's tunic. She had had no wish to put on memory every morning with a symbol which had outlasted the giver and would outlast her, to make grief and loss public knowledge with every gesture of her hand. It was an easy platitude to say that the dead lived on in the memory of the living, but what substitute was memory for the loving voice and the strong enclosing arms? And wasn't this the stuff of nearly all the world's poetry, the transitoriness of life and love and beauty, the knowledge that time's wingèd chariot had knives in its wheels?

There was a low knock on the door and it opened. She swung round and saw Inspector Miskin. For a moment they stood regarding each other and Emma saw no friendliness in the other's eyes.

Then the Inspector said, 'Father John said I'd find you here. Commander Dalgliesh has asked me to put everyone in the picture. He's returned to London and I shall be staying on for the present with Inspector Tarrant and Sergeant Robbins. Now that security locks have been fitted to the guest sets it's important that you lock yourself in at night. I'll be in the college after Compline and will see you to your set.'

So Commander Dalgliesh had gone without saying goodbye. But why should he have said goodbye? There were more important matters on his mind than a casual courtesy. He would have said his formal farewells to Father Sebastian. What else would have been necessary?

Inspector Miskin's tone had been perfectly polite and Emma knew she was being unjust in resenting it. She said, 'I don't need to be escorted to my set. And does this mean that you think we're in danger?'

There was a pause, then Inspector Miskin said, 'We're not saying that. It's just that there is still a murderer on this headland and until we make an arrest it's sensible for everyone to take precautions.'

'And do you expect to make an arrest?'

Again there was a pause, then Inspector Miskin said, 'We hope to. After all, that's what we're here for, isn't it, to make an arrest? I'm sorry I can't say any more at present. I'll see you later then.'

She went out, closing the door. Standing alone by the bed, looking down at the folded cap and tunic and with the ring still on her finger, Emma felt tears welling in her eyes but didn't know whether she was weeping for Miss Betterton, for her dead lover or a little for herself. Then she replaced the ring in its envelope and set about completing her task.

15

The next morning Dalgliesh drove before first light to
the Lambeth laboratory. Rain had been falling steadily
all night and although it had now stopped, the changing
red, amber and green of the traffic lights cast their
trembling and gaudy images on roads still awash, and
the air held a fresh river smell borne on a full tide.
London seems to sleep only for the hours between two
and four in the morning, and then it is a fitful slumber.
Now, slowly, the capital was waking up and the workers,
in small preoccupied groups, were emerging to take
possession of their city.

Material from Suffolk scenes of crime would normally
have been sent to the Huntingdon forensic science laboratory but that laboratory was overloaded. Lambeth was
able to offer Premium One priority, which was what Dalgliesh requested. He was well known at the lab and was
greeted with warmth by the staff. Dr Anna Prescott, the
senior forensic biologist who was awaiting him, had given
evidence for the Crown in a number of his cases and he
knew how much success had depended on her reputation
as a scientist, on the confidence and lucidity with which
she presented her findings to the court and on her calm
assurance under cross-examination. But, like all forensic
scientists, she wasn't an agent of the police. If Gregory
were ever brought to trial, she would be there as an independent expert witness with allegiance only to the facts.

The cloak had been dried in the laboratory drying cupboard and had now been spread out on one of the wide search tables under the glare of the four fluorescent lights. Gregory's track suit had been taken to another part of the lab to avoid cross-contamination. Any transferred fibres from the track suit would be recovered from the surface of the cloak with adhesive tape and then be examined by comparison microscopy. If this initial preliminary microscope examination suggested that there was a match, a further series of comparative tests would be undertaken including the instrumental analysis of the chemical composition of the fibre itself. But all that, which would take considerable time, was in the future. The blood had already gone for analysis, and Dalgliesh awaited the report without anxiety; he had no doubt that it had come from Archdeacon Crampton. What Dr Prescott and he were looking for now were hairs. Together, gowned and masked, they bent over the cloak.

Dalgliesh reflected that the keen human eye was a remarkably effective instrument of search. It took them only a few seconds to find what they were seeking. Twisted in the brass chain at the neck of the cloak were two grey hairs. Dr Prescott unwound them with delicate care and placed them in a small glass dish. She immediately examined them under a low power microscope and said with satisfaction, 'Both have roots. That means there's a good chance of getting a DNA profile.'

16

Two days later at seven-thirty in the morning the message from the laboratory was telephoned to Dalgliesh at his Thames-side flat. The two hair roots had yielded their DNA, and it was Gregory's. It was news that Dalgliesh had expected but he still received it with a small surge of relief. Comparison microscopy of fibres on the cloak and on the top of the track suit had given a match but the results of the final tests were still awaited. Replacing the receiver, Dalgliesh paused for a moment's thought. To wait or to act now? He was unwilling to leave it longer before making an arrest. The DNA showed that Gregory had worn Ronald Treeves's cloak and the fibre-match could only confirm this main incontrovertible finding. He could, of course, ring Kate or Piers at St Anselm's; both were perfectly competent to make an arrest. But he needed to be there himself and he knew why. The act of arresting Gregory, of speaking the words of the caution, would in some way assuage the defeat of his last case when he had known the identity of the murderer, had listened to his quickly withdrawn confession, but hadn't sufficient evidence to justify arrest. Not to be present now would leave something incomplete, although he was unsure precisely what.

As expected, the two days had been more than usually busy. He had returned to a backlog of work, to problems which were his responsibility and others which laid their weight on his mind, as they did on the minds of all senior officers. The force was seriously understaffed. There was an urgent need to recruit intelligent, educated and highly motivated men and women from all sections of the community at a time when other careers offered this sought-after group higher salaries, greater prestige and less stress. There was the need to reduce the burden of bureaucracy and paperwork, to increase the effectiveness of the detective force and to tackle corruption in an age when bribery wasn't a £10 note slipped into a back pocket but a share in the huge profits of the illegal drugs trade. But now, at least for a short time, he would return to St Anselm's. It was no longer a place of unsullied goodness and peace but there was a job to be finished and people he wanted to see. He wondered if Emma Lavenham was still in college.

Putting aside thoughts of his crowded diary, the weight of files requiring attention, the meeting planned for the afternoon, he left a message for the Assistant Commissioner and his secretary. Then he rang Kate. All was quiet at St Anselm's – abnormally so, Kate thought. People were going about their daily business and with a kind of subdued intensity, as if that bloody corpse still lay under the *Doom* in the church. It seemed to her that the whole house was waiting for a consummation half longed-for and half dreaded. Gregory hadn't shown himself. He had, at Dalgliesh's request, handed over his passport after the last interrogation and there was no fear that he would abscond. But flight had never been an option; it was no part of Gregory's plan to be hauled back ignominiously from some inhospitable foreign refuge.

It was a cold day and he smelled in the London air for

the first time the metallic tang of winter. A biting but fitful wind scoured the City and by the time he reached the A12 it was blowing in strong, more sustained blasts. The traffic was unusually light except for the trucks on their way to the east coast ports, and he drove smoothly and fast, his hands lightly on the wheel, his eyes fixed ahead. What had he but two grey hairs as the frail instruments of justice? They would have to be enough.

His thoughts moved from the arrest to the trial and he found himself rehearsing the case for the defence. The DNA could not be challenged; Gregory had worn Ronald Treeves's cloak. But the defence counsel would probably claim that Gregory, when giving that last Greek lesson to Treeves, had borrowed it, perhaps complaining of feeling cold, and that at the time he had been wearing his black track suit. Nothing was less likely, but would a jury believe that? Gregory had a strong motive, but so had others, including Raphael. The twig found on the floor of Raphael's sitting-room could have blown in unseen when he left his set to go to Peter Buckhurst; the prosecution would probably be wise not to make too much of it. The telephone call to Mrs Crampton, put through from the box in the college, was dangerous to the defence but it could have been made by eight other people, and possibly by Raphael. And then there was a case to be made against Miss Betterton. She had motive and opportunity, but had she the strength to wield that heavy candlestick? No one now would know: Agatha Betterton was dead. Gregory had not been accused of her murder, nor of murdering Margaret Munroe. In neither case had there been sufficient evidence even to justify his arrest.

He made the journey in under three and a half hours. Now he was at the end of the approach road and saw before him a waste of turbulent sea, white-specked to the horizon. He stopped the car and rang Kate. Gregory had left his cottage some half an hour previously and was walking on the beach.

Dalgliesh said, 'Wait for me at the end of the coast road, and bring cuffs with you. We may not need them but I'm taking no chances.'

Within minutes he saw her walking towards him. Neither spoke as she got into the car and he reversed and drove back to the steps leading to the beach. They could see Gregory now, a lone figure in an ankle-length tweed coat, the collar turned up against the wind, standing at the side of one of the decaying groynes and staring out to sea. As they scrunched over the shingle a sudden gust tore at their jackets making it difficult to stand upright, but the howling of the wind was scarcely heard above the thunder of the sea. Wave upon wave crashed in explosions of spray, boiling around the groynes and setting balls of spume dancing and rolling like iridescent soap bubbles on the high ridges of shingle.

They walked side by side towards the still figure and Gregory turned and watched them coming. Then, when they were within twenty yards, he stepped with deliberation on the edge of the groyne and walked along its length to a post at the end. It was only about two feet square and less than a foot above the inrushing tide.

Dalgliesh said to Kate, 'If he goes in, ring St Anselm's. Tell them we need the boat and an ambulance.'

Then, with equal deliberation he stepped up on to the groyne and moved towards Gregory. When he was within eight feet he stopped and the two men stood facing each other. Gregory called out strong-voiced, but his words only just reached Dalgliesh above the tumult of the sea.

'If you've come to arrest me, well here I am. But you'll need to come closer. Isn't there some ridiculous rigmarole of a caution you need to pronounce? I take it I have a legal right to hear it.'

Dalgliesh did not shout a reply. For two minutes they stood in silence regarding each other and it seemed to him that that brief stretch of time covered half a lifetime of transitory self-knowledge. What he felt now was something new, an anger stronger than any he could remember. The anger he had felt when he had stood looking down at the Archdeacon's body was nothing compared with this overwhelming emotion. He neither liked it nor distrusted it, but simply accepted its power. He knew why he had been reluctant to face Gregory across that small table in the interviewing room. By standing a little apart he had distanced himself from more than the physical presence of his adversary. Now he could distance himself no longer.

For Dalgliesh his job had never been a crusade. He knew detectives for whom the sight of the victim in his or her pathetic final nothingness imprinted on the mind an image so powerful that it could only be exorcized at the moment of arrest. Some, he knew, even made their private bargains with fate; they wouldn't drink, go to the pub or take a holiday until the killer was caught. He had shared their pity and outrage but never their personal involvement and antagonism. For him detection had been a professional and intellectual commitment to the discovery of the truth. That wasn't what he felt now. It wasn't only that Gregory had desecrated a place in which he had been happy; he asked himself bitterly what sanctifying grace was bestowed on St Anselm's by the mere fact of Adam Dalgliesh's happiness. It wasn't only that he revered Father Martin and couldn't forget the priest's stricken face as he looked up at him from Crampton's body; or that other moment, the soft brush of dark hair against his cheek and Emma trembling in his arms so briefly that it was difficult to believe that the embrace had ever happened. This overpowering emotion had an additional and more primitive, more ignoble cause. Gregory had planned the murder and carried it out when he, Dalgliesh, was sleeping within fifty yards. And now he planned to complete his victory. He would swim out to sea content in the element he loved, to a merciful death by cold and exhaustion. And he planned more than that. Dalgliesh could read Gregory's mind as clearly as he knew Gregory was reading his. He planned to take his adversary with him. If Gregory went into the water, so would he. He had no choice. He could not live with the memory that he had stood and watched while a man swam to his death. And he would be risking his life not out of compassion and humanity, but out of obstinacy and pride.

He assessed their relative strengths. In physical condition they were probably about equal, but Gregory would be the stronger swimmer. Neither would last long in the bitterly cold sea, but if help came quickly – as it would – they could survive. He wondered whether to move back and instruct Kate now to ring St Anselm's and get the rescue boat launched, but decided against it;

if Gregory heard cars racing along the cliff path he would hesitate no longer. There was still a chance, however faint, that he would change his mind. But Dalgliesh knew that Gregory had one almost overwhelming advantage: only one of them was happy to die.

And still they stood. And then, almost casually, as if this were a summer day and the sea a shimmering stretch of blue and silver under the radiance of the sun, Gregory dropped the coat from his shoulders and dived.

For Kate the two minutes of confrontation had seemed interminable. She had stood immobile as if every muscle were locked, her eyes fixed on the two motionless figures. Involuntarily but carefully she had edged forward. The tide swept over her feet but she was unaware of its cold bite against her legs. Through stiff jaws she had found herself muttering and cursing, 'Come back, come back. Let him be', urging with an intensity which must surely reach Dalgliesh's unyielding back. Now it had happened and she could act. She stabbed out the college number and heard the ringing tone. There was no reply and she found herself mouthing obscenities she would never normally have uttered. The ringing continued. And then she heard Father Sebastian's measured tones. She tried to keep her voice steady.

'It's Kate Miskin from the beach, Father. Dalgliesh and Gregory are in the water. We need the boat and an ambulance. Quickly.'

Father Sebastian didn't question her. He said, 'Stay where you are to mark the place. We'll be with you.'

And now there was an even longer wait, but one she timed. It was three and a quarter minutes before she heard the sound of cars. Gazing across the leaping waves she could no longer glimpse the two heads. She ran to the end of the groyne and stood where Gregory had stood, oblivious to the waves slurping over the post and the slash of the wind. And now she had a sudden sight of them – the grey head and the dark, only a couple of yards apart – before the sleek curve of a wave and a burst of spray hid them from sight.

It was important to keep them in view if she could, but from time to time she glanced towards the steps. She had heard more than one car but only the Land Rover was visible parked at the edge of the cliff. It looked as if the whole college had arrived. They were working swiftly and methodically. The doors of the shed had been opened and a launch pad of slatted wood rolled out over the gritty slope of the beach. The rigid inflatable was pushed down it, then lifted with three men each side. They ran with it to the edge of the sea. She saw that Pilbeam and Henry Bloxham were to make the rescue and felt a little surprised that it was Henry instead of the stronger-looking Stephen Morby. But perhaps Henry was the more experienced sailor. It seemed impossible that they could launch the craft against this crushing weight of water, but within seconds she heard the roar of the outboard engine and they were heading out to sea, then coming towards her in a wide sweep. Again she had a brief glimpse of the heads and pointed towards them.

And now neither of the swimmers nor the boat could be seen, except momentarily when it crested a wave. There was nothing more she could do and she turned to join the group running along the beach. Raphael was carrying coiled rope, Father Peregrine had a lifebelt and Piers and Robbins had hoisted two rolled canvas stretchers on to their shoulders. Mrs Pilbeam and Emma were there, Mrs Pilbeam with a first aid box and Emma with towels and a pile of bright coloured blankets. They came together in a little group and stared out to sea.

And now the boat was returning. The sound of the engine was louder and it suddenly appeared, rearing high on a wave before plunging into the trough.

Raphael said, 'They've got them. There are four on board.'

They were coming in fairly strongly now, but it seemed impossible that the boat could survive in so rough a sea. And then the worst happened. They no longer heard the engine, and saw Pilbeam desperately bending over it. And now the boat was powerless, thrown from side to side like a child's toy. Suddenly, within twenty yards of the shore, it reared up, was for a couple of seconds motionless and upright, then capsized.

Raphael had tied the end of the rope to one of the uprights of the groyne and now, fixing the other end round his waist, went into the sea. Stephen Morby, Piers and Robbins followed. Father Peregrine had thrown off his cassock and now hurled himself under the advancing waves as if this turbulent sea were his element. Henry and Pilbeam, helped by Robbins, were managing to fight their way ashore. Father Peregrine and Raphael took hold of Dalgliesh, Stephen and Piers of Gregory. Within seconds they were thrown on to the bank of shingle and Father Sebastian and Father Martin hurried forward to help drag them up the beach. They were followed by Pilbeam and Henry who lay gasping while the waves broke over them.

Only Dalgliesh was unconscious and, running to where he lay, Kate saw that he had struck his head against the groyne and that blood mixed with sea water was running over his torn shirt. There was a mark on his throat, red as the flowing blood, where Gregory's hands had grasped him. She pulled off the shirt and pressed it against the wound, then heard Mrs Pilbeam's voice. 'Leave him to me, miss. I've got bandages here.'

But it was Morby who took control. He said, 'Let's get the water out of him first,' and, turning Dalgliesh over, started resuscitation. A little apart, Gregory, naked except for a pair of shorts, was sitting with his head between his hands gasping for breath, watched over by Robbins.

Kate said to Piers, 'Get some blankets round him and a hot drink into him. As soon as he's warm enough and fit to understand what you're doing, charge him. And put the cuffs on him. We're not taking chances. Oh, and you may as well add attempted murder to the main charge.'

She turned again to Dalgliesh. Suddenly he retched, spewed water and blood and muttered something indistinct. It was then that Kate was first aware of Emma Lavenham kneeling, white-faced, at his head. She didn't speak but, catching Kate's glance, got up and moved a little apart as if realizing that she had no place there.

They could hear no ambulance arriving and had no idea how long it would take. Now Piers and Morby lifted Dalgliesh on to one of the stretchers and began trudging with it to the waiting cars, Father Martin at Dalgliesh's side. The group who had been in the water stood shivering, blanket-wrapped, passing a flask from hand to hand, then began making their way towards the steps. Suddenly the clouds parted and a frail ray of sunlight illuminated the beach. Watching the young male bodies towelling their wet hair and jogging to restore circulation, Kate could almost believe that this was a summer bathing party and that at any moment they would begin chasing each other across the sand.

They had reached the top of the cliff and the stretcher was being loaded into the back of the Land Rover. Kate was aware that Emma Lavenham was at her side.

Emma said, 'Will he be all right?'

'Oh he'll live. He's tough. Head wounds bleed a lot but it didn't look deep. He'll be discharged and back in London within days. We all shall.'

Emma said, 'I'm going back to Cambridge tonight. Will you say goodbye to him for me and give him my best wishes?'

Without waiting for a reply, she turned away and joined the little group of ordinands. Gregory, handcuffed and shrouded in blankets, was being pushed into the Alfa Romeo by Robbins. Piers moved over to Kate and both of them looked over to Emma.

Kate said, 'She's going back to Cambridge this evening. Well, why not? That's where she belongs.'

Piers said, 'And where do you belong?'

He didn't really need an answer but she said, 'With you and Robbins and AD. Where did you suppose? This is my job, after all.'

BOOK FOUR

An End and a Beginning

Dalgliesh came to St Anselm's for the last time on a perfect day in mid-April in which sky, sea and the quickening earth conspired in a soft compliance of settled beauty. He drove with the car roof down and the rush of air against his face brought with it the essence – sweet-smelling, nostalgic – of the Aprils of boyhood and youth. He had set out with some misgivings, but they had been thrown off with the last eastern suburb, and now his inner weather matched the calm of the day.

The letter had come from Father Martin, a warm invitation to visit now that St Anselm's had been officially closed. He had written: 'It will be good to have the opportunity to say goodbye to our friends before we leave, and we are hoping that Emma will also be with us for the April weekend.' He had wanted Dalgliesh to know that she would be there; had he also warned her? And if so, would she decide not to come?

And here at last was the familiar turning, easy to miss without the ivy-clad ash. The front gardens of the twin cottages were massed with daffodils, their brilliance in contrast to the soft yellow of the primroses clumped in the grass verge. The hedges on each side of the lane were showing their first green shoots and when, with a lifting of the heart, he first saw the sea, it stretched in untroubled bands of shimmering blue to a purple horizon. High overhead, unseen and hardly audible, a fighter aircraft shed its tattered ribbon of white across a cloudless sky. Under its radiance the mere was a milky blue, unthreatening and peaceful. He could imagine the gleam of shining fish sliding beneath that untroubled surface. The storm on the night of the Archdeacon's murder had broken up the last timbers of the sunken ship and now not even that black fin of wood remained, and the sands stretched untrodden between the bank of shingle and the sea. On such a morning Dalgliesh couldn't even regret this evidence of time's obliterating power.

Before turning north along the coastal road he drew to the edge of the cliff and switched off the ignition. There was a letter he needed to read again. He had received it a week before Gregory had been sentenced to life imprisonment for the murder of Archdeacon Crampton. The writing was firm, precise and upright. There was no superscription; only on the envelope had Dalgliesh's name appeared.

I apologize for this writing paper which you will understand is not my choice. You will have been told by now that I have decided to change my plea to guilty. I could claim that my reason is to spare those pathetic fools, Father Martin and Father John, the ordeal of appearing as witnesses for the prosecution, or my reluctance to see my son or Emma Lavenham exposed to the somewhat brutal ingenuity of my defence lawyer. You will know me better. My reason is, of course, to ensure that Raphael doesn't all his life suffer the stigma of suspicion. I have come to realize that there is a very real chance that I might be acquitted. My lawyer's brilliance is almost proportionate to the size of his fee and he early made it plain that he was confident that I could get away with it, although he was careful not to use those particular words. I am after all so very middle-class, so very respectable.

I had always planned to be acquitted if the case ever came to court and had no doubt that I would be. But then I had planned to murder Crampton on a night when I knew Raphael would not be in college. As you know, I took the precaution of calling in at his set to check that he had in fact left. Had I found him in his room, would I have gone ahead with the murder? The answer is no. Not that night, and perhaps never. It is unlikely that all the conditions necessary for success would have so fortuitously come together again. I find it interesting that Crampton died because of Raphael's simple act of kindness to a sick friend. I have noticed before how often evil comes out of good. As a parson's son you are more competent than am I to address this theological conundrum.

People who, like us, live in a dying civilization have three choices. We can attempt to avert the decline as a child builds a sand-castle on the edge of the advancing tide. We can ignore the death of beauty, of scholarship, of art, of intellectual integrity, finding solace in our own consolations. And that is what for some years I have tried to do. Thirdly, we can join the barbarians and take our share of the spoils. That is the popular choice and in the end it was mine. My son's God was chosen for him. He has been in the power of those priests since he was born. I wanted to give him a choice of a more contemporary deity – money. Now he has money, and will find that he's unable to face giving it away, not all of it. He will remain a rich man; time will show whether he remains a priest.

I imagine that there's nothing I can tell you about the murder which you don't know. My anonymous note to Sir Alred was, of course, designed to stir up trouble for St Anselm's and Sebastian Morell. I could hardly have expected that it would bring to the college the most distinguished of Scotland Yard's detectives, but your presence, so far from deterring me, added challenge to expediency. My plan to entice the Archdeacon to the church worked perfectly; he could hardly wait to view the abomination which I had described to him. The tin of black paint and the brush were conveniently ready for me in the sanctuary and I confess I enjoyed my vandalizing of the Doom. It's a pity Crampton had so little time to contemplate my artistry.

You may be wondering about those two deaths for which I was not charged. The first, the suffocation of Margaret Munroe, was a necessity. It required little planning and her death was easy, almost natural. She was an unhappy woman who probably had little time left, but in that time she could have done damage. It didn't matter to her whether her life was shorter by a day, a month or a year. It did matter to me. I'd planned for Raphael's parentage to be known only after St Anselm's had been closed and the furore of the murder had died down. Of course you early realized the nub of my plan. I wanted to kill Crampton and at the same time throw suspicion on the college without providing conclusive evidence against myself. I wanted the college closed early, preferably before my son was ordained, and I wanted his inheritance to be intact. And, I must confess, I also took pleasure at the prospect of Sebastian Morell's career ending in suspicion, failure and ignominy. He had ensured that mine should end in just that way.

You will wonder perhaps about the unfortunate death of Agatha Betterton, another unhappy woman. But that was merely taking advantage of an unexpected opportunity. You were wrong if you thought that she was at the top of the stairs when I made that telephone call to Mrs Crampton. She didn't see me then. She did, however, see me on the night of the murder when I was returning the key. I could, I suppose, have killed her then, but I decided to wait. She was, after all, regarded as mad. Even if she accused me of being in the house after midnight, I doubt whether her word would have stood up against mine. As it was, she came Sunday evening to tell me that my secret was perfectly safe. She was never a coherent woman but she gave me to understand that no one who had killed Archdeacon Crampton had anything to fear from her. It wasn't a risk I could take. You do realize that you wouldn't be able to prove either of those deaths? Motive isn't enough. If this confession is used against me I shall repudiate it.

I have learned something surprising about murder, about violence generally. It's probably known to you, Dalgliesh; you are after all an expert in these matters. Personally I find it interesting. The first blow was deliberate, not without a natural squeamishness and some repugnance, but a matter of summoning the will. My mental process was unambiguous: I need this man dead; this is the most effective way to kill him. I had intended a single blow, two at most, but it's after the first strike that the adrenalin surges. The lust for violence takes over. I

went on striking without conscious will. Even if you had
appeared at that moment I doubt whether I could have
stopped. It is not when we contemplate violence that the
primitive instinct to kill takes over, it is only when we
strike the first blow.

I have not seen my son since my arrest. He has no wish
to meet me and no doubt it's just as well. I have lived all
my life without human affection and it would be
awkward to indulge in it now.

And there the letter ended. Folding it away, Dalgliesh
wondered how Gregory would endure imprisonment
which might well last for ten years. Provided he had his
books he would probably survive. But was he even now
looking out from his barred window and wishing that
he, too, could smell the sweetness of this spring day?

He started the car and drove straight to the college.
The front door stood wide open to the sunlight and he
stepped into the emptiness of the hall. The lamp still
burned at the foot of the statue of the Virgin and there
still lingered on the air the faint ecclesiastical smell compounded of incense, furniture polish and old books. But
it seemed to him that the house had already been partly
stripped and that it now waited with a quiet resignation
for the inevitable end.

There was no sound of footfalls, but suddenly he
was aware of a presence and, looking up, saw Father
Sebastian standing at the head of the stairs. He called,
'Good morning, Adam, please come up.' It was the first
time, thought Dalgliesh, that the Warden had used his
Christian name.

Following him into his office, Dalgliesh saw that there

had been changes. The Burne-Jones picture no longer hung above the fireplace and the sideboard had also gone. There was a subtle change, too, in Father Sebastian. The cassock had been put aside and he now wore a suit with a clerical collar. And he looked older; the murder had taken its toll. But the austere and handsome features had lost none of their authority or confidence, and something had been added: the controlled euphoria of success. The university Chair he had gained was prestigious and it was one he must have coveted. Dalgliesh congratulated him.

Morell said, 'Thank you. It is said to be a mistake to go back, but I hope that for me and for the university it will prove otherwise.'

They sat and talked for a few minutes, a necessary concession to politeness. It was not in Morell's nature to feel ill at ease but Dalgliesh sensed that he was still irked by the distasteful thought that the man now sitting opposite him had once regarded him as a possible murder suspect, and he doubted whether Morell would ever forget or forgive the indignity of his fingerprinting. Now, as if feeling under an obligation, he brought Dalgliesh up to date with the changes in the college.

'The students have all been found places at other theological colleges. The four ordinands you met when the Archdeacon was murdered have been accepted at Cuddesdon or St Stephen's House, Oxford.'

Dalgliesh said, 'So Raphael is going ahead with his ordination?'

'Of course. Did you think he wouldn't?' He paused, then added, 'Raphael has been generous, but he will still be a rich man.'

He went on to speak briefly about the priests but with more openness than Dalgliesh had expected. Father Peregrine had accepted a post as archivist in a library in Rome, a city to which he had always been anxious to return. Father John had been offered the job of chaplain to a convent near Scarborough. Since, as a convicted paedophile, he was required to register any change of address, it was felt that the convent would offer as safe a refuge as had St Anselm's. Dalgliesh, suppressing a smile, privately agreed that no more suitable post could have been found. Father Martin was buying a house in Norwich and the Pilbeams would move in to look after him, inheriting the house when he died. Although Raphael's right to his inheritance had been confirmed, the legal position was complicated and there was much to be decided, including whether the church would be taken into the local group ministry or deconsecrated. Raphael was anxious that the van der Weyden should be used as an altar-piece and an appropriate place was being sought. The picture was at present safely locked in a bank security vault, as was the silver. Raphael had also decided to give the Pilbeams their cottage and Eric Surtees his. The main building had been sold as a residential centre for meditation and alternative medicine. Father Sebastian's tone conveyed a nicely judged distaste, but Dalgliesh guessed that he thought it could have been worse. In the meantime the four priests and the staff were temporarily staying on at the request of the trustees until the building was handed over.

When it was apparent that the interview was over, Dalgliesh handed Father Sebastian Gregory's letter. He said, 'I think you have a right to see this.'

Father Sebastian read in silence. At the end, folding it and returning it to Dalgliesh, he said, 'Thank you. It is extraordinary that a man who loved the language and literature of one of the world's greatest civilizations should be reduced to this tawdry self-justification. I have been told that murderers are invariably arrogant, but this is arrogance on the scale of Milton's Satan. "Evil be thou my Good." I wonder when he last read *Paradise Lost*. Archdeacon Crampton was right in one criticism of me. I should have taken more trouble in choosing the people I invited to work here. You're staying the night, I believe.'

'Yes, Father.'

'That will be pleasant for us all. I hope you will be comfortable.'

Father Sebastian didn't accompany Dalgliesh to his old apartment in Jerome, but summoned Mrs Pilbeam and handed over the key. Mrs Pilbeam was unusually talkative, checking carefully in Jerome that Dalgliesh had all that was necessary. She seemed almost reluctant to depart.

'Father Sebastian will have told you about the changes. I can't say Reg and I much like the idea of alternative medicine. Still, the people who came round seemed harmless enough. They wanted us to stay on in our present jobs, and Eric Surtees too. I think he's happy enough, but Reg and I are too old for change. We've been with the Fathers a good many years now and we don't fancy getting used to strangers. Mr Raphael says we are free to sell the cottage, so we may do that and put a bit by for our old age. Father Martin probably told you that we're thinking of moving to Norwich with him.

He's found a very nice house with a good study for himself and plenty of room for the three of us. Well, you can't really see Father Martin looking after himself, can you, not at over eighty? And it will be nice for him to see a bit of life – for us too. Have you got everything you want now, Mr Dalgliesh? Father Martin will be pleased to see you. You'll find him on the beach. Mr Raphael's back for the weekend and Miss Lavenham is here too.'

Dalgliesh moved his Jaguar to the back of the college and set out to walk to the mere. In the distance he saw that the pigs at St John's Cottage were now roaming freely on the headland. They seemed, too, to have increased in number. Even the pigs, apparently, seemed to know that things were different now. As he watched, Eric Surtees came out of his cottage, bucket in hand.

He walked along the cliff path to the mere. From the top of the steps he could at last see the whole stretch of the beach. The three figures seemed almost wilfully to have distanced themselves. To the north he could see Emma sitting high among the pebbles, her head bent over a book. On one of the nearer groynes Raphael was sitting, dangling his legs in the water and looking out to sea. Close to him on a sandy patch Father Martin seemed to be constructing a fire.

Hearing the scrunch of Dalgliesh's shoes on the shingle, he levered himself up with difficulty and smiled his transforming smile. 'Adam. I'm glad you could come. You've seen Father Sebastian?'

'Yes, and congratulated him on the Chair.'

Father Martin said, 'It's the one he's always wanted, and he knew it would become vacant in the autumn.

But of course he wouldn't have considered accepting the offer if St Anselm's had remained open.'

He crouched again to his task. Dalgliesh saw that he had scooped a shallow hollow in the sand and was now building a small wall of stones round it. Beside it there was a canvas bag and a box of matches. Dalgliesh sat down, leaning back on his arms and thrusting his feet into the sand.

Without ceasing his work, Father Martin said, 'Are you happy, Adam?'

'I have health, a job I enjoy, enough food, comfort, occasional luxuries if I feel the need of them, my poetry. Given the state of three-quarters of the world's poor, wouldn't you say that unhappiness would be a perverse indulgence?'

'I might even say that it would be a sin, something to be striven against anyway. If we can't praise God as he deserves, we can at least thank Him. But are those things enough?'

'Is this going to be a sermon, Father?'

'Not even a homily. I'd like to see you marry, Adam, or at least sharing your life with someone. I know that your wife died in childbirth. That must be a continuing shadow. But we can't set aside love, nor should we wish to. Forgive me if I'm being insensitive and impertinent, but grief can be an indulgence.'

'Oh it isn't grief, Father, that's kept me single. Nothing as simple, natural and admirable. It's egotism. Love of my privacy, reluctance to be hurt or to be responsible again for another's happiness. And don't say that pain would be good for my verse. I know that. I see enough of it in my job.' He paused, then said, 'You're a bad

545

matchmaker. She wouldn't have me, you know. Too old, too private, far too uncommitted, perhaps with hands too bloodstained.'

Father Martin selected a smooth round stone and placed it with precision. He looked as happily occupied as a small child.

Dalgliesh added, 'And there's probably someone at Cambridge.'

'Oh, with such a woman there probably is. At Cambridge or elsewhere. That means you will have to take trouble and risk failure. That at least would be a change for you. Well, good luck, Adam.'

The words sounded like a dismissal. Dalgliesh got to his feet and looked towards Emma. Then he saw that she too had got to her feet and was walking towards the sea. They were only fifty yards apart. He thought, I'll wait, and if she comes to me, that at least will mean something, even if it's only to say goodbye. And then the thought struck him as cowardly and ungallant. He had to make the first move. He moved to the edge of the sea. The small sheet of paper with the six lines of verse was still in his wallet. He took it out and, tearing it into small pieces, dropped them into the next advancing wave and watched them slowly disappear in the creeping line of foam. He turned again towards Emma, but when he began moving he saw that she too had turned and was already walking towards him on the strip of dry sand between the bank of pebbles and the receding tide. She drew close and, without speaking, they stood shoulder to shoulder looking out over the sea.

When she spoke her words surprised him. 'Who is Sadie?'

'Why do you ask?'

'When you were coming round you seemed to expect that she was waiting for you.'

God, he thought, I must have looked a mess, dragged half-naked up the shingle, bleeding, covered with sand, spewing water and blood, spluttering and retching. He said, 'Sadie was very sweet. She taught me that, although poetry was a passion, it needn't be the whole of life. Sadie was very wise for fifteen and a half.'

He thought he heard a low satisfied laugh but it was caught in a sudden breeze. It was ridiculous at his age to feel this uncertainty. He was torn between resentment at the adolescent indignity of it, and a perverse pleasure that he was capable of so violent an emotion. And now the words had to be said. Even as they fell dully upon the breeze he judged them in all their banality, their inadequacy.

He said, 'I would very much like to see you again if the idea doesn't repel you. I thought – I hoped – that we might get to know each other.'

He told himself, I must sound like a dentist making the next appointment. And then he turned to look at her and what he saw in her face made him want to shout aloud.

She said gravely, 'There's a very good train service between London and Cambridge now. In both directions.'

And she held out her hand.

Father Martin had finished preparing his fireplace. Now he took from the canvas bag a sheet of newspaper and bunched it into the hollow. Then he laid the Anselm papyrus above it and, crouching, struck a match. The paper caught fire immediately and it seemed that the flames leapt at the papyrus as if it were prey. The heat for a moment was intense and he stepped back. He saw that Raphael had come beside him and was silently watching. Then he said, 'What are you burning, Father?'

'Some writing which has already tempted someone to sin and may tempt others. It's time for it to go.'

There was a silence, then Raphael said, 'I shan't make a bad priest, Father.'

Father Martin, the least demonstrative of men, laid a hand briefly on his shoulder and said, 'No, my son. I think you may make a good one.'

Then they watched together in silence as the fire died down and the last frail wisp of white smoke drifted over the sea.

ff

Faber and Faber is one of the great independent publishing houses. We were established in 1929 by Geoffrey Faber with T. S. Eliot as one of our first editors. We are proud to publish award-winning fiction and non-fiction, as well as an unrivalled list of poets and playwrights. Among our list of writers we have five Booker Prize winners and twelve Nobel Laureates, and we continue to seek out the most exciting and innovative writers at work today.

Find out more about our authors and books
faber.co.uk

Read our blog for insight and opinion on books and the arts
thethoughtfox.co.uk

Follow news and conversation
twitter.com/faberbooks

Watch readings and interviews
youtube.com/faberandfaber

Connect with other readers
facebook.com/faberandfaber

Explore our archive
flickr.com/faberandfaber